Books by Michael Craft

FLIGHT DREAMS
EYE CONTACT
BODY LANGUAGE

Published by Kensington Publishing Corp.

BODY LANGUAGE

MICHAEL CRAFT

Kensington Books
http://www.kensingtonbooks.com

KENSINGTON BOOKS are published by

Kensington Publishing Corp.
850 Third Avenue
New York, NY 10022

ISBN 1-57566-554-9

First Kensington Hardcover Printing: June, 1999
First Kensington Trade Paperback Printing: May, 2000
10 9 8 7 6 5 4 3 2

Printed in the United States of America

The author is indebted to Agatha Christie, master of this genre, one of whose stage plays inspired the core idea for this story. Further, he thanks Mari Higgins-Frost and Joel Wallen for their assistance with various plot details. As always, the author expresses his gratitude to Mitchell Waters and John Scognamiglio for bringing this series to print.

—M.C.

Naturellement,
à Léon

Contents

PROLOGUE

This Afternoon

My new life seems bogged by funerals, peppered by the last rites of passage into some vast unknown. The mourners who surround me are watching the spectacle of grief played out at the altar. With a numb sense of detachment, they mime the prescribed motions and mouth psalms about sheep, lost in their memories, as I am lost in mine.

This journey, this launch of a faithful soul to its presumed reward, mirrors my own journey north to this town, seeking a future still rooted in my past. While the events that led me here were personal and introspective—selfish, some might say—the circumstances of this funeral, and the one that preceded it only days ago, have deeply bruised the public psyche of this town. Wondering what thoughts are harbored by the others here in church today, I am tempted to make a few notes.

Reaching beneath my topcoat, my hand brushes the spiral of a steno pad as I remove from my pocket the wonderful old pen I carry everywhere, even here. In the course of my career, I've known legions of reporters, but none other have used a fountain pen for notes—idiosyncratic perhaps, and not entirely practical, but it's a luxurious affectation that is by now second nature to me. Rolling the Montblanc in my fingers like a fine cigar, I remove the cap and examine the gold band beneath the nib. Engraved there in tiny letters is the name MARK MANNING, barely legible through the years of wear.

The priest drones through the script of his fill-in-the-blanks sermon, eulogizing "this allegiant child of the church." Heads bob, some sob, but most try to huddle deeper into their scarves; outside, the midday sun may glare in a crystalline sky, but inside, the building's old boiler is no match for the January cold spell that now grips central Wisconsin.

Pulling the notepad from my coat, I flip it open and poise my pen, searching for the first words of a story that wants to be told. After all, the events of the past few weeks are the stuff of sensational journalism. I know a great story when I see one, and my reputation stems from an ability to report it. Groping now for that opening phrase, I find that words seem to resist the tangibility of ink. But why? This one has it all—deceit, greed, secrets, and lust. Not to mention murder.

And it dawns on me. I'm too close to this story. This is family. This is *me*. Though page-one material, this will never carry my byline. This is a tale I can spin only in my mind.

PART ONE

Three Months Ago

Where to begin? The roots of this story trace back to my boyhood, some thirty-three years ago when I first visited Dumont, Wisconsin. And there were even earlier chapters, with a hidden prologue written prior to my birth in Illinois forty-two years ago. But the events that led to the tragedies of the past few weeks are not nearly so distant. The main action of this tale began just three months ago.

It was autumn, mid-October in Chicago, arguably the most pleasant weeks of the year—cool, dry, and invigorating. Kids were back in school, the opera and symphony seasons were in full swing, and the world got busy again with the productive grind of life. For all of these reasons and countless others, I have always enjoyed fall.

But last October was different. A mild despondency had gnawed at me all year, and by the time the leaves began to yellow, I found myself in the throes of full-blown depression. On the surface, this condition could be glibly diagnosed as a common case of midlife crisis. Indeed, like most men in their forties, I had begun to contemplate my mortality, and my staunchly rational creed did not permit the safety net of an afterlife. At the suggestion of an attorney friend, Roxanne Exner, I even wrote a will.

The truth was, though, that while I wasn't getting any younger, there wasn't a thing physically wrong with me. I was (and still am) as fit as most at thirty. So it is simply inaccurate to say that my depression was caused by the pull of the grave. What was really eating me was my job.

Doubtless, there are many who look back at their life's work and wonder why they've bothered. All too often, visions of a changed world are dead-ended by the realities of a future that doesn't measure up to the plan.

My career, however, exceeded all expectations. Back in the seventies, as a journalism student at Champaign-Urbana, I didn't dare dream that success might await me in Chicago, where I managed to land a reporting job at the *Journal*, one of that city's two major dailies. Over the years, I honed my skills and eventually secured a reputation as the most respected investigative reporter in the Midwest—a statement that verges on boasting, perhaps, but it is not with empty pride, because I did, in fact, deliver a unique brand of journalism in a city that's known as a newspaper town.

Most notably, last summer's big story dealt with a civic festival of the arts and sciences. When I took on the assignment, I had no idea—no one did, other than a handful of conspirators—that the festival was related to a bizarre scheme with insidious social implications for the entire country. During the course of my investigation, several of my coworkers were killed, and while there were many who considered me a hero in these developments, I myself had a hard time shrugging off the notion that I had played a role in these deaths.

This notion may have been shared by the Partridge Committee, that august body of publishers and scholars responsible for handing out the Partridge Prize (investigative journalism's highest award, known among reporters as "the coveted brass bird"). When the nominations were announced last fall, my efforts were again ignored, and the elusive prize was awarded posthumously to a reporter who was felled by the events of my story. Ironically, this was his *second* Partridge. The one awarded to him in life meant little to him—he treated it like a knickknack, a gaudy paperweight.

I am a reasonable man, self-analytical and perhaps overly logical, hardly prone to fits of peevishness. But that story was easily the highlight of my reporting career—any journalist would drool at the prospects of typing his byline over it. A combination of circumstances, luck, and my own best efforts produced an investigation that was hailed by my editor as the story of the year, if not the decade. Public acclaim was overwhelming, but the Partridge people ignored me. And this has happened before. I believe this is the result of a particular prejudice against me. I believe this is a reaction to the fact that I am gay.

Recognition of prejudice is not a persecution complex, and my insistence upon maintaining this distinction is not mere defensiveness. People are free to believe whatever they wish, and if, as a result of their beliefs, they don't "like" me, so be it—I'm not apt to like them, either. But the Partridge Foundation, while private, functions in the public arena, claims open-mindedness, and parades a veneer of objectivity. By any objective standard, I was screwed.

In other words, last October my career at the *Journal* maxed out. I had taken the job as far as it was likely to go, and while my performance was recognized by the adulation of my readers and the respect of my cohorts, I was convinced that my reporting would never be endorsed by that one evasive plum it deserved. Further, assignments like the festival story don't come along every day—subsequent stories fired no passion within me. And there was still that nagging thought that I had played a role in the death of friends.

I was beginning to grapple with awareness of the unthinkable: my reporting days at the *Journal* were drawing to an end, and I had no idea where I was headed.

All was not bleak, however, not by a long shot. Though the stability of my professional life was approaching a crisis of uncertainty, I had achieved emotional bedrock at home with Neil Waite. Meeting him, learning to love him, had precipitated a different kind of crisis—an identity crisis—some three years earlier. Approaching forty, I was single, straight, frustrated, and curious when an intriguing young architect, barely in his thirties, came to Chicago on business from Phoenix. At first glance, I judged him athletically handsome; during our first evening of conversation, I came to understand that he was intellectually rigorous as well. I was doomed (perhaps "destined" has a less pejorative ring) to fall in love with him, and my lifetime of fears became meaningless.

Roxanne introduced us, a courtesy she learned to regret, as she'd set her sights romantically on both Neil and me over the years. By the time Neil made his decision to relocate to his firm's Chicago office, it was obvious to both of us, as well as to Roxanne, that he and I belonged together. We were relieved when Roxanne ultimately reconciled herself to the role of unwitting matchmaker, and she has since been our closest friend.

The other aspect of my life that was anything but bleak last autumn was finances. As the *Journal's* star reporter, I was well paid, of course, but that was just the beginning. When I solved a prominent missing-person case nearly three years ago (at the time I met Neil), I received a substantial cash award from the woman's estate. Not long after that, I learned that I had inherited a large house from an uncle in central Wisconsin— Dumont, Wisconsin—which I had seen only once during a boyhood visit. Since both Neil and I were then anchored to our jobs in Chicago, I sold the house to an architecture buff and his wife from Madison, a Professor and Mrs. Tawkin.

The proceeds from all this were used to customize a cavernous loft apartment in Chicago's Near North area, which I had bought and Neil redesigned. The renovation took nearly two years, but we both enjoyed the process despite the upheaval. We were literally building our life together, and our home was the tangible symbol of that commitment.

The loft project, while substantial, did not exhaust my windfall, and I proved myself a shrewd investor of the remaining funds, watching with bemused disbelief as they multiplied. Then, last summer, after my investigation of the festival story made page-one headlines worldwide, I found myself in constant demand as the recipient of outrageously inflated lecture fees, which fueled my investment hobby with additional capital.

No, money wasn't a problem. Nor was my home life the problem. The problem, as I have said, was my job. I wanted out.

"So just quit," Neil told me. "Take a breather. Or take an early retirement." We were at home one evening at the loft, and he waved his arms at our lavish surroundings, all paid for. "You don't *need* to work."

"But I do need to work." I handed him one of the two cocktails I had just poured, Japanese vodka over ice with a twist of orange peel—more of a summer drink, actually, not quite right for October, but ever since the evening we first met, this had been "our" drink, our ritual.

Taking the glass, he said, "Concentrate on your investments. You're good at it."

"Just because I'm good at it doesn't mean I enjoy it." I sat next to him on a sofa facing a tall bank of windows looking east toward Lake Michigan. "I'm no bean counter. I'm a journalist."

"Then write a book."

A tempting thought. I knew very well, though, that books get written by people who have something to say, not by people who are merely in search of a literary pastime. I told Neil, "Someday, sure, I'll try my hand at a book. Now, I'm still absorbed in the day-to-day mind-set of newspapers—that's all I've done, and that's really all I know. But it's time for a change."

We'd had this discussion before, frequently, so Neil was aware that I was wrestling not with idle musings, but with an active attempt to solve a dilemma. He'd been wholly sympathetic in these talks, but knowing that any major change in my life would surely affect his as well, his sympathy was tempered by a measure of caution. He said, "If you need to stick with newspapers, you could easily get a reporting job somewhere else. You'd be welcome in any newsroom on the planet. Please, though, not New York—I'm just not ready for it."

I laughed. It felt good, as my mood had ranged from funky to somber over the previous few weeks. Setting my drink on a table in front of the sofa, I took Neil's hands into mine. He still held his glass, and its icy condensation spread through his fingers to mine. "Set your mind at ease, kiddo," I assured him. "I won't let this come between us. You're far more important to me than my professional wanderlust. You've uprooted yourself once already to be with me. I wouldn't dream of confronting you with such a choice, not again."

"But you've got to be *happy*," he insisted, setting his own drink next to mine and leaning forward, his face close to mine. I felt his breath as he continued. "You're at the top of your profession, Mark. I can't expect you to take some beat reporter's job in Podunk. You need to move *up*, and there aren't many options—none within driving distance."

I smiled, wanting to tell him how much I loved him, but that might have led to some carnal diversion, and there was something I was eager to discuss with him. "I've had an idea," I told him, "and I think it might work, and it wouldn't disrupt 'us' at all."

"Oh?" Intrigued, he reached for his glass again and sipped. "I'm all ears."

Pausing, I grinned. "What if I *bought* a paper? Nothing on the scale of the *Journal*, of course—that's impossible. But with other investors, I might be able to swing a small-town daily somewhere, maybe in the suburbs. It would be a big investment, certainly a gamble, but one that I would really care about. And here's the point: It would be a new challenge. Acting as a publisher, I *would* be moving up, 'steering the ship of journalism'—a small ship, granted, maybe a measly punt, but it would be mine and I'd be in charge." Twitching my brows, I asked Neil, "What do you think?"

"Mr. Manning," he told me, kissing me before passing judgment, "I think you're a genius." Then his face turned quizzical. "How do you go about buying a newspaper? Check the want ads?" He wasn't serious.

"There are various trade journals," I explained, "and if I need to field some discreet queries, Gordon said he'd help."

"You've already discussed this with *Gordon?*" asked Neil. "He'd be the *last* person I'd tell."

We were speaking of Gordon Smith, the *Journal*'s acting publisher, recently promoted, waiting for the nod to take over the position permanently. Before his promotion, he served as managing editor, and I'd worked with him on a daily basis for years. He always took a fatherly interest in my career, pride in my success. Much of what I achieved at the *Journal*, I owed to Gordon's mentoring.

"Gordon is remarkable," I told Neil. "He seems almost as concerned about my welfare as you do, and he knows that I'm itching to try something else. I can tell that he's sick at the prospect of losing me, though."

"Who wouldn't be?" asked Neil. Then we sat quietly for a while, weighing the future's uncertain prospects, but secure in the knowledge that we'd hit upon a workable plan.

Later that week, I was at my desk in the *Journal*'s newsroom, at work on a story about some routine autumn scandal in the county treasurer's office, when I took a phone call, grateful for the interruption.

"Good morning, Mr. Manning," said the thin voice of an older man on the line. "This is Elliot Coop. Do you remember me?"

I hesitated. The name was familiar. He continued. "I'm the lawyer from Dumont who handled the sale of your uncle's house on Prairie Street."

"Of course. Forgive my memory lapse, Elliot. It's nice to hear from you—it's been a while."

"Nearly three years," he tittered. "I got a phone call from Professor Tawkin yesterday, and I thought you'd want to know about it. You do remember the Tawkins, don't you?"

How could I forget? Elliot Coop prattled on about something, but his words were a blur against the din of the newsroom as I recalled the day some three years ago when I first met both the lawyer and the Tawkins.

I hadn't seen the house on Prairie Street in over thirty years, when I first visited Dumont as a boy of nine. Even then, the house struck me as a place of uncommon beauty—masculine beauty—but its restrained grandeur seemed tainted by an unspoken past. Like its occupants, it guarded secrets, and those bits of missing history puzzled me until the day I returned, the day I met Elliot Coop.

The first I knew of Elliot was a few weeks prior, when I received a FedEx from him informing me that I had inherited the house from my uncle, Edwin Quatrain, who had recently died. Uncle Edwin, my mother's brother, was a wealthy man, patriarch of the huge Quatro Press, a web-fed printing business in Dumont, situated in the central Wisconsin area known for its paper mills. His children grown and his wife long dead, Uncle Edwin had no other family with him during his latter years in the house on Prairie Street, just the live-in housekeeper who had helped raise the children. Her unlikely name was Hazel.

Both Neil and our lawyer friend, Roxanne Exner, were with me in the Chicago loft on the evening I opened Elliot's FedEx. They were as astounded as I to learn of my good fortune. "Wow," said Neil. "Your uncle had no kids?"

"As a matter of fact, he had three."

Roxanne asked, "Then why would *you* inherit the house?"

"I'm not sure." Then I added, "There was also a printing business, big enough to make them *all* rich," as if the house were merely an afterthought, a trinket for a distant nephew.

"What's it worth?" asked Neil, never one to dance around delicate subjects. I had mentioned the house before, and he was intrigued by it, but we would not be moving into it. We were both city mice finding scant allure to the prospect of life in central Wisconsin. Of *course* it would be sold.

"Plenty," I told him. "Hundreds of thousands—maybe three, maybe five, depending on the market up there."

Roxanne asked, "Going up to see the place?"

"Probably. The lawyer's letter says they've already got a prospective buyer. They'll let me know when they need me. God, talk about a nostalgia trip."

And a nostalgia trip it was. A few weeks later, I was summoned to Dumont by Elliot Coop, the Quatrains' longtime family lawyer who was handling the estate. He'd found a buyer for the house, the architecture buff from Madison who planned on moving up to Dumont to live in it. We would be meeting him at the house with his wife—she held the purse strings and still needed a bit of convincing.

Driving north in a slick new Bavarian V-8, I was thrilled by the satisfaction of having finally bought the car I'd always wanted. Neil had accused me of counting chickens before they hatched, but it turned out that my estimate of the house's worth was well on the low side, so the car would barely make a dent in the windfall that would come of that afternoon's transaction. Besides, I told myself, Uncle Edwin would surely approve—I could still smell the leather in the magnificent imported sedan he drove when I first visited Dumont as a boy.

As I turned onto Prairie Street, the house filled my view, and the sight was no less imposing than when I first saw it thirty years before. An agent's spec sheet, which was sent to me, described the house as "vintage Prairie School, Taliesin-designed." It was, in fact, the work of one of Frank Lloyd Wright's students at Spring Green, Wisconsin. An expansive Palladian window across the third-floor façade was not at all typical of the style, a design eccentricity that made the house even more appealing to the man from Madison, a professor of architectural history. The spec sheet further confirmed that the house was every bit as big as I remembered it—six thousand square feet, two thousand on each floor. Plus basement. My most enduring memories of the place focused on the third floor of the house, where there was a beautiful and (in my child's mind) mysterious loft space. The spec sheet described this attic great room as "a fabulous mother-in-law apartment/ retreat."

Parked at the curb that day were two cars, the lawyer's and the buyers'. I hesitated for a moment, then pulled into the driveway—it and the house were, after all, mine, if only for the day. As I got out of the car, the lawyer hobbled toward me, extending his hand. "Good afternoon, Mr. Manning. Elliot Coop. Thank you for driving all this way. Let me introduce you to Professor and Mrs. Tawkin."

The wife cooed, "Introductions are hardly necessary. It's an honor, Mr. Manning." We all shook hands, then followed the lawyer in through the front door.

It took less than an hour to tour the house and convince the wife. In the attic great room she told us, "I was skeptical, I admit, but I'm totally won over. Shall we sign some papers?"

Mission accomplished. We trundled down the stairs, out the door, and back to our cars, with the lawyer giving directions to his office. Once the Tawkins were in their car, Elliot walked with me toward mine, telling me, "Before your uncle died, while he was reviewing his will, he gave me a letter and asked me to deliver it into your hand." He produced the envelope. "There, Mr. Manning. Done."

"Are you still there, Mr. Manning?" Elliot Coop's voice buzzed through the phone at my desk in the newsroom.

"Sorry, Elliot," I told him, snapping back to the moment. "You were saying something about Professor Tawkin?"

"Indeed," he replied in a breathless tone, giddy with some pent-up gossip. "They're divorcing! It's uncontested, and they've retained me for arbitration."

"Oh." I wasn't sure how I was supposed to react to this news—or why Elliot thought I'd be interested.

He bubbled onward. "I don't need to remind you that *she* controls the finances. She *hates* life in Dumont, and—guess what—she's pulling the plug on the mortgage. So they've instructed me to sell the house, at a substantial loss if necessary. 'Just *dump* it,' she told me. So I was wondering, Mr. Manning, if you might have any interest in reacquiring it. It's a magnificent home, as you know, and with your family roots in Dumont, I thought—"

"Thanks, Elliot," I interrupted him, "but Dumont is a bit out of the way for me." Even as I spoke, though, another thought occurred to me. The local paper up there, the *Dumont Daily Register*, had long been known as a fine small-town daily. I recalled picking up a few copies during my brief visit three years ago when I sold the house, and the *Register* measured up handsomely to its reputation. What's more, its venerable founding publisher was due for retirement. So my phone conversation with the lawyer took a different turn. "Excuse me, Elliot, but is the *Dumont Daily Register* still being run by its founder?"

"My, yes," he assured me. "Barret Logan has manned the helm for nearly fifty years. With Bonnie gone now, it's his whole life."

"Do you think he'll ever retire?"

"Depends." Elliot chuckled. "In the market for a newspaper, Mr. Manning?"

"Depends." I thought a moment. "Do you have his phone number handy?"

The lawyer recited it. "That's his direct line. He answers his own phone, and he's usually at his desk till noon."

"Thanks, Elliot. I appreciate the information."

He asked, "What about the house?"

"Depends." I laughed at his persistence. "I'll have to get back to you."

Within a minute, I had dialed the number he gave me and a man answered, "Good morning. Barret Logan."

"Hello, Mr. Logan. This is Mark Manning, a reporter for the *Chicago Journal*. My mother was originally from Dumont; she was Edwin Quatrain's sister."

Logan laughed gustily. "I know who you are, Mr. Manning—who doesn't? And to what might I owe the unexpected pleasure of your call?"

An hour later—it was well past noon by then—he said, "I'm late for a lunch appointment, Mark, so I really must go. Let's both have our people review these numbers; then let's talk again. Soon. I'm so very glad you called."

With my mind spinning, I said, "I am, too, Barret. I think we've laid the groundwork for a promising transaction. I've got a lot of thinking to do, and I know that you do, too. But we *will* talk again. Soon."

That evening, I waited at the loft for Neil to return from work. I considered having cocktails ready for his arrival, but reconsidered, knowing that this conversation would require a clear head. When he walked through the door, we exchanged a kiss and some small talk. I suggested, "Let's take a walk along the lake. There's a bit of daylight left, and I want to discuss something with you."

"Uh-oh." A wary glance. "How about a run together? It's been a while."

"Maybe later, Neil. But now, let's just walk, okay? An opportunity presented itself at the office today, and I need to know what you think of it."

So, still dressed for the office, minus jackets, we headed out. It would be a week till the ritual of setting back the clocks, and shafts of orange twilight angled between the buildings toward the shore. An easterly breeze striped the surface of Lake Michigan with whitecapped waves. Colliding with the cement embankment, they disappeared in rosy mist. Out near the horizon, a few hardy sailors leaned their masts toward harbor, conceding at last that summer was gone.

"What's up?" asked Neil after we had crossed through the traffic on the Outer Drive and settled into an easy saunter along a stretch of beach.

"Remember the house I inherited from my uncle Edwin in Dumont?"

"I never saw it, but sure, I remember it. It paid for our work on the loft."

"Right. Well, today I learned from a lawyer up there that the house is on the market again, and I could get it back cheap."

Neil shrugged an I-don't-get-it. "Why would you want it?"

Obliquely, I answered, "I also learned that the local paper up there, the *Dumont Daily Register*, might be available to the right person. I talked to the publisher, Barret Logan. He thinks I'm the right person, and he's ready to retire. I think I could swing it. I'd have to go heavily into debt, and I'd probably have to take on some investors, but it sounds doable—*if* you go along with it."

Neil's pace slowed, stopped. He eyed me askance. With an uncertain inflection, he said, "Dumont is—what?—three hours' drive from here?"

I confessed, "Closer to four."

"That's a hefty commute." There was no humor in his understatement. Nor in his afterthought: "And I doubt if there's much need for high-powered architectural talent in central Wisconsin." Eyeing me, he asked, "Where would that leave 'us'?"

I strolled him toward a park bench anchored in the sand,

telling him, "I've struggled with this all afternoon. I do want the *Register*, but I want you more, and I won't push for anything that would jeopardize 'us.' "

We both sat down, legs touching. Neil gazed out at the water. I peered at him, saying, "So I'd like to propose an arrangement."

He grinned. "Yes?"

"I would buy back the house on Prairie Street, but I'd also keep the loft here in Chicago. I'd take over the *Register* and work up there, and you'd stay here at your job. *But*—and here's the crucial part—we'd spend every weekend together, alternating locales. We'd try this for a solid year. It wouldn't be easy, but it would be a commitment to buy some time. After a year, we'd reevaluate the arrangement. By then it should be obvious what we need to do. Maybe circumstances would allow us both to settle happily in either Dumont or Chicago. Maybe we'd extend the arrangement. Maybe we'd explore other options we haven't thought of yet."

I stopped talking, as there was nothing else to add. All that mattered now was Neil's reaction. I waited.

He turned to me and rested an arm across my shoulder. "Some 'arrangement.' You don't ask much, do you?"

"Neil, I could flop big-time up there, but I have to find out if . . ."

"Shhh," he stopped me, pressing a finger to my lips. "I know you need to do this. You're working your way through some sort of midlife guy-thing, and the last thing I want is for our relationship to be a casualty of this crisis. I don't much like the 'arrangement,' but I'm willing to go along with it. Like you said, we're buying time. I can deal with inconvenience for a year. What I can't deal with is the thought of not spending my life with you."

How could I react other than to pull him into my arms? I nuzzled his neck and told the back of his head, "I love you so much. I really don't deserve you."

"No, you don't," he agreed. "You're the luckiest man in the world."

News spread fast that I was leaving the *Journal* for—of all places—Dumont, Wisconsin. Roxanne Exner was first to get wind of it, hearing it directly from Neil, and she wanted more details. So she suggested that we meet for dinner at Bistro Zaza, a loud, trendy, but good Near North restaurant that had of late become our favorite haunt.

Parking at the door, giving my car keys to the valet, I entered Zaza's with Neil, asking him, "Will Carl be here, too?"

I was asking about Carl Creighton, a recently appointed Illinois deputy attorney general, formerly a senior partner at Roxanne's law firm. When Carl entered political life, he left the firm and promoted Roxanne. As of that Saturday evening last October, they had been romantically involved for about a year. Neil and I often wondered aloud whether they would take the plunge into "the *m*-word." Roxanne had never struck either of us as the marrying type, so we rarely breathed the actual word, referring to it in code.

Neil answered me, "Rox didn't mention Carl, but I assume he'll be here tonight. It seems they're always together now."

The man at the host's podium, black-garbed and sunken-cheeked, greeted us like old friends. (I couldn't recall having ever met him, but then, I was forever confused by the help at Zaza's, who all looked like cloned models from some depraved perfume ad.) He escorted us through the noisy metal-raftered room toward the booth where Roxanne and Carl awaited us. We leaned to kiss Roxanne; Carl rose to shake our hands. We all got situated around the table, ordering drinks from the man in black.

"You look fabulous tonight, Rox," said Neil. And indeed she did. At thirty-seven, she was successful, smart, stylish— and sober. She'd sworn off drinking nearly three years ago, not long after introducing Neil and me. The new challenges she had recently undertaken at Kendall Yoshihara Exner obviously agreed with her, and she sat there radiating a confident smile that, worn by anyone else, might appear smug.

She nodded a wordless thank-you for Neil's compliment,

then returned it. "Again, it seems, I've stumbled into the good fortune of being surrounded by three devastatingly attractive men."

Her statement had the ring of hyperbole, but I realized as she said it that she was sincere—we *did* look good that night. At thirty-four, Neil was the youngest of us, and the advantage of his years was augmented by his designer's eye; he always seemed to dress with an instinctive appropriateness to the occasion, as evidenced by the combination of the casual but expensive slacks and sweater he wore that night. The eldest at the table was Carl, forty-nine, whose prematurely white hair was countered by his lanky frame and the aggressive energy that flashed from his eyes; his breeding and bearing were Brooks Brothers all the way, a correct but laid-back dressiness perfectly attuned to his role in the world. And between them sat I, forty-two, wearing my favorite gabardine suit, a nattier wool version of the khakis and blazer that I habitually wore to the office.

Carl got to the point. "There must be something in the air to account for this epidemic of career-tweaking—my move into politics, Roxanne's name on the door at the firm, and now word of your rather stunning intentions, Mark." He laughed, slapping my shoulder. "Is it true? Are you really folding your tent at the *Journal* and heading north to . . . *Wisconsin?*" He, Roxanne, and Neil leaned toward me, waiting to hear it from my lips.

Our drinks arrived—bourbon for Carl, the usual vodka for Neil and me, mineral water for Roxanne. We exchanged a quick toast; then the group fell instantly silent, still waiting to hear my story.

I confirmed the whole plan, detailing the arrangement that Neil had agreed to. "So, probably sometime after the first of the year, I'll take over as publisher of the *Dumont Daily Register*—assuming I can pull the finances together."

"A *desk* job?" scoffed Roxanne. "That doesn't sound like you, Mark."

"I'll be the boss," I reminded her, "so I can take on any duties that suit me. As publisher, I'll be responsible not only for the *business* of the paper, but also for its thrust, direction, and stature—that's the whole point of this move. I confess I don't know much about the day-to-day logistics of running a paper, so I'll need a good number two. Barret Logan's managing editor is nearing retirement age, so I'm sure they'll leave together, and that's just fine. I'll need to build my own team anyway, so I'll start with the managing editor."

"But what about investigative reporting?" asked Neil. "That's what you've always done, what you've always loved. Won't you miss it?"

"The paper *has* a reporting staff," I assured him, "and it's known to be a good one. If a particularly juicy story should come along, though, I can always don my old hat and do a bit of sleuthing."

"In sleepy little Dumont?" asked Roxanne, her voice heavy with sarcasm. "Somehow, Sherlock, I think your whodunit days are over."

We all laughed. "You're probably right," I conceded.

Little could I imagine how wrong we were. Though I have never placed the least credence in superstition, I can only conclude that our flippant humor that night must have nettled some fractious gremlin of fate.

By the next week, word of my intentions had spread further, and I began to receive queries, by letter and phone, regarding the managing editor's position in Dumont. I was surprised— both pleased and humbled—to discover that so many of my journalism colleagues, some of whom I had never met, had such unswerving faith in my new undertaking that they were willing to uproot their own lives and follow me to a smallish town they had never seen.

At first I just stuffed the résumés into my briefcase, but the collection thickened to the point where I had to dump it on the kitchen counter at home one evening. Neil and I had no plans that night, so we spent a couple of hours together sorting through the applications, commenting on likely candidates while sipping a cocktail or two.

"Wow," he said. "Guess who wants to move to Dumont with you."

I looked up from the cover letter I was reading. "Who?"

He passed the papers across the kitchen island. "Lucille Haring."

Sure enough, the letter, the résumé, the supporting documents—all crisply laser printed on heavy white Strathmore—were hers. Lucille Haring worked upstairs at the *Journal* in the publisher's office, a computer specialist with a military background and a stiff, efficient manner to match. While I was immersed in my investigation of the festival conspiracy last summer, she provided me with key information that helped crack the story. I also learned that she was a lesbian, a guarded aspect of her private life that she had kept well removed from the job.

"Lucy?" I mused aloud. "Gordon says he finds her indispensable, which surprises me—he's such an affable sort of backslapper, and she, well . . . isn't. But I have to admit that she's smart, dedicated, and no-nonsense. If she feels she could handle the Dumont job, she'd probably make a hell of an editor." I fell silent.

Neil prompted me, "But . . ."

"But I'd hate to raid Gordon's staff. I mean, he's already losing *me*."

"He'll live," Neil reminded me, smirking.

I laughed, putting Lucy's application aside, tucking it back in my briefcase for future consideration. I swirled the ice in my empty glass, asking Neil, "Another?"

"Sure," he said. "I'll get it." He rose from the stool where he sat, picked up both glasses, and crossed the kitchen to the refrigerator, saying over his shoulder, "We'd better plan to eat soon, or we'll be smashed—on a weeknight, no less."

"God forbid." Absentmindedly, I opened the next envelope and skimmed the cover letter. Intrigued, I read it again in detail, then flipped to the résumé and studied it. "Hmm."

"Who is it?" asked Neil, setting down my glass, snooping over my shoulder.

"Someone named Parker Trent."

Neil shrugged. "Never heard of him."

"Me neither, but he has nearly thirty years' experience with credentials as a hardworking editor at lots of papers, large and small."

"Sounds kind of old," Neil said under his breath. With curiosity slaked, he returned to the far side of the island, preparing to dig deeper into the slushpile of applications.

"He's fifty-one," I admonished Neil, reminding him, "only nine years older than yours truly."

"Whatever. If this guy's so hot, why has he moved around so much?"

A reasonable question. "He says he's been in search of the perfect position. He wants to 'make a difference.' And get this: he's currently managing editor of the *Milwaukee Triangle*."

Neil's brows rose reflexively. "The gay paper?"

"Yeah." I passed Parker Trent's material across the counter, and Neil began perusing it. I continued. "The *Triangle* is one of the best gay weeklies around, known for its solid reporting as well as its tough stance on gay issues. This guy's at least partly responsible for that reputation."

Impressed, Neil acknowledged, "He writes a good letter. Listen: 'I can think of no more rewarding career move than to work at the side of Mark Manning, helping to shape the *Register* into a top-notch daily.' Pretty smooth. Does he jump to the top of your interview list?"

"With any luck, he'll be the *only* interview. He's qualified, he's nearby, he wants to work with me—and he's gay."

Neil beaded me with a stare. "Remember now. No casting-couch antics."

"Hardly," I assured him. "Even if the thought crossed my mind, I wouldn't get far with you in the room."

"*Me?*" Neil looked up from sipping his vodka. "Why would I be in the room?"

"Because I insist. Whoever ends up as my managing editor will be working with me on a daily basis, sometimes day and night. It's bad enough that you and I will be spending our weeks apart—I certainly don't want to burden you with 'casting-couch' suspicions. So I won't hire anyone without your approval."

Neil sucked an ice cube into his mouth and rolled his tongue around it. Dropping it back into the glass, he grinned, telling me, "This interview process may take longer than you think."

The process began that Saturday. I had phoned Parker Trent the day after reading his application, and he was eager to meet with me. Milwaukee is an easy two-hour drive from Chicago, and he offered to make the trip that weekend. So I suggested that we meet at the loft late on Saturday afternoon. Neil would be there, as I wanted, and if the meeting went well, I could suggest that we all go to dinner together.

That day the city basked in perfect autumn weather. The loft's eastern wall of windows framed a spectacular lakescape under cumulus clouds like mountains of froth in some trompe l'oeil fantasy. Overhead, the room's skylights admitted brilliant shafts of light that played against the interior surfaces, heightening the sculptural quality of Neil's design of the space. Within these great oblique beams, motes of dust silently danced.

"This place is a mess," Neil fretted while spritzing a table with Endust.

In fact, the place was immaculate, and I couldn't help laughing. "He's supposed to impress *us*, remember."

Neil glanced about. "Well, we don't want him to think we live like pigs."

Dryly, I told Neil, "I doubt that he'll draw that conclusion." While setting my notepad on a table near the sofa, I checked my watch. Nearly four—Parker Trent should arrive soon.

Stowing his cleaning paraphernalia in a cupboard, Neil asked, "When you talked to him, what did he sound like? I mean, cute?"

We both knew that his question was ridiculous, but I had to admit that I, too, had been wondering what Parker Trent would look like. He had enclosed no photo with his résumé, forcing me to ponder whether this signaled political correct-

ness, true professionalism—or a wizened old mug. I answered
Neil, "He sounded . . . nice enough. You'll have to judge for
yourself whether he's 'cute.' But remember, he's fifty-one."

This speculation was ended by the sound of the door buzzer.
Glancing at my watch, I told Neil, "He's on the dot—I like
that." Then I buzzed him up.

Neil followed me to the door, where we waited the half-
minute that it took Parker Trent to come up from the lobby.
When he rapped on the door, I opened it.

"Well, hello," he said, smiling, surprised to find two of us
waiting for him. He looked from my face, to Neil's, then back
at me.

"Hello, Parker," I told him, extending my hand. Though
we'd talked at length on the phone, I recited the ritual of
introducing myself.

"It's a pleasure, Mark, an honor," he told me, shaking hands;
in his left hand he carried a portfolio, which undoubtedly
contained samples of his work. "I've long wanted to meet you."

I turned. "This is Neil Waite, my lover." As they shook
hands, I explained, "Neil is an architect, and all of *this*"—I
gestured toward the expansive interior of the loft—"is the
product of his talents."

Parker gazed into the apartment, telling us, "It's sensational.
Congratulations to both of you. Your success and, I presume,
happiness is a rousing model for the gay community."

Neil chuckled. "That's a bit thick, Parker, but thanks.
Hey—come on in." And he ushered Parker into the room,
closing the door behind him.

I suggested that we move to the sofa and chairs that were
grouped by the big window, and as Parker walked toward the
center of the room, I had the chance to get a good look at
him.

He stood about my height (not quite six feet), with a lean,
trim body. His hair thinned a bit at the crown, but otherwise
it was thick and wavy with handsome dashes of silver. A neat,
short beard framed the features of his face, giving him an
ageless air. He looked believably fifty and fit, or believably
thirty, like an actor playing a role. His clothes made no particu-

lar fashion statement—khaki slacks, oxford shirt, a nice vest—but they were right for the weather, right for this casual meeting at home, and exactly right for the man who wore them. Most striking, though, his style of movement was youthful, loping, and self-assured, a body language that was uniquely his and unforgettable.

Equally unforgettable (and there is no genteel way to relate this), he strutted a simply fabulous ass. As he leaned in front of the sofa to place his portfolio on the coffee table, I was treated to a full, unobstructed view of his muscular, khaki-clad butt, a sight that actually made me gasp. Parker didn't hear me—he was saying something at that moment, God knows what—but Neil picked up on my reaction, and, in fact, he shared it, mouthing an exaggerated, silent *Wow!*

My mind was in a momentary spin, caused not only by the unexpected, delightful display of Parker Trent's posterior, but also by a memory that it triggered. Many years earlier, when I was a mere boy, at the very onset of my sexual awakening, I had experienced a similar rush upon viewing a similar sight. In a boy of nine, these new feelings were confusing and a bit frightening, but, most of all, thrilling. It had happened at Christmastime, during my first visit to Dumont. In the Chicago loft with Parker and Neil on that Saturday afternoon last fall, Dumont was very much in the back of my mind. I was planning the career move that would take me there. Clearly, it was my subliminal preoccupation with Dumont that fired my powerful response to Parker's physique.

Parker said, "I've brought along some tear sheets of my better work—editorials, extended series, special features. Ultimately, the work itself will tell you more about my background than a résumé can." He unzipped the portfolio, flopped its cover open, and began sorting through a pile of full-page newspaper samples, handing them to Neil and me.

Sitting in a cluster around the coffee table, we began a quiet discourse of the various samples, Parker explaining the background of each project, Neil and I voicing our approval. While Neil was more interested in the design of the pages, I focused on their content and the solid research that backed each story. We both agreed that all of it was first-rate, and I grew steadily more convinced that Parker would make an outstanding managing editor for the *Dumont Daily Register*.

When Parker finished with one stack of pages and prepared to make room for another, Neil rose, offering to get us drinks. Parker asked for juice or tea, and I had no taste for alcohol yet— it was still before five—so Neil stepped away to the kitchen, promising to concoct some sort of herbal infusion that he felt would suit the autumn afternoon.

Parker and I thanked him; then Parker turned to ask me, "May I bore you with some more of my samples?"

"I'm not the least bit bored," I assured him. "What else have you got?"

The coffee table was by now covered with the sheets of newsprint. "Let's see," he said, "somewhere here I've got a three-part series on a funding controversy at an upstate AIDS clinic. I didn't do the actual reporting, but I dreamed it up, assigned it, and provided the hard research. I'm proud of it, Mark. I think you'll agree that it's good, solid journalism. Ah— here we are."

He made a clearing on the table and spread the funding series before me. As I leaned forward to study it, he gathered together the various pages I had already reviewed and glanced about for somewhere to put them, mentioning, "Let me get these out of the way." Vacantly, I told him, "Anywhere's fine," already engrossed in my reading. With one knee on the floor, he picked the stack of clippings off the table and reached away to place them on the carpet, bending away from me, his rump aimed squarely in my direction.

That broke my train of thought. I found it difficult to continue reading—hell, I couldn't even focus on the type. Instead, my eyes were again glued to Parker Trent's beautiful khaki ass. The sight of him kneeling there, bending over, with those sharp creases running up the back of his thighs, reminded me of my boyhood visit to Dumont.

My mind spun back thirty-three years. It was several days before Christmas when my adventure began. I was nine and alone, bundled up and packed onto a northbound bus, laden with gifts for my as-yet-unmet extended family, including several pounds of margarine for Aunt Peggy, who had a heart condition. Mom had stuck some cheap self-adhesive bows on the waxy cartons, explaining, "They make so much butter in Wisconsin, margarine is actually *illegal* up there. You can be a real hero by smuggling these in for her."

The bus ride took most of the day, as I traveled a few hundred miles from my Illinois home into Wisconsin, headed for a town called Dumont. Though the weather at home was cold, it hadn't snowed yet, so I was anxious to set foot in the faraway land where I assumed all Christmases were white. As the long afternoon shadows grew darker around our bus, the driver announced that we had arrived, and I was disappointed to see that the ground was still green. I had presumed that Dumont was nestled somewhere in the great north woods, a mere clearing in the pines, but it turned out to be a substantial little city, larger than my own hometown. And though there were plenty of trees, they did not, even collectively, constitute a woods—certainly not the primeval forest that had rooted in my mind.

At the bus stop, I was the only child to get off the Greyhound, so my uncle easily spotted me in the crowd. "Mark," he said, rushing forward and squatting to hug me, "I'm your uncle Edwin, your mother's brother. Welcome to Dumont."

In the car, he told me how anxious my aunt Peggy was to meet me. She was at home helping the housekeeper with dinner. (Mom had told me that her name was Hazel—right! The *real* Hazel wouldn't need help fixing supper.) "The kids," Suzanne and Joey Quatrain, were dying to show me around (I'll bet). And the older son, Mark (same first name as mine), wouldn't be home from college till tomorrow. Uncle Edwin did most of the talking, as if he could fill me in on a lifetime of missing details during the short ride from the bus station. He mentioned his printing business, "the new plant," and I remembered Mom's frequent comment that our family must have printer's ink in its blood.

The car was a real beauty, imported, which was something of an oddity back then. I found the strange controls on the wood-inlaid dashboard far more engrossing than my uncle's chatter. "Here we are," he said at last, turning onto Prairie Street. And then I saw it.

Big and brick, square and stately, it looked more like a bank than a house, conspicuous among its fancy-gabled neighbors. Its clean, strong lines rose from the earth and shot three stories high, topping the giant elms that edged the street. The pitch of the roof was so shallow that it appeared flat, overhanging the walls with broad, shading eaves. Though the house was more than twice my age, its many windows gave it a modern airiness that belied its structural heft. The most prominent of these windows was a half-circle of glass on the third floor, like a mammoth eye peering out from under the eaves.

My uncle laughed at my awed reaction to the house, mentioning a famous architect who ran a school in Wisconsin. One of the students had designed this house, and everybody got all gushy once when the head architect paid a visit and said he "liked" it. (Big deal!)

We entered through the heavy front door, and I was met by the entire household, who fluttered around me with such excitement, you'd think they never had company. Aunt Peggy was nice, but a little stiff; I was expecting someone more like Mom. She thanked me for the margarine, saying, "That's very thoughtful, dear," then handed it to Hazel, who held the stuff as though it might explode. Hazel wasn't anything like the maid on TV. She was not plump, she did not have red hair, she wore thick glasses, and she had a husband, Hank Healy, who was the handyman around the house (too bad he didn't have any snow to shovel).

As for "the kids," Suzanne, an eighth grader, was pretty and friendly, but sort of stuck-up, the way girls get when they're set for high school. I knew right away that we wouldn't be spending much time together. Joey, on the other hand, was ready to be my new best friend, at least for a week. A fifth grader, he was a year older than I was, but shorter, which evened the score. From the way he darted around, snatched at gifts, and generally caused a commotion, he seemed *younger* than me. He would do as a companion for the length of my visit, but he really wasn't my type. Not that he was dirty or anything, but he seemed, well . . . messy.

They all showed me through the house, which was so big that I often felt lost. Downstairs were all the rooms you'd expect—living room, dining room, kitchen, and kind of a den-place for Uncle Edwin. The furniture was woody and expensive, and the Christmas tree in the front hall looked department-store-perfect. A big open staircase led to the second floor, where there were mostly bedrooms, including my guest room, which was nice. There was a second stairway at the back of the house leading down to the kitchen and up to the third floor. No one offered to take me up there, so I assumed it wasn't used much, like an attic. But then I remembered that big window and wondered if maybe it was a ballroom or something. As we began heading down the stairway to the kitchen, I turned and asked, "What's upstairs?"

Everyone stopped in their tracks. Uncle Edwin cleared his throat and told me, "Just extra space. We don't use it anymore. You can have a look sometime if you like." Joey didn't need any prompting: "*I'll* show it to you. It's *neat* up there." Aunt Peggy said, "Tomorrow, dear." Then we all went downstairs.

Next day, my oldest cousin, Mark, returned from college. A freshman, he had never really been away from home before, so it was a big deal when he arrived. Mark was very handsome, with wavy brown hair, and I could tell that Suzanne was jealous of all the attention he got. He wore tan pants, like soldiers wear, and I thought they looked really good on him. I liked his belt buckle, too, and his hands. Everyone else was hugging him; I wanted to, but thought I shouldn't. I wanted to be friends with him, but didn't think he'd care to hang around with a kid. Trying to think of something clever, I told him brightly, "We've got the same name." He smiled and said, "How about that?" Then he mussed my hair with his hand, and I really liked the way his fingers felt on my head. I'm usually fussy about my hair—but I didn't straighten it out for a while.

Later that afternoon, Mark was playing records in his room. Joey and I were horsing around, killing time before dinner, in

Joey's room. He had his own typewriter, a portable Smith-Corona. Its metal case was painted harvest gold, and its ribbon printed either black or red, which was really neat. But something was out of whack, and you couldn't make it print all black or all red—no matter how you fiddled with the little lever, the letters always printed red on the bottom. Joey didn't know how to type (he just punched at the keys, which is probably how the ribbon got messed up), but I had already learned, so he let me use the machine whenever I wanted. I thought of a little story that I tried to write, but Joey was too noisy and I gave up on the idea.

Bored with Joey's clowning around, I strolled out into the hall. Hearing music from Mark's room, I took a look inside, and there was my older cousin with his shirt off—he still had those nice tan pants on—unpacking a suitcase and sorting through his records. Seeing me standing there, he said, "It's their new album. You like the Beatles?" I didn't much care for them and didn't know how to answer, so I shrugged my shoulders and told him, "Sure," then went back to Joey's room.

A while later, Joey was busy scribbling in a coloring book (he acted very babyish) when I noticed that the music coming from Mark's room had changed, and this time I recognized it—Mozart, something about "night music"—Mom said it was a famous serenade. So I sneaked out of Joey's room and walked down the hall again, figuring I'd impress Mark and make up for shrugging off the Beatles. When I got to his doorway, I was ready to say something, but, looking inside the room, I stopped short. There was Mark, kneeling on the floor, reaching for an album that had slipped behind the stereo table. His backside was toward me, and I felt a little embarrassed, but I couldn't take my eyes off him—those tan pants looked so nice, somehow. And the hard creases of the cloth on the back of his legs made sort of an arrow, pointing right at his butt. I felt lost for a moment, like I didn't know where I was. I wanted to walk over to him and just, well . . . *touch* him. Could I do that? Would that be wrong? Would he think I was weird?

"Hey," said Joey, popping up behind me. I froze, wondering

if he knew what I was thinking. "Hey!" he repeated. "Wanna see the upstairs?"

"Hey!" Neil laughed. I blinked. Both Neil and Parker were staring at me, and their expressions betrayed a measure of concern as well as mirth. The iced tea Neil had promised to prepare already sat on the table—his and Parker's half gone, mine untouched, sitting in a pool of its own sweat. Neil asked me, "Lost in space?"

With a chagrined, apologetic laugh, I told them, "Sorry, guys. I was lost in the past for a moment. Lost in Dumont, in fact. I've never thought much about my roots before, but with the big move looming, a lot of forgotten memories seem to be bubbling to the surface."

Parker flopped back in his chair with a whistle of relief. "I was afraid my funding series had lulled you into a trance, induced by sheer boredom."

"Hardly," I told him. "I'm highly impressed with everything you've shown me—it's well conceived, beautifully researched, and painstakingly edited. Are you free this evening, Parker?"

He leaned forward, elbows on knees. "I was hoping you'd suggest something."

"Great. Why don't the three of us go out for dinner and discuss a few details?"

My suggestion met with everyone's enthusiastic approval, and Neil got on the phone to see if Zaza's could take us on such short notice. No problem, they assured him. Parker then excused himself, needing to use the bathroom, which gave me an opportunity to compare notes with Neil.

"Well?" I asked him. "What do you think?"

Carrying the glasses of tea to the kitchen, Neil paused and flashed me a sidelong glance, answering, "Nice buns."

"Ah, you noticed," I replied coyly.

"He's a hot man for—how old, fifty-one? Khaki, too." Neil dumped the glasses into the sink.

I strolled up behind him and held his hips. "That's a plus, I admit. But I don't think it would be in anyone's best interest to hire him on the basis of a fetish. The important question is: Would he make a good managing editor for the *Register?*"

Neil turned to face me. "He seemed professional, affable, and eager, but I'm in no position to judge his work. That's for you to decide."

"I won't hire him without your approval," I reminded him.

"Mark"—Neil framed my face with his hands and kissed me, just a peck—"hire the guy. I presume I can trust you to stay out of his pants, however alluring the package. Just remember that I love you. And save your libido for the weekends."

The three of us shared a wonderful evening at Zaza's. It started with champagne, and during a toast to the future, I offered Parker Trent the number-two position at the small daily newspaper I would soon own. He accepted on the spot. Neil obligingly excused himself to the men's room for a few minutes so that Parker and I could talk money. Upon returning, he asked, "Everything ironed out?"

Parker answered, "All systems go. Forgive me if I sound soppy, but this is probably the biggest night of my life. This is all I've ever wanted, Mark. You're the best in the business, and I'm sure there were dozens of other qualified editors eager to work at your side. I'm overwhelmed that you would choose me, and I'll work my ass off to guarantee that you won't regret your decision."

At Parker's reference to his own posterior, Neil and I each concealed a grin with a sip of champagne, not daring to let our eyes meet.

"And Neil," continued Parker, "it's a pleasure to meet you as well. I hope we'll all become best of friends. It's no secret that you're the man who helped Mark discover his own true gay identity, and for that, if nothing else, the entire gay community owes you a medal."

"Believe me," said Neil, dismissing Parker's fulsome flattery, "bringing Mark out was its own reward."

I leaned over to him in the booth and kissed his cheek. "Thanks, kiddo. I've never been happier." And I realized as I said it that I *was* happy that night. Despite the morbid ruminations that had bugged me since summer, despite the career angst and general sense of depression that had discolored my vision, I knew that I had successfully negotiated a dangerous turn, that I was now prepared to begin a new phase of my journalistic life.

Discussing logistics of the move north, we decided that Neil would drive up to Dumont with me during Christmas week, helping me settle into the big house on Prairie Street. At the same time, Parker would move from Milwaukee, and I offered to let him stay at the house until he was able to lease a place of his own, sometime after the transition at the *Register*. Assuming that the transaction with publisher Barret Logan proceeded on schedule, I would be taking over at the *Register* in mid-January, giving both Parker and me a few weeks to acclimate ourselves to the community and our new jobs there.

Neil suggested, "As long as we're all going to be in Dumont for Christmas, why don't we invite Roxanne and Carl to come up for the holiday? They're always looking for an excuse to get out of the city."

"Great idea," I told him. "Let's make it a big Christmas dinner. I'll invite my cousins, the Quatrains, over for the day—I haven't seen them in thirty-three years—both you and Parker ought to meet them. And I almost forgot that there's someone *I've* never met. One of my cousins, Suzanne Quatrain, has a son named Thad who must be a teenager by now. Believe it or not, I'm the boy's guardian. So it'll be a 'family' Christmas."

"It sounds like one highly unconventional family," Neil commented before draining the last hefty slug of champagne from his glass.

Parker rapped the table with his fingertips, saying, "Until the laws in this country are changed in such a way that they recognize and validate our relationships, our families will never be more than second-class social oddities."

Silence hung over the table for a moment as Neil and I exchanged a sidelong glance. Then Parker grinned, telling us, "Or I could bag the polemics and save it for the editorial page."

We all laughed heartily, our tacit agreement that this was

a night for celebration. The injustices of the world would have to wait—they could be tackled later. For now, I was focused on the next chapter of my life with an eager sense of adventure. For the first time in many months, I embraced the future with unbridled optimism.

PART TWO

Three Weeks Ago

Christmas morning in Dumont should have been a time of lazy repose, a relaxed respite at the end of a hectic weeklong move-in. The previous week, I had trucked some things up to the house on Prairie Street; then Neil and I drove up in my car, packed to its ceiling with my clothes, files, and cartons of afterthoughts that had missed the van. We arrived as planned on Monday, December twentieth, meeting Parker Trent, who drove the shorter distance from Milwaukee.

Hazel Healy greeted us at the house. The Quatrain family's longtime housekeeper had stayed on the job for Professor and Mrs. Tawkin, and though she was now sixty-seven, she had agreed to stay on with me for a while as I settled into the big house and made it my home. She was not at all the woman I remembered from my boyhood visit thirty-three years ago, and, of course, I was no longer that boy of nine. So when we met again at the front door, neither of us recognized the other, and we awkwardly introduced ourselves, like in-laws at a reunion. In a word, her youth was gone, and the passing of years had taken its toll not only on her appearance, but also on her vision—the lenses of her pop-bottle glasses were even thicker now. What's more, she was essentially alone in the world—she had not only outlived her usefulness to the Quatrains, but she had also outlived her husband, Hank, who died some twenty years ago. So, the week before Christmas, she helped to get a new household settled on Prairie Street, pointing out where things were, showing us how things worked, reciting her perspective of Dumont's who's who.

Since the house was changing owners, it had not been decorated for the holidays, and although my own take on Christmas had long been decidedly secular, even cynical, I was nonetheless a sucker for its trappings, so I asked Hazel to direct the decking of the halls. There was plenty to keep me busy arranging an office in Uncle Edwin's old den off the first-floor foyer, but Parker and Neil eagerly volunteered to help Hazel spiff the place with pine, tinsel, and lights. Hazel found and unpacked things; Parker provided the brawn of lifting, hauling, and climbing; and Neil brought it all together with his keen designer's eye. By Thursday night, the place looked even better than it had during my boyhood visit, complete with a tree in the front hall that stood at least twice my height.

Friday morning, the day of Christmas Eve, I met with retiring publisher Barret Logan at the *Register*'s offices, which would close early, at noon. Parker went with me, we greeted the skeleton staff on duty that day, and we outlined with Logan details of the transition that would put me in charge of the paper three weeks from Monday.

Arriving at the house that afternoon—amid a flurry of hugs, kisses, gifts, and best wishes—were Roxanne Exner and Carl Creighton, joining us for the long holiday weekend. The weather had turned cold the last few days, and Roxanne was grateful for it, as it gave her an excuse to parade her new fur coat, a full-length nutria, which Carl had given her sometime that week as an early Christmas present. Roxanne's mind-set is about as urban as they come, so I was pleased when she took me aside to tell me that she found Dumont "utterly charming, if a tad quaint," and the house, she decreed, "is simply to die for." She met Parker Trent for the first time that day, and while he and Carl carried luggage up the front staircase, Roxanne, grinning wide-eyed, turned to confide in me, "Hot cross buns!" Her stage whisper was heard by everyone in the room. Carl and Parker shrugged off the remark as if they didn't get it. Hazel bustled away toward the kitchen to fuss with something. Neil laughed so gustily, I thought he'd cry. As for me, knowing that Roxanne would skewer me if I claimed indifference to her comment, I kidded, "Why do you think I hired him?"

A light snow had started to fall—the first of the season,

perfectly timed—so Neil and I carried armloads of logs indoors and stoked the several pine-swagged fireplaces throughout the house. We were setting the scene for a perfect Christmas Eve, and the entire household soon got into the spirit of warmth and merriment.

Until the mail arrived. During the few days since arriving in town, I hadn't received much mail—a bill or two, some paperwork from Elliot the lawyer, one day nothing at all. But Friday afternoon's delivery, the last before the holiday weekend, was remarkable because of its sheer bulk. There were dozens of envelopes, all addressed by hand to me, none with return addresses. I wondered if they were Christmas cards, but they didn't have that shape or stiffness. Opening a few, I discovered that these were hardly season's greetings. No, this was hate mail.

There was a heap of it—none of it signed. All the letters had the same basic message: As an openly gay man, I was not welcome in Dumont, and if I did not get out of town, I was to be the victim of various vague threats. Oddly, some of the letters referred to my homosexuality as an "abomination against Mother Nature," but none of them railed, as I would have expected, about sin or the Bible.

So while Christmas morning should have been a time of lazy repose, I was not able to spend it lolling in front of a fire, or opening gifts with friends, or taking an easy run in the snow with Neil. Instead, I met with Douglas Pierce, sheriff of Dumont County, who was kind enough to come to the house on Prairie Street that morning at nine. "Merry Christmas, Mr. Manning," he told me, shaking my hand at the front door, stomping snow from his shoes. "Sorry your arrival in Dumont has begun on such a sour note."

Taking his coat, escorting him into the den—once Uncle Edwin's office, now mine—I apologized for dragging him out on police work on Christmas morning. He assured me that such inconveniences were a predictable aspect of his job, that he could easily have sent a deputy detective, but that he was eager to meet me and happy to be of service. His gracious manner caught me off guard, and I felt ashamed for expecting less. Decades of city living had taught me to judge small-town officials as bureaucratic rubes, but Douglas Pierce didn't fit my stereotype.

He didn't even *look* like a sheriff—no Mayberry cop trappings, no badge on his chest, no six-shooter at his hip. He struck me as a true professional, nicely dressed in civilian clothing (camel-hair blazer, pleated charcoal wool slacks), with a discreet pager on his belt and the glint of a polished leather shoulder holster under his jacket. He seemed a few years older than I, two or three at most, with an easy bearing that complemented his well-educated but disarmingly unpretentious speech. "Your call yesterday came as a disappointment," he told me, "not because it was Christmas Eve, but because the circumstances cast our community in such a negative light. Please, how can I help?"

I invited him to sit opposite me in a chair facing Uncle Edwin's stocky old mahogany partners desk. Yesterday's mail lay scattered on a suede blotter between us, but before getting into it, I offered, "Coffee, Sheriff?" Hazel had shined up a coffee service that remained at the house, and it sat within arm's reach at the edge of the desk, its silver surfaces aflutter with reflected flames from the fireplace on an adjacent wall.

"Yes, thank you. Black," he answered. Then he added, "But please, Mr. Manning, feel free to call me Doug."

Further impressed by his amiable nature, I, of course, insisted that he call me Mark. Pouring coffee for both of us, I told him, "I don't mean to do your job for you, but I couldn't help noticing a curious thread that runs through all of the letters. While they were clearly written by different people, their similar messages and their arrival in one clump suggest a bit of collaboration."

Taking the first sip of his coffee, Pierce nodded, saying, "A letter-writing campaign. Do you have any idea who might have instigated it?"

I reminded him, "I'm new in this town, Doug."

"I've lived here all my life," he told me, "except for college. Now tell me about this 'curious thread.' "

I leaned over the desk toward him, unfolding letter after

letter before him, pointing out similar passages, the repeated references to Mother Nature, and the conspicuous lack of fundamentalist screed. I told him, "In the back of my mind, I almost *expected* some flack from the local chapter of the religious right, but this has me baffled." I sat back in my chair, drinking from the cup I now held in both hands, watching over its rim as Pierce paged through my mail.

Slowly, his stern features spread into a grin as he placed the last letter atop the pile and looked up at me. "I appreciate how upsetting this is, Mark, but, honestly, I wouldn't lose sleep over it. This can only be the work of Miriam Westerman."

The obvious question: "Who?"

He relaxed in his chair, explaining, "There's a feminist group here in Dumont. It was founded twenty-odd years ago by Miriam Westerman, a local gal, after she returned from college. She still has a trace of the charismatic flash that made her a natural leader in the seventies, but now she comes across as something of an aging hippie in search of a cause. Her group has championed everything from feminism and environmentalism to paganism and animal rights."

Intrigued, I leaned forward. "What do they call themselves?"

Pierce laughed. "I thought you'd never ask." He paused for a moment, fingers to his forehead, making sure he could remember correctly. "Get this—they're the Feminist Society for the New Age of Cosmological Holism, FSNACH for short, or Fem-Snach among Miriam's detractors, and she has many."

I broke into laughter, joining Pierce, who enjoyed imparting this morsel of local history. As our guffaws waned, I wiped a nascent tear from the corner of my eye and, thinking of something, frowned. "There's something I don't understand, Doug. The group you've described sounds liberal to the core. Why pick on me? I should think they'd count gay rights among the causes they've loaded on their bandwagon."

"Oh, they do," he assured me. "To a degree."

I stared at him blankly. "What am I missing here?"

Pierce leaned forward, elbows on desk. With a blank expression, he explained, "It is widely rumored that Miriam herself is a lesbian." My eyes widened with interest. He continued. "She apparently views this . . . 'choice' as the logical and ulti-mate extension of feminism. On the other hand, she views male homosexuality as wholly abhorrent."

Stunned, I wasn't sure what to say next. Pierce saved me the trouble: "Fortunately, her rhetoric is worse than her bite. These threats"—he wagged a handful of the letters—"are empty words. Miriam loves a good battle, and she uses rhetoric as a weapon, but I seriously doubt that she'd stoop to violence. These letters make oblique warnings of physical harm to you, your home, and your new business, but Miriam's a peacenik, remember. Assault is not her style."

I leaned close to him over the desk, asking, "What about her followers? A charismatic leader, she could lure her faithful into taking action of their own"—I tapped the pile of letters with my index finger—"then wash her hands of it, claiming she was misinterpreted by overzealous disciples."

"Mark," said Pierce, raising his hands in a calming gesture (I noted that he wore no wedding ring), "I know these people, and I don't think you're in danger. Nonetheless, I'll have a talk with Miriam and forewarn her against any mischief. Also, there's a woman in the department who's had a passing interest in Fem-Snach. She still goes to some of the weekly meetings, and I'll ask her to keep her ear to the rail for me. Most important, you've got the law solidly on your side. Do you realize that Wisconsin was the first state in the union to enact statewide gay-rights legislation? Further, we've got a hate-crimes provision that takes a very dim view of gay bashing. And in Dumont County"—he smiled—"the citizens have elected a sheriff who is determined to see that our community's most prominent new resident is safely, happily at home here."

The conversation lapsed for a moment, and I shook my head, amazed—and highly grateful—to find Pierce so reassur-ing and concerned. His words had produced their intended effect, and I let myself relax. Standing, I picked up my coffee cup, walked to the fire, and turned back to face him. "Thanks, Doug." I grinned, asking him, "Are you accepting checks for your next election?"

"That's a ways off." He grinned back at me. "But I'll remember the offer."

I crossed from the fireplace to the front window and looked out toward the quiet town. Snow-dusted lawns stretched down Prairie Street beneath black-branched elms, reminding me how I'd wished for snow when I first arrived for my boyhood visit and found the town still green. Still gazing through the glass, I said to Pierce, "I'm not generally a sentimental sort, but I do sense that I have roots here, and I look forward to being, as you say, 'safely, happily at home' in Dumont." I turned to face him. "But it takes a while to settle in—not just the house and the job, but I need to reconnect with my family here. So this afternoon, it's Christmas with the Quatrains."

"What's left of them," Pierce reminded me with no intended sarcasm.

Indeed, the family had shrunk considerably since I was nine, when I met them. Uncle Edwin had died nearly three years ago, when I inherited the house, and his wife, Peggy, had died many years earlier. Hazel had long been widowed. And my oldest cousin, Mark Quatrain, my fantasy cousin had . . .

Pierce continued. "Of course there's new blood now. Have you met Suzanne Quatrain's son yet?"

"No, but Suzanne is bringing Thad to the house for Christmas dinner this afternoon, along with her brother Joey. I haven't seen my cousins in over thirty years—we were all kids then. Are you aware that I'm Thad's guardian?"

"No," said Pierce with a chortle, "I'm not." Rising from his chair, he refilled his coffee cup. "You've never even met him—and Thad's sixteen now."

"I know," I told him, scratching my head at the unlikeliness of the situation, "but I didn't even know Thad existed till ten years ago."

"Care to share the story?" he asked, hoisting the pot, offering more coffee.

Crossing to the desk, I extended my cup, which Pierce filled. I told him, "It was a busy afternoon at the *Journal*—I think there was a Chicago election in the works—when I answered the phone at my desk, and out of the blue, it was Suzanne. I couldn't even figure out who she *was* at first. I mean, the last time I'd seen her was when I visited Dumont one Christmas as a boy. I was nine then, she was fourteen, and we spent no time together that week, except at family meals."

I sipped some coffee while gathering my thoughts, then continued. "So there we were on the phone, all grown up, virtual strangers, and she gave me the pertinent update on life in Dumont. In a nutshell: She was working her way up the executive ladder at her father's business, Quatro Press, serving as executive vice president. She'd had a baby, but never married. Her son, Thad, had turned six, and she recognized that it was time to make out a will, for his sake. Then *bang*, the question: Would I consent to be named as Thad's guardian? She could tell by my stammering that I was stunned, so she went on to assure me that it was a meaningless provision, that it would only take effect if she died before he reached adulthood, that she was in perfect health, and so on.

"When I could finally muster sufficient wits to speak, I said, 'I'm enormously flattered, Suzanne. But why me?' She explained that the boy's only closer relatives were her own father, Edwin, who was already too old to serve as the boy's father, and her brother Joey, who was mildly retarded and would not be fit to look after the boy. This last bit of news intrigued me, as I could vividly remember Joey's goofy behavior when he was ten—I'd been too young to realize that he was obviously handicapped by some sort of learning disability. So Suzanne and I discussed Joey's condition briefly, until something else occurred to me. I asked her, 'Hey, what about your brother Mark? Couldn't *he* look after Thad?' "

My storytelling stopped short as my eyes met Sheriff Pierce's. He strolled toward the fire, already knowing what I had learned on the phone from Suzanne. What he couldn't imagine, though, was that my own thoughts were again overpowered by the unshakable memories, images, and dreams of my handsome older cousin—dreams that, for thirty-three years, had lived within me.

" 'Mark is dead,' Suzanne told me, her voice a dull buzz over the phone. I literally jerked the receiver away from my ear as if it had bit me. Then, catching my breath, I asked, 'How? When?' "

Sheriff Pierce picked up the dialogue, answering for Suzanne, "Mark Quatrain died in Vietnam thirty years ago."

I nodded, feeling the same sense of loss as when I'd learned of Mark's fate on the phone. "Did you know him, Doug?"

Pierce nodded. "He was several years older than me, but *everyone* knew Mark Quatrain, or at least *of* him. Oldest son of the richest man in town. Star athlete in swimming and track. Top student in high school. Then he majored in English at college, but he was never the nerdy bookworm type. Everyone was amazed that he was so well-balanced with both academics and sports. Good-looking guy, too."

"I remember that." Pierce couldn't possibly fathom the extent of my understatement. With a wistful shrug, I dismissed the memory of Mark Quatrain. "Anyway," I told Pierce, "I reluctantly consented on the phone that day, and that's how I came to be Thad's guardian, if only on paper. Before hanging up, Suzanne and I agreed that we really ought to get to know each other better, but the years quickly passed, with no further contact other than Christmas cards from her, New Year's cards from me."

Pierce gave me a quizzical look, so I explained, "I'm not religious."

"Oh." He nodded, finished his coffee, and set the cup on the mantel.

"Nor am I straight, which the whole world seems to know by now. And that makes me wonder if Suzanne has had any second thoughts about naming me her son's guardian—her phone call was years before I came out."

Pierce suggested the obvious: "Ask her. You'll see her this afternoon."

"In spite of their French Catholic heritage, the Quatrains have always struck me as a liberal-minded clan, but I ought to at least give her the opportunity to back out of the agreement gracefully if she wants to. It's not as if I'd feel slighted—like I said, I've never even met the kid."

Pierce raised his brows, puckering a silent whistle. "Don't judge him too quickly, Mark. Okay?"

That was ominous. "What do you mean?"

"Well," Pierce hesitated. "Let's just say that Thad has had something of a troubled childhood. No serious scrapes with the law, but he's been going through something of a rebellious stage lately. On the positive side, I've heard that he's highly intelligent and a good student when he applies himself. Being raised by a single mom may be politically correct for the times, but let's face it—it's not the perfect setup, regardless of the family's wealth."

Nodding my accord, I asked, "Thad carries the Quatrain name, right? What happened to the father?"

"His name was Austin Reece. I'm not really sure what happened to him, except that he left town before the baby was born."

"Cold feet about marriage, huh?"

"Hardly." Pierce stepped close to me, continuing, "Suzanne jilted *him*. Apparently Reece presumed they were headed for the altar, but the rumor has always been that Suzanne just wanted to make a baby with him. So he left town—some say in anger, others in despair. In any event, he hasn't been back since."

I laughed. "This is starting to sound like a soap opera."

Pierce checked over both shoulders, as though someone might be listening. "There's more."

"Christ." I gestured that we should both sit again at the desk. Leaning toward each other over the blotter, I asked a silent *Well?*

He cleared his throat. "This is no longer official business."

"No"—I grinned—"this is gossip. Let's have it."

He leaned even closer. "The story comes full circle. We're back to Miriam Westerman. Leading up to the time when Suzanne had her baby, she went through a period when she embraced radical feminism and—you guessed it—joined Fem-Snatch. For a while, Suzanne and Miriam were really close, although there was never any suggestion that the two of them got 'romantically' involved. Rather, they were sisters in a cause, women making it on their own in a man's world. In those days, the group had socialist leanings and was something of a commune, so when one of their members gave birth, the baby was claimed as a child of the Society."

I rolled my eyes. "Uh-oh."

"Right. Suzanne has always had an independent streak, which fed her interest in feminism, but she drew the line at sharing her child. Suzanne named the boy Thad, but Miriam always insisted on calling him something else, some goofy name. So that was the beginning of the end between Suzanne and Fem-Snach."

"The beginning?" I asked. "What did it take to cinch the rift?"

"The green movement, environmentalism. By the time Suzanne had the baby, she had started on her way toward the executive suite at Quatro Press. It's her family business, and she loves it, and she's always taken enormous pride in the management skills she's exhibited there. However, as far as Miriam Westerman is concerned, Quatro is 'big business,' and in her eyes, that's bad. She's been relentless over the years in campaigning for impossible pollution standards, and while the printing business is a relatively clean industry in the first place, that didn't stop her from having Quatro hounded by the EPA at every turn—biodegradable inks, aqueous coatings, scrap recycling, you name it."

I couldn't help smiling. "And Suzanne didn't like that."

"God, no. It came to a head when Miriam led a protest march of Fem-Snachers on Quatro property and Suzanne herself phoned my office to have the woman bodily removed from the premises. Miriam resisted, of course, and spent the night in jail, a martyr to her cause."

"Whew. Sounds like open warfare between them."

Pierce leaned back in his chair. "Philosophically, yes, they were through with each other, and Suzanne completely distanced herself from Fem-Snach. Tactically, however, the war was over. Deadlocked by each other's strength, Suzanne and Miriam simply lapsed into a long period of truce—or denial. Neither woman will even acknowledge the other's existence."

Pondering all this, I began to form a picture of my cousin Suzanne that was altogether different from the lingering memory of a blithe little girl I'd met only once. The prospect of that afternoon's family dinner now filled me with even greater curiosity—and a jot of apprehension. I told Pierce, "I can't thank you enough, Doug."

Sensing that our meeting was over, he stood, asking, "For what?"

I stood, too. "For spending your Christmas morning horsing around with this nonsense." I gestured toward the pile of hate mail, then added, "I also appreciate the scoop on the Quatrains."

Crossing to the door to retrieve his overcoat from the hook where I'd hung it, he told me, "I thought some background information might add a little—shall we say, spice?—to your Christmas dinner." With a quiet laugh, he winked.

I had the sudden urge to invite him to return later and join us all for dinner. Since he wore no wedding ring, chances were good that his day included no fatherly duties. Maybe he had nothing to do, nowhere to go.

But I decided that these thoughts were presumptuous. While I sensed that Doug Pierce could become a valued friend in my new hometown, Christmas dinner on the day we met might be pushing things. Better to let this evolve.

Walking with me from the den and through the front hall, he stopped near the foot of the staircase that led up to the third-floor great room. In the turns of the stair stood the tall pine that Neil and Parker had decorated. Pierce gaped at it. "It's perfect, Mark," he decreed. "May it bring nothing but warmth and peace to your life in Dumont."

Sensitive comment, coming from a cop. I liked him.

That afternoon, the pace of things grew hectic at the house on Prairie Street. My meeting with Pierce had convinced me that I could dismiss the venom of Miriam Westerman's minions, and I was able to concentrate instead on preparing to

celebrate Christmas with friends and family—family I'd not
seen since I was a boy.

Hazel took charge of the meal once the menu was agreed
to. Earlier that week, Neil had suggested goose, hoping that
our dinner would be strictly traditional. However, no one else
shared his enthusiasm for the idea (Roxanne claimed she might
gag—and did a credible job of miming it), so roast beef was
discussed, which struck everyone as too pedestrian. In a spirit
of compromise, then, we settled on turkey, in spite of the fact
that we'd all had our fill of it at Thanksgiving.

The heady aroma of roasting fowl filled the house as Hazel
basted away in the kitchen, having chopped and clattered since
dawn. By noon, everyone else was up and dressed and ready
to pitch in. Parker Trent played backup to Hazel in the kitchen.
Neil and Roxanne set the table and arranged flowers. Carl
Creighton and I replenished the fireplaces with logs and kindling, ready for the match. By one or so, everything was in
order. The Quatrains were due at two. We planned to sit down
at three.

Shortly before the Quatrains arrived, I was tidying the grate
in the dining room when Hazel came in from the kitchen to
survey the table. She seemed satisfied, turned to leave, then
turned back, bug-eyed. "Mr. *Manning!*" she gasped, hand to
chest. "Too many places have been set."

There were nine chairs. Counting on my fingers, I said,
"There's Neil and me, Roxanne and Carl, and Parker—five.
Suzanne, Joey, and Thad Quatrain—that's eight. And you,
Hazel, make nine."

Her jaw sagged, as if I were out of my mind. "Mr. *Manning!*"
she gasped again. "I couldn't possibly dine with the family."

I laughed. "Don't be silly, Hazel. You're more a part of
this family than I am. We'd love to have you at the table with
us."

She shook her head with quick, tiny wags. "I wouldn't think
of it," she said flatly, removing a setting from the table. "I'll
eat in the kitchen. Of course." And she trundled out of the
room, dragging a chair to the wall as she left.

A while later, I was fussing with something at the back of

the house when the doorbell rang. I checked my watch. Two o'clock—the Quatrains had arrived. From somewhere down the hall, Neil called, "Shall I get that, Mark?"

"Thanks," I said, rushing toward the door, "but I'd better greet them myself." After all, Suzanne and Joey Quatrain had grown up in this house, and it wouldn't seem right for them to find a total stranger at the door. But then, they wouldn't recognize me either—it had been thirty-three years.

"My God, Mark, it's really you!" said the woman at the door as I opened it. Rushing over the threshold, leaving two men behind, she hugged me tight, effusing, "I'd know you anywhere!"

We both laughed. "Come on, Suzanne"—I gambled that it was she, but she didn't look at all familiar—"don't try to tell me that I haven't changed. I was *nine*."

She held me at arm's length. "And I was fourteen. But *you've* become a renowned journalist, and I've seen your picture many times." I remembered her as an especially pretty little girl, and now she was a beautiful, stylish, self-assured woman of forty-seven. She turned to the door and waved the others in. "Joey? Do you remember your cousin Mark?"

A middle-aged man stepped timidly into the house, looking about the entry hall, getting his bearings. He carried an armload of gifts, picking absentmindedly at their ribbons, fidgeting with the oversize buttons of his topcoat. I peered into his face, and yes, I could discern the features of the hyperactive kid who had hounded me with his friendship during my long-ago visit. It was Joey.

He was followed by a teenager who carried one small package, shivering because he hadn't worn a coat. He had not yet grown out of his adolescent gawkiness, and while his face showed the promise of some handsome features, they had not yet gelled. His slunky bearing telegraphed that he'd rather be anywhere else, and he absolutely refused to let his eyes meet mine. It was Thad.

Neil was there in the hall as well, and I managed a round of introductions, bravely referring to him as my lover, briefly explaining the arrangement we had agreed to regarding our alternating weekends. Suzanne took an instant liking to him, curious about his architectural practice. Joey, in a word, was confused—polite enough, but his only interest seemed to lie with the house itself, as he hadn't been inside it since his father Edwin's death three years ago. Thad was downright rude, refusing to shake either my hand or Neil's.

By now Roxanne and Carl had wandered in, so I introduced everyone again, explaining that Roxanne was the attorney friend who had brought Neil and me together. As Roxanne stood there gushing about Carl Creighton's recent exploits in the Illinois attorney general's office, I realized that she bore a remarkable resemblance to my cousin Suzanne—they even had similar names. Suzanne was older than Roxanne by about ten years, but otherwise, they had a twinnish air about them. In their speech patterns, their style of dress, and their languid laughter, they appeared to imitate each other.

"My *dear*," Suzanne cooed at Roxanne, "you must feel utterly out of your element, up here in the provinces."

"Actually," she replied, "it feels a bit like a homecoming. I've always liked Wisconsin—I went to law school at Marquette."

"Really?" I butted in. "I didn't know that."

"First in her class," Carl bragged, hugging her waist.

Suzanne and Joey still had their coats on, and I offered to take them. Referring to the presents Joey and Thad carried, I said, "We have some things for you, too, but let's save them till after dinner. You can put them under the tree for now."

Joey managed to get his coat off without dropping the gifts, then eagerly got busy arranging things under the tree. Thad stood smirking, refusing to move. Suzanne prompted, "Thad, darling. Put your uncle Mark's present under the tree."

He pitched the small box underhand across the floor to where Joey squatted at the base of the tree.

"Thad!" his mother yelped. "That was a Tiffany *clock*."

He shrugged, looking proud of himself. I wanted to slap him.

Roxanne broke the tension with a confused little laugh. "Just a moment," she said. "I don't think that Mark is Thad's *uncle.*" She put her fingers to her lips, thinking. "No. Mark and Suzanne are cousins, and Thad is Suzanne's son, so unless I'm mistaken, that makes Mark and Thad cousins once removed, sometimes called second cousins."

Carl Creighton laughed. "That's my Roxy—always the stickler for detail."

"That's *way* over my head," I told the group.

Suzanne ushered Thad to my side and studied the two of us together. "I just don't see them as *cousins,*" she told Roxanne, " 'removed' or otherwise. For simplicity's sake, let's stick with 'uncle.' "

"And 'nephew,' " I agreed, resting my hand on Thad's shoulder.

His head snapped toward me, and for the first time he looked me in the eye. Jerking his shoulder out from under my hand, he skulked out of the hall and wandered back toward the kitchen. I heard him greet Hazel there, and his tone was warm and amiable, as if the scene in the hall had never happened.

His mother apologized to the group. "Thad's going through a rebellious phase. He even refused to wear his coat today. I hope to God he grows out of it—and fast."

We all did our best to assure Suzanne that Thad's behavior was typical, ignoring the minor detail that not one of us had ever raised a child. I made a mental note to take her aside later and attempt to beg out of my guardianship.

Joey kept interrupting our discussion, pestering us about wanting to see the rest of the house.

"Joey, love," Suzanne said to her brother as if addressing a child, "you spent most of your life here. What could you possibly want to see?"

He stood quietly for a moment in our midst, then explained, "Things look different. There's been other people living here," which made me feel like an intruder, an invader of ancestral ground.

Suzanne looked about, gesturing toward the various rooms visible from the hall. "But, Joey. Everything's been beautifully restored. Professor and Mrs. Tawkin were very careful about that. If you ask me, the place looks even *better* than when we grew up here."

Joey stamped a foot. "But it's not the *same!*" At forty-three, a year older than I, he still exhibited the petulant behavior that had marred my boyhood visit, when he threw tantrums at the slightest provocation.

Worse still, I vividly remembered that he had frequently threatened, "I'll hold my breath till I turn blue and die!" Sometimes he attempted to do this, which threw the whole household into a panic, and, on one occasion, he actually blacked out. Mark, his older brother who was home for Christmas from his first semester of college, had just returned to the house from swimming at the local Y. Ten-year-old Joey was lying unconscious in the upstairs hallway with everyone circling him and yelling. Mark bounded up the stairs, dropping his gym bag as he fell to his knees and gave his younger brother mouth-to-mouth resuscitation. I stood there mesmerized by the whole procedure, watching as my older cousin seemed to swallow Joey's mouth. I was too young to identify the emotion that welled within me, but it was base jealousy—I wished that *I* had been the one there on the floor, straddled by those khaki pants, my lips being gulped by Mark Quatrain.

Joey now stamped his foot again. "I want to see my *room!*"

I said to the others, "We could tour the house—why not?" Joey's mood immediately brightened, and I suggested to him, "Let's start down here, in the kitchen. Wouldn't you like to see Hazel?"

"Sure!"

I told Suzanne, "I'd like you to meet someone, my new managing editor from Milwaukee. He seems like a great guy. Last time I saw him, he was helping Hazel."

"Lead the way, Mark," Suzanne told me. "You're lord of the manor now."

So the six of us (Suzanne and Joey, Roxanne and Carl, Neil and me) piled into the kitchen, where Hazel had taken a break from her basting in order to feed Thad a sample of her mince-meat pie. The kid must have liked Hazel more than the pie, for he made a polite effort to swallow a few of the ugly brown gobs that he pushed around the plate with his fork.

"Suzie! Joey!" said Hazel as we entered. "Merry Christmas, my darlings." Joey rushed to hug her, and Suzanne leaned through their embrace to give Hazel a kiss as the woman wiped a nostalgic tear from her cheek, a tribute to Christmases past.

Everyone talked about the delicious smells, gabbed about the menu, offered to help. Suzanne noticed that the Tawkins had updated the kitchen appliances, and Hazel conceded that the changes were a distinct improvement. Roxanne told us, "Historic preservation is a laudable goal, but in my book, it ends at the kitchen door." We all laughed our agreement.

I glanced about, looking for Parker, whom I intended to introduce to Suzanne, but he was no longer in the room. Then I thought of something else.

"I just remembered," I told Suzanne. "When I bought the house back from the Tawkins, they mentioned having found some things in storage here that may be of sentimental interest to the family—some old toys, the three Quatrain children's baby books, that sort of thing. I'm barely settled yet, and I haven't run across any of it, but when I do, I'll send it all over to you."

"Thank you, Mark. That would be most kind," said Suzanne while helping herself to a glass of wine that Carl had just decanted for dinner. I poured a glass for myself, as did Carl and Neil. Joey joined Thad, having some milk. Hazel and Roxanne drank nothing.

Hazel said, "When things calm down some next week, I'll do a thorough cleaning and keep an eye out for the toys and such." Wistfully, she added, "If you don't mind, Suzie, I'd love to take a look through those baby books."

"Of course, Hazel," Suzanne answered, then noticed that Thad was looking at her with dumb curiosity. She said to him, "You know what a baby book is, don't you, Thad? It's sort of a scrapbook that parents fill with hospital footprints, locks of hair, first words, report cards. I still keep *yours* up to date, honey."

Predictably, Suzanne's doting only annoyed the kid, who grunted while grinding more pie with his fork.

Joey finished his milk. "Come on," he urged us. "Let's go upstairs."

We all looked at each other and shrugged—there was no point in putting off the tour any longer. Joey was already in the doorway and ready to go exploring. Hazel said, "That's a fine idea, Joey. If you'll all be on your way, I can get some work done." She turned her back to us and began mashing potatoes. The rest of us filed out of the kitchen like chastened schoolchildren, following Joey into the hall.

Suzanne leaned to tell me quietly, "Hazel is a treasure, really. You'll grow to love her, just as we all do."

Unconvinced, I summoned an I-hope-so smile.

Our little crowd made its way through the hallway past the dining room, living room, and den. In the entry hall, we gawked at the tree for a moment, then started up the stairs. As I did this, I noticed the back hall doorway open. Parker stepped indoors with two bags of groceries, apparently last-minute supplies for Hazel.

"Parker!" I called. "Come meet the Quatrains."

As I herded the group back down to the Christmas tree, Parker hesitated at the back door, hefting the bags as if to say that he was needed in the kitchen. "Come on, Parker"—I laughed—"this'll only take a moment." And I led Suzanne a few steps down the hall to meet him.

Parker looked about for somewhere to put the groceries, placing them on the floor near the kitchen doorway; then he stepped toward us, still bundled up for the cold weather, complete with muffler and knit cap. His beard was frosty, his sunglasses fogged.

As he removed his cap and shook his wavy hair, I told Suzanne, "This is Parker Trent, whom I've hired as my new managing editor at the *Register*." As he unwound the scarf from his neck, I told him, "And this is my cousin, Suzanne Quatrain, chairman of Quatro Press."

She extended her hand. "A pleasure, Mr. Trent. Welcome to Dumont."

He shook her hand and removed his sunglasses, telling her, "It's an honor, Miss Quatrain. After Mark offered me the job here, I did a little research on Quatro. I discovered that Dumont's largest industry has enjoyed a boom period under your recent leadership." He smiled. "Congratulations."

"Thank you," she said, sounding a little flustered—I wasn't sure if she was responding to Parker's flattering words or his physical charm. "But, please," she added, "do call me Suzanne."

"And I, Suzanne, am simply Parker."

She paused in thought. "So," she said, "you're a researcher."

"A highly skilled one," I answered for Parker. "He's been responsible for some first-rate journalism, and I'm eager to put him to work here in Dumont."

He granted, "Research has always interested me, and I guess it is, in fact, one of my strong points."

She nodded. "After you settle into the job, perhaps we could talk. I've been involved in a little research project of my own lately, and I could use some advice."

Unzipping his coat, he said, "Glad to help, if I can. What's the focus of your project?"

"It's of a scientific nature. Specifically, DNA."

"Sounds interesting. Maybe we could—"

"I'm bored," Joey interrupted. "Can we please go upstairs now?"

The rest of us laughed. Joey had been sidelined long enough, so we all headed upstairs. Parker ran back to deliver the groceries to Hazel, then joined our group, draping his heavy ski jacket over the banister at the foot of the stairs. Arriving in the upstairs corridor, we toured the rooms on either side of the hall—six bedrooms.

The two most lavish of these were originally occupied by my uncle and aunt, Edwin and Peggy Quatrain. While separate bedrooms for a married couple now strike me as a civilized notion, it was highly unusual back in the sixties when I first visited the house, and, even as a boy, I was curious as to why Mr. and Mrs. Quatrain didn't sleep together. Now, Neil and I had claimed my uncle's room as our own, where we did indeed sleep together. We decided to use my aunt's beautiful room as our principal guest room, and it was occupied that weekend by Roxanne and Carl.

Of the four remaining bedrooms, three were originally for each of the Quatrain children, and the last was the guest room where I slept as a boy. (Hazel's little suite was still in its original location, downstairs off the kitchen, except that now she lived there alone, as she had since the death of her husband, Hank the handyman.) Now these four smaller bedrooms were mostly in disarray, except for the room that had been my cousin Mark's, which Parker Trent had spruced up as his temporary quarters until able to lease an apartment of his own.

As we passed through the hall, Suzanne paused to look inside her room. It still had the pink floral wallpaper and frilly tieback curtains she had known as a girl, and I expected her to linger in the doorway, sharing with us some fond memory of awaking there with the giddy excitement of a long-ago Christmas morning. But she said nothing. She simply stepped back from the room, and it was impossible to read any thoughts whatever from the blank expression on her face.

Joey was eager to see his old room, and he raced ahead of the crowd to open its door. We followed and watched as he wandered to the center of the room, little more than a clearing amid the piles of boxes and other miscellany that had been stored there. I expected him to react with indignation at the discovery that his childhood sanctuary was now used as a junk room, but, to the contrary, his face lit up with fascination, and I remembered that even as a boy, he defied Hazel's best efforts to bring some order to his constant mess.

"Hey!" he said. "Look at this, Thad." We all craned into the room as Thad joined his uncle, helping him extract something from the bottom of a box. As they worked together, I realized that Thad—who had thus far comported himself as an absolute snot—was actually capable of displaying a spark of interest in someone else's life. It was also clear from his manner that Thad liked his uncle Joey, sympathetic to his disability.

"It's my *typewriter*," said Joey as they lifted it out of the carton. "I wondered where it went." And sure enough, there was the old Smith-Corona portable that Joey had lent to me during my visit. He carried it to his bed and flumped down with it, setting it on the same plaid bedspread that had remained there for years. He blew some dust off the machine, rolled a piece of paper into its carriage, and started awkwardly but patiently pecking at the keys—his technique had improved some in the thirty-three years since I last saw him attempt this. Thad tapped his uncle on the shoulder, then placed the typewriter on a child-size desk at the bedside, as if to tell Joey that he could work more easily there. Joey smiled at his nephew, sat on the little chair, and continued to peck away. Moments later, he yanked the paper from the machine and rushed over to present it to me. It read, "Merry Christmas, everybody. Have a happy New Year, Mark," printed half red, half black. I was surprised to see that Joey had spelled and punctuated his message correctly. While I still harbored some serious philosophical quibbles with the Catholic education that both Joey and I had been subjected to, I was forever grateful to those nuns for their unrelenting focus on grammar.

"Excellent," I told Joey. "I didn't realize our family was riddled with writers." He grinned proudly and showed his brief missive to the others in the hall, who wished him a merry Christmas in return.

Continuing down the hallway, we stopped at the door to Parker's bedroom. Joey rambled to the others, ". . . and this was my brother Mark's room, but he's dead now."

"Yes, Joey," his sister Suzanne told him, "we all know that."

But Neil, Roxanne, Carl, and Parker all flashed me a quizzical glance—this was a detail of family history that I found difficult to discuss, that I had simply never mentioned. So I mumbled, "Vietnam," a single, sufficient word of explanation that prompted the others to nod their understanding.

In that quiet moment, standing there looking through Mark Quatrain's doorway, I wondered what he would look like if he were still alive that day, if he were there with us to celebrate my move to Dumont. Would he still wear those khaki slacks that triggered my own lifelong fetish? Would he muss my hair again? Would I feel the same erotic charge from the touch of his hand?

"Hey," said Joey, popping up behind me. I froze, exactly as I had done on the afternoon when Joey caught me looking through this same doorway, staring at his older brother's ass. "Hey!" he repeated, just as before. "Wanna see the upstairs?"

"What *is* upstairs?" chimed Roxanne, who had not yet wandered up there.

"I was wondering about that myself," said Carl.

"There's one way to find out," Suzanne suggested, gesturing toward the front staircase, which continued up to the third floor. "Follow me," she said. "I'll be happy to show it to you." Then she stopped herself, adding, "That is, of course, if Mark doesn't mind." She had forgotten that, while this was her childhood home, the house had a new owner.

"Of course I don't mind," I told her. "Do lead the way."

And she did, escorting the eight of us up the front stairs.

But in my own mind, not far below the surface of consciousness, I was still staring into Mark Quatrain's bedroom. Joey still asked, "Wanna see the upstairs?" He grabbed my elbow and started tugging me toward the steep back stairway.

Barely above a whisper, I asked, "Are you sure it's all right? Your parents acted so weird about it."

"Sure," said Joey, "it's not as if it's *locked* or anything."

Even so, there was something sneaky about the way we climbed those back stairs. As he reached to open the door, I expected to feel a rush of cold air from the unused top floor, but it was plenty warm up there.

To my surprise, the door led to a kitchen, which looked a lot like the one downstairs, but with a much higher ceiling. There was no food around, but there was a toaster and such on the counter, and you could see gold-edged dishes through the glass doors of the cupboards. Everything was neat, nothing was dusty, but you could tell that no one lived there. "C'mon," said Joey, heading through a doorway toward the front of the house.

I followed. A hall—with a bedroom on one side, an office on the other—led to the main room and its arched window across the front wall. I stood gaping at the vast space. The ceilings were slanted, like an attic's, only much, much higher.

The furniture and paintings and rugs all looked like they came out of Mom's decorating magazines. At the back end of the room, chairs faced a brick fireplace that was tall enough to walk into. It had shiny brass things like big chessmen that kept the logs in place, and there was a metal rack that held a bunch of long fireplace tools. Along the side walls, there were rows and rows of built-in bookcases with cabinets beneath them. There must have been tons of books, but now and then there were gaps on the shelves, and these were filled with old things like candlesticks and framed pictures and marble statues of guys' heads. At the front end of the room, everything faced the wide half-circle window. Through it, you could see the bare branches of the treetops and, beyond them, most of the town and, farther still, fields. Near the window, there was an unusual railing that looked like the banister of the front stair- case down in the entry hall, but it didn't go anywhere. Every few feet along the top of the railing there was a fancy piece of carved light-colored wood that looked like some kind of plant.

Joey saw me looking at these, so I asked what they were.

His eyes got wide as he told me, "King-things!"

"Huh?"

"Watch this," he told me, walking over to one of the wooden plants—they looked sort of like pineapples, but without the leaves on top. He took hold of it, and, to my surprise, it lifted right off the railing. Attached to the bottom of the plant was a round wooden stick, maybe a couple of feet long, that slipped out of a hole drilled in the top of the banister. "They're all this way," Joey explained, then lifted it in the air, kind of like a drum major. "See?" he said. "It's a king-thing." He started marching around the room with it, waving at unseen crowds with his other hand, and you could practically see some big furry cape hanging from his neck. I have to admit, it was pretty funny, and he liked it when I laughed, but he himself couldn't laugh—he was the king, and I guess kings have to be serious.

He kept this up for a while, but as far as I was concerned,

the game was over. (It was sort of babyish, if you ask me.) So I ambled around the room looking at things, touching things, and I decided it was the most beautiful room I'd ever seen. I hoped that someday I could live in a place like this, which didn't look anything like the house where Mom and I lived at home in Illinois.

Like the kitchen, the big room was clean and tidy, but clearly not lived in. The rooms were kept this way for a reason, I figured, but I had no idea why. It was as if someone had gone away, and these rooms—separate from the rest of the house, a home in and of themselves—were being kept presentable so that they might be rented or something. I asked Joey, "Who lived here?"

He stopped marching around and thought for a moment. Then he shrugged his shoulders. "It's *always* been this way. Hazel comes up and cleans now and then, and Hank fixes things that need fixing. I like to come up and look around or snoop out the window or play king, but otherwise"—he slipped the king-thing back into its hole—"no one's ever up here."

"They're artichokes," I heard Neil telling the crowd, and I snapped out of my thoughts. I'd been so wrapped up in my recollection of first seeing the upstairs great room, I could not now remember climbing the front stairs with the others—but there I was. Neil had his hand on one of the banister's carved wooden finials. "They were a common motif," he explained, "at the time the house was built, but it's not typical of the Prairie School. Interesting. And the Palladian window—really just a huge, simple lunette—is out of character for Prairie-style residences, though these were sometimes used in commercial structures."

I reminded him, "When Professor Tawkin bought the house three years ago, it was the window that intrigued him most. He saw it as a key selling point."

"To each his own," Neil conceded. "It's a stunning view, though."

It was. The panorama that day looked much as it had on the afternoon when I first saw it with Joey, except that there were no longer fields on the horizon—Dumont had grown.

We all stood facing the window, cooing at the vista, save Thad, who'd have walked on coals before showing the slightest sign of enthusiasm.

Roxanne and Carl, who were seeing the third floor for the first time, were genuinely awed by the space, bringing to mind my own reactions as a child. "My God, Mark," said Roxanne, "this is fabulous. You could practically *live* up here."

I told her, "That's exactly what Mrs. Tawkin said when we showed her the house before she and the professor bought it. They're the ones who reopened the front staircase—it had been closed off for years."

"Really? Why?"

I hesitated. "That's a long story. Maybe later."

Suzanne rescued me. "As I recall, you practically *did* live up here when you visited the family as a boy. Remember, Joey?"

"Yeah," he said with an ardent nod. "Mark spent all his afternoons up here. I let him use my typewriter."

Roxanne eyed me askance. "*How* old were you?"

"Nine," I answered. "I had just gotten interested in creative writing, and I tried my hand at a few short stories that week. That was a formative period for me, and this space had an influence on it."

Parker asked, "Did you ever stop to think that there's a similarity between this space and your loft in Chicago? I mean, the decorating is all different, but the volume of the space is about the same, with the feeling of—what?—an aerie."

Neil and I chuckled. I told Parker, "As a matter of fact, we've discussed that."

While our conversation continued, Carl wandered about the room, exploring some of its features. From the fireplace he called to us, "Jeez, look at these magnificent andirons."

The group crossed the room toward him. Roxanne added, "And those tools!" An array of wrought-iron pokers, brushes, shovels, and log forks—each with a long handle topped by a brightly polished heavy brass ball—stood at the ready, warmed in the glow of a picture-perfect fire that burned behind an oversize mesh curtain. She continued. "Those things look like medieval *weapons*. What a perfect setting this would be for some dastardly crime."

We all laughed. I admitted, "That's crossed my mind more than once. Even as a child, I thought of this room as highly 'mysterious,' and the little stories I wrote up here were mostly about the room itself: What was it for? Who lived here? What happened up here? And why was the stairway closed off?"

Everyone looked expectantly at me. "Well?" asked Roxanne. "The answers?"

Again I hesitated, and this time I enjoyed tantalizing my audience. Coyly, I informed her, "Maybe later."

"You turkey," she told me amid the others' laughter. "Speaking of which," she added, "I smell dinner."

We all did by now, and I realized that I had grown hungry for our midafternoon meal. Checking my watch, I told the others, "It's not quite time to sit down, but I'll bet Hazel could use some last-minute help pulling things together. Neil? Could you check downstairs with me?"

"Natch," he agreed. And Parker joined us, descending the back stairs to the kitchen. As I left the great room, I said to the others, "Please make yourselves at home—you've got the run of the house."

Joey didn't need further prompting and shot down the front stairs, presumably to spend some time in his old bedroom. Thad went after him. Suzanne hesitated a moment—I think she wanted to visit with Roxanne—then decided she'd better look after Joey and Thad, so she, too, went down the front stairs. Roxanne and Carl remained in the great room, browsing among the books, the busts, and other artifacts.

A short while later, Neil was settled in the kitchen, mastering his technique with a potato slicer. I delivered some serving dishes to the dining room and was arranging them on the table. Parker had just brought more wood from the outdoor shed and was replenishing the dining room fireplace when Suzanne appeared, framed in the portal from the hall. "Anything I can do to help?" she asked.

The offer seemed genuine enough, but I didn't think that the town's richest woman (possibly the town's richest citizen, period) would actually enjoy any form of kitchen duty, so I assured her, "Everything's under control." I pulled one of the dining chairs sideways for her so we could chat while I fussed with the table. "I hope you're enjoying the day."

She sat. "Truly, I am. It's good to spend some time in the house again, and I'm glad it's back within the family—you may have built your fame as a Manning, but remember, Mark, you're half Quatrain."

"How could I forget—especially here in Dumont?" I'd intended the comment as a meaningless throwaway, but then I realized that it carried a deeper truth. "Actually," I told Suzanne, "the Quatrains were the only extended family I ever had. I never knew my father's side of the family."

She rested back in the chair, thinking. "When did Mark senior die?"

(Yes, there were three men in my family who shared the name Mark: myself, my father, and my cousin.)

"I was only three," I told her. "I barely remember him."

"What a shame. I'm sorry I never met him."

Joey burst into the room. "Guess what Thad and I found!"

Joey's appearance startled Parker, who had been methodically stoking the fireplace, his back to Suzanne and me. (As usual, Parker wore khaki that day, and his squatting at the hearth made it difficult for me to concentrate on Suzanne.) At the sound of Joey's voice, Parker lost his balance momentarily, but he caught himself before toppling. Standing, he clapped the grime of logs from his hands.

Suzanne obligingly asked Joey, "What did you find, dear?"

"A box of my old toys. The Etch A Sketch was broke, but all the model cars are fine. Look." He held forth a sixties vintage Riviera for her inspection.

Before Suzanne could comment, Hazel entered from the kitchen bearing a stack of small dishes, muttering, "We forgot to set bread plates—what would people think of us?" And she began setting them above the dinner plates.

Joey followed her around the table, sticking the car in front of her face, yammering about the various treasures he had unearthed from the mess in his room. "We even found my typewriter, and I wrote Mark a Christmas card!"

Hazel showed motherly restraint in dealing with the retarded man she had helped rear. "That's very exciting, Joey," she told him, placing the eighth plate on the table. "I don't suppose you found the baby books as well?"

"I'm not real sure what they look—"

Parker interrupted. "Baby books?"

Hazel told him, "The previous owners ran across the three Quatrain children's baby books. They left them behind, but we're not sure where. I'd love to have a look at them—sentimental me." And she fluttered off to the kitchen.

"Oh," said Parker, and he returned to stoking the fire.

Roxanne and Carl then strolled into the room, and Joey bounded out again, heading upstairs in search of old toys. Carl said to everyone, "I don't know when I've enjoyed a Christmas more. This charming house, the perfect company"—he hugged Roxanne's waist—"the wonderful smells coming from that kitchen. Mark, this bodes as a propitious beginning to your new life in Dumont."

I was about to concur when Roxanne reminded him, and me, "Don't forget the hate mail."

"Well, yes," he granted, "but Mark said the sheriff dismissed it as . . ."

"What?" asked Suzanne. She had appeared lost in thought since Hazel left the room, but the talk of hate mail caught her attention. "What happened?"

I told her about the mail that had arrived the day before and about my morning meeting with Sheriff Pierce. "The letters did contain some vague threats, but Pierce felt certain they were groundless."

"Get this," said Roxanne, picking up the story. "The mail came from some wacko feminist group." At that moment I realized that while I had conveyed much of Pierce's information to Roxanne, I had not told her about the bad blood between Suzanne Quatrain and Miriam Westerman. I hoped that Roxanne wouldn't take this any further. But she did: "From what Mark tells me, they're a bunch of lesbian Communists who call themselves Fem-Snach—can you imagine? Their fearless leader is some burned-out hippie named Miriam Westerman." Then Roxanne thought of something. She asked Suzanne, "Do you happen to know her?"

I held my breath, not knowing what reaction to expect.

Suzanne sat perfectly rigid at the edge of her chair. With a flat inflection, she said through pinched lips, "Never heard of her."

And that was that. Suzanne again drifted into her thoughts—an almost trancelike state—as Roxanne, Carl, and Parker matched wits in a search for puns regarding Fem-Snach. At a particularly crude juncture in their quipping, Roxanne lowered her voice and said as an aside, "I hope the kid's not listening," referring to Thad—but he was somewhere else in the house.

Then their gabbing was interrupted by Suzanne. "Excuse me," she said, standing. She did not seem upset, merely preoccupied. "Do we still have a few minutes before dinner, Mark?"

"I think so, yes."

"If you don't mind," she said, sidestepping out of the room, "I'd like to go back upstairs." She was already moving toward the front hall as she explained, "I want to see if I can find something." And she was gone.

The rest of us exchanged a puzzled shrug; then each set about some last-minute tasks before the official call to dinner. The exact sequence of what happened next is impossible to reconstruct, as the entire household was by then in a state of merry confusion. Hazel, Neil, and I tried to whisk hot food to the table, but countless forgotten details sent us scurrying in different directions for a packed-away platter, a better corkscrew, more peppercorns for an empty mill. Parker was in and out of the house for kindling, fresh holly sprigs for the table, a special lightbulb for the chandelier. Roxanne and Carl had procrastinated wrapping some presents, and they were rushing to secret these under the tree in time for the later festivities. Joey and Thad were all over the house playing hide-and-seek or engaged in some other equally annoying antics. And Suzanne was upstairs in the great room trying to find something.

I must have passed everyone in the halls at one point or another, and there was a procession of people up and down both stairways, with a steady stream of questions asked over disappearing shoulders: Where's Mom? Where's Hazel? Where's Joey? Where's Thad? Where's Mark? Where's Mom?

"Where's Mom?" asked Thad as we all finally gathered around the table. Hazel had outperformed my most optimistic expectations, delivering a holiday meal that would have sent Norman Rockwell scampering for his brushes. She hovered proudly near the kitchen doorway as we began to settle into our chairs, one of which remained conspicuously empty. Neil asked, "Where *is* Suzanne?"

"She went upstairs," I told him, "to see if she could find something."

Thad sprang from his chair and leaned through the portal into the main hall, yelling, *"Hey, Mom!"*

The obliging host, I stood, dropped my napkin onto the seat, and told the others, "I'll get her." Neil began pouring wine for the others as I left the room and climbed the stairs.

Arriving at the second-floor landing, I leaned on the banister, stretching toward the third-floor great room, and called, "Suzanne? Dinner is served." But there was no response.

So I climbed the last flight of stairs. I laughed as I emerged into the lofty space above, asking, "Hey, Suzanne, what's so interes—"

I stopped. Gaped. Caught my breath. At the far side of the room, on the floor near the fireplace, Suzanne lay sprawled on a Persian rug in a syrupy pool of her own blood. "My God"—I inhaled the words unvoiced. Rushing to her side, I knelt and could feel her still-warm blood soaking through my pants to my knees. The side of her head was crushed, presumably bludgeoned by some classic "blunt instrument." The room contained any number of possible weapons, and the immediate area was littered with several of them: The fireplace tools had been knocked askew. A pair of hefty candlesticks had toppled from a sideboard. A small alabaster bust of de Tocqueville stared at the ceiling, having fallen from nearby shelving amid a pile of other curios and books—there were books everywhere.

And then the shouting started. Wondering where I was, the others had left the dining room and now called to me from both the front and back stairways. They laughed and hooted that they were waiting for us, that dinner was getting cold, that Hazel was getting angry. I wanted to shout that something terrible had happened, that someone should get help, that Suzanne had been killed. But the words stuck in my throat as I stared at my cousin's pallid, broken face.

An eyelid fluttered! Left for dead, she had willed herself to cling to some few moments of consciousness. Her eye opened and she saw me. Her lips parted. She positioned her tongue between her teeth, preparing to speak, but she was unable to summon the breath for it. I leaned close to her face and cradled her head in my hands, lifting her neck an inch to help her get air. I said, "Tell me, Suzanne." As the commotion downstairs intensified, she swallowed. Footsteps were bounding up the front stairs when she managed to speak a single word into my ear: "Thad." Her head went limp, and I knew that her assailant's work was now finished.

In that same instant, into the room bounded Parker Trent, followed closely by Thad Quatrain. "Hey, Mark," began Parker. Then, seeing me, he stopped in his tracks, rear-ended by Thad.

I rose and faced them. There was blood on my hands. "I found her," I explained. "I'm so sorry, Thad."

With swollen, feral eyes, the boy looked from me, to his mother, then back at me. He freaked, and for the first time in his life he spoke to me, screaming, *"You fucking, lying queer!"* Then he bolted downstairs to sound the general alarm.

Dumbfounded, I mumbled to Parker, "I heard her dying word. It was 'Thad.' But she couldn't have been *accusing* him, could she?"

With a purposeful stride, Parker crossed the room toward me. Facing me squarely, he grasped my shoulders and said, "Don't worry, Mark. I'm here for you. Count on me to say or do whatever it takes to help you solve this."

Within an hour, Sheriff Douglas Pierce was back at the house. Ironic. That very morning, I'd wrestled with whether to invite him to return later in the day for Christmas dinner. Though I'd decided against it, here he was again, bringing with him not a bottle of wine for our table, but a couple of deputies, a lieutenant detective, and the county coroner.

With his crew busy taking away Suzanne's body and photographing the crime scene in the upstairs great room, Pierce called the entire household into the living room to discuss what had happened. All eight of us—Neil and me, Roxanne and Carl, Joey and Thad, Parker and Hazel—were assembled on sofas in a semicircle facing the fireplace, where Pierce stood asking questions, taking notes.

During a lull in this session (Pierce had checked his watch and was scribbling some extended details), Roxanne leaned from her sofa to the one where I sat, telling me, "This is getting way too Agatha Christie. I'm surprised we weren't herded into the drawing room."

Though the circumstances were anything but humorous, I had always appreciated how well she had honed her sarcastic wit. "We don't *have* a drawing room," I reminded her. "This'll have to suffice."

She rolled her eyes and lolled against the back cushion, feigning boredom with the whole rigmarole. In truth, though, she was almost certainly rehearsing a much embellished version of the day's events to recite at the office next week. *It was the Christmas I'll never forget . . .*

Neither would I, of course. Because I barely knew Suzanne, I could not yet appreciate the full impact of her murder, but ours was a very small family, and we were cousins. What's more, the timing of the tragedy was ominous, falling on Christmas, of all days, during the first weekend in my new home. If that weren't upsetting enough (having a relative bludgeoned under my own roof), there was also the matter of Parker Trent's disquieting vow to "say or do whatever it takes" to help me—

what was *that* all about? Yes, there was plenty on my mind that afternoon—issues ranging from merely vexing to downright grim—so Roxanne's sarcasm provided a welcome, if brief, note of comic relief.

When Sheriff Pierce finished writing, he asked me, "When you found the victim, then, she was still alive?"

Before I could answer, Thad stood, pointing a finger at me, telling Pierce, "He didn't 'find' the victim, he *killed* her. That fag killed my mother—me and Parker caught him!" I didn't know whether Thad's schooling was Catholic or not, but one thing was certain—he'd never had a run-in with a nun.

Parker muttered some calming words in Thad's direction, and, to my surprise, the kid sat down and shut up. I heard Pierce telling Thad that I had no motive to kill his mother, that everyone needed to cooperate in order to bring the killer to justice. But I wasn't really listening to this exchange. I was far more fascinated by whatever made Thad tick.

I now understood clearly that his atrocious behavior toward Neil and me earlier that day had been triggered by garden-variety adolescent homophobia. I didn't like it, not at all, but at least I could understand what motivated his hostility, and I appreciated the insight. Also, it was apparent that Thad presumed Parker to be straight. If Thad learned otherwise, would his hostility then be vented toward Parker as well?

These thoughts were interrupted by the Avon-chime of the front doorbell. Hazel rose uncertainly. "Shall I see who it is, Mr. Manning?"

News had spread fast that Suzanne Quatrain had been murdered, and the caravan of police vehicles in front of the house heightened the sense of public drama. Reporters I could deal with, having pestered my share of the grief-stricken at moments of misfortune, but the bland statements of "no comment" and "pending investigation" had already been issued, and the local press had sense enough not to hound its new publisher. Anyone ringing that bell must have explained his way past an armed deputy, so chances were good that he belonged here. I looked to Pierce, who nodded to Hazel that she should answer the door.

We all listened as Hazel left the room. The door clacked open. Several lines of subdued dialogue were exchanged, enough for me to decipher that our visitor was Elliot Coop, the Quatrains' old family attorney who had helped me sell the house, then buy it back. Hazel escorted him into the room. He carried a slim briefcase.

After a cursory round of condolences and introductions (he was visibly impressed to find in our midst Roxanne Exner, senior partner at one of Chicago's most prestigious law firms), he told Sheriff Pierce, "I wonder if I might meet privately with you and Mr. Manning for a few minutes." He patted his briefcase. "It's a matter of some importance."

Pierce asked me, "In your den?"

"Fine." I led them toward the front hall, then paused. "Actually, Elliot, I'd like to have Miss Exner present." It appeared we were about to delve into paperwork, and I had absolute trust in Roxanne's opinion of legal matters. "Neil, too—I can have no secrets from him. And Parker—he'll be my right-hand man at the *Register*." I assumed that all three of them would later pressure me for details of what had transpired, so I could save some bother by letting them hear it from the source.

With a bow of his head, Elliot told me, "As you wish, Mr. Manning."

I led them through the hall, opened the door to my office, and the six of us piled inside. The fire I'd built there had dwindled to embers, but the room was still hot. I raised a window a few inches, and icy air gushed over the sill. So I reduced the opening by half.

Elliot had already situated himself in one of the chairs at Uncle Edwin's partners desk, disgorging his briefcase onto the blotter. I asked Roxanne to sit in the opposite chair, but she demurred, insisting that she was present only as a casual observer. I sat down.

With Elliot and me facing each other over the desk, the others gathered around us, trying to glimpse the papers that the old lawyer had brought to discuss. He began, "By the terms of Suzanne Quatrain's will . . ."

"Already?" I asked. "God, Elliot, she hasn't been dead two hours."

He raised a finger in mild admonishment. "Mr. Manning," he reminded me, "your cousin Suzanne was a wealthy and powerful woman, captain of the area's largest industry. News of her death traveled instantly here, as her passing has enormous implications for the town's economy. Naturally, the key executives who survive her at Quatro Press have urged me to disclose the stipulations of her will—not motivated, I might add, by greed, but by the genuine need for direction at this time of unexpected loss."

"Of course." I had known Suzanne only as family, a distant cousin. It was easy to forget that she also played a central role in the life of this community. As soon-to-be publisher of Dumont's daily newspaper, my success here would be tied, at least in part, to the town's general prosperity. Suddenly concerned by this new angle, I asked the lawyer, "What *were* the stipulations of her will? Had she taken steps to ensure that the business wouldn't founder?"

Elliot slouched in his chair, chuckling. "Oh my, yes, Mr. Manning." He took off his glasses and rubbed the bridge of his nose. "Quatro Press will survive and prosper. Suzanne was an extraordinary manager and saw to it that all key positions were filled with able, dedicated people. She often told me, 'A chief executive's highest responsibility is to phase oneself out.' So she built her team in such a way that the company could run itself without her. And now it will do just that."

"What about her family—Thad and Joey?"

Elliot leaned forward and thumbed through the document. "Joey Quatrain, her brother, is, of course, disabled, and he'll be comfortable for the rest of his life. Suzanne, like her father Edwin before her, made sure that Joey could never wrest control of the company—he's barely capable of managing his own life, let alone a giant printing business, but he's well paid for his menial office duties, and he's now beneficiary of trusts ensuring that he will always have a home and income."

I asked, "What does Joey do at Quatro?"

Elliot had to think for a moment. "I believe they have him pushing papers in the human resources department."

From the side of her mouth, Roxanne asked, "*Why* doesn't that surprise me?"

I gave her a visual jab, an appeal for her to behave herself, before asking Elliot, "And Thad?"

With a smile, he flipped his palms in the air and explained, "Master Quatrain has inherited the vast majority of Quatro stock, to be held in trust until his twenty-fifth birthday." Elliot tapped Suzanne's testament. "As the boy's duly appointed guardian, Mr. Manning, you have also been named executor of the entire estate."

Kettle drums. Although sitting, I felt my knees buckle. Certainly, I was well aware of the issue of Thad's guardianship, having discussed it mere hours ago with Doug Pierce. Suzanne's murder, however, had so completely overshadowed the events of the day, I'd been temporarily blinded to one dizzying detail: With Suzanne's last heartbeat, I became foster father to a bigoted little hellion.

"Oh, Mark," cooed Roxanne. "How sweet! This is so sudden."

Neil looked at me with unbelieving eyes. Parker Trent covered his mouth to stifle a laugh. Doug Pierce took notes.

I tried not to make eye contact with anyone, save Elliot. "But I, uh . . ." Grasping my chair, I tried to think of something to say.

"It is also my duty to inform you, Mr. Manning—"

Now what?

"—that Suzanne has left you a very . . . *hefty* cash inheritance, far more than is actually necessary to assure Thad's proper upbringing. Hazel Healy, the family's longtime housekeeper, has also inherited a substantial little nest egg."

At that moment, I wasn't thinking about Hazel. I wasn't thinking about the circle of curious onlookers. I was thinking about "hefty." I asked, "Elliot? When you refer to my inheritance as 'hefty,' what exactly do you mean?"

He stated the figure. My jaw dropped. My brain danced with neurons performing mental math. The millions were probably a pittance by Quatrain standards, a mere tip, a gratuity for an obliging relative, but in my book, they amounted to a fortune. I would easily be able to pay off the investors who were helping me acquire the *Register*. I'd have to invent ways to spend the rest. I might even get serious about philanthropy. Suzanne—how could I ever thank her? And Thad—the dear, sweet child.

Hold on. What was I *thinking?* I had zero interest in playing daddy to that monster, and it was inconceivable that he would be willing to live under the same roof with me. This could never work. Baldly (there was no other way), I asked Elliot, "Is my inheritance contingent upon fulfilling my duties as guardian?"

"Well, I," he sputtered, "I'm not sure." He replaced his glasses and started leafing through the will. "Why ever do you ask?"

"The boy hates me," I answered flatly, "and to be honest, I don't like *him*, either. Surely, other arrangements could be made—couldn't they?"

Elliot fumbled with his paperwork. "This will take a bit of study, Mr. Manning. Can I assume the boy will have somewhere to sleep tonight?"

I noticed that it was now nearly dark outside. I looked at the faces around me, unsure of how to respond, unprepared to be making these decisions. I asked Neil, "Is it all right—I mean, at least for tonight?"

"He has to sleep *somewhere*," Neil told me, but I could tell from his tone that he didn't like the idea any more than I did.

There was plenty of spare room upstairs, so at least the boy could have some space to himself. With any luck, we simply wouldn't need to deal with him until a saner plan could be devised.

Elliot folded his documents and returned them to his briefcase, snapping it shut. He rose, extending his hand; I rose, shaking it. He said, "I'll get back to you with an opinion as soon as possible, Mr. Manning. Meanwhile, do accept my heartfelt sympathies on the passing of your cousin." I thanked him, escorting him to the hall, where he retrieved his hat, coat, and gloves from Hazel, then left.

Returning to the den, I was greeted by the mute stares of Roxanne, Neil, Parker, and Sheriff Pierce. Rubbing the nape of my neck, I could think of no comment more original than, "What a day."

Roxanne caught my eye. "It's certainly had its ups and downs."

Parker said, "You're a wealthy man, Mark."

Neil added, "You're also a father. Suddenly, *we're* parents. Something tells me that Thad's not going to be happy with this—and neither will we."

Roxanne reminded us, "The inheritance may be tied to the brat. To get the loot, you may *have* to raise him, and if Suzanne's will isn't explicit on the point, it'll all end up in probate court. If I were you, I'd play daddy long enough to pack that kid off to a good Swiss boarding school."

"That's a thought," Neil granted.

With a humorless chuckle, I told them, "It seems I have a dilemma."

Sheriff Pierce had taken no part in this conversation, watching us from a corner of the room. Now he stepped forward to tell me, "You have more than that, Mark."

We all turned to face him. "What do you mean, Doug?"

"Now you have a motive."

Gulp. Again I asked, "What do you mean?" But I knew where he was headed.

"The kid has accused you of murdering his mother. He and another witness—Mr. Trent here—caught you kneeling over her body with blood on your hands. Your explanation that you had simply 'found' the victim was perfectly plausible, so long as you had no motive to kill her. Now, however, we've all just learned that you have profited enormously from Suzanne Quatrain's death."

Roxanne stepped right up to him. "My God, Sheriff," she said in his face, "Mark had no idea that he was named a beneficiary in Suzanne's will—you yourself saw his stunned reaction to the news. What's more, he's had no desire to be saddled as Thad's guardian, which he knew would happen only in the event of Suzanne's untimely death. Most important, though: Mark Manning is probably the most highly principled man I've ever met."

Pierce answered not Roxanne, but me. Stepping past her, he grasped my upper arm. "I know that. I don't believe for a minute that you're guilty of this crime. However, Harley Kaiser might."

In unison, we asked, "Who?"

"He's district attorney of Dumont County. Pressure will be intense to solve this case fast and win a conviction. I'll feel it, too, of course, but Kaiser is up for election this spring, and he's shrewd enough to understand that any perception of laxity in solving the Quatrain murder will very likely cost him his job."

Suddenly in sync with Pierce, Roxanne told him, "I've dealt with enough DAs to understand that they fall into two categories. This Harley Kaiser, is he a just and competent prosecutor—or a hot dog?"

Pierce grinned. "The latter, I'm afraid. But you didn't hear it from me."

Roxanne nodded confidentially.

Pierce continued. "It goes without saying that the Quatrain murder is, to date, the biggest case of Kaiser's career—mine as well. The difference is, he'll be pressuring me for an arrest based on expediency and public relations rather than the solid police work that this case demands. I've decided to head up the investigation myself, and you needn't worry, Miss Exner— I'm not hotdogging—I rose through the ranks of the department as a detective, and a good one."

"Do forgive me, Sheriff," she told him with absolute charm, "if I gave any impression of skepticism."

I told Pierce, "Thank you, Doug, for attending to this. I have every confidence in your ability to see that justice is served."

He laughed. "Truth is, I'm clueless. You have a reputation, Mark, as a reporter who knows how to dig. You'll rarely hear this from a cop, but I encourage you to bring your own investigative talents to the fore—if only in your own defense. Extenuating circumstances aside, you're a strong suspect. You were found with the body, and you've profited from the victim's death. Help me prove otherwise."

Parker Trent stepped into the conversation. "Not so fast. You're forgetting, Sheriff, that there were *two* major beneficiaries to Suzanne's will, Mark and Thad."

"True," Pierce conceded, "but there's nothing unusual in an only child's inheritance. And while the kid has a weird streak, I know of nothing in this case that would cast suspicion on him."

"Neither do I," I quickly volunteered, sensing where Parker was leading me, but preferring not to go there.

Neil and Roxanne nodded that they, too, knew of nothing that would incriminate Thad, but Parker beaded me with a stare. "Mark?"

I didn't answer. There was an awkward pause.

Watching this exchange, Pierce frowned. "Mark"—his tone was soothing—"what aren't you telling me?"

I hesitated, but Parker was right. This needed to be said. I told Pierce, "As you know, when I found Suzanne, she was on the verge of death, but still conscious. What I didn't tell you is that she spoke to me."

Pierce, Neil, and Roxanne looked from me to each other with surprise. Pierce flipped his notebook open and began to write. He asked me, "What did she say?"

"She mustered the will to say one word before dying. That word was 'Thad.' "

Neil gasped audibly. Roxanne merely raised her hand to her mouth. Pierce looked up from his note taking.

I added, "My impression is that Suzanne was expressing a mother's dying wish for her son's future welfare, spoken to the man who had consented to be the boy's guardian. At the same time, I'm well aware that others might conclude that she was naming her killer, and that's why I've been reluctant to divulge this."

Pierce nodded. "This could be important, Mark. We need to consider it. And it takes some of the heat off you."

"I know." But I wasn't happy with this turn.

"It would be even better for you," Pierce told me, "if there'd been a witness to this exchange. But you were alone with Suzanne at that time, correct?"

"Correct."

"No," Parker butted in, "I was nearing the top of the stairs when it happened. I heard her voice clearly. She said, 'Thad.' "

I found this improbable, as Suzanne barely had sufficient strength to speak the word into my ear. Was Parker making good on his promise to "say anything" to help me? In any event, this was Parker's claim, not mine, and I saw no point in contradicting him. Maybe he did hear Suzanne—it would certainly help my case.

While I pondered this, Neil and Roxanne voiced their relief and Sheriff Pierce updated his notes. Then Parker caught my eye. He winked at me.

Minutes later, we all emerged from my office and found the rest of the household in the dining room, where Hazel had rearranged our untouched Christmas dinner as a cold buffet. Carl Creighton picked without enthusiasm at the platter of already dry turkey, smothering a few slices with cranberry sauce in hopes of rehydrating it. Joey sat sniffling over a plate heaped with Christmas cookies and cold yams. Thad dug angrily at a dish of Neapolitan ice cream.

Sheriff Pierce and I had agreed that the first order of business was to talk to Thad and determine whether he was aware that his mother had appointed me as his legal guardian. Needless to say, I was dreading this encounter, half hoping that the boy's strident homophobia would serve to convince everyone that I was simply not the man to raise him. Seeing the food, I lamely proposed to the den crowd, "Why don't we all eat something?" Yes, I was hungry—starved by then, in fact—but the underlying motive that spurred my suggestion was to postpone, if only for a few more minutes, the discussion with Thad.

It was not to be, however. I had just picked up an empty plate when Thad asked anyone, "What'd the old gasbag want?"

I gave him a moment's cold stare before answering, "Mr. Coop, who is not a gasbag but your mother's trusted attorney, deserving of your respect, was good enough to bring to our attention some important provisions of your mother's will. Do you understand what a 'will' is, Thad?"

"Yeah," he said through a mouthful of ice cream. "What'd I get?"

Truly appalled by his callousness, I glanced at the other faces in the room before telling him point-blank, "For starters, you got *me*—as your legal guardian."

"No way," he grunted, tossing his spoon over his shoulder, whipping a strand of ice cream against the wall. "No fucking fag is gonna tell me what to do. Me and Joey can live together."

I slammed my plate and spun toward him. "*What* did you say?" Enraged as I was by his use of both *f*-words, I was all the more disturbed by his abuse of the objective case. No kid of *mine* would start a sentence with "me" and not hear about it.

I yanked him up from his chair and jabbed a finger at his chest. "Me plenty pissed," I spat at him. "You get this straight, young man: You're well past the age of confusing 'me' and 'I,' and I don't ever want to hear it again. If you honestly don't know the difference"—I started calming down—"I'll get you a book."

That was a gamble, I admit. He might have dismissed me as a ranting psychopath, or, worse, a prissy schoolmarm. But I had a hunch that he'd find my reaction so unexpected and bizarre, he just might listen to me.

And he did. To the surprise of everyone in the room, he straightened his shirt, picked his spoon off the floor, and sat again. In a civil tone, he told me, "Joey and I can live together. Better?"

"Much better," I told him. "And it might not be a bad idea."

"Uh, Mark"—Pierce stepped toward me and took me aside—"I'm afraid that *is* a bad idea. Joey needs almost as much supervision as Thad does. They're in no position to take care of each other. That's why Suzanne asked you to consent to the guardianship in the first place."

While trying to spin an argument for some way out of this, I was distracted by the ring of the doorbell. Hazel had been boohooing by the sideboard, but stalwartly tucked her hankie in her sleeve and marched down the hall to the door. A moment later, she returned to the dining room with another woman in tow. She announced dryly, "An unexpected guest."

Whisking a heavy woolen cape from her shoulders, the new arrival struck a pose, framed by the portal to the hall. Middle-aged and lanky, with straight, graying hair, she wore a long crinkly skirt, primitive jewelry, and no makeup. " 'Visionary!' " she declaimed, quoting from a source unknown to me. " 'Thy paradise would soon be violated by the entrance of some unexpected guest.' "

Roxanne perked up. Recognizing the passage, she continued, " 'Like Milton's it would only contain angels . . .' "

" '. . . or men sunk below,' " the other woman added. Then she and Roxanne laughed like old friends reviving a long-dead joke.

Roxanne cited the passage: "Mary Wollstonecraft, *The Rights of Woman*, 1792."

"*Brava!*" shouted the unexpected guest, rolling the *r*, applauding with such gusto, her beads rattled.

Uncertain how to react to this performance, the rest of us watched in silence. Finally Sheriff Pierce addressed her, "Merry Christmas, Miriam. What brings you here, of all places, this afternoon, of all times?"

Uh-oh. It was Miriam Westerman, founder of Fem-Snach.

She told Pierce, "I had to dash right over as soon as I heard the *tragic* news." Her tone was far from grieving—it was almost euphoric. "I've come to console Ariel"—she rushed to Thad—"you poor, motherless angel!"

He recoiled from her touch. "My name's not Ariel. I'm Thad."

"No, dear, no," she explained. "On the day you were born,

the Society celebrated your birth and called you Ariel, our child of the mists."

"That sounds like a *girl's* name," he said, his voice heavy with revulsion. "Mom would never do that to me."

"Your name is Ariel, my child." Her tone was now firm. "Get used to it."

"Get over it," he shot back, and I realized that his spunk had a certain appeal.

Pierce asked, "What's this about, Miriam? I don't think your presence is much appreciated in this house, especially after that letter-writing campaign, which you obviously instigated. Shame on you."

She sailed right past the reference to the hate mail. "I've come to take Ariel, of course. It was Suzanne's wish that I serve as his foster mother in the unlikely event of her own untimely passing. Little did we know, alas, how prophetic that conversation would prove to be."

Huh? It was news to me, and it was promising—was I really to be let off the hook so easily?

Pierce questioned her, "When was this? There's been bad blood between you and Suzanne for years, and everyone knows it. What's more, Suzanne's will stipulated that her son's guardian was to be her cousin, Mark Manning. By the way, have you met?"

I mumbled some formula courtesy at her, but she stood rigid and silent, glaring down her shiny nose at me.

When she spoke, she would not address me, but replied to Pierce, "It was mere weeks ago when dear Suzanne and I had a complete rapprochement. We met to discuss plans for a project we had first formulated during our much younger years, the building of a school. During Suzanne's active years with FSNACH, she set up an irrevocable trust that would, upon her death, endow the Society with sufficient funds to build a school as part of the group's growing complex—the first holistic/environmentalist/paganic school in Dumont—or in Wisconsin, for that matter."

I heard Roxanne mutter, "Or in the world, for that matter."

"Then," said Miriam, "our conversation turned to Ariel . . ."

"Mom *never* called me that."

"Don't interrupt, dear. Our conversation turned to Ariel, and she expressed concern over his recent phase of belligerent behavior. I, of course, recommended that she place him on a steady course of Saint-John's-wort brownies. She asked me for the recipe, which I happily provided."

Thad rolled his eyes, meeting mine. I grinned. As for the others in the room, Pierce was taking notes again; Joey was paying no attention, busy with his cold yams; Neil, Roxanne, Carl, and Parker listened in gaping disbelief; and Hazel had retreated to the kitchen to indulge in another crying jag.

Miriam continued. "It was then that Suzanne revealed to me that she had displayed the poor judgment some years ago to name her cousin as her son's guardian. That was well before certain changes occurred in her cousin's life, before he became a revolting, flagrant penis-cultist." She sniffed.

"Let me remind you," I told her, "that you happen to be in my home. You were not expected, and now you are not welcome. Please leave."

"Come along, Ariel." She held out her hand.

Thad laughed at her.

She told Pierce, "Sheriff, do your duty. Carry him to my car."

He answered, "Frankly, Miriam, I don't believe a word you've said. Show me some documentation of these claims."

"When we discussed Thad's future, Suzanne was perfectly healthy and saw no immediate need to fiddle with the paperwork, but her intentions were perfectly clear, and I intend to honor them. As for the trust fund"—she pulled an envelope from the folds of her cape—"I believe you'll find everything in order. This document dates back a bit, prior to Ariel's birth, but counsel has assured me that its terms are still binding. Construction of my new school will begin as soon as this claim is probated."

She handed the envelope to Pierce, who opened it, offering me a look. I motioned for Roxanne and Carl to join us in perusing it. It was dated nearly eighteen years ago and specified a sum that, compounding interest over that period, would now allow construction of a school.

Roxanne said to Pierce, "This is a cursory opinion, of course, but it appears to be a well-drawn trust." She looked to Carl, who nodded his agreement.

Pierce said, "Suzanne's signature appears genuine. Elliot Coop should be able to verify this—it was drawn up by a former partner in his office, who's now dead."

Miriam snatched it back. "I'll be visiting Coop as soon as his office reopens after the holiday. Meanwhile, I'm prepared to discharge my motherly duties at once. Ariel," she demanded with a finger snap. "Come."

"I'd rather starve on the streets, you old witch."

I was grateful that Thad had restrained himself from calling Miriam a bitch, but, in truth, either word applied.

Thad added, "I'd even rather live with *him*," jerking his head in my direction.

Though a backhanded compliment, it was a distinct improvement over his earlier performance, and I was surprised to feel a change of heart regarding what was best for Thad's future. I told Pierce, "The woman is obviously lying about the guardianship—Suzanne showed no qualms whatever about my life with Neil. At the same time, I know that Thad has serious misgivings about living with me, and that's his right. Ultimately, I feel that this is a decision that should rest with Thad himself and, if necessary, the courts. For the short term, though, I feel that Thad should stay here in the house on Prairie Street."

Pierce turned to the boy. "What do you think, Thad?"

"Why can't me and Uncle Joey"—he caught it—"can't Joey and I live together?"

Pierce smiled. There was a tender quality to his voice as he said, "Now, Thad, you know that's not a good idea. Yes, Joey loves you, and he's a wonderful uncle, but I don't think he's able to act as your parent. Do you understand that?"

Thad quietly answered, "Yes."

"So then," said Pierce, "your uncle Mark thinks that it should be your own choice whether he or Miss Westerman

will take care of you. But sometimes these things get complicated, and the courts have to help us sort it out. We'll see
about that later. Tonight, though, it's up to you. Where would
you like to stay—here, or with Miss Westerman?"

For the first time, I actually felt sorry for Thad, being
faced with a decision between two options that he found so
unappealing. Anguishing with his choice, he at last answered,
barely above a whisper, "I guess I'll stay here."

"Okay," said Pierce to the room as a whole, his voice now
carrying the ring of authority, "the boy will stay here for now,
at least till things get sorted out better."

Miffed, Miriam scurried to Thad's side and poked his arm,
telling him, "Don't take any chances, Ariel. You be sure to
lock your door tonight—and I mean lock it good and tight!"

"That's *enough*," I told her. "I'm sick of your insults. Get
out."

She glared at me. Everyone else in the room beamed at the
prospects of a delicious confrontation. Pierce asked me, "Shall
I escort her to the door?"

"Thank you, Sheriff, but I'll handle this myself." I marched
toward Miriam and, pointing toward the hall, repeated, "Get
out of my house."

She crossed her arms with a defiant smirk.

So I grabbed one of her arms and dragged her into the hall.
She hadn't expected that, and she started yelping about male
aggression and sexual harassment and lawsuits and my penis.
"Sheriff!" she hollered. "Do something!"

By then we had reached the front door, which I opened
with my free hand. "Get the hell *out*," I told her, shoving
her over the threshold, slamming the door behind her. I was
tempted to open the door again and shout a profanity into the
darkness, but I'd already made my point, and it would have
been rude to disturb the neighbors.

Everyone in the dining room had watched from the portal,
and by now they were enjoying a hearty round of laughter,
Thad included. "Can we finally *eat?*" someone asked, and the
little crowd herded back to the table.

Still standing at the door, I caught my breath and felt my

adrenaline subsiding. Then I noticed that Hazel was not with the others, but there in the front hall, watching from near the Christmas tree. When our eyes met, she approached me. With lowered voice, she said, "Mr. Manning, there's something I need to discuss with you."

"I'm sure there is," I told her, guessing the topic. "Thad's room—we need to put one of the spare bedrooms in order. Could you help with linens?"

"Certainly, sir. But that's not what I meant to discuss." She checked over her shoulder, then touched my arm, as if preparing to tell a secret. "It's regarding *Mizz* Westerman." She wagged her head, signaling general disapproval of the woman.

I led her to the den, and we stepped inside the doorway to talk. I told Hazel, "I've been wondering about something. How did Suzanne ever get involved with Miriam's group in the first place? I can understand Suzanne's general interest in feminism—she was a talented and strong-willed woman—but I can't imagine how she could support the Society's belief in paganism. The Quatrain family is Catholic to the core."

Hazel sighed. "Suzie had a strong Catholic upbringing like the other children, but she broke from the Church many years ago, way back in high school." Hazel wrung her hands, offering no more details—there was something else she was anxious to broach.

Again she touched my arm. Leaning close, she told me, "I thought you'd want to know that *Mizz* Westerman was here at the house earlier today." She removed her heavy glasses, waiting for me to react.

"Oh?" My brows arched. "When?"

"During all the confusion just before dinner, just before poor Suzie was butchered. Miriam Westerman came to the back door with a fruitcake—an *organic* fruitcake, if you can believe it—with her 'belated best wishes for the winter solstice.' I told her we'd tolerate no such heathen nonsense in this house, and then *she* had the gall to get huffy with *me*—right there in the back hall by the service stairway. I was getting pretty well steamed, and not feeling right about fighting on Christmas, when the oven timer went off, praise the Lord. So I bit my tongue, thanked her for the 'gift,' and excused myself to the kitchen."

I couldn't help laughing at the scene Hazel had sketched. I asked her, "What did Miriam do?"

"That's my point," said Hazel, replacing her glasses and peering tensely into my eyes. "I assumed the woman would *leave*—the back door is right there, just around the corner from the kitchen. Once I'd put down the fruitcake and checked the oven, I noticed that I hadn't heard the door open and close, so I poked my head into the hall to ask her if she wanted something else. But she wasn't *there*, Mr. Manning. Glad to be rid of her, I went back to work in the kitchen. Now, though, it's plain enough what happened."

Hazel folded her arms resolutely, concluding, "I'll bet that woman slipped up the service stairs to clobber the life out of poor Suzie."

It had been a harrowing day, and by ten o'clock, Roxanne and Carl were tucked in for the night in Aunt Peggy's lovely former bedroom. Grudgingly, Thad settled into the old guest room, hastily arranged for him. Hazel retreated to cry in her quarters near the kitchen. And Joey had gone home hours ago (at the same time Sheriff Pierce left the house), not quite grasping the gravity of the day's events.

Neil, Parker, and I sat up later than the others, talking in the den. There was a tidy group of stuffed furniture near the fireplace, and we sat there finishing a drink together. Neil and I had our usual—Japanese vodka on ice, garnished with orange peel—we both knew instinctively that it was important to maintain our rituals, since our relationship would now be tested by separate living arrangements. As for Parker, he drank Scotch, single malt, neat.

"Help me sort this out," I asked my companions. "What do we know so far?"

Neil shrugged. "Suzanne Quatrain was murdered upstairs in the great room."

Parker continued. "And we don't know who did it, how, or why."

"Thanks, guys," I told them under my breath before sipping some vodka. Gathering my thoughts, I recalled aloud, "During the minutes leading up to the murder, the household was in a state of happy holiday mayhem, with people all over the place involved in various tasks—no one person's actions can be mapped for the entire time. Since the third-floor apartment where the murder occurred is served by both a front and a back stairway, it's impossible to focus on the killer's access to the scene. And since there were no screams, Suzanne probably knew her killer. It could have been anyone in the house."

Parker nodded. "Who was here? There were the three of us. And the three Quatrains—Joey, Thad, and victim Suzanne. Roxanne and Carl were here. And Hazel. That's nine, minus Suzanne."

"Plus Miriam Westerman," I told them, "assuming Hazel was on the level with me, and I can't imagine why she wouldn't be. So the way I see it, we have three suspects: Me . . ."

"Stop that," Neil interrupted. "Parker and I *know* you didn't do it."

"Thanks," I told him, "so do I. But we have to be at least as objective as the DA will be, and right now I'm at the top of his list—I was found with the victim with her blood on my hands, and I'm suddenly a wealthy man as the result of her death. *We* know I'm innocent, but the only way to prove it is to prove someone else's guilt."

"Which leads us," said Neil, "to your two other suspects."

Parker guessed, "Thad and Miriam?"

"Right. Thad had even more to gain from Suzanne's death than I did, and we've all seen enough of his awful behavior to know that he has a rebellious streak. Most compelling, of course, is the fact that Suzanne's dying word was 'Thad,' but I never really felt that she was naming her killer. Further, while Thad is indeed ill-mannered and immature, I have no reason to believe that he was sufficiently motivated to kill his own mother. He's snotty, not heinous."

Neil grinned. "What about Miss Fem-Snach?"

"She's another story entirely. I'm willing to believe that Miriam Westerman is capable of anything. Consider: There was a history of feuding between her and the victim; there was trust money at stake for her school; she spoke longingly of Thad as 'Ariel, my child'; and she was reported to be in the house at the time of the murder, her presence known only to the maid."

Parker leaned forward with his drink between his hands. "What do you make of that business about the trust—and Miriam's story that she and Suzanne had recently kissed and made up?"

"The document looked genuine," I answered, "and if her lawyer assured her that its terms are still binding, chances are good that Miriam is about to land some serious cash. But I simply don't believe her story about the rapprochement with Suzanne. Two reasons: First, shortly before the murder, while Suzanne and Roxanne were talking, Roxanne mentioned Miriam, and Suzanne reacted with a cold 'Never heard of her.' Second, Miriam said that Suzanne found my homosexuality 'revolting,' but this afternoon, she greeted me with open arms and took an instant liking to Neil. Our relationship didn't bother her in the least—in fact, she seemed intrigued by it."

Parker wore a confused expression. "If Suzanne was still on the outs with Miriam, why would she leave her all that money?"

"Suzanne must have simply forgotten about the trust. The original endowment wasn't all that much—it's been inflated by eighteen years' interest."

"Hmm," said Neil, swirling his ice. "Miriam sounds like a strong suspect."

"And at this point," I told him, "everyone else who was in the house is above suspicion. Both of you guys, as well as Roxanne and Carl, barely knew the victim and had nothing to gain from her death. On the other hand, Hazel Healy and Joey Quatrain knew Suzanne all her life, and there's no reason to think those relationships were anything but loving—they were both shedding tears today."

"Conspicuously," added Neil, "neither Thad nor Miriam showed any outward signs of grief."

"Good observation," I told him.

Neil sucked the last of his drink and set down the glass. "I'm shot," he said. "Time for bed."

Stifling a yawn, I told him, "I've still got a bit of *Register* business to discuss with Parker, but you go on up, kiddo. I'll join you soon."

He rose and stretched, then gave me a kiss, Parker a hug. Amid an exchange of good nights, he left the den and went upstairs.

For the first time that day, the house was calm. In the stillness, nothing moved, save the fire in the grate; all was quiet, save its hiss. Everyone had been talking, it seemed, all day long, and now it felt good to say nothing. But there were things that still needed to be said, which is why I'd asked Parker to remain there with me. Contrary to what I'd told Neil, though, it was not the *Register* that was on my mind. It was Parker's lie to Sheriff Pierce about hearing Suzanne's dying word, which injected a worrisome note of doubt into my decision to hire him as my second-in-command at the paper. While searching for the words to broach this, I heard his voice.

"I'm the outsider here." He laughed quietly, rubbing the neatly trimmed bristles of his short beard. His eyes shone in the firelight.

"How so?" I asked him.

"This house was filled today with your friends and family. This house itself was *built* by your family. I'm honored to be here now, but I've got that weird feeling of being the new kid on the block. Think about it, Mark—I first met you and Neil only last month, and I'm a total stranger to everyone else who was here today."

I reminded him, "I barely know the others myself. They may be family, but we've hardly been close. As for Thad, I'd never even met him till this afternoon."

"Sure, I know," he said, brushing my observation aside with a wag of his hand, "but you've got *roots* here. You belong in Dumont."

Finishing my drink, I held the glass in my lap. "I was born in Illinois. I've lived my whole life there, till now. And my only significant exposure to Dumont was during a week's visit as a kid."

"You've mentioned that," said Parker, leaning forward with interest. "You gave the impression that the visit was memorable for some reason."

I laughed. "Lots of reasons."

"Care to enlighten me?"

Did I really want to get into this? It was getting late, and I was tired. But my memories had, in fact, been stirring all day, and the wood-and-leather setting of the den was conducive to the spinning of a tale. "Okay, Parker. Need more Scotch first?" He shook his head and settled into his chair.

I told him, "As you know, the house was built by my uncle Edwin. He grew up in Dumont with my mother, Eden Quatrain (everyone called her Edie), and their younger sister, Edna. Edna later moved away to California, and my mother moved to Illinois, where I was born—where my father died when I was three. I never met my aunt Edna, but it was because of her illness thirty-three years ago that I first visited this house."

Telling him the background of that early visit to Dumont, I slipped back to my childhood and relived the events with absolute clarity:

One afternoon when I was in fourth grade, I came home from school and was surprised to find my mother waiting for me. She had taken over my father's modest printing business when he died—a gutsy decision for a woman in those days—and didn't normally get home till well past five. We lived a comfortable life. She enjoyed running the business, which boomed under her reins, and I enjoyed my few hours of independence after school. Late afternoons were a quiet time, and I had begun to appreciate the solitude that allowed me to indulge in some youthful experimentation as a writer.

She met me at the kitchen door that day and leaned to kiss my forehead. "This morning I got a call from your aunt Edna in California," she told me, blowing cigarette smoke sideways so that it wouldn't hit me full in the face. "Her cancer's spreading. I have to go see her."

"But, Mom," I said, putting my books on the counter, unzipping my heavy coat, "Christmas is coming."

"I'm sorry, dear, but I have to go, and the holidays are a good time for me to be away from the plant. You'll be off from school, but you wouldn't enjoy this trip. So I phoned my brother, your uncle Edwin, and he says you're more than welcome to spend Christmas with them in Wisconsin."

I opened my mouth to protest, but she continued. "Everything'll be fine, honey. It's time you met Edwin and Peggy anyway, and you'll have a grand time with your cousins—Mark, Suzanne, and Joey. In fact, Joey's not much older than you. And just wait till you see that house! They even have a maid."

This might not be too bad, I decided, pouting just enough to assure Mom that I would miss her when she took off alone for California, but not enough to convince her to change plans and drag me along to visit her sick sister. So I spent a whole day on a bus to Dumont, and on the evening I arrived, I met the Quatrain family, including my cousins, except Mark, of course.

"He had died, right?" Parker's question interrupted my story, and my mind snapped back to the present. "In Vietnam?"

"No no no," I explained. "At the time of my visit, Mark Quatrain was a freshman in college. When I arrived at the house, he was still at school. I met him the next day, when he came home for semester break. I'm sure he finished college, so it would have been at least four years later when he went to Vietnam, but I've never known the details." I paused to calculate the years. "Yes, that would have been right in the thick of it."

Parker nodded his understanding of this chronology, saying, "I've met Joey and—briefly—Suzanne. What was Mark like?"

"I never really got to know him. He was nine years older than I, twice my age, so we simply didn't interact much during my visit. But"—long pause—"he was easily the most handsome young man I'd ever seen. He stirred feelings in me that I couldn't possibly fathom at that age. Looking back, I understand that meeting my older cousin signaled the onset of my own sexual awakening."

"Whew. Heavy." Parker got out of his chair and stepped to the hearth. The fire was low, and he dropped to one knee, poking the embers.

"Years later, when Suzanne told me on the phone that her brother was dead, I felt as if someone had robbed me of something. But I'll never lose the memory of him—more of a fantasy, actually."

I was about to amplify on this—to explain my early fixation on Mark Quatrain's khaki pants, to attempt a humorous confession of the fetish that followed me into adulthood—when I found myself transfixed by the movement of Parker's own fabulous khaki ass as he knelt there stirring the fire. To my chagrin, I realized that I was now firmly aroused by these thoughts and sights.

This was nuts. The purpose of this quiet talk with Parker was simply to question him about the odd vow he had made to me at the murder scene, and here I was, practically drooling at the sight of his butt. My childhood tale was finished. It was time to confront this. "Uh, Parker . . . ?"

There was something in my tone of voice that caused him to turn from the fire, facing me with puzzled apprehension. "Yes, Mark?"

"I need to talk to you about something important." I gestured that he should sit again, which he did. I continued. "I want to follow up on what you said this afternoon in the great room, right after Suzanne was killed."

"Mark," he stopped me, smiling, "I'm glad you brought this up. I was waiting for an opportunity to explain, but, well, it's awkward."

I laughed. "Why?"

Though his glass was now empty, he picked it up and rubbed a finger around its rim. "What I said upstairs must have seemed absurdly out of the blue. Sorry."

That was all? I waited for more.

He dithered with his thoughts before speaking, and when

he did, his tone was oddly academic. "It may seem that I overstated my determination to help you, Mark, but you're not fully aware of the context from which I spoke those words."

Did I really want to hear this? "What 'context,' Parker?"

He leaned toward me, though the movement was barely perceptible, a nudge of the base of his spine. He said softly, "The context of love. Though you've never known it, Mark, I've loved you—from a distance. And now I'm here with you. I'm here *for* you."

I'd had a mounting, uneasy sense of where his words were headed, but that didn't soften their impact. While I found the man unquestionably attractive, my feelings for him could never advance beyond physical allure to that heady emotional state commonly labeled "love"—or so I assumed.

Mustering a semblance of composure, I told him calmly but bluntly, "I'm flattered, Parker. But surely you realize that I'm committed to Neil. Nothing is possible between you and me other than our working relationship—and, of course, our friendship, *casual* friendship. I have to warn you, though: harboring any notions of . . . carnal involvement will work against you, against us, and against my 'marriage' with Neil. You and I need to work closely at the *Register*, long hours, too, and any nonprofessional overtones will simply be bad for business. Plus the fact, you're living here with me at the house for a while. This is middle America, and we need to be above reproach. I have a lot at stake here."

There. I'd laid it out. Had I overstated my position? Would Parker suddenly see me less as a gay journalistic trailblazer and more as a relic of my square, closeted past? My struggle with all this must have shown in my face. He leaned further from his chair to pat my knee, and I was relieved to sense that this physical gesture carried no hint of a come-on.

"I understand," he assured me. "Listen, Mark. This discussion, please forget it. I've been grappling with these feelings all day, trying to decide whether to open up to you. Then, sitting here, you *asked* me to do just that. And I blurted out something that should have remained unsaid. It would now be dishonest of me to *retract* what I told you—because it was true—but I promise that these feelings will be kept well below the surface. I'll do nothing that could lead you to question your decision to hire me. Fair enough?"

He had said precisely what I wanted to hear. "Fair enough," I told him, signaling with a smile that a potential crisis had passed. Relaxing in my chair, I was curious about something. Confident that we were now on the same wavelength, I felt comfortable enough to ask, "How did this get started? I mean, you said you've 'loved me from a distance.' What does *that* mean?"

"Mark," he explained, equally relaxed now, "I told you when you first interviewed me in Chicago that you're the best in the business, that your coming out and your open relationship with Neil has set an enviable model for the entire gay community. I don't mean to embarrass you, but please understand that as a struggling gay journalist—struggling with my career as well as with my gay identity—I've practically *idolized* you. I've read everything you've written, and everything that's been written about you, since you first came out a few years ago."

Such flattery was unexpected, and I felt guilty for having fished for it. Wagging a finger, I told him, "We'll have no more hero worship," trying to inject a lighter note into our discussion.

Parker hesitated, then said, almost shyly, "It's not just hero worship, Mark. You're a very attractive man, and I'd be lying if I tried to tell you that I don't find you desirable. It certainly doesn't hurt that you're—what?—nine or ten years younger than me."

I grunted. "I'm no spring chicken."

"Everything's relative."

I was tempted to console him on the age issue, to return his compliment and let him know that both Neil and I found him highly attractive. I even considered confiding in him that his khaki pants—

But no. That would simply reopen a door that I meant to close. It was time to conclude. I heaved a thoughtful sigh, then told him, "Now that we're here, past glories or failures—or fantasies—are irrelevant. We've got a job to do at the *Register.*"

He nodded with purpose. "That sounds great. To repeat what I told you that first night in Chicago: This is all I've ever wanted. Thanks, Mark, for your confidence in my ability to do the job. I'll be the best managing editor you could possibly have hired."

"I'm sure you will be, Parker." And with that, I rose. Our conversation had ended on exactly the right note, and I was tired. I switched off a table lamp.

Then Parker reminded me, "You'll never find anyone more loyal to you. After all, I lied for you—to Sheriff Pierce—about hearing Suzanne's dying word."

Sunday, the day after Christmas, dawned colder than before, and most of the household slept late. I had no way of knowing whether the others were simply indulging in a long winter's nap, or if they, as I, had found it difficult to fall asleep the night before, bedded under the great room where Suzanne had just been murdered.

Hazel was up, busy in the kitchen, trashing the last of the detritus generated by our failed holiday feast. Pastries, along with coffee, were set out in the dining room, and I could tell by their arrangement that I was the first to pick at them. Deciding against the kringle—a large horseshoe-shaped Danish, something of a specialty in the area—I poured a cup of black coffee and took it to the den.

I had dressed warmly for the day, but the room felt cold, so I built another fire atop yesterday's ashes. Settling down with my coffee, I realized that something was missing—the *Dumont Daily Register.* I wanted it not only because I have *always* read the morning paper while having my coffee, and not only because I was soon to take over as its publisher, but especially that morning because I was curious about the treatment of Suzanne's story. Surely, this was big news.

Stepping to the window nearest the front door, I looked through the curtains, trying to see if the paper had been delivered yet. What caught my attention, though, was the traffic outside the house. Prairie Street was one of Dumont's quieter boulevards, and the Sunday following Christmas should have been quieter still, but a steady stream of cars paraded slowly by, faces pressed to foggy windows to glimpse the site of a great civic tragedy.

As I watched, a woman walking on the street turned onto my sidewalk and approached the house, her pace brisk against the wind. As she drew nearer, I judged her to be older than I, perhaps fifty or so, a lady of striking bearing and somewhat eccentric appearance. In spite of the cold, her legs were bare below the knees—attractive legs, I noted, shown to best advantage atop a pair of spiked heels that pecked the cement. Her manner of dress was conspicuously fashionable by Dumont standards, and she carried an enormous purse, sort of a flat leopard-spot carpetbag. She climbed the several stairs from the sidewalk and stepped across the porch toward the door.

Realizing that she was about to ring the bell, I rushed out of the den to the entry hall, hoping I could beat her finger to the punch, not wanting the chimes to disturb those who were still asleep. I opened the door in time to catch her squatting at the mat, picking up the rolled bundle of the Sunday *Register*. Presenting it to me, she said, "Your paper, Mr. Manning— glee savage features." Big smile. Big red lips.

"I beg your pardon?"

She laughed, extending her hand. "My name is Glee Savage. I'm features editor of the *Register.*"

"Oh . . ." I echoed her laugh, shook her hand. "Do come in—is it *Miss* Savage?"

"Yes," she answered, stepping through the doorway, "but do call me Glee."

"And I hope you'll call me Mark," I told her.

She eyed me askance. "Mr. Logan would never permit that." With a grin, she bumped the door closed behind her.

"In case you haven't noticed, Barret Logan and I are the products of different generations. I'm a first-name kind of guy."

"And you're soon to be my new boss," she mused. "I didn't

get a chance to meet you last month when you drove up to discuss the buyout with Mr. Logan." Looking me up and down, she said, "I approve." Then she added, "Your eyes—they're so uncommonly green—and arrestingly handsome."

"Thank you." I may have blushed. "May I take your coat?" She removed her coat and gloves, passing them to me, keeping her hat and purse. I ushered her into the den and hung her things, asking with feigned formality, "May I inquire as to the nature of this visit?"

"Well, my condolences, of course." She gently grasped my forearm with both of her hands. "What a terrible tragedy. Such a grisly welcome to our fair city. I'm so sorry, Mr. Manning— Mark."

I thanked her for the sentiments, explaining, "The truth is, I barely knew Suzanne. I think her loss will be felt much more deeply by the town as a whole." As I spoke, I unrolled the *Register* on my desk. Its headline trumpeted: SUZANNE QUATRAIN KILLED! There was a photo of her bagged body being carted out the front door of the house, with an italic subhead: *Quatro Heiress Bludgeoned in Childhood Home.* I tapped the newsprint, telling Glee, "That explains all the traffic this morning—I was wondering."

She made no response to my comment, but fidgeted with the top edge of her purse (it really was the biggest I'd ever seen, nearly two feet square). Then she said, "There's another reason I decided to come over this morning—and I do apologize, by the way, for this early intrusion. There's a matter of some delicacy I want to discuss with you, and I didn't want it to wait till next week."

"Oh?" I gestured that we should sit. She chose the love seat near the fire, I the adjacent chair. "May I get you some coffee?" Mine was at hand on a nearby table.

"Thank you, no." Wryly, she added, "Too many stimulants already today."

Joking, I added, "Then how about a *drink?*"

To my surprise, though it was not yet nine o'clock, she paused to consider my offer. "Still a bit early, thanks—even for me!"

We shared a laugh, and when it subsided, I prompted her, "I'm all ears, Glee."

She collected her thoughts, then began. "This goes back thirty years, come spring. No lady enjoys dating herself, but I'll admit that it was during my first year out of journalism school, when I was twenty-two. I was a cub reporter at the *Register*, where I have subsequently spent my entire career. In those early days, long before I had an inkling that I would one day serve as the paper's features editor, I worked on what was then termed the 'women's page'—softer news, the social scene, weddings, food, and such. Covering preparations for the Dumont High spring cotillion (God, I *am* dating myself!), I was assigned to work up profiles on candidates for queen of the formal event, including Suzanne Quatrain."

"Ahhh." I leaned forward to ask her, "Should I be taking notes?" My pen, as always, was clipped inside my pocket, but I would need to find a pad.

She shook her head. "There's not much detail, just my own speculation. I wish I had more."

"Tell me what you know." I reached for my coffee, swirled the cup, and swallowed some. Finding it tepid, I returned the cup to the table.

She snapped open her bag and extracted first a delicate pair of half-frame reading glasses, perching them on her nose, then a folded newspaper clipping. Careful not to tear the creased old newsprint, she examined it briefly and passed it to me. Faded mug shots of a dozen high school girls, all with the same ratted hairdo, smiled up at me from the foxed and musty page.

Glee said, "Suzanne was seventeen then, a junior. As you can see, she was truly a beauty." Sure enough, posed alphabetically between Missy Palmer and Heidi Renquist was the pretty Suzanne Quatrain I had met during my boyhood visit. The photo was snapped three years later, but still, it captured the essence of the perky young lady I'd known when I was nine. Glee continued. "Suzanne's charming appearance, combined with her family's wealth and her own gregarious personality, made her the most popular girl in her class, a shoo-in for cotillion royalty." Glee paused, leaning toward me. "But something peculiar happened."

I looked up from the murky image of grayed dots on yellowed paper. "What?"

"She withdrew from the running." Glee crossed her arms.

This was not the climax I'd expected. I wondered, So what?

Glee amplified, "She withdrew from the running—without explanation—then missed the dance and nearly a week of school, claiming some routine ailment. But there was other evidence that Suzanne left town for that period, and there was a general consensus that she was never quite the same after she returned. Needless to say, I smelled a story."

"I don't blame you. What'd you do?"

"Nothing. Barret Logan wouldn't hear of it. The Quatrains were far too important to the community, he said, to be hounded by the local press. Case closed. But I have *always* wondered what that episode was about, and now I wonder if it could possibly relate to Suzanne's murder."

I stood, puzzled. Crossing to the fireplace, I turned to tell Glee, "I don't follow that. Sure, Suzanne's earlier disappearance is intriguing, but why would you think it has some connection to her murder, thirty years later?"

Glee also stood, stepping near to explain, "Over the last year or so, Suzanne spent a lot of time at the *Register*'s offices, doing research in the paper's morgue."

"She mentioned some sort of project," I recalled.

"It's not clear what she was digging for, but all of her research focused on the year or two after her high school graduation." Glee bit her lip, smearing lipstick on her front teeth. She concluded, "There *was* a story there—I'm sure of it. And I think that Suzanne had almost discovered its last chapter."

"**A**bortion?" suggested Neil.

"A reasonable theory," I answered. "It's the first thing that occurred to me."

It was around noon that day, and we were out for a run.

Neil had slept late that morning while I met with Glee Savage and, later, perused the *Register*. When Neil appeared in the doorway to the den, he was already wearing sweats and running shoes. "We're getting fat," he told me.

We weren't getting fat, but the message was clear enough—we'd been lax in this routine since our arrival in Dumont. I returned his grin and, without a word, put down my paper and trotted upstairs to change. Within three minutes, I was back in the front hall, where Neil was doing some stretches at the foot of the stairs. Leaving the house together through the front door, we jogged down the sidewalk toward the street, and I was grateful to note that the earlier gapers' block had thinned to an occasional slow drive-by. I told Neil, "Maybe everyone's in church."

I wore a heavy sweatshirt, but no sweatpants, just my usual running shorts, knowing I would generate enough heat of my own to keep me comfortable. Sunday morning had turned bright, and while it was still cold—well below freezing—there was no wind. The light snow that had fallen Christmas Eve still stuck to the grass and the branches of trees, but the streets were clear of ice, splotched with salty puddles that steamed in the sunlight. All in all, conditions were pleasant for a run.

We were heading down a side street toward a park I thought I remembered, exploring the neighborhood, enjoying each other's company, trying to clear our heads of yesterday's grim events. But it was impossible, of course, to dismiss Suzanne's murder, and I related to Neil the "matter of some delicacy" broached to me by Glee Savage.

Continuing our discussion of the abortion theory, I told him, "It all fits—the secrecy, the travel, the timing. Abortion wasn't legal in Wisconsin till *Roe v. Wade*, but there was a period prior to that when a lot of people flew to New York, where it was legal. Suzanne's incident fits that time frame."

Running at my side, Neil commented, "That would certainly explain why everything was so hush-hush about Suzanne withdrawing from the cotillion. The pregnancy itself would have been scandal enough in those days. Add an abortion to the plot, and you've got a doozy."

"I'll say," I told him, "especially when you consider that the Quatrain family has always been staunchly Catholic, right down to its French roots. Hazel mentioned to me yesterday that Suzanne had distanced herself from the church sometime during high school."

Neil snorted. "Now we know why—if our theory is correct."

"That's a big 'if,' " I reminded him. "The abortion theory is pure speculation, and it leaves a lot of details unanswered."

Neil broke stride. "Like what?" he asked, then caught up with me.

I stopped. "How'd she get pregnant?"

Neil stopped, turned, faced me with a grin. "The usual way, I imagine."

I walked the few paces between us, standing in front of Neil. "I mean"—my steamy breath mingled with his as I spoke—"was it a simple matter of a dumb kid getting knocked up, or was there more to it, something more . . . serious?"

Panting, thinking, Neil nodded. "Intriguing thought. But we'll never know."

"Probably not." The park lay just ahead now, and our run had been interrupted, so I suggested, "Care to stroll for a while?"

"Sure. Show me the park. Chances are, there'll be no crowds to contend with."

He was right, of course. There were no other people in sight, not even a car. Our pathway narrowed between banks of pines, and the houses of the town disappeared. Spreading before us was nothing but the glacial moraine that had carved the area's rolling landscape ages before it was settled by the French or the Indians or even the deer. A tarry scent of balsam mingled with the midday chatter of invisible birds who lunched on morsels of nothing high in the trees. Below, down a ravine, the silver thread of a creek lay frozen in time. Something furry foraged at its bank.

Stopping at the path's edge, gazing at it all, I sighed a wordless appreciation of the quiet spectacle.

Neil stood before me and draped his arms over my shoulders. With his lips nearly touching my face, he said, "Let's horse around."

That was unexpected. "Here?" I asked, assuming he was joking. In case he was serious, I added, "It's cold." Running had kept me plenty warm, but our ambling walk hadn't burned many calories, and my bare legs now stung against the December air. "Besides, the district attorney would be more than happy to book me on suspicion of murder—no point in compounding it with a public-indecency charge." My tone was jocular, but I couldn't have been more serious.

A glint caught Neil's eye. "Race you home," he challenged. "That'll warm you up. Maybe there?"

"Maybe there," I agreed, "but no race—let's just enjoy the run home together."

And we did. Watching Neil trot at my side, I thought of the first time we ran together on Christmas morning three years ago in Phoenix, where he then lived. There was no need to bundle against the cold that day—we ran bare-chested. And when we returned to his mountainside home, I made love to a man for the first time in my life. No wonder the shared act of running continued to be so erotically charged for both of us, often a prelude to sex.

I knew, though, that our return to the house on Prairie Street would not precipitate a tumble before the fire. The house was still full of guests, and the anxieties of both the move and the murder had taken their toll on our passions. Neil and I had not engaged in any meaningful intimacy since our arrival in Dumont a week earlier. So I looked forward to the following weekend, New Year's, when, by terms of our arrangement, I would "visit" Neil at our loft in Chicago. Visions of a second honeymoon danced in my head. A black-tie dinner at Zaza's, perhaps a concert, then back home for champagne, a few ounces of beluga . . .

"Thad certainly seemed sullen this morning," Neil interrupted my thoughts.

With a cynical laugh, I observed, "He's not the bubbly type." (I must have still had the New Year's bottle of Dom on my mind.)

Neil looked over at me. "I mean, his mother was murdered yesterday. You'd think he'd be *grief*-stricken, but he just acts like he's pissed."

We dashed along for a few moments, our legs moving in unison, while I mulled this. "People react differently to sudden loss. Maybe he hasn't quite grasped it yet. I haven't seen him yet today. What was he doing?"

"He was in the kitchen with Hazel. She's the only one in the house he opens up to. Get this: He wasn't interested in breakfast. He was going out with friends. He borrowed money for a burger."

We turned onto Prairie Street, and the house was in sight, a block away. "I suppose I should try talking to him, but I doubt that he'll listen."

Neil suggested, "Read him the riot act on split infinitives. *That*'ll get his attention."

Because Christmas had fallen on Saturday, Monday was part of a long holiday weekend, so all of the houseguests were still in Dumont. The Chicagoans (Roxanne, Carl, and Neil, but not I) would drive home later that afternoon.

That morning, Neil and I decided to go for a run again, this time inviting Parker Trent to join us. When we gathered in the front hall, I noticed at once that the soft, conforming fleece of Parker's sweatpants displayed his ass to even greater advantage than did his chinos. This was a detail that Neil would not be likely to miss, and I could predict with near certainty that as our run progressed, we would jockey to let Parker take the lead.

"You'll freeze out there," Parker told me, gazing at my bare legs.

Stubbornly, I had again decided against sweats, even though the weather was a few degrees colder still. I assured Parker, "If we keep the pace up, I'll be fine." To Neil I added, "No dawdling in the park this time."

"Yes, master," he quipped, then opened the front door.

Sheriff Douglas Pierce was trudging up the walk, huddled into the collar of his topcoat. Neil turned back to me. "Uh-oh."

" 'Morning, Doug," I called to him. "Come on in."

He rushed the final few steps and, closing the door behind him, greeted the three of us in the front hall.

I explained, "We were just going out for a run."

"You'll freeze out there," he told me, glancing at my knees while rubbing his gloved hands together.

"So I've been told—but I may need to postpone it, now that you're here."

"Thanks," he said, unbuttoning his coat. "We really should talk."

I turned to Neil and Parker. "Sorry, guys. I have a hunch this may take a while. Why don't you go ahead without me?"

"We can wait," they assured me. "It's no problem."

"No," I decided for them, "go ahead. I'll try to get out later." I opened the door for them. Neil gave me a hug, Parker cuffed my shoulder, and they both took off down the sidewalk. Leading Pierce into the den, I asked, "What's up?"

"We need to do some brainstorming," he told me, removing his coat, hanging it behind the door. "Harley Kaiser, Dumont's esteemed district attorney, is already pressuring me to make an arrest."

"And the short list of suspects," I guessed, "includes a certain journalist, a recent transplant from Chicago." I gestured that we should sit, not at the desk today, but in the more comfortable grouping of furniture near the fireplace.

"Right," he confirmed, settling into an armchair. "So I'm looking for ideas to broaden the investigation."

I sat on the love seat, and we made an incongruous-looking pair. He was dressed as before in his dapper gray flannels, this time with a sportcoat of muted sage plaid and a nubby silk tie with a perfect Windsor knot. By contrast, I wore an old (very old) Illini sweatshirt, a pair of loose cotton running shorts, and Reeboks.

With a laugh, I asked him, "What makes you so sure I *didn't* do it?"

"Instinct, I guess. For whatever reason, I trust you. But

Kaiser doesn't. You're the outsider in this case, and that's a strike against you in his book. He's very reluctant to pursue anything against Thad—the boy's name may have been on his dying mother's lips, but he's a Quatrain. As for Miriam Westerman, she has denied your housekeeper's claim that she was here at the time of the murder, and Kaiser will be willing to give her the benefit of the doubt—he and Miriam have forged something of an odd political alliance. The bottom line is this: If I'm unable to divert Kaiser with some reasonable alternate theories, he'll expect me to haul you in. So let's put our heads together."

Without further comment, we both fell into thought, and the room grew momentarily quiet. In the stillness, my thinking was interrupted by a noise in the hall—a little noise, like cautious footsteps. I caught Pierce's eye and directed his attention to the open door. A moment later, Hazel entered the den and walked to the desk, not seeing us seated by the fireplace. Leaning over the desk, she moved a few items. "May I help you find something?" I asked her.

She gasped, turning toward me. "I didn't *see* you, Mr. Manning. I'm *sorry.*" Backing toward the door, fumbling with her glasses, she explained breathlessly, "I thought you'd gone out. I didn't know you had a guest. I was going to do some cleaning. I'll leave it till later." And she was gone. I heard her footsteps retreat toward the kitchen.

Pierce arched his brows, amused by an unconvincing performance. I signaled with my hand that we should wait to speak; then I got up and closed the door. Turning back to Pierce, I asked, "What do you make of *that?*"

He stated the obvious: "She was looking for something, and you caught her."

Returning to the love seat, I perched on its arm near Pierce's chair, thinking. "I hate to cast aspersions on the woman," I told him, "but you'll recall that when Elliot Coop met with us about the will, he mentioned that Suzanne left Hazel a 'substantial little nest egg.' "

Pierce nodded. "Money always makes a good motive."

I leaned toward him. "And she seemed more than eager to

tattle that Miriam Westerman was in the house at the time of the murder, which Miriam denies. Miriam might be lying—it wouldn't surprise me—but on the other hand, Hazel might have lied in order to draw suspicion away from herself. Do you think there might be more to this?"

"It's worth looking into," Pierce answered, lolling back in his chair.

At that moment, for the first time during our discussion, I was struck with the feeling that Pierce was . . . *looking* at me, sort of drinking in the sight of me. And I realized that I may have been sending signals that invited him to do exactly that. I was sitting there in a pair of running shorts with my crotch at his eye level, and my mounting enthusiasm for a "Hazel theory" had nudged me steadily nearer the man. I had not intended to entice him with my body language, but he seemed to be responding to it. On his first visit to the house, Sheriff Douglas Pierce had proven himself gay-friendly. Was he also, perhaps, gay?

He continued. "If nothing else, this new angle should buy me some time with the DA, and, right now, that's precisely what we need." He pulled a notepad from his jacket pocket and clicked a ballpoint over it.

I stood and crossed to the desk, wanting to check some of my own notes—had Hazel wanted to get a look at them, too? I told Pierce, "I've got another idea for you, Doug. Thad's father—here it is, Austin Reece—might he have had some motive to want Suzanne dead? You told me that she jilted him, that he left town in either anger or despair. Those are plausible motives."

"You're right," he said, finishing a note. Rising, he joined me at the desk. "Austin Reece is a long shot at best—I haven't a clue as to where he went when he left Dumont—but there are ways to find out."

"There now." I smiled. "You arrived this morning with three suspects, and you're leaving with five. A productive meeting, wouldn't you say?"

"Yes," he said, rubbing his neck, "but now *I'm* the one who has to sort this out." Then he rested a hand on my shoulder. "The things I don't do for friends."

It was a lighthearted comment, not quite a joke, but I knew that his underlying reason for saying it was to let me know that he did, in fact, think of me as a friend, not just another citizen involved with another case. And I was happy to hear it—not so much because of the special attention it implied that I would be accorded, but because I'd felt since our first meeting that Doug Pierce's friendship was well worth nurturing. Conspicuously, I twisted my head to eye his hand on my shoulder. Then I looked him in the face and asked, "Do you know Glee Savage?"

Laughing at this non sequitur, he flipped open his notebook and clicked his pen. "Of course," he answered. "She's a great gal. Do you suspect *her*, too?"

"Hardly. But she paid a visit yesterday, telling me an intriguing tale about Suzanne's high school days when she disappeared for a week and withdrew from the running for queen of a cotillion."

Pierce paused in thought. "I forgot all about that," he said. "Suzanne was two years ahead of me in school, and the cotillion didn't interest me anyway, but now that you mention it, I do recall that there was something of a stir back then. I was just a freshman—I never understood what it was about."

"Neither did Glee," I told him, "but she certainly sniffed a story, and I presume she suspected an unwanted pregnancy." I elaborated, telling Pierce about Suzanne's mysterious ailment, the trip out of town, the timing with regard to *Roe v. Wade.*

"Interesting," said Pierce. "But so what? It's water under the bridge."

"That's just how I reacted. But then Glee informed me that Suzanne had been doing a lot of morgue research at the paper lately—Suzanne herself mentioned this. And according to Glee, the research focused on a brief period immediately after high school. She thinks that Suzanne had stumbled onto something that got her killed. She thinks the murder is related to the high school 'ailment.'"

Pierce shook his head. "Glee's been reading too many pot-boilers. It sounds like a stretch to me."

"You're probably right," I told him, "but could you at least take a look at the police records from that period? See if there were any suspicious incidents that might relate to Suzanne's brief disappearance."

"Okay," he said, adding to the list on his pad. "Anything else?"

I shrugged. "Nope. That ought to do it."

He crossed to the door and got his coat. "I've got to run."

"Me, too." I laughed, glancing down at my Reeboks.

He took a lingering look at me. Grinned. "You'd better put some pants on."

Late that afternoon, Neil was preparing for the drive down to Chicago. The week before, he had ridden up in my car, which would now stay in Dumont, so he was returning with Roxanne and Carl. Upstairs in our bedroom, zipping one of his bags, he told me, "I've been thinking about it, Mark—maybe it would be a good idea if I came back up here next weekend."

"New Year's? I was planning a night on the town for us. Besides, I don't want to renege on the 'arrangement' already—it's my turn to visit you."

"I know that," he said, hugging me in a loose embrace, "and I appreciate your determination to live up to our deal, but you've got a lot going on up here. You're not settled into the house yet, and you take over the *Register* in three weeks."

"Not to mention," I said, voicing the concern that he had kindly left unspoken, "it might look bad for me to leave town while Suzanne's murder is unresolved."

"That, too," he admitted, and we agreed that his offer made sense.

Joey Quatrain had come over to the house that afternoon to visit Thad, who spent most of his time in his room, when he wasn't out with friends. Joey was confused about who actually lived in the house now, and he was surprised to learn that

Neil, Roxanne, and Carl were going home—he thought they *were* home. But he enjoyed the excitement of everyone packing, and he helped carry luggage downstairs, to be loaded in the car.

It was a tight fit. Roxanne had never known the virtue of traveling light, and added to her and Carl's things were Neil's, plus an array of Christmas booty that needed to be hauled back. Hazel brought out a hamperload of snacks for the trip, which went onto the backseat with overflow from the trunk.

At last we were all assembled in the driveway—even Thad deigned to make an appearance—when Neil remembered, "Oh, God, the wastebasket." We had been shopping a few days before Christmas, when Neil found a wastebasket that would look good in the kitchen of the loft. "It's still in the trunk of your car," he told me.

Eyeing the load in his own car, Carl Creighton asked, "Will it fit?"

"I'll carry it on my lap if I have to," Neil answered. "It's bulky, but not heavy."

Parker stepped forward, volunteering, "I'll get it." Joey added, "Me, too. I want to see Mark's nice car." So I thanked them, giving Parker the keys, and he and Joey walked together to the garage.

"Parker's a neat guy," Neil told me. "I think you made the right choice."

"I think so, too—at least I hope so. You enjoyed your run together?"

"Yeah. We had a good talk, mostly about you. He's fast—and I don't just mean fast 'for his age'—he's a well-trained runner."

Roxanne sidled into our conversation. "If *that's* how he built those killer buns, I'm ordering a treadmill tomorrow!"

We were laughing at this comment when Parker returned with Neil's wastebasket. Roxanne asked Parker if his ears were burning.

Before he could answer, Thad asked him, "What happened to Joey?"

"He's still in the car—hope you don't mind, Mark. He loves it."

"Hell, I'm flattered."

And it was time for good-byes, accompanied by a round-robin of hugs and kisses and wishes for safe travel. "I'll miss you, kiddo," I told Neil.

He reminded me, "I'll be back in four days. Now, behave yourself." And everyone was in the car.

Carl revved the engine, and Roxanne opened a window. "I'm still licensed to practice law in Wisconsin," she told me. "If things heat up, I'll happily defend you." Though the crack was meant to be funny, no one found much humor in it, and the car drove away.

It was barely four-thirty, and night had already fallen. Parker went to the garage to shag Joey out of my car while Thad, Hazel, and I went inside the house. We were hanging around the kitchen when Parker returned. Tossing me my keys, he told us, "Joey thought he'd better go home. He said to tell you good-bye, Thad."

The kid grunted his thanks.

I sighed. It had been a harrowing Christmas for everyone, an inauspicious prelude to my new career in Dumont. I could easily have slipped into a depression at that moment, but I willed my spirits back up, determined to conquer the postholiday icks. "Hey," I told everyone, "let me take you out to dinner."

"Thank you, Mr. Manning," Hazel said, "but that would be inappropriate." Turning her back to me, she began rinsing something in the sink, telling me over her shoulder, "I'll be cooking for myself and for anyone else who remains."

Thad said, "I'm eating here with Hazel," and left the room.

"I'll go, Mark," Parker told me. "With pleasure, of course. What time?"

"Early, okay? How about six?"

"Sounds great. Where are we headed?"

"There's that nice place on First Avenue near the *Register*'s offices."

Hazel informed me, "That's the First Avenue Grill."

Parker winced. "I'll bet they don't go by their initials."

He and I shared a vigorous laugh while Hazel ground up something in the garbage disposal—it sounded like forks.

At one minute before six, Parker and I walked through the doorway of the First Avenue Grill. The handsome dining room occupied a converted storefront on the town's main street, and its contemporary furnishings gave the place a surprisingly urban look—though its white linen tablecloths, sturdy nurse-uniformed waitresses, and fish-free menu told me I'd traveled some million miles from Bistro Zaza.

When I'd called an hour earlier, the hostess assured me that I wouldn't need a reservation, and, indeed, the dinner crowd was sparse that night. Though it was Monday, it felt like Sunday, and most people were probably at home eating leftovers or ordering pizza, keeping the next morning's work demons at bay for a few more hours. The hostess already knew me (I'd lunched there with Barret Logan on the day I drove up to negotiate the buyout), so she seated Parker and me at a comfortably large table in a prime location between a window and the fireplace. Handing us menus, she told me, "I'm so sorry about your cousin, Mr. Manning. We'll all miss Suzanne terribly. Have the funeral arrangements been announced?"

"No, not yet," I told her, thanking her for her concern. Then we ordered a cocktail—vodka for me, Scotch for Parker—and she left the table.

"If you don't mind my asking," said Parker, "what *about* Suzanne's funeral?"

"It's up in the air," I answered. "The Quatrain family has belonged to one of the town's Catholic parishes for genera-tions, and even though Suzanne split with the church years ago, the good father is itching to put on a show. Ditto for Fem-Snach. It's sort of an all-purpose group, mainly political but also quasi-religious (if you think of paganism as a religion), and Miriam Westerman wants to officiate at Suzanne's burial. Suzanne's will left no indication of her desires, so Elliot Coop, the old family attorney, thinks the decision should rest with the family. But who is 'family'? There never was a husband, and Suzanne is survived only by a minor son, a handicapped brother, and me, her cousin and executor. So it's a mess."

The hostess returned with our drinks, lighting a candle at the table. We asked for some time before ordering, and she left us.

Parker raised his glass to me. "To the future, Mark. Good luck to both of us."

I returned his toast, and we drank, but my mind didn't spring to the future. I was still absorbed in the past. I told Parker, "All this business about the funeral. It strikes me that the emerging history of my roots in Dumont seems highlighted by . . . death."

Parker gulped. "What do you mean?"

"Christmas night, you and I sat up talking in the den. I told you about my childhood visit to Dumont. Remember, the whole reason for that trip was that my mother needed to visit her sister, Edna Quatrain, in California. Aunt Edna had lung cancer, and she died that next spring."

"People die, Mark. And that was a long time ago."

Leaning closer, I told him, "But it's almost as if that was the start of a 'trend,' the first of many dominoes that would fall. Consider: My older cousin, Mark Quatrain, died in Vietnam just a few years after my visit, and his mother, my aunt Peggy, died the same year he did. My own mother died when I was in college, and Uncle Edwin attended the funeral. It had been more than ten years since I first met him, and I would never see him again. I inherited the house when he died three years ago. And when I finally moved up to the house last week, Suzanne was killed there."

I rested my case, as if there were some great mystery of interconnectedness linking these events.

Again Parker said, "People die, Mark." He patted his hand on the table, stopping just short of touching mine. "It's the natural order of things. Sickness, old age, warfare—these are forces that lead inexorably and *naturally* toward death. Each loss, while surely sad, is nothing ominous."

"There was nothing 'natural' about Suzanne's death," I pointed out.

"Yes"—he nodded—"she's the tragic exception in the litany you've recited, but her murder does not imply some doomful conspiracy of death within your family." He eyed me squarely, grinning. "Wouldn't such a view be a tad irrational?"

I smiled. He'd caught me flirting with the illogical, bemoaning the bugbears of fate, and I was glad to be chastened for it. "Thanks for the reminder," I told him, lifting my glass to sip my drink.

In a much lighter tone, I mused, "Something happened at my mother's funeral that intrigued me for years—and this does relate to my early visit to Dumont."

Parker leaned back in his chair. "I'd be happy to hear about it," he told me, drinking some of his Scotch.

"As I've mentioned, Mom died while I was in college, victim of the same cigarettes—the same brand, in fact—that had killed her sister eleven years before. Ours was a small family, so the funeral was little more than a discreet memorial service. Preoccupied with my own loss, I hadn't realized that Uncle Edwin might attend, but he did, and he seemed as surprised to see me as I was to see him. Not that he wouldn't expect to see me at my own mother's funeral, but he was unprepared to see me *as a man*. 'My God, Mark,' he said as we embraced, 'you'd have no way of knowing, but you've grown into the very image of your father.' Then he repeated something he'd told me during my boyhood visit to Dumont: 'You're such a special young man, not at all like the others.' And he kissed me. Right on the lips."

Parker's jaw dropped. I expected him to comment on the kiss, but instead he asked, "What 'others' was your uncle talking about?"

"I assumed he meant his own children."

Parker seemed baffled by this. "What did he mean when he said that you were different from them?"

I leaned forward to explain something that I thought should already be obvious. "Parker, the man kissed me on the mouth. I wasn't a little kid anymore, but a junior in college. He said that I wasn't like the others because he sensed that I was gay—long before I myself figured it out. And I wondered, standing near my mother's grave, if *he* was gay."

"Was he?"

At that moment, I was distracted by the distinguished figure of Barret Logan entering the restaurant. The *Register*'s retiring publisher saw me as well and headed straight for our table. Parker and I stood. He offered condolences on Suzanne's death, wished Parker and me a belated merry Christmas, and took off his coat. Since I'd previously had lunch with Logan at the First Avenue Grill, I quipped, "Do you take *all* your meals here, Barret?"

"In fact, I do," he answered with a laugh. "Or at least it seems so. I've been a widower for some years now, and there's no appeal in cooking for myself. Besides, this is easily the best place in town." He wore a dark business suit that night, which struck me as a bit overdressed (Parker and I were dressed nicely, but casually). I wondered if Logan was *always* attired this way, or if tonight he had spiffed for his outing to "the best place in town."

I asked if he would care to join Parker and me for dinner. He thought about it, but not for long, and readily agreed. The hostess whisked away his coat and brought him a place setting; they both understood that he didn't need a menu. "Would you like a drink, Mr. Logan?" she asked. "Yes, please," he answered. "Lillet." The woman went away to fetch it, a French apéritif. I was surprised that they had it, up here in the hinterlands, and I suspected that it was laid in at Logan's request.

Our small talk quickly returned to the murder, and I mentioned the irony of circumstances that had pegged me as a prime suspect. I was relieved to note from Logan's tone that he harbored no such suspicions himself. "The investigation is in good hands with Douglas Pierce," he assured me. "He's a dedicated professional. What's more, he has a genuine hunger that justice be served."

"I've already learned that," I told Logan. "We've come up with a handful of potential suspects, and I'm sure the investigation is grinding away, even as we speak. He's an impressive guy." We all paused as Logan's Lillet was delivered. Exchanging a silent toast, we drank. Then I told Logan, "I was also impressed with one of your staff. Glee Savage visited me yesterday."

Logan sat back in his chair with a broad smile. "She's a great gal—and a damn good writer, too. She's added a lot to the *Register* over the years. You'll enjoy working with her." His expression turned quizzical. "Why the visit?"

I explained to Logan—and also to Parker, who had not yet heard details of my discussion with Glee—that she had told me about Suzanne's mysterious high school "ailment," her disappearance from town for a week, and her recent research in the *Register*'s morgue. "In a nutshell, Glee has a theory that the research was related to the 'ailment' and that the murder is related to both. Glee wasn't specific on this point, but I got the impression that Suzanne may have dealt with an unwanted pregnancy."

Parker listened to this story with wide-eyed interest, but Logan merely nodded, deep in thought. He told me, "I recall the incident—some thirty years ago. I also recall that Glee was eager to work up an exposé. I spiked it before it was written."

"Glee mentioned that," I admitted.

"Mark," he told me, "you're calling the shots on this now. In three weeks, you'll be sitting at my desk down the street, and the issues you've raised relate to your own family. My policy has always been to treat the Quatrains with kid gloves, but you're welcome to take any approach that suits your own journalistic philosophy. Just be aware"—he raised a cautionary finger—"that a Quatrain scandal, for the sake of mere headlines, will serve neither the town nor the paper well."

"But"—I, too, raised a finger, countering his—"if a scandal is the result of bared secrets that help solve a high-profile murder, the scandal is an unavoidable consequence of serving the public's best interest."

"That's a tough call," Logan conceded. With a chuckle, he added, "I *am* looking forward to retirement."

Parker had been itching to enter this discussion, and now

he did so. "Mark," he said, practically leaning out of his chair, "Suzanne *mentioned* that research to me. She asked me to *help* her, remember? Mr. Logan, I don't know what kind of systems you have in place at the *Register*, but chances are, I could retrace whatever it was she was digging for—research almost always leaves a trail. Mark, what do you think? This could be valuable in helping to clear you with the DA."

He had a point. "Let me think about it," I told him. Turning to Logan, I asked, "Do you mind if Parker and I pay another visit to the *Register*'s offices tomorrow? There's still staff I haven't met, and Parker could check out the morgue."

"Mark," Logan assured me, "you needn't ask permission to visit the *Register*. Drop in anytime, announced or otherwise, and we'll all try to be on our toes."

"That's gracious of you, Barret. But I just don't want to give the impression that I'm . . . *usurping* anything."

He laughed. "Hell, Mark, you're *buying* it—lock, stock, and barrel." He was right, of course, and Parker and I shared his laughter.

The hostess sent a waitress over to take our order, and Logan recommended that night's special, a meat loaf that he claimed was extraordinary. Meat loaf? I hadn't had it since I was a kid, and I had never much missed it, but suddenly it seemed appealing—comforting—and I joined Logan in ordering it. Parker ordered steak, a strip, rare. We all decided on the ubiquitous Caesar salad, only Parker opting for anchovies. And we needed another drink, Logan switching to Bordeaux.

Try as we might to focus our conversation on carefree matters, we could not avoid the topic of Suzanne's murder. "Aside from the possible economic implications for the community," lamented Logan, "there's the tremendous personal toll on Suzanne's son."

"And her brother," I added. "Poor Joey. I don't think the loss has hit him yet."

"How well do you know him?" Logan asked me.

"I've spent a bit of time with him this weekend," I explained, "but I knew him better as a child. He was ten then; I was nine.

Even as a kid, I could tell there was something not-quite-right about him."

"It's a pity," said Logan. "Joey's ability to learn never progressed much beyond the level you witnessed as a child. Suzanne told me that test results described him as having a twelve-year-old brain in a middle-aged body. He's a good-natured soul, but emotionally, of course, he's highly immature. At least he's learned to take care of himself, and a few years ago, he finally got a driver's license, with restrictions. Thank God—because he's on his own now."

Parker said, "He's secure at Quatro Press, isn't he?"

"Certainly," said Logan. "He's held a job there—personnel, I think—his entire adult life, and that will continue to take care of him. But he's aware that he ought to be sitting behind his father's desk by now, and he's incapable of understanding why his learning disability has hobbled his natural desire for fulfillment."

"It's pathetic," I agreed. "But Joey is obviously unable to run a business."

"Can you imagine?" asked Logan with a restrained laugh. "When Joey heard that I was finally ready to sell the *Register*, he wanted to buy it himself. He offered me twice what you're paying, Mark. But I wasn't tempted."

Unprepared for this bit of news, I told him, "Then I must have gotten a real bargain—thank you, Barret."

With a not-so-fast gesture of his hands, Logan explained, "I refused Joey's offer because, first, he hasn't a clue as to how to run a newspaper. And second, he hasn't a dime—at least not beyond the generous trusts that were established to care for him. In short, Joey has no grip on reality, and as he's grown older, he's grown increasingly confused and frustrated about his role in the world."

Parker shook his head. "One thing's certain. He'll never fill his sister's shoes—talk about an emasculating notion."

"And in their father's eyes, Suzanne never filled her older brother Mark's shoes, in spite of the circumstances."

Parker and I exchanged a confused glance. I asked Logan, "What circumstances? His death in Vietnam?"

"That's part of it," said Logan, "certainly." But his manner was now highly reticent, and I understood that he had ventured into sensitive territory that he assumed, incorrectly, was familiar to me. I could tell that he would have been more comfortable dropping the topic of Mark Quatrain, but the door had been opened, and I waited for more. At last he elaborated, "There were circumstances surrounding your elder cousin's death that you apparently never knew. I'm sorry, Mark, to have been so insensitive to broach this. You've been through a lot already this weekend."

"Please, Barret, fill me in. I need to know what happened."

He fingered the empty glass in front of him, searching for the fortification of alcohol. "Very well," he told me. "Your cousin Mark was drafted fresh out of college—he'd majored in English, taking his degree with highest honors. Predictably, he ended up in Vietnam. As you know, he died there. What you've never heard is that, before he was killed, he got into trouble there. Serious trouble."

Logan paused. "Mark Quatrain raped, then killed, an Asian girl in Vietnam. He was awaiting a military trial there when he died, along with most of his platoon, in an ambush—a hideous massacre that left Mark and many of his compatriots butchered beyond recognition. There were very few survivors of the attack, and Mark was identified among the casualties on the basis of his dog tag and personal effects." Logan swallowed. "I apologize for relating this at table, but his body had been mutilated, with most of his head missing." Again he paused. "Mark's mother, your aunt Peggy, was, of course, highly distraught by this news. As you know, she suffered from what we then simply called a 'weak heart.' News of her son's death, and the details surrounding it, literally killed the woman. Peggy died the same week. The *Register* reported the deaths of both mother and son, of course, but I never saw reason to reveal in print the crimes that Mark committed in Asia—the family had been through enough."

At some point during Logan's recounting of this, I had stopped breathing. Uncounted moments of suspended silence followed; then the waitress reappeared with our second round of drinks, saying, "You have a phone call, Mr. Logan—one of your editors." I gulped for air as he excused himself. As I watched him cross the room to take his call, my mind spun to grasp all that he had told me.

Though I was thinking about a beautiful young man who had lived as a fantasy in my subconscious for over thirty years, I said to Parker, "Wouldn't you think that a man like Barret Logan would carry a cell phone, or even a pager? Maybe there's a lesson here, Parker. Maybe the ultimate luxury, the height of sophistication, is to be *dis*-connected. If people really need to reach you, they can somehow figure out . . ."

"Mark," Parker stopped me, "you don't have to bury your emotions about this, not from me. You told me how you felt about your cousin. I understand. It must be devastating."

"It's not devastating," I lied, "just unexpected. I'll deal with it, Parker. But I do appreciate your concern."

Then he patted my hand and repeated something I'd already heard from him more than once: "This is all I've ever wanted."

I had a dream that night, an eerie exercise in déjà vu.

I'm a boy of nine, visiting the house on Prairie Street for the first time. It's the second day of my visit, and I've met everyone in the household except my oldest cousin, Mark Quatrain, who's returning that morning from college. Everyone's excited because it's the first time he's been away, and they all miss him.

Then somebody opens the door, and I see my cousin Mark for the first time. He's very handsome, with wavy hair, and I can tell that Suzanne is jealous of all the attention he's getting. He's wearing tan pants, like soldiers wear, and they look really good on him. Everyone else is hugging him; I want to, but think I shouldn't. Trying to think of something clever, I tell him, "We've got the same name." He smiles and says, "How about that?" Then he musses my hair with his hand, and I really like the way his fingers feel on my head.

Later that afternoon, I'm in Joey's room, and I'm getting bored with him, so I stroll out into the hall. Hearing music from Mark's room, I look inside, and there's my older cousin with his shirt off—he still has those nice tan pants on— unpacking a suitcase and sorting through his records. Seeing me, he says, "It's their new album. You like the Beatles?"

So far, the dream is just a replay of everything that really happened. But then, things start to get different. When he asks me about the Beatles, I answer, "I like Mozart better." And he tells me, "I'll play some, if I can find it."

He kneels on the floor, reaching for an album that has slipped behind the stereo. His backside is toward me, and I feel a little embarrassed, but I can't take my eyes off him— those pants look so nice. And the creases of the cloth on the back of his legs make sort of an arrow, pointing right at his butt. I feel lost for a moment, like I don't know where I am. Then I walk over to him and just, well . . . *touch* him.

"Hey," says Mark, getting up fast, "what are you doing?" I don't know what to say because I really don't *know* what I'm doing. Finally I tell him, "I just wanted to touch you."

He laughs—not *at* me—he's being nice. "Then touch me." And I do. I feel his belt buckle, and I put my arms around his waist and squeeze him against me. He starts looking at the ceiling with his mouth open, and he puts his hands in my hair again, and he pulls, and it sort of hurts but feels good anyway. He says, "I want to touch you, too, Mark."

I was hoping he'd say that. So I take one of his hands and put it between my legs, and he sort of cups it, and I feel warm and hard there. He looks into my eyes and tells me how green they are, and I laugh because people are always making a big deal out of it. And I tell him, "Show me your cock. Fuck my mouth."

I can't *believe* I said that, but then I realize that I'm not a little kid anymore. I'm no longer nine, but about his age, eighteen. We're the same height, same build, same name, same khaki pants. There's sort of a twin-thing going on, and it heats up fast. We're down on the floor, we're into each other's clothes, and we're doing things to and for each other that feel like love. "Mark, oh, Mark," we both whisper from the jumble of our bodies.

"Hey," says Joey, popping into the room. But I can't see him, and I don't care—I'm busy with Mark. "Hey!" he repeats. "Wanna see the upstairs?"

Mark grabs my hair again, mussing and pulling, and I know I'm on the verge of orgasm. "Are you ready to come?" I ask him. He answers with a groan that sounds like pain. I reach to grab his hair, wanting to feel those beautiful, wavy locks twisted around my fingers, but my hands can't find his head. My hands feel warm, my fingers are wet, and I know something is wrong. "Mark," I ask, "are you ready?" But he doesn't answer, and his whole body goes limp, and then I can *see* what's wrong: His body has been mutilated, most of his head is missing, and there's blood on my hands. "Mark!" I scream.

"*Hey!*" Joey screams louder. "*Wanna see the upstairs?*"

And I awoke.

It was Tuesday morning, still early, still dark, not quite dawn. I reached blindly to switch on my bedside lamp. Squinting against the assault of light, I examined my hands and determined that they were not bloody, that no one had been mutilated, that Joey was not standing in the doorway—that yes, it was only a dream. I breathed a heavy sigh, dried my brow with a swipe of my arm, and lay there thinking, booting my brain to full consciousness.

It was the first night I'd spent alone in my new bed—Neil had been with me those first seven or eight nights since move-in. The dream was an ugly kickoff to the reality of our "arrangement," a planned separation that I myself had devised and sold to Neil against his every instinct. Once again I was faced with an omen that my future in Dumont was ill-fated. And once again I had to remind myself that I held no faith whatever in such irrational flights of mysticism. My future was in my own hands, not at the mercy of some supernatural portent. My future might yet be wrenched by chance, but it would not be doomed by destiny.

Secure in this knowledge, I dismissed the dream for what it was—the product of my churning subconscious combined with my shock at hearing Barret Logan's ghastly revelations of the previous evening, as well as the general state of horniness that had been hounding me for several days. There would be three more nights without Neil, I counted. Masturbation might be fun—it would at least relieve the pressure—but my bout of self-analysis since waking had focused my mental energies in a less earthy sector of my brain, and I found that I'd simply lost interest in an overdue hand job.

Swinging my feet to the floor and sitting on the edge of the bed, I reviewed the day that lay ahead. My only appointment was later that morning, when Parker and I would visit the *Register*. Otherwise I was free to concentrate on desk work regarding my move and the takeover of the paper. In the back of my mind, of course, I would continually wrestle with the questions surrounding Suzanne's murder—the who and the why. And, of course, there was still a thicket of legal issues to resolve concerning my inheritance and Thad. Perhaps I should try to spend some time with the boy that day.

Gray daylight now tinged the bedroom curtains, and I switched off the lamp. It was still too early to rouse the household with the racket of showering, so I decided to throw on some clothes, go down to my den, and see if the morning paper had arrived.

Padding downstairs in my stocking feet, crossing the entrance hall, I quietly unlatched the front door and cracked it open. A gush of cold air hit me, making me instantly more awake than coffee could. Coffee, I thought—that's what I needed. But first the paper. I grabbed the *Register* and pulled it inside.

Taking it to the den, I spread it on the desk and switched on the reading lamp. The front page was, of course, covered with news of the murder investigation. CORONER STUMPED read the main headline. The story explained that the coroner had not yet filed a final report and that the murder weapon was still unknown. Investigators had therefore requested postponement of Suzanne's funeral, which was now tentatively scheduled for next week, Monday, January third, location to be announced. Father Nicholas Winter, pastor of Saint Cecille parish, was preparing to file a court petition to have the body remanded to the church for burial, in an effort to block what he called "the sacrilegious plans of Miriam Westerman to inter this faithful daughter of Christ in unhallowed ground." I stifled a laugh, taking delight, even at that early hour, in any form of ecclesiastical squabbling.

My reading was then interrupted by voices somewhere in the house. Curious, I went to the hall and listened. The voices—there were two of them—came from the kitchen. The tone made it clear that they were arguing, and though they tried to keep it quiet, tension was building. So I sneaked farther down the hall, closer to the kitchen, in order to hear better. From where I stood, I could smell coffee brewing. I could also discern that the voices belonged to Thad and Hazel.

"I was *there* that day, at your mother's house," Hazel told Thad. "We hadn't had a nice visit in weeks, and I offered to fix lunch. I was in the kitchen when you two started yelling, and I heard every word of it."

"It didn't mean anything. She yelled at me a lot."

"A mother's *supposed* to yell at her kids when they act like you do."

"I wasn't acting up. I wanted to get a job."

"A *job*." Harrumph. "Your *job's* at school . . ."

"You sound like *her* now."

Hazel plowed on, "Your *job's* to get some decent grades. Your *job's* to grow up and stop acting like . . ."

"I *am* grown up," he insisted. "That was the whole point, in case you missed it. Are you deaf as well as blind?"

At that moment, I sincerely hoped that the next sound I'd hear would be the smack of her hand on his face.

"Owww!" he whined. (I smiled.) "I'm sorry, Hazel. But what I *mean* is, is that I just wanted to move out of the house and get an apartment—you know, with friends. And she was like, 'You're too young.' And I'm like, 'But my friends are older. They can handle it.' And she's like, 'You can't be unsupervised,' or whatever. And I'm like, '*They'll* look after me.' So, of course, she's like, 'What about money?' So I'm, '*That's* why I need to get a job—just part-time—it won't hurt school.'

But she wouldn't let me, so I asked for more allowance, and she laughed at me. And . . . And . . ."

"And," Hazel picked up the narrative, "you *warned* her. You warned your own mother that if she didn't stop treating you like a baby, she'd be *sorry*. You threatened to take matters into your own hands. 'One way or another,' you yelled at her, 'I'm getting out of this frigging house.' "

"Oh, brother"—Thad smirked audibly—"I'd never say 'frigging.' "

"Then you know good and well what you *did* say, and I won't repeat that word."

Thad challenged her, "So long as you were snooping on us, you know what happened next."

"Indeed I do. She threatened you with boarding school."

Hmm. Suzanne and I had been thinking along the same lines.

Hazel continued. "Not just any boarding school, mind you, but a good, strict military academy. The discipline would serve you well, young man."

"I'd *never* go there. Never!"

"And that's just what you told your mother. Exactly. Then you said"—Hazel choked on the words—"you said you'd kill her first."

There was a long pause. I heard my heart pounding, fast. When Thad spoke, he seemed to be fighting back tears. "I'd never hurt Mom!" he blurted.

"Then why did you say such things, Thad?"

"I don't *know*. We had a lot of fights lately. We both said lots of things we didn't really mean." He repeated, "But I'd never hurt Mom."

I'd heard enough. Thad and Hazel's argument had climaxed and was winding down. Retreating through the hallway to the foot of the stairs, I wondered, Is Thad sincere now about being incapable of hurting his mother? Or is he merely squirming? Was Suzanne's dying word, "Thad," in fact meant to name her killer? And what about Hazel? On the day of the murder, she did her best to paint Miriam Westerman in a suspicious light, so what was her motive in precipitating today's quarrel with Thad? What game was she playing?

I needed time to weigh all of this. My more immediate need, however, was caffeine. So I crept up a few stairs, then bounded back down, calling, "Anybody up yet? Hazel? Coffee ready?"

Around eleven that morning, I took Parker over to the offices of the *Dumont Daily Register*. He had been there only once with me, briefly, on Christmas Eve day, and had not yet seen the operation running at full tilt. I found a parking spot on First Avenue within a block of the paper and, while backing my black Bavarian V-8 into the space, wondered when I could legitimately claim one of the prime spots in the executive lot behind the building. Walking toward the offices with Parker, I told him, "Barret Logan should write a textbook on publishing a well-run small-town daily. He's not only managed to attract top talent, but he's also reinvested the company's profits in a continual modernization of its physical plant."

"Sounds like the ideal setup," said Parker. "I'm eager to be a part of it."

Stepping through the glass doors into the vestibule, I noticed that our names had been displayed on the welcome board. A well-dressed receptionist (CONSTANCE said the plaque on the counter) greeted us warmly on sight. "Good morning, Mr. Manning. We've been expecting you." I introduced Parker as the new managing editor, and she told us, "Mr. Logan said to send you right up."

By now I had a sense of the building's general layout. The editorial department was upstairs on the second floor, advertising on the ground floor, circulation below. The actual printing plant, along with its warehouse and loading docks, occupied a separate larger building behind the offices. I led Parker up to the editorial floor, telling him, "Welcome to your new domain."

The newsroom was fully staffed at that hour, but I recognized the activity level as low—with a single morning edition, the *Register*'s next deadline would not hit until late afternoon. Phones rang sporadically, but it was not the din of breaking news. So I felt comfortable mingling with the staff a bit, introducing Parker, on our way to the executive offices.

Logan saw us coming and came out from behind his desk to greet us. If he had any misgivings about passing the torch after so many years, they were not the least evident. He spoke of "your office" (meaning mine), and I had to wonder if his sparky nonchalance would wane as the day of the actual takeover neared. In three weeks' time, when he woke up retired, without a desk to report to, would he don the same dark three-piece suit (navy blue, with the faintest gray chalk stripes) that he wore that Tuesday morning? Or would he think, The hell with it, and lounge in a bathrobe till lunch?

Glee Savage turned an aisle and beelined toward us. "I *heard* you were in the building." Big smile. Big red lips. "Good morning, gentlemen!"

As she had not yet met Parker, I introduced them, explaining that Parker, an experienced researcher, was interested in exploring the *Register*'s morgue.

Logan interjected, "I understand, Glee, that you're pushing to resurrect that exposé idea." He wagged a finger.

"Only if it's of interest to the new publisher," she answered demurely—while reminding the old publisher that his days were numbered.

If they were sparring, it was a mannerly match, one that had apparently been enacted countless times over the years. Logan checked his watch and apologized, "I'm afraid I need to spend some time preparing for a lunch meeting—Rotary, you know—so perhaps Glee could squire you gentlemen through the offices. With *her* tenure, she knows where everything is." He winked at her.

Without comment to Logan, she come-hithered us with her finger, asking, "May I take your coats?"

Once she mentioned it, I felt warm, having worn my long topcoat since entering the building. I had already unbuttoned it, but I was glad to be rid of it entirely, handing it to her with my thanks.

Parker wore a heavy Eisenhower jacket. Its snug waistline showed his butt to particularly fine advantage that morning—an anatomical nicety that now magnetized Glee's stare. I thought she might pounce and bite him. Parker also noticed her interest, taking it in stride, returning the compliment with a wolfish innuendo as he passed her the jacket, a muffler, gloves.

She placed our things in her own office, which we passed while traversing several corridors on our way to the reference room. Arriving at the morgue, Glee introduced us to the reference staff, who took turns explaining various aspects of how the paper's records were stored, cataloged, and retrieved.

Parker was impressed. "I'm amazed," he said. "Your setup here is more typical of much larger papers. What a wonderful resource."

He was right. The thoroughness and organization of the clippings, photos, and other records reminded me of the *Journal*'s morgue in Chicago. The *Register* operated on a much smaller scale, of course, but technologically, all the bases were covered, with electronic systems in place to complement the older collections of microfiche and hard copy.

Parker questioned the staff about the research that Suzanne Quatrain had been pursuing, and they voiced their willingness to help him try to trace it. "I'd like to dig right in," he told me. "Do you mind if I get to work?"

I was still uneasy playing boss, but Logan had already given me carte blanche on the whole issue of the Quatrains, so I told Parker, "Enjoy yourself."

"Hold on," said Glee. "I was planning to take you guys to lunch. Mr. Logan has Rotary today, but he asked me to flex the house account for you at First Avenue Grill—best in town, you know."

Somehow I got the feeling I'd be seeing a lot of the Grill. "I'd be delighted," I told her. "Parker, how about you?"

He hesitated. "I'm really not hungry. And I really do want to delve into this. Would you mind terribly if I bugged out?"

"Terribly." Glee pouted. "I was hoping to get to know the new number two." She was talking to his face, but staring at his pants.

"Rain check?" he asked. "Sometime soon—I'd like that."
He winked.

"Oh, very well," she groaned, resigned to lunch without
Parker. "I guess it's just us," she told me, linking an arm with
mine.

We were about to return to her office for coats when someone at the research desk said, "You have a call, Mr. Manning."

Parker, Glee, and I exchanged a quizzical shrug; then I
crossed to the desk and took the receiver. "Mark Manning,"
I answered.

"Tag—I found you," said a familiar voice. "Hi, Mark. Doug
Pierce."

"Did it require an APB," I asked the sheriff with amiable
sarcasm, "or did you deduce that if I was not at the house,
you might find me here?"

"The latter," he admitted. "Hazel was evasive about your
whereabouts—she does have something of a shifty streak—but
I figured, Try the *Register*. Logan's secretary put me through
pronto. I'm surprised you're not more 'connected.' Haven't
you gone wireless?"

Again that sense of déjà vu swept over me: The previous
night, Barret Logan was tracked down with a phone call at
the Grill, and I found it remarkable that he was able to function
unfettered by electronics. I explained to Pierce, "Back in Chicago, I was on call via every gizmo known to science, but those
toys belonged to the *Journal*, and they stayed there. Up here,
I'll wait and see."

"It's a modern world," he reminded me.

Standing there with the phone in one hand, I pulled the
antique Montblanc from my jacket pocket and rolled it in my
fingers. "Get this," I told Pierce. "I still use a fountain pen."

"A what?" He was joking.

I asked him, "What can I do for you, Doug?"

His tone was instantly more serious. "There have been
some developments on the case. We should meet again."

"Is it urgent? I could come right over to the department."

"No," he said, "there's no need to interrupt your day.

Tomorrow morning would be good, though, if you're free. I could stop at the house."

Flipping through my pocket calendar, uncapping my pen, I told him, "The day's wide open. How's nine or ten?"

"I'll be there at nine," he said. "And, Mark? Try to keep an open mind, okay?"

"What does that mean?"

"You'll find out soon enough—tomorrow at nine. Thanks, Mark." We hung up.

Noting the appointment, I returned the pen and calendar to my jacket, telling Parker, "Something's up. Details tomorrow."

"I'd better get busy. Maybe we can come up with something by then."

I thanked him, checked my watch, and turned to Glee. "Time for lunch?"

We left the morgue together, returning to her office for coats. Helping her on with hers—a flashy ocher-colored sort of smock with wide sleeves and a thick fur collar—I said, "I'm glad you came to see me at the house on Sunday. As you probably know, I'm considered a suspect in this case, so I need to explore every possible angle."

Returning the courtesy, she helped me into my own coat. "I hope it proves useful to you, but that wasn't my motive for telling you about Suzanne's high-school episode. There's a *story* there, Mark. If it pans out, will you let me write it?"

"Absolutely." I liked her candor. I liked her persistence. "Let's go."

"I just need to grab my purse." From behind the door, she hefted another portfolio-size carpetbag, identical to the one she carried before, except that it was patterned with tiger stripes instead of leopard spots.

Out on the street, walking the block or so to the restaurant, we both donned sunglasses against the glare of a clear winter day. Though the low noontide sun cast an appearance of warmth, the illusion was dispelled by a sharp, cold wind that played havoc with Glee's purse. Struggling to anchor it under the flapping sleeve of her coat, she barely flinched—such was the price of fashion.

Pacing briskly to the snap of her heels on the sidewalk, she asked, for no apparent reason, "How old is Parker?"

I had to think for a moment, recalling his résumé. "Fifty-one." I also recalled that during Glee's Sunday visit, she mentioned being twenty-two when she started working at the *Register* thirty years ago. So she and Parker were about the same age.

"Jeez, he sure doesn't look it. Seems raring to go."

"Yes," I confirmed, "he's eager. I was lucky to find him, and I think we'll all enjoy working with him."

"I know *I* will." Glee swung her head toward me. "Say, boss—do you have any particular policy on workplace romance?"

With a chortle, I replied, "Why do you ask?"

"Well ..." she singsonged coyly, "new blood is always welcome here, and my prospects have been somewhat limited of late, and he seems unattached ..."

"*Parker?*" I stopped in my tracks.

"Why not?" she asked. The peck of her heels ceased. "He's hot."

"Glee"—I was laughing openly, loudly there on the street, with passersby pausing in dismay to observe my boisterous behavior—"he's gay!" I would not normally be so quick to out an associate, but Parker's near-militant homosexuality was a matter of public record, and I was certain that he would not want Glee to harbor false assumptions on this issue.

"I don't believe it," she told me flatly, removing her sunglasses.

"He was editor of the *Milwaukee Triangle*, for Christ's sake, and I can show you a pile of first-person editorials in which he crusades for every gay cause, from employment rights to adoption." I could have added that the man had professed his love for me on Christmas night, but that was a detail she didn't need to know. I simply told her, "You're barking up the wrong tree."

She fixed me with a skeptical stare for a moment, then resumed walking toward the restaurant. I followed. With a pensive shake of her head, she said to me, "I've always had a sixth sense about these things, and I'm never wrong. Mark, he was flirting."

"Glee," I assured her, "your radar needs adjusting."

Wednesday morning, working in my den, I heard the slam of car doors at the curb, then the muffled sounds of conversation. It was nine o'clock. I expected Sheriff Douglas Pierce, but who was with him? Glancing out the window, I was stunned to see Miriam Westerman walking with him toward the front door.

I bounded from my desk into the hall and opened the door as they were mounting the porch steps. Looking past Pierce as if he didn't exist, I told Miriam with a flat inflection, "Go away. I don't want you here."

Pierce rushed to meet me in the doorway and placed a restraining hand on my shoulder. "Mark, you agreed to keep an open mind."

With my eyes fixed on Miriam, I told Pierce, "Now I understand why you wouldn't explain that comment. I don't want her in my house, Doug."

"I know how you feel about her," Pierce leaned close to tell me (though she could obviously hear him), "but Miriam may have something useful to contribute to this investigation. I wouldn't steer you wrong, Mark—I think it's in your best interest to ask her in."

There was a brief, tense round of stares and counter stares. "Oh, all right," I said, scuffing one foot like a reticent child.

I stood aside and let both of them enter, closing the door. They followed as I walked directly to the den, making no offer to takes coats. Standing rigid at my desk, I asked, "What's this all about?"

Miriam jumped in. "I have no idea why Sheriff Pierce wished to see you," she sniffed, "but as for me, I have a short agenda of two items to share with you." She removed her cape and flung it over the back of the love seat. "First, of course, is Ariel's welfare."

"His name is Thad," I reminded her sternly.

"I want you to be aware, Mr. Manning, that I am taking legal action against you regarding Ariel. I have spoken with Harley Kaiser, district attorney for Dumont County, regarding the most expedient procedure for having Ariel removed from your household. As you know, I maintain that I am rightfully the boy's guardian, and I seek to have this claim upheld by the courts."

I turned to Pierce. "Is this her 'useful contribution,' Doug, or is there something else?"

Pierce unbuttoned his coat and, with strained temper, told her, "You promised not to get antagonistic, Miriam. Let's talk about Hazel Healy."

That caught my interest, and I flashed Miriam an inquisitive look.

She smiled smugly, fingered her heavy primitive necklace (it looked like painted bones and teeth), and plopped herself in one of the chairs by the fireplace. "It may come as some surprise to you, Mr. Manning, that I do *not* consider you to be a likely suspect in Suzanne's murder."

She was right—her statement did surprise me. Warily, I asked, "Why not?"

She paused, leaning forward in her chair. "Because Hazel killed Suzanne."

Before continuing the discussion, I thought it best to close the door. I did so, then sat across from Miriam at the fireplace. Pierce hung his coat behind the door, then joined us. With hushed voice, I asked Miriam, "How can you make this accusation?" I noticed that Pierce was not taking notes—he'd apparently already heard the answer.

Making no effort to subdue her stentorian speech, Miriam began, "Contrary to Mrs. Healy's assertion, I was *not* in this house on Christmas Day prior to Suzanne's murder. Hazel lied to you. And the obvious motive for her deception was to cast suspicion away from herself. It is now common knowledge that she was named to receive a sizable inheritance from Suzanne. Hazel may be getting old, and she may be going blind, but she's suddenly a woman of considerable means." Miriam paused, letting innuendo hang heavy in the air.

"Money can be a motive," I allowed, "and you've raised a point that I myself have considered, but your conclusion is purely speculative."

"Hardly!" She crossed her arms, clattering her bones. "Only days before your arrival in Dumont, Mr. Manning, Suzanne made the fatal mistake of *telling* Hazel about the generous terms of her will. I visited Suzanne at her home that day to pursue the issue of Ariel's guardianship. But Suzanne was preoccupied. She recounted the discussion she had just finished with Hazel, and she was concerned about the effect that the news had had on her. To hear Suzanne tell it, and these were her exact words, 'Hazel waltzed out of here with dollar signs in her eyes.' "

Again there was a pause as Miriam's words sank in. "That's very ... interesting," I told her, glancing sideways toward Pierce, not at all sure that I believed the woman, in spite of the fact that her story worked to my advantage.

Pierce said, "Thank you, Miriam. We'll try to work with this."

She rose, straightening the folds of her tunic. "I'm sure you will," she said vaguely to both of us. Whisking up her cape, she crossed to the door and opened it. Framed by the doorway leading to the hall, she told me, "The Feminist Society for the New Age of Cosmological Holism will break ground for its new school come spring. My son Ariel will be among its charter enrollees. *Don't* try to stop me, Mr. Manning." She smiled. "I'll see myself out."

She turned on her heel and, in the swirl of her cape, disappeared through the front door, which closed behind her with a sturdy thud. It was as if she had vanished into thin air, and I would not have been surprised to hear her cackle. Instead, I heard the knock of her clogs crossing the porch toward the street.

I arched my brows, blew a silent whistle, and suggested with a jerk of my head that Pierce should join me at the desk— somehow, I felt, it would be easier to focus our discussion there. He rose from his chair near the fireplace and sat at my uncle Edwin's partners desk, as he had done when we first met on Christmas morning. Seating myself opposite him, we again faced each other over the blotter.

"What do you make of her story?" I asked him.

He shrugged. "It's her word against Hazel's. The only person who could corroborate Miriam's story is Suzanne—who is now conveniently indisposed."

"Do you think Miriam is simply getting back at Hazel for accusing her of being at the house at the time Suzanne was murdered? Hazel's wacky fruitcake story is similar to the story Miriam just told us—it's one woman's word against the other's."

"Hey," said Pierce with a snap of his fingers, "we should ask Hazel to show us the 'organic fruitcake.' I wouldn't quite classify it as hard evidence, but it would at least lend *some* support to her story."

I shook my head. "I thought of that last night and talked to her about it. She called the fruitcake 'loathsome pagan garbage.' She threw it out with the rest of the trash on Christmas. It was picked up and hauled away yesterday. If, in fact, there *was* a fruitcake, I think we'd have a hard time identifying it at the dump among the thousands of others that were surely pitched last weekend."

We both laughed. It was hard to believe either woman's story—they seemed equally implausible. Yet either one, if true, would get me off the hook with district attorney Kaiser, and I was in no position to dismiss blithely any accusations that worked to my advantage. This brought to mind something else:

"Yesterday I overheard a quarrel," I told Pierce, "between Hazel and Thad."

"Should I take notes?" he asked, reaching inside his jacket.

"I think so," I told him. "The argument was inconclusive, but maybe you can sort it out." Then I told him what I had heard, eavesdropping outside the kitchen: Hazel essentially accused Thad of killing his own mother, and while Thad denied the murder, he did not deny that he had threatened Suzanne over issues relating to his rebellious desires for greater independence.

Dotting his notes with a period, Pierce said, "That's pretty juicy, but I think we'll have to keep this angle in reserve for a while. I've told you before, Mark, that Harley Kaiser needs, politically, to avoid implicating a Quatrain in this case. What's more, he could easily conclude that you fabricated the quarrel to save your own skin—and Hazel and Thad could easily deny that it ever occurred. From Kaiser's perspective, your story would have no more credibility than Hazel's tale of Miriam's organic fruitcake."

"That's heartening." So I pursued the only other angle I had. "Any luck tracking down Thad's father?"

"We've begun a search to trace the whereabouts of Austin Reece, but it's too early for results. Even if we find him, though, it's a long shot that he had either the motive or the means to kill Suzanne."

Nodding, I asked, "So where does that leave us?" I answered my own question, summarizing, "We currently have five suspects, with Austin Reece as little more than a specious hunch. The four remaining—Miriam, Hazel, Thad, and myself—all had plausible motives to want Suzanne dead, and there is reason to believe that each of us had the opportunity to act on those motives. Miriam has accused Hazel; Hazel has cast suspicion on both Miriam and Thad; Thad is convinced that I did it; and the DA, like Thad, would like nothing better than to convict me and be done with it."

"That's about it," said Pierce, clicking his ballpoint.

"So where do we go from here?"

His blank expression told me he was stumped; then his eyes widened with a new thought. He suggested, "Why don't we go upstairs?"

I had not set foot in the murder scene since four days prior, when I discovered the body. In the back of my mind, I had recently questioned my failure to return to the third floor, dismissing this as an oversight that could not be construed as active reluctance. But of course I was kidding myself. The upstairs great room, which had so intrigued me as a child, instilling a lifelong appreciation of the aesthetic it so dramatically embodied, had now become for me a place of deep foreboding, as if it were cursed. It was time for my rational brain to overrule this senseless angst. I told Pierce, "Let's go."

We left the den together, climbed the front stairs, passed the second-floor landing, and continued up the last flight to the room above. Pierce was talking about some aspect of the investigation, but I wasn't listening, absorbed in thoughts of Christmas Day. It would be hard to shake the memory of mounting the last few stairs and catching my first glimpse of Suzanne's bloodied body near the fire.

Arriving at the top of the stairs, I saw that the body was gone, as I knew it surely would be, and with this observation, the room's demons dispersed. Gone with Suzanne's body was the florid rug on which she bled, taken, I presumed, as evidence. Crossing the room, I noted, too, that various objects were missing—heavy, blunt objects that might have been the weapon: the fireplace shovel, the candlesticks, the bust of de Tocqueville had all been bagged and tagged and taken away. Aside from the bared area in front of the fireplace, though, the room looked much as it always had, and the mess of spilled books that had littered the floor was now returned to the shelves, either by the police or by Hazel—I wasn't sure.

"The missing items will be returned," Pierce told me, "as soon as it's determined they have no evidentiary value."

"Don't bother with the rug," I said, not needing to explain that it was hopelessly stained.

"We'll get rid of it," said Pierce, making a note. "The coroner needs more time with the rest. So far, he's drawn nothing but blanks in identifying the weapon."

As he spoke, we strolled through the room. At its center, midway between the fireplace on the back wall and the arched window in front, there was a grouping of leather-upholstered furniture beneath the ceiling's highest point. The sofas and chairs were draped with warm, handsome throws, and I gestured that we should sit there. A large worktable with a single desk chair stood nearby, perpendicular to the banister below the window. Overhead hung an oversize wrought-iron chandelier of whimsical design, dangling huge crystal prisms that caught light from either the window or the fireplace, depending on the time of day.

Pierce continued to explain some technicalities of the investigation, but my mind, busy with the surroundings, could not absorb his words. The lofty space had always affected me this way, awing me with its sheer scale, filling me with imagined tales of its past, tugging at my own memories of the place.

Again I recalled my visit to Dumont three years ago, after inheriting the house from Uncle Edwin. At the recommendation of Elliot Coop, the family attorney, I had driven up from Chicago to meet Professor and Mrs. Tawkin, who were interested in buying the house from me. We met outside the house that day—it was spring, and the elms were green. Having somehow survived the pestilence that felled so many of their brothers, the trees appeared even loftier than I remembered them from my boyhood. Elliot took us all inside.

Though thirty years had passed since I'd last seen it, the house still matched my memory of it. Some furnishings had changed, and certain features had been updated, but the general character of the place had been faithfully retained. Winding our way through the rooms, with the lawyer and the professor pointing out countless details to the wife, I grew impatient to see the upstairs again. At last Professor Tawkin said, "Now the best part, pumpkin—the third floor."

We climbed the back stairs, and a flood of memories rushed over me as we stepped into that pristine kitchen. The wife gabbed excitedly as we followed Elliot through the hall and into the big front room. In that instant, I was transported back to the quiet afternoons when I claimed the great room as my private domain, dreaming and writing my most private thoughts and fantasies.

The other three were talking rapidly, tossing around comments, ideas, questions. The wife wagged the agency's spec sheet. "*Mother-in-law* apartment? God, we could *live* up here."

The professor told her, "Look at this terrific banister, still intact. We could easily break through to the main staircase."

Of course—I realized—obviously. The front stairs had originally led directly up to the third-floor great room. The remodeling, which suddenly appeared rather clumsy, had not been apparent to me as a child. I asked Elliot, "Do you happen to know—what *was* this space used for? It's always baffled me."

"The upstairs hasn't been used in a long while, Mr. Manning. But many years ago, when the house was built, your uncle Edwin had a partner. They'd built up their printing business together, and then they built this house together. Your uncle and his young family—there was just the one baby then, your cousin Mark Quatrain—lived on the first two floors, and your uncle's partner, who was not married, lived up here. An odd setup, but it seemed to work. For a few years. Then there must have been a falling-out, because the partner suddenly left the business—and the house. These rooms weren't needed anymore, so they just weren't used."

"*We'll* use them," the wife assured us. She told her husband, "I was skeptical, I admit, but I'm totally won over. Shall we sign some papers?"

Mission accomplished. Outside, the Tawkins got into their car, and Elliot walked with me toward mine, telling me, "Before your uncle died, while he was reviewing his will, he gave me a letter and asked me to deliver it into your hand." He produced the envelope. "There, Mr. Manning. Done."

"Hey, Mark"—a hand touched my knee—"is something wrong? You haven't heard a word I've said." It was Sheriff Pierce, leaning from the leather sofa, trying to get my attention.

With an embarrassed laugh, I told him, "Sorry, Doug. I was lost in thought. This room has had quite an impact on my life."

He looked confused. "Why?" he asked, sitting back. "Suzanne's murder would be enough to shake anyone, certainly, but was there more?"

"I've loved this room since the first day I saw it, but it turns out—and it was many years later that I learned it—this room has a history, a significance that I could never have fathomed."

Pierce set aside his notes. "You've captured *my* attention. What happened?"

"About three years ago, shortly after I inherited the house, I drove up here and sold it, as you know, to the Tawkins. Elliot

Coop gave me a letter that day, left for me by my uncle." I paused, not sure I was ready to tell this.

But Pierce was hooked. "A letter? Yes? Then what?"

"Elliot said that before my uncle died, he'd instructed Elliot to deliver the letter into my hand. He gave me the envelope right outside the house, as I was getting into my car. I placed the envelope on the passenger seat and started the car, needing to follow the buyers and Elliot to his office for some paperwork. The letter was addressed, simply, 'Mr. Mark Manning, Jr., Chicago.' I couldn't quite take my eyes off it as I backed out of the driveway and pulled into the street. The other cars were well on their way, but my curiosity demanded satisfaction— then and there—so I pulled over to the curb and, in the shadow of the house, opened the envelope."

This, of course, was an important juncture in my narrative, and I again paused, reluctant to continue.

"Well?" said Pierce, leaning forward. "What *about* the letter?"

"I read it," I answered, "and I still have it."

Pierce flumped back, tossing his hands. "*That's* anticlimactic." His disappointed tone conveyed that he knew I would not complete the story.

"There's more," I conceded, then vaguely added, "maybe later." Since I really wanted to set our conversation on a different course, and since we had already ventured into personal territory, I turned the tables, saying, "You've mentioned that you grew up here, Doug. What was it like?"

"Great," he said with a blank expression, caught unawares by my question. Then, collecting his thoughts, he became more articulate. "I may be prejudiced, but Dumont is a special kind of place. If I didn't feel that way, I'd have taken my career elsewhere—God knows, there are other communities in far greater need of able law enforcement. By *their* standards, Dumont is a quiet town. Violent crime is rare, Suzanne's case notwithstanding, and gangs are nonexistent. Believe me, it's a fulfilling, even *noble*, challenge to keep it that way."

"Bravo," I quietly cheered him.

"I'm not looking for flattery," he assured me. "A job well

done is its own reward. And my reward is knowing that Dumont is still the kind of place where I'd want to raise a kid of my own."

"You never married." Though the words were meant as a question, I spoke them as a statement, seeking confirmation.

"No." His tone was colored by the slightest awkwardness. "The right girl never came along."

Chortling, I told him, "I know *that* feeling." My comment was intentionally flip, meant to acknowledge my homosexuality. I did not intend to imply, however, that the right girl had evaded him for the same reason. Regardless of how he read my remark, he did not respond to it.

He continued. "Of the people I grew up with, many moved away, but there are many others I still see every day, and we all feel we have a stake in this town. Our *roots* are here, and now that we've passed into middle age, we're *running* the place. Whether we're collecting a paycheck and parenting, or serving in a public capacity as sheriff or district attorney—"

I interrupted, "You grew up with Harley Kaiser?"

"As a matter of fact, I did. Miriam Westerman, too. We all went to school together—we're about the same age—I'm forty-five. Harley and I were close friends through high school, but now we have nothing in common other than our work."

"Were you close to Miriam?" I wondered aloud.

Pierce shook his head. "Not really. She was just another girl in class, unremarkable except for her height. But things changed after we graduated. Miriam went away to Berkeley, fried her brain, got her degree, and came back with a lot of addled ideas. Sometime in the seventies, she got Fem-Snatch up and running, and during the early eighties, she first attracted Suzanne to the group."

This was starting to get interesting, so I got up and crossed to the desk, looking for paper. "Mind if I take a few notes?" I asked Pierce.

"Be my guest," he said, rising to face me.

I slid a sheet of white bond out from a drawer in the work-table, then sat at the chair, uncapping my pen. Sketching the chronology Pierce had just related, I said, "You mentioned on

Monday that Harley Kaiser and Miriam have forged some sort of political alliance. What was that all about?"

"The story fast forwards to a few years ago," he explained, "when Miriam spearheaded a campaign to pass a local 'obscenity ordinance.' The idea was to shut down some adult bookstores you may have noticed along the highway on the outskirts of town."

I rolled my eyes. "Porn shops?" I asked.

"Exactly. Miriam and Fem-Snach took the position that pornography is (get this) 'violence against women,' so they sought to write a Dumont County ordinance duplicating a statewide law that had recently passed judicial scrutiny. Earlier attempts had been ruled unconstitutionally vague, but the Bible thumpers eventually managed to get something to stick in Madison."

"If there was already a state law," I asked, "why would Miriam bother with the local ordinance?"

With a frustrated toss of his hands, Pierce answered, "Miriam wanted it debated locally so that county board members would have to go on the record, for it or against it—she was trying to identify her future targets. Needless to say, most board members didn't want to get *near* such a volatile, no-win issue, so the county executive deferred to both my office and Kaiser's, seeking opinions regarding the practical, administrative implications of the proposed ordinance."

Guessing the answer, I asked, "What was your position?"

Pierce approached the desk, standing opposite of where I sat. "I told them outright to forget it. I doubt that I need to detail my reasoning for you."

Looking up from my note taking, I reminded him, "I'm a First Amendment kind of guy, Doug."

"I am, too, and as far as I could always tell, so was Harley. Believe me, he had never been even remotely religious, and since these censorship campaigns are typically the work of the right-wing Christian crowd, he had no taste whatever for the ordinance. So he originally responded to the county board that he was philosophically neutral on the issue but that such a law would be difficult and expensive to enforce."

"A sane response. Then what happened?"

"He began to sniff political pay dirt. Miriam's radical feminists had gone to bed, figuratively, with the conservative Christians, so Harley capitulated and found sudden enthusiasm for so-called family values. He stood by quietly as the ordinance passed by a lopsided margin, then sought to enforce it with a vengeance. Off the record, Mark, the man sold his soul."

I stood, shaking my head. "Somehow," I predicted, "this guy and I just aren't going to get along." I stepped around the worktable and walked to the Palladian window, looking out over the town where this political drama had been enacted.

Pierce's tone brightened some. "For whatever it's worth, Harley's hotdogging hasn't paid off so far. He's used my department to collect evidence that these stores are dealing in obscenity—we've bought a few videotapes—then he's hauled them to trial. But he's had a tough time finding juries who agree on what's 'obscene.' The community is starting to lose patience with this nonsense, and he's responded, without much savvy, by yapping to the press like some guardian of public morals. Common sense should tell the man that he should distance himself from Miriam now, but, instead, they've been closing ranks."

"Huh?" Something caught my eye from the window. "Speak of the devil."

"Harley's out there?" asked Pierce, stepping beside me for a look.

"No," I said (I'd never set eyes on Harley Kaiser, so I wouldn't have known him if I'd seen him), "it's Miriam Westerman, and she's snooping around my car." There had been some jockeying of vehicles back near the garage last night, so I'd left my car in the driveway, up front near the street. Miriam's nose was pressed to the driver's window. "What the hell is *she* still doing here?"

Pierce laughed, explaining, "That's a magnificent automobile, Mark. We don't see many like that up here. It's drawn a lot of interest."

Though the sun would not set for another hour, it was already reduced to a dim glow in a gray sky, lolling near the southwest horizon. Damp and bleak, the day had nonetheless warmed some, blanketed by thick clouds that clogged the afternoon.

Shortly after three, Parker Trent returned to the house from his day of digging in the *Register*'s morgue. I was in the kitchen, on a coffee break from the den, when Parker clomped across the back porch and swung open the door, whipping off his cap. Neither of us quite expected to encounter the other, and we shared a grin that made me realize we were both happy to have each other's company.

We were eager to report on our day's activities—his research and my meeting with Pierce—but before we could open that exchange, Parker suggested, "Why don't we go for a run? There's still some light, it's not too cold, and we can talk."

I hadn't run in three days, since Sunday with Neil, and I had missed Monday's run with Parker. "I'll meet you in the front hall in five minutes," I told him.

But it took us only four minutes to change, and we met on the second-floor landing, emerging from our bedrooms. Once again, Parker wore those flattering gray fleece sweatpants. I, too, wore sweatpants that day—everyone seemed more dismayed than impressed by my bravado of wearing shorts in December. I also wore a zippered jacket over my T-shirt, while Parker wore a sweatshirt with a towel tucked around his neck.

Out on the street, we fell into a comfortable gait together and turned without comment in the direction of the park—I assumed Neil had shown Parker the route when they ran without me on Monday. Curious about Neil's assessment of Parker as a well-trained runner, I picked up the pace and found that Parker had no difficulty matching it. I could have gone faster still, but there was no point in it. This wasn't a race, and, besides, if we ran much faster, we wouldn't be able to talk.

"How'd it go at the *Register* today?" I asked him.

He turned to flash me a self-satisfied smile. "I may be on

to something. Yesterday afternoon, I came up dry, but I was still getting the hang of their systems. Today went much better. I'm starting to reconstruct the sequence of materials that Suzanne was researching, but I'll need more information before I can make sense of it. It's just a matter of time."

"Time is the one commodity that may be running out for me," I told him.

"Why?" His tone carried genuine concern. "What happened?"

"The meeting with Sheriff Pierce this morning was less than encouraging. The DA is itching for an arrest, and I'm still his most politically expedient suspect. Fortunately, Pierce and I are armed with some other possibilities." I reviewed for Parker what we then knew about Miriam, Hazel, Thad, and Thad's father, Austin Reece. "For whatever it's worth," I concluded, "Miriam Westerman is convinced that I'm not the culprit. She's accused Hazel of the murder, but her story is weak."

We were reaching the perimeter of the park, and I slowed to a more leisurely pace, preferring to enjoy the serene surroundings unencumbered by the grind of aerobics. Parker's instincts matched my own, and he slowed the pace further, walking at my side. A wintry fog hung over the grounds, and distant banks of trees receded into layers of gray, with pines pointing black into the dusk. We both gaped a wordless appreciation of the hushed setting, its quietude broken only by our panting and by the crunch of icy gravel beneath our treaded soles. Watching the movement of Parker's feet, the scissoring motion of his legs, the general character of his body language, I was again reminded of my cousin Mark. Like my nine-year-old self, I just wanted to . . . touch him. But of course I wouldn't. What was I thinking?

"I was thinking," Parker's voice cracked the silence. "As long as Neil is coming back to Dumont this weekend, maybe you could invite Roxanne and Carl back as well—they could share the ride."

We were approaching a pavilion near the frozen lagoon. There were some benches arranged in a lit alcove, sort of an open porch, offering a sense of shelter from the falling night. We sat next to each other, huddling leg-to-leg—a natural thing to do, a means of conserving our warmth, but I was well aware that it carried an erotic overtone, and I enjoyed the feel of his calf and thigh muscles against mine, buffered by the soft layers of our sweatpants.

Regarding his suggestion to invite Roxanne and Carl up for the weekend, I told him, "I'd enjoy having everyone at the house again. We could have a proper New Year's party. And let's face it: our big Christmas weekend was a flop, to put it mildly." We both laughed, grateful to find some shred of humor in the situation.

Then Parker told me, "A party would be great, but the weekend would also give you and Roxanne some time together to do some serious planning. I mean, logistics—if worse comes to worst."

That wiped the smile off my face. Had I been taking the district attorney's prejudices too lightly? Was it obvious to Parker that I should line up some high-powered legal talent? After all, Roxanne had offered to return and defend me . . .

"Hey, gosh, I'm sorry, Mark." From the tone of Parker's soothing words, my face must have told him that I was shaken by his suggestion. "Look"—he placed his hand on my knee—"I didn't mean to upset you. We all know that you're innocent of this crime, and you've got a lot of people on your side working to help you, myself included. Doesn't it just make sense, though, to recruit someone like Roxanne for your team?"

I fixed him in my stare. "I loathe sports phraseology," I told him. Though my tone had the ring of humor, I couldn't have been more serious. "Don't ever let it creep onto the editorial page."

"No, sir!" he said, grinning. Laughing, he added, "It won't happen again, coach." Then he lifted his hand from my knee—I saw it coming, as if in slow motion—and he playfully mussed my hair.

I felt the warm touch of his fingers on my scalp as my hair parted and clumped. I felt the instant onset of an erection burning the folds of my sweatpants. I felt transported in time, sucked back to the confusion of my boyhood when I first met my handsome older cousin and tried to be clever, telling him brightly, "We've got the same name."

My cousin smiled and said, "How about that?" Then he mussed my hair with his hand, and I really liked the way his fingers felt on my head. I'm usually fussy about my hair—but I didn't straighten it out for a while.

Christmas came and went. Uncle Edwin and I phoned Mom in California to ask about her visit with her sick sister. She said that the weather was like summer (who'd want to spend Christmas *there?)* and Aunt Edna was worse.

In the days that followed, my cousins Mark and Suzanne spent lots of time away from the house with their older friends; Joey spent every waking moment with *me.* I was grateful for his company—to a point—but I missed the private time I always had at home in the late afternoon, when I could think about things, maybe do some writing. So I told Joey that there was a school project due after vacation and that I needed to spend some time working on it alone.

"You're going to the *library?*" he asked as if he'd rather eat glass.

"Nah. I'll just work on it upstairs. May I borrow your typewriter?"

And I did. Each afternoon I climbed the back stairs and claimed that big attic room as my private world. I imagined living there and pretended to make phone calls, inviting unnamed friends over to see the place, asking Mark up for lunch, telling my mother she simply *had* to drop by the next time she flew in from California. Then I would settle into a chair at the worktable under the curved window and type things—sometimes poems (they didn't always rhyme), but mostly little stories. They looked sort of strange, with the type both red and black, instead of just black, but they looked much neater than if I had written them by hand. I wrote about my trip. I wrote about my new home, "Upstairs on Prairie Street," revealing gory secrets of its past. And I wrote about Mark, including the way I felt when he mussed my hair, but I changed his name to Marshall.

On New Year's Eve, I stayed upstairs later than usual, as it was the last full day of my visit. When I came down the stairs around five-thirty with Joey's typewriter and my folder of stories, Uncle Edwin was in the hall outside his bedroom carrying a tuxedo in a cleaner's bag (big party that night). He said, "Hi there, Mark. Care to keep me company while I get this monkey suit together?"

"Sure." I'd always been comfortable with adults and was glad to spend the time with Uncle Edwin. I hadn't realized that he and Aunt Peggy had their own bedrooms, which was nifty—I'd hate to share *my* room.

He showed me all the goofy stuff that went with his tuxedo—shoes like bedroom slippers, jewelry for buttons, and this sash-thing he called a "crumb catcher." He told me about growing up with Mom and Aunt Edna. And he told me how everyone had enjoyed my visit. "Joey tells me you've been working upstairs on a project. Something for school?"

"That's right," I told him (okay, I lied a little). "Some poems and stories."

"Really?" Uncle Edwin seemed surprised—and pleased. "Creative writing can be somewhat personal, but is there any of it you'd care to share with me?"

Happy that he was curious, I said, "You can read it *all*, if you want," and handed him my folder. "I won't need it back till tomorrow."

"Not till tomorrow," said Parker, "but I'd be happy to give her a call for you."

"What?" There on the park bench, we were discussing Roxanne, but I'd been absorbed in the memory of my cousin, and I could recall, line for line, parts of the story I had written about him thirty-three years ago. I recalled the exact wording I used to describe what I felt when he mussed my hair—feelings I could not possibly understand. My uncle Edwin, however, was to read that story during the last night of my visit, and he would understand it perfectly.

"I said," Parker repeated, "that we won't be able to reach Roxanne at her office till tomorrow. Shall I call her?"

"No," I answered, "I'll phone Neil first, then her. But thanks."

"Good. Settled." He stood. "It's getting dark—and cold. Time to head back?"

I nodded, got up, stretched a bit; then we started our run back to the house. The pace was easy, and we may have chatted along the way, but I was still focused on an uncomfortable mix of memories and emotions. My fantasies of Mark Quatrain were safely buried in the past, I told myself, but I could not allow those fantasies to spill into the present, to color my relationship with Parker Trent, who was very much alive there at my side, returning home with me to sleep under my roof— while Neil caught up with his work, two hundred miles away.

Shortly past noon on Thursday, I entered the First Avenue Grill with Thad, and we instantly spotted Joey waiting for us at a table. Arranging the simple lunch outing had not been easy. My cousin Joey was eager enough to meet us, but when I proposed it to Thad, he at first refused, citing plans with "friends," and he wasn't going to waste one of his last days of Christmas vacation on family.

"That's just the point," I told him. "We *are* family, and, like it or not, we'd better pull together and get used to each other. You and Joey and I are all that's left of the Quatrain clan in Dumont."

"You're not a Quatrain," the kid told me.

"My mother was," I reminded him. "Just like yours. We're equally qualified to claim the name. And we're going to lunch."

Thad's protests notwithstanding, we did indeed hop into my car at noon and left the house for downtown. While Thad made it clear that he had no interest in sharing a meal with me, I was surprised to note that he seemed to enjoy sharing the ride—my car was high on the list of "guy things" that had irresistible appeal for him, and, in his eyes, the fact that I'd shown sense enough to buy the Bavarian V-8 gave us our first shaky toehold on common ground.

In truth, my motives for calling the lunch were mixed. Yes,

we were family and it seemed the right thing to do. And yes, there was family business that needed discussion, such as the venue for Suzanne's funeral. But also, I'd heard Hazel stop just short of accusing Thad of killing his own mother—a murder, believed by some to be my own doing—so I wanted to spend some noncombative time with him and try to get into his head.

Inside the restaurant, already bustling with its lunch crowd, I shook hands with Joey and removed my coat. Thad had refused to wear a coat, insisting that the bulky sweater hanging past his hips was sufficient. He and Joey hugged warmly, and for the first time I saw Thad as the orphaned child he truly was.

We sat down, and when the waitress asked for drink orders, Joey wanted cocoa, which sounded good, so we all had some. Joey and I exchanged some small talk, and I quickly learned that his interests and world view were severely limited—the weather, the menu, the murder. Remembering that publisher Barret Logan had described Joey's "twelve-year-old brain in a middle-aged body," I treated him as an adult and mustered a show of interest in his discussion of snow and bread sticks and the many sympathy cards he was receiving from coworkers at Quatro Press.

Thad watched our conversation silently, but I did not, for once, interpret this behavior as sulking. It was obvious that he felt genuine affection for his retarded uncle—perhaps he even felt protective of him—and the fact that I treated Joey kindly must have earned me a measure of respect in Thad's eyes. When I leaned forward, elbows on table, to say, "There's something important that the three of us have to talk about," Thad also leaned into the conversation, asking, "What's that?" His tone was entirely civil.

"Suzanne's funeral is scheduled for next Monday," I told them both, "but there's still some question as to where the service will be held. It's up to us."

Joey told us, "Father Winter says it ought to be at Saint Cecille's. He came to work and talked to me about it yesterday." Joey's eyes widened as he recounted the meeting. There was a foamy mustache of cocoa on his upper lip. "He said that the

Quatrain family goes way back with Saint Cecille's, and that it's time for Suzanne to come home, whatever that means. And I told him that I remembered something about people who were murdered—I thought that priests weren't supposed to bury them, and that had me sort of worried. But Father Winter said no, I was thinking about people who killed themselves—that's a sin, and the church doesn't like that, but Suzanne's murder was just fine, and they'd be happy to handle it."

Thad and I glanced at each other and shared a silent laugh—another small step, I noted, along the bumpy road toward bonding.

"But Mom never went to church," Thad told his uncle.

Joey answered, "She did when she was little."

I said to Joey, but more for Thad's benefit, "I used to go to church, too, but sometimes people's ideas change as they grow older."

Joey told us, "Father Winter said it was never too late for Suzanne to come back. He called her a 'prodigal.' "

"I don't know," said Thad with a skeptical shake of his head. "Mom never had very nice things to say about Father Winter. Sorry, Uncle Joey, I know he's a friend of yours."

"There *is* another option," I reminded them. They both turned to me with the same puzzled look, apparently unaware of the squabbling reported in the *Register*. "Miriam Westerman, the Fem-Snatch lady, says that she and Suzanne became best of friends again." Thad and Joey both laughed their disbelief. I continued. "Miriam wants to officiate at Suzanne's funeral. It would be some sort of New Age ceremony held on the grounds of the Society."

"What does *that* mean?" asked Thad.

I chuckled. "I'm not exactly sure. Miriam's Society believes that nature itself is sort of a god, so they have this loosely structured religion geared toward it. Some people call it paganism."

Joey turned pale. "That won't do at *all*, Mark. That would be sinful, I'm sure. Even if Suzanne didn't much like Father Winter, we *can't* get her into trouble with God. She *has* to be buried at Saint Cecille's!" His voice was beginning to rise, and people at adjacent tables were turning to look. I recognized a pattern here—Joey's boyhood petulance was emerging again, as it had on Christmas Day. Then the old threat. "If Father Winter doesn't get to do the funeral, I'll, I'll . . . I'll hold my breath till I turn blue, and this time I'll die!" And with that, he crossed his arms, puffed his cheeks, and closed his eyes so tight, his brows were nearly swallowed by the wrinkles.

I sat there stunned as our lunching neighbors gasped, dropping forks. Someone hailed the hostess, wondering what should be done. But before anyone could act, Thad took over, having learned from experience how to handle these snits. He simply leaned over and tickled his uncle's armpits. Joey burst into laughter, loving Thad's attention. Uneasily, the others in the restaurant turned back to their food and attempted to pick up lost conversations.

When things had calmed down at our own table, Thad told me, "I haven't decided about God, but I do know that Miriam Westerman is a bitch on wheels—a lying, crazy bitch on wheels. I say there's no way in hell she's gonna bury Mom."

"I'm with you, Thad." I patted his shoulder, and he did not pull away. "Joey seems to feel pretty strongly that Suzanne should have a Catholic burial. I'm not entirely comfortable with that, but at least they'll put on a good show. Besides, there aren't any other options." I didn't honestly think that Suzanne would have cared for *either* option, but since she had left no instructions, we were stuck with our best judgment. And in my judgment, if we went with the priest, we'd piss Miriam but good. It sounded like a plan. "Are we agreed then, guys? Should I tell the lawyer that the funeral will be at Saint Cecille's?"

"Sure. Yeah," they told me, making it official with a round of shaken hands.

The rest of our lunch was considerably less eventful. We returned to Joey's chitchat about the weather and the food, and Thad volunteered a few comments about school—he'd enjoyed driver's ed., he wasn't into sports, and, surprisingly, he even had some cogent thoughts regarding *As You Like It*, his first exposure to Shakespeare. "By the way," he told me, leaning back in his chair with an air of triumph, "Shakespeare started lots of sentences with 'me' instead of 'I.' "

I should have seen that coming. "Methinks thou art a mite confused, Thad. 'Methinks' is not 'me.' What's more, it's Middle English and archaic. Trust me."

I wasn't sure how he would react, but he accepted my correction with good humor. Methinks he knew that I respected him for gaming with me on the issue.

Sometime during dessert (three chocolate sundaes—what is it about cold weather that makes ice cream so appealing?), Elliot Coop, the Quatrain family's old attorney, entered the restaurant with a couple of businessmen. They ended up at a table on the far side of the room, but as soon as Elliot noticed me, he excused himself from his companions and walked over to us. "Gentlemen, good afternoon," he told us brightly. "So nice to see everyone getting along so well. Suzanne would be delighted, I'm sure." He shook hands with me, mentioning, "It didn't take you long to discover the best place in town." Then he gave a genial nod to both Thad and Joey.

I told him, "Glad we ran into you, Elliot. We were just discussing the controversy regarding Suzanne's funeral. The *family* has decided"—I gestured with my hands that the word referred to all three of us—"that Saint Cecille's will bury her. Could you convey our wishes to Father Winter, please?"

"Delighted, Mr. Manning." His head bobbed with a deferential bow. Then he chuckled and, turning to Joey, told him, "I thought perhaps *you* had called this meeting—to do a bit of arm-twisting regarding the house."

Joey looked up from the sundae he was spooning. "Huh?" There was chocolate on his chin and a dab of whipped cream hooked at the end of his nose. Though Joey's response was far from eloquent, it summed up my own reaction to Elliot's statement—I had no idea what he was talking about.

The lawyer continued, telling me, "When word got out that the Tawkins were divorcing and the house would be sold, Joey came over to my office and made an offer to buy the place." Elliot gave me a big obvious wink. "It was twice what you were willing to pay for it."

Interesting. This had a familiar ring. Monday night, in this very restaurant, Barret Logan told me that Joey had tried to buy the *Register* at twice what I was offering. Logan concluded that Joey was growing increasingly confused and frustrated about his role in the world. Now, hearing this news of a similar incident with the house, I saw the accuracy of Logan's assessment.

Joey seemed embarrassed that the lawyer had mentioned his offer. He put down his spoon and told me, "I just thought it would be nice to keep the house in the family. But it's okay, Mark—you're family, too."

"Thanks, Joey." I patted his arm. "I'm glad you feel that way."

Oblivious to these emotional dynamics, Elliot prattled on, telling me, "While sifting through the details of disbursing Suzanne's estate, I ran across a bundle of files that she had left with me for safekeeping. I'm not sure what should be done with them, but as you've been named her executor, Mr. Manning, I thought I'd offer them first to you."

My reporter's instincts were suddenly on full alert. "Thank you, Elliot," I told him, trying not to appear too interested. "What sort of files are they?"

"I haven't had time to study them—it's rather a thick bundle, after all, and Suzanne's instructions were simply to hold them for her, not to act on them—but they appear to have been compiled by various private investigators around the country. One might call them 'dossiers,' but that has such cloak-and-dagger overtones, don't you think?"

Semantics aside, I told him, "I'll be happy to take them off your hands, Elliot. Shall I come to your office?"

"That won't be necessary. They're already packed in my car, so I'll deliver them to your house."

I was tempted to suggest that we dash outside to the curb and move them to my own car, but that might appear impatient, and, besides, he needed to get back to his table. So I thanked him for his thoughtfulness, and we wished each other a pleasant afternoon.

When we had finished dessert, I paid the check, and we

prepared to get up from the table. Glancing at my watch, I said, "I really need to get over to the *Register*'s offices—Parker is expecting me. Did you drive today, Joey? I wonder if you could give Thad a ride back to the house."

"Sure," said Joey, eager to help. "No one cares if I'm late getting back to work."

Standing, I asked Thad, "Do you mind? I'm late already."

"No, no problem. But I have to tell you, Mark"—I noted that it was the first time he spoke my name—"I'd rather be seen in *your* car any day."

I thanked him for the compliment and handed Joey his overcoat from a nearby hook. While shrugging into my own coat, we all headed for the door. Then I thought of something. "Thad," I asked, "you've started driving, haven't you?"

"Yeah, I got my license in the fall."

"I know you're planning to go out with friends tonight." I paused. Did I really want to make this offer? Was the risk outweighed by the possibility of some shred of the kid's affection? "Would you like to take my car?"

He stood speechless for a moment, not believing his ears, wondering if I was joking. When I did not burst into laughter and retract the offer, he said, "*Would* I!" He nodded stupidly. "Thanks, Mark. That's really nice of you. I appreciate it."

Within five minutes, I had walked the block or so to the First Avenue offices of the *Register*, said hello to Connie, the ground-floor receptionist, and climbed the stairs to the newsroom. The pace of activity there was rising, so I did not linger while greeting the staffers who noticed me, though it was satisfying to note that I could now actually remember some of their names. While unbuttoning my overcoat, I zigzagged through the maze of desks toward the back of the building, passing by Barret Logan's office (he was working on something beyond the glass wall that separated him from his secretary, who acknowledged me with a smile and a nod) and Glee Savage's office (her quarters were considerably smaller than Logan's, without a secretary—Glee sat working on a story, wearing a feathered hat, and she glanced up from her computer to wave as I passed). Then I turned into the corridor that led to the morgue.

A woman at the desk saw me enter and offered to take my coat, draping it over an extra chair. I asked about Parker, and she told me he was at work in the stacks, pointing the way. Making my way through a narrow aisle of metal bookshelves, which housed not books but folders filled with photos and clippings, I emerged into a clearing where Parker sat working at a round library table. He looked up from the heaps of material he'd pulled from the shelves. "Oh, hi, Mark," he said, rising, checking his watch as though he'd lost all track of time.

"You need to come up for air now and then," I told him. He laughed, sitting again, and I joined him at the table.

"Did you manage to drag Thad to lunch?" he asked.

"As a matter of fact, I did, and it was productive. He, Joey, and I decided that Saint Cecille's will bury Suzanne—so that's *one* issue resolved."

Parker nodded. "Yeah, but what about the *tone* of it? Did Thad behave?"

"He was fine. This may be premature, but I think his hostility toward me is actually beginning to wane. It didn't hurt that I offered to lend him my car."

"Hey"—Parker laughed—"whatever it takes."

"In fact," I continued, "if there was any difficult behavior, it came not from Thad, but from Joey. He worked himself into a little snit at one point and made quite a scene. I think the hostess was ready to dial nine-one-one."

"Oh, no. Really?" Parker shook his head in amused disbelief. "Not one of his threats about turning blue?"

"Exactly. But Thad snapped him out of it, and we had a nice lunch. Then, during dessert, who should arrive but Elliot Coop?" I leaned toward Parker, elbows on the table, knowing the next bit of information would be of great interest to him. "Guess what. Suzanne had been collecting personal files, dossiers compiled by private investigators around the country. They were left with Elliot for safekeeping, and he asked if I'd like to have them."

"Well?" said Parker, rising an inch or so from his seat. "Where *are* they?"

"They're still in Elliot's car," I answered calmly. "I didn't want to appear too anxious. He's going to drop them off at the house."

Parker literally rubbed his hands together, hungry to get at them.

"It's intriguing, to say the least," I said, "but I can't imagine what's in them."

Without hesitation, Parker said, *"I've* got a theory. And it fits what I've been finding here. Look"—he slid a pile of folders across the table toward me, opening the one on top—"I've begun to reconstruct Suzanne's morgue research, and it seems to have focused on two areas. First, her older brother, Mark Quatrain."

I glanced through the folders he had given me, and, sure enough, they contained newspaper accounts of my older cousin's high school and college achievements, his victories as a swimmer and a runner, his being sent to Vietnam, his death there. Conspicuously, there was nothing mentioning his rape and murder of the Asian girl. The photos were old, stiff, and unnatural. Anyone could see that he was handsome, but he had the look of being frozen in time, in an earlier generation, without those vital sparks that had let him live in my imagination for so many years. Missing were the sound of his voice, the touch of his hand in my hair, the way he moved—his body language.

"Second," said Parker, sliding another pile of folders toward me, "her research also focused on the period three years ago when her father died."

The second group of clippings reported Edwin Quatrain's death with page-one headlines, accompanied by various retrospectives of his work at Quatro Press, founding it with a long-gone partner and nurturing it into the county's biggest industry. There were less flashy stories, consigned to the paper's business pages, detailing the probate investigation of his estate, which was ultimately resolved, without incident, naming Suzanne Quatrain as his principal heir. The photos of my uncle were far more recent than my memories of him, and it surprised me to see him in his seventies. His image, like his son's, was now frozen in time, though this wizened Uncle Edwin seemed to peer at me not from a past generation, but from an age I had not yet known.

The photos of both my cousin and my uncle stirred emotions that sapped my reasoning, and I found myself unable to analyze the hard facts within the files. "I'm sorry," I told Parker, "but I don't know what to make of all this."

Parker scooted his chair closer to mine, as if he needed to speak confidentially. Leaning nearer, he touched his shoulder to mine. With lowered voice, he said, "I have a theory, and it may sound farfetched, but hear me out. Before she was murdered, Suzanne went to a lot of effort to review, first, details of her brother's death and, second, details of the probate investigation when her father died. Maybe she had reason to see some correlation between those two events."

"Maybe," I agreed. "That's not at all farfetched, but I can't imagine what that correlation could be—can you?"

"*Yes,*" he said forcefully, but his voice was now barely above a whisper. "Mark Quatrain may still be alive."

The words caught me totally off guard, and I felt my jaw muscles slacken. Reacting to my dumbfounded expression, Parker amplified, "More to the point, I think that *Suzanne* may have thought that her older brother could still be alive."

"*Parker,*" I said at full voice, pulling back from him as if to clear my head and force us back to reality, "what on *earth* leads you to such a conclusion?"

"Hear me out," he repeated, fixing me with his stare, luring me close again. "Consider: Barret Logan told us a few nights ago that Mark Quatrain's body was so badly mutilated in the ambush, his remains were identified on the basis of his dog tag. Some thirty years later, Edwin Quatrain died, leaving an enormous estate to be settled by a haggling crew of probate lawyers. I suspect that the lawyers, leaving no stone unturned, reviewed the circumstances of Mark Quatrain's death in Vietnam and concluded that someone with a motive could have switched identities with a dead man on the battlefield."

Listening, I realized that Parker's theory was not so far-fetched. It made sense. I recalled, "At the time of the ambush, Mark Quatrain was awaiting a military trial on charges of rape and murder. That would make him plenty motivated to change identities and start a new life—if he actually survived the attack and if circumstances permitted him to make the switch."

Parker reminded me, "Suzanne said, within minutes of first meeting me in your front hall, that she was involved in a big research project, that it related to DNA. And, in fact, I've traced numerous books and articles on that very topic, which she checked out from the *Register*'s morgue."

"And DNA," I picked up his reasoning, "is used, forensically, to identify people. It fits. She may have been searching for her brother, who was presumed but not proven dead. She may also have employed private investigators in hopes of locating him, which would explain the existence of Elliot Coop's dossiers."

"Exactly," said Parker. He leaned back in his chair. "I doubt, however, that I need to point out to you that this theory, while compelling, still lacks something."

"Exactly," I echoed him, standing. "The 'why.' Why would Suzanne expend so much time, effort, and money researching the mere *possibility* that her brother was still alive? After all, her father's estate was settled—uncontested—and she was the principal beneficiary. Did she simply want to make sure that there would be no future claims against her?"

"A possible obsession, but not likely," said Parker, standing. "Or, was she just hell-bent on avenging her brother's murder of some unknown Asian girl, a total stranger?"

"Another possible obsession," I admitted, "but again, not likely."

"We've got some thinking to do."

"I'll say." I couldn't help laughing at the puzzle we'd created for ourselves. I stepped to him and clapped him on the shoulder. "Good work, Parker. You've taken this further than I thought you could—and you're not even on the payroll yet."

"Soon enough," he assured me, "but first things first. If we don't clear you of suspicion with the DA, I could be out of a job before it starts."

He was right. I had not yet gotten used to the idea that a lot of people would soon depend on me for their livelihood—all the more reason to resolve Suzanne's murder quickly, to clear my name before any rumors could hurt the *Register* or its staff. I mused aloud, "I should have listened to Glee Savage that first morning she came to visit me."

"Oh?" said Parker, unsure of what I meant.

"She said that she sniffed a story here all along. What's more, she felt that it was all tied to Suzanne's recent research. If your 'brother from the grave' theory pans out, Glee's going to have one hell of a story on her hands. She asked for the assignment, and I gave it to her."

"You assigned it to Glee? I mean, she's features—soft news."

"Have you read her stuff? She's one hell of a writer. Just as important, she has a real passion for this story. In fact, this probably wouldn't even *be* a story if it weren't for her persistence in pursuing it. She deserves the assignment."

"Fine," said Parker, busying himself with the files on the table. "I didn't mean to question you. It struck me as an odd decision at first, but if nothing else, Glee should bring a unique slant to the story." His words were agreeable enough, but his manner in handling the files seemed uncharacteristically slipshod, and I could not help wondering if he resented my assigning the story without consulting him. As managing editor of the *Register*, he could expect to be routinely responsible for such decisions, but as publisher, of course, I could take an active role in any matters that interested me—and this story interested me greatly.

As I mulled over whether this incident signaled potential trouble in my future working relationship with Parker, the morgue librarian emerged from the stacks to tell me, "You have a call, Mr. Manning. The switchboard sent it to my desk."

I thanked the woman, excused myself from Parker, and returned to the front of the reference room to answer the phone. "Good afternoon. Mark Manning."

"Hello, Mark! It's Roxanne. Hard at work up there?"

"Yes, actually." I laughed. "Did Neil talk to you about this weekend?"

"He called this morning, right after you called him; then I had to reach Carl. Another winter holiday in the north woods sounds fabulous, Mark—we'd *love* to come. But there's one small hitch. Carl has an important meeting here in the city, so we won't be able to drive up with Neil tomorrow for New Year's Eve. But we could leave first thing Saturday, New Year's Day, if that's okay with you."

"Sure," I told her, delighted to hear it. "You won't miss much on Friday—we're planning a small party at the house. As for the rest of the weekend, I promise it will be quiet and uneventful—at least compared to Christmas."

"Neil tells me that Suzanne's funeral will be held on Monday. Carl and I are planning to attend. Then we'll drive back to Chicago. Unless"—she hesitated—"unless I'm still needed up there. If that's the case, Carl can ride back with Neil, and I'll stay on with the car."

"That sounds perfect. Thank you, Roxanne." As I was speaking, Parker appeared from the rear of the morgue with his jacket—he was overdue for lunch. Hearing me mention Roxanne's name, he looked at me as if to ask, Are they coming? I gave him a thumbs-up, and he returned the gesture.

"Oh," said Roxanne, thinking of something, "how's the weather up there?"

"No more snow. The roads should be dry." But I knew she wasn't concerned about the drive—she was planning her wardrobe. I added, "Clear skies mean cold temperatures, and, come January, it's time for the deep freeze. So be prepared."

"Gotcha." She sounded preoccupied. I'd swear she was ticking items off a checklist that included multiple furs, muffs, and boots. "We should arrive Saturday at noon or so. See you then, Mark." We said good-bye and hung up.

I turned to Parker. "They can't make it till Saturday, but Roxanne is willing to stay on if I need her. Thanks for suggesting that I invite them, Parker."

"My pleasure." He zipped his jacket and was about to say

something else when Glee Savage interrupted, poking her head through the door from the hall.

She told me, "Mr. Logan wants you in his office, Mark. It sounded important."

"Parker"—I wagged a finger—"whatever it is, I want you in on it."

Glee whimpered like an abandoned puppy. I said, "You, too, Glee. Come on."

I led Parker out of the reference room, and Glee joined the parade, the three of us striding through the corridor to the publisher's office. His secretary waved us in, and we joined Logan at his desk. "What's up, Barret?" I noticed that the newsroom staff had seen us pile into the glass-walled office, and some of them started drifting near, discretion outweighed by curiosity.

"We just got word over the city newswire," said Logan, "that the coroner has filed his report." He handed me the text.

I skimmed it for pertinent details, then told the others, "The murder weapon has not yet been identified, but the coroner has concluded that the blunt instrument that killed Suzanne was something like a baseball bat. His report says, 'There were microscopic traces of both varnish and white-ash hardwood in the victim's fatal wound. However, a pattern of indentations in the wound was found inconsistent with the smooth design of a baseball bat.'"

As I finished reading, my brows reflexively wrinkled. There was something, I knew . . . but the thought wouldn't click.

Friday was a busy day at the house. Neil had gotten an early start on his drive from Chicago, arriving well before noon. I hadn't expected him yet, so I was surprised to see him pull into the driveway as I sat at the desk in my den, studying still more documents related to the *Register* buyout. I rushed through the hall to the back door without a coat and met him on the porch as he carried things to the house from the car.

"What time did you leave?" I asked, planting a big kiss on his mouth.

"Crack of dawn," he told me, holding me in an awkward embrace that included several shopping bags. "You'd better get inside—Christ, it's cold!"

It *was* cold, not much above zero, and it would worsen through the afternoon. As I'd told Roxanne on the phone the day before, New Year's always seemed to signal the onset of the season's coldest weather. It was true in Chicago—and even more so up here.

Neil had brought up some party supplies for an elegant dinner we'd planned for that night. In the kitchen with Hazel, I helped him unload the shopping bags, which included several ounces of the caviar I'd hoped to share with him in the city. I handed the little jars to Hazel, who eyed the stuff warily— it reminded me of her reaction to the margarine I'd smuggled up to Aunt Peggy when I was a boy.

"Who's coming tonight?" asked Neil.

"It's still sort of in flux," I explained. (I noticed Hazel roll her eyes as she banged around in a cupboard, extracting a broiler pan.) I counted, "Parker, Thad, you, and I are four. Joey will be coming. And when Parker left this morning for another day's research at the *Register*, I suggested that he ask Glee to join us. That would be six. Seventh at the table—and I insist this time—is to be Hazel."

"Mr. *Manning*"—she turned to face me from where she worked at the counter—"I really don't feel . . ."

"Tut-tut," I told her. "I won't have you eating alone in the kitchen tonight. We've all been through a lot lately, and you deserve to enjoy our friendship, as well as a spectacular meal."

She turned back to her work, offering no further protests.

"A possible eighth," I told Neil, "would be the sheriff, Douglas Pierce. He's not married, and I get the impression he doesn't have a 'significant other,' so he may not have plans tonight. What do you think?"

"Sure," said Neil, sampling a finger-swipe of crème fraîche from the tub he was placing in the refrigerator, "why not?"

So I telephoned Pierce and, not finding him at his office, left a message for him to call me. Early that afternoon he phoned back, and I said, "I was wondering, Doug, if you have plans for this evening."

The question seemed to throw him—he must have thought I was calling to ask about the coroner's report. "No," he answered with a reluctant tone, "just thought I'd aid the effort to keep Dumont's streets safe. New Year's can get dicey."

"We're having a late dinner here at the house," I continued, "and Neil and I were wondering if you'd care to join us. There'll be six or eight of us—you've met everyone—and I'll do my best to keep shop talk to a minimum. How 'bout it?"

He hesitated. "Thanks, Mark, that sounds great, but I think it might be better if I decline—better for both of us."

It was an odd response that I was simply not prepared for. "Why?"

"Well," he squirmed. "The investigation. It might look bad for us to be socializing while . . . while you're still under suspicion. Once this thing is behind us, though, I'd be honored. Anytime."

"Oh, sure, Doug," I told him, as if to say it was no big deal, but my voice carried the unmistakable ring of disappointment. I couldn't help wondering: Did he think of me first as a murder suspect and second as a friend? Or was he uncomfortable with the idea of socializing with openly gay people? After all, law enforcement is traditionally among the more homophobic of professions, despite his own tolerant views. Might his own tolerance have sprung from something deeper that he was still trying to hide?

"I'm sorry," he said after a pause, as if he'd been reading my thoughts, as if there were coworkers standing around him and he could offer no truthful explanation for refusing the invitation. We both understood that, for now, nothing more would be said of this. Then he added, "I'm afraid I have some disturbing news for you."

"Let's hear it, Doug." I was in no mood for circumlocution.

"Miriam Westerman has made good on her threat of Wednesday morning. She has persuaded Harley Kaiser to file an injunction that would forcibly remand Thad into her custody."

"So she actually got the district attorney to play along with her." Talking on the phone at the desk in my den, I glanced up and in my mind's eye saw her twirling her cloak in the doorway to the hall, cackling—the old witch. "You were right, Doug. If Miriam killed Suzanne, we're going to have a rough time convincing the DA of it."

"One small consolation," Pierce added. "Because of the holiday, the injunction won't be acted upon until after the long weekend, Tuesday at the earliest. By the way, has the situation calmed down during the past week? I mean, has Thad shown any signs of adapting to living there at the house?"

"Ironically, he has." I allowed myself a feeble laugh, but there was no humor in it. "Just last night, I let him borrow my car for an outing with some friends of his. He was away for only a couple of hours with it, brought it back in one piece, and delivered the keys into my hand with profuse thanks. He's been bragging on the phone all day—I think he had a great time."

"I'm *sure*," said Pierce. "The way to a boy's heart is through a set of keys, and *those* keys would soften even the hardest heart. I've said it before, Mark: that's a magnificent automobile."

I offered, half in jest, "Would you like to drive it sometime?"

"Really? You'd let me? I'd love to—maybe next week?"

I had to laugh. For whatever reason, Pierce was reluctant to socialize with me in my home, but he wouldn't think twice about being seen behind the wheel of my car. After making a tentative date for a drive the following week, Pierce promised to keep me posted on the custody matter; then we exchanged New Year's wishes, and I hung up the phone.

The issue of the guardianship had implications beyond the question of where Thad would be living for the next few years. There was still the legal technicality of whether my inheritance from Suzanne was contingent upon my fulfilling the role of Thad's foster father. And now a new wrinkle. What if I were willing to become Thad's new dad, but the courts sided with Miriam and gave her custody? These questions gnawed at me throughout the afternoon, until I finally decided that a call to

Elliot Coop was in order. But it was after four-thirty, and I suspected I would not find him in his office.

I gave it a try, but my hunch proved correct. Elliot's secretary said that she herself was just on her way out the door and that I had missed the lawyer by only a few minutes. Coincidentally, though, he had mentioned that he planned to stop and see me—there were some files he needed to deliver. I had almost forgotten about the dossiers from Suzanne's private investigators, so now I was doubly anxious to see Elliot. I thanked his secretary and wished her a happy New Year.

I had barely hung up the phone when I noticed Elliot pull up to the curb under a streetlight in front of the house. He got out of the car, opened the trunk, and removed with difficulty a hefty bundle of manila folders packed to overflowing in a cardboard box. Though spry for his age—well into his seventies—he had to struggle with his load, and I was suddenly concerned that an unseen patch of ice on my sidewalk could spell real trouble for both of us.

Bounding to the front door, I switched on the porch light and met him coming up the walk. "Let me help you with that, Elliot."

"Don't be crazy, Mr. Manning," he scolded. "You'll catch your death out here."

He had a point. The temperature was now well below zero. Our spent breath mingled in a shared cloud of frozen vapor that trailed us to the house.

"I didn't realize there was so much of it," I told him as we carried the box inside. I nudged the door closed behind us and continued directly to the den, where we set the box on my desk with a weighty thud.

"Whew!" He removed his gloves and rubbed his hands, recovering from both the exertion and the cold. He wore no hat, but rather a fulsome pair of fur earmuffs—beaver, I think. The muffs, combined with his distinctive skittering manner, gave him something of a gnomish air that evening.

I asked, "Can I offer you a libation, Elliot? Something to warm you up and toast the New Year?"

"Thank you, Mr. Manning," he tittered, "but no. I'll be

doing quite enough of that later. And the night, as they say, is young."

I laughed. "May I at least take your coat? If you have a few minutes, I'm wondering what you've determined about Suzanne's will—regarding my inheritance and Thad's guardianship."

He made no move to unbutton his topcoat. "The terms of her will, as I mentioned before, are ambiguous on this matter, and I've sought another opinion that I am not yet able to report to you. I presume you've heard by now that Miriam Westerman is taking legal action with regard to the boy."

I noticed that he was speaking a tad louder than was his habit, and I wondered if it was because his ears were still muffed. I confirmed, "Yes, Sheriff Pierce phoned me about Thad earlier."

"The upshot is this." He twisted his gloves, thinking. "The custody issue appears destined to be settled by the courts. I'm still hoping, however, that the issue of your inheritance can be settled as a matter of simple disbursement of the will, as specified by its own terms, without need for court involvement."

I hardly needed to tell him, "That's exactly what I'm hoping."

"The whole matter requires more study, I'm afraid. But you can rest assured that I am according it my full attention. And with that, Mr. Manning, I really must dash—I need to put myself together for the bar association's annual fête at the country club."

"Have a wonderful time, Elliot," I told him, draping my arm across his shoulder as I walked him to the door. "I need to get busy myself. We're throwing a little dinner party here at the house tonight."

"How splendid," said the old lawyer. "Have a happy New Year, Mr. Manning, and do extend my greetings to your guests."

We shook hands, and I opened the door for him, watching as he scampered into the darkness toward the pool of light surrounding his car.

Returning to the den, I was of course curious about the contents of the files he had delivered. I knew, though, that if I delved into them, I would be hooked for the night—and I had a party to host. So, resolving not to open a single folder, I simply fingered through them, glancing at some of the covers. They were labeled with names, men's names. Inside, presumably, were reports on their whereabouts and activities, which would be consistent with Parker's theory that Suzanne was having ambush survivors investigated. Excited by this prospect, I was tempted to crack open just one of the folders to confirm whether it was a dossier on a Vietnam veteran. But no, there would be plenty of time to study these over the weekend, and at the moment, I was running short of time for the evening's preparations.

Lifting the box of files from the partners desk that had been my uncle's, I carried it to a deep cabinet, a sort of credenza, that stood along an adjacent wall under a bookcase. That particular cabinet had a lock, and though it would prove easy picking for anyone skilled with a hairpin, it at least sent the message that anything within was private. If Suzanne had seen fit to leave these documents with a lawyer for safekeeping, I figured that I should now handle them with a similar measure of caution, at least until I determined what was in them.

Opening the cabinet door, I slid the box in and was relieved to find that it just fit, but not without some rearranging of other items I had placed there, including an imposing heap of contracts and other paperwork relating to the purchase of the house and the *Register*. Least conspicuous of these other items, however, was a plain white envelope that contained a letter. The envelope was addressed, simply, "Mr. Mark Manning, Jr., Chicago."

I placed the envelope on its edge between the box of dossiers and the wall of the cabinet. Then I locked the cabinet door.

Compared to the confusion and tumult of Christmas, our celebration of New Year's Eve was smooth and flawless—at least through the end of the meal.

Parker returned home from his day's research at the *Register* shortly after five, just missing Elliot Coop's visit. He told me, "Glee said she'd be delighted to join us. I think she canceled other plans—she wasn't about to turn down an invitation from the boss."

"Which boss?" I asked him, grinning. "Me or you?"

He explained, "You, of course," surprised that I would ask.

I wagged a finger. "Don't be so sure. I happen to know that Miss Savage has set her sights on you." He looked at me with disbelief. I assured him, "It's true. Walking to lunch with her on Tuesday, she expressed her interest in you (in no uncertain terms, by the way) and went on to ask if I would object to an office romance. What's more, she'd gotten the distinct impression that you were flirting with her." My serious tone gave way to laughter.

"I hope you set her straight, if you'll pardon the expression."

"Of course I did—or at least I tried—but she seemed undaunted by your yen for men. It's a wrinkle that only heightens your allure."

Parker paused in thought. "Ah, yes. The challenge of converting a gay man. Thanks for the tip, Mark. I'll be on my toes."

I then asked Parker to help me ready the fireplaces on the first floor of the house—dining room, living room, and den. They would add a festive touch, to say nothing of warmth, to our celebration of a dangerously cold night. Our plan was to gather at eight, when Joey Quatrain and Glee were due to arrive, sharing an evening of conviviality (and cocktails) until our late dinner, scheduled for ten, ending with the traditional champagne toast at midnight.

Joey arrived well before seven, nicely dressed in a dark business suit for the evening but more than an hour early. He busied himself in his old bedroom for a while, happily sorting through the junk there till his nephew Thad was ready, joining him. I was pleased to see that Thad had made an effort to get into the celebratory spirit of the night, wearing a nice pair of corduroys instead of his usual threadbare jeans and a pair of dark hiking shoes instead of his dirty white tennies.

Neil and I opted for tuxedos that night—lords of the manor. Shortly before eight, we appeared in the upstairs hallway from our bedroom just as Parker was emerging from his. Seeing us, he froze in his doorway and flattered us with a wolf whistle. "I won't be held responsible for my actions this evening, gentlemen. You're both drop-dead!"

"You're looking damn hot yourself," Neil told him, and the compliment was well warranted. Parker didn't wear a tux— that just wasn't his style, and I doubt if he even owned one— but he'd put together an all-black outfit, casually chic, with the right measure of theatricality for a New Year's at home. He'd chosen wool slacks, silk shirt, and dressy vest, with a flash of silver here and there. Other than the couple of times I'd seen him in sweatpants, that evening was the first time I'd seen him not wearing khaki, and, in truth, I did not get the same charge from his ass in dress slacks. But that was a highly personal prejudice, I recognized, noting that the cut of his vest left his backside fetchingly displayed for those who might harbor a fetish for flannel. Perfectly groomed, as always, he had trimmed his neat beard in a more severe fashion that gave his face a rakish edge. Parker was ready to party.

As the three of us went downstairs together to the front hall, I asked Neil, "Did you get the stereo working? I heard a few blasts this afternoon." The house had seemed too quiet when all the company left after Christmas, so I bought a sound system during the intervening week, but left it boxed for Neil to deal with. Odd—there was a time when I'd have torn into that project like a kid with a present, but middle age had brought with it a singular disinterest in electronics.

"Thad helped me set it up," Neil told me, revealing that his own fascination with black boxes was waning at thirty-four. "It sounds great," he continued, "and you needn't worry—I took care to hide all the wires. Everything's out of sight."

"Thanks," I told him, giving him a kiss as we reached the foot of the stairs. Then I remembered, "Music—I didn't shop for any music."

"I'm way ahead of you," he assured me, pausing to pouf my bow tie. "You mentioned on the phone that you'd bought the new equipment, so I brought a bunch of favorite old CDs up with me—no Christmas carols, either."

"Where would I be without you?" In answer to my own wistfully rhetorical question, I gave him another kiss. Comically synchronized with the peck of my lips, the doorbell rang.

"Yow," said Neil, feigning a swoon, "I heard bells."

Laughing, Parker offered, "Shall I get it?"

But before he could act, Hazel bustled past us toward the door, wiping her hands on the apron that covered her Sunday-best navy-blue dress—not her typical kitchen garb by a long shot, so I concluded that she had grown more comfortable with the idea of joining us at table that night. As she passed, she commented, "My, we're all looking spiffy!" And she opened the door.

Glee Savage stepped inside, accompanied by a gush of cold air that made my nipples go hard, scratching against the stiffly starched bib of my shirt. Hazel got the door closed, taking our guest's coat as I stepped forward to greet her. Glee handed me a bottle of something wrapped with foil and ribbon, which I passed along to Neil. Neil extended his hand, saying, "Neil Waite, Mark's friend from Chicago."

"I'm *sorry*," I told them both. "I forgot that you hadn't met. Glee, please meet Neil Waite, my lover and better half, a Chicago architect. Neil, this is Glee Savage, features editor of the *Register*." They exchanged the expected pleasantries about having heard so much about each other, but I wasn't really sure that I'd given either of them much to go on.

Glee told Neil, "You and Mark certainly make a handsome couple. Will we be seeing much of you here in Dumont?"

As Neil explained to her our arrangement—the alternating weekends—I couldn't help but notice that he and I did indeed make a good-looking couple, and our "couplehood" was accentuated that night by our nearly identical dress. We looked like a pair of grooms on a gay wedding cake. Good thing, I decided, in case Glee had a taste for younger men. While she may have doubted my word about Parker's homosexuality, there could be no doubt, in this context, about Neil's.

Neil reinforced this conclusion when he told Glee, "By the

way, your outfit is a real knockout. It's always interested me the way fashion trends are sometimes a harbinger of broader stylistic changes that can even ripple into architecture. I'd enjoy discussing it with you at length sometime."

Outright captivated by Neil and by his comment, she gushed, "My *dear*, what a fascinating premise for a fashion feature. I'd love to interview you, soon, for a page-one story in our Trends section. It could double as a personality profile, introducing you to the community. Do let me make a note of this." And she snapped open her big bag, fishing for a steno book.

The purse she carried that night was identical to the two others I'd seen, but this one was finished not in tiger or leopard, but zebra stripes. The black-and-white theme, so starkly appropriate to New Year's, carried through her entire ensemble, its various elements boldly patterned with everything from railroad-gate stripes to polka dots. Topping it all off was a black pillbox hat sporting a lavish white ostrich plume, which of course she did not remove. The sole exception to the monochromatic palette of her attire was the oily ruby gleam of her lips. While all this may sound tasteless in the telling, its total effect was quite the opposite—she was a dynamic woman of confident bearing who could flout the rules and draw envious stares from the more timidly correct. I was happier than ever to know she would be on my staff.

"Good evening, Glee," said Parker, stepping into the conversation. He gave her hand a friendly clasp. "Nice to see you outside the office for a change."

She offered him her arm. "Parker," she told him, "it's always a pleasure to see you, at work or at play."

I flashed him a discreet I-told-you-so. Motioning toward the living room, I suggested to everyone, "Shall we?"

Parker led Glee out of the hall, Neil and I following. As Glee disappeared through the portal into the living room, she stole a glance behind Parker, below his vest. Neil whispered to me, "I wonder if he has *any* idea that we've all been staring at his butt." I laughed loudly, but it drew no reaction from either Parker or Glee—we were getting into a party mood.

"Why don't you start some music?" I suggested to Neil, sending him ahead. I stopped at the foot of the stairs and called up to the second floor, "Thad? Joey? Come on, boys—" I stopped myself, regretting having called Joey a boy, an understandable mistake, as it was difficult not to think of him as a child. I rephrased, "Come on, guys. The party's begun."

Within a few minutes, the evening was under way. Neil had selected an album of not-too-raucous club tunes that thumped brightly in the background. The cocktail cart was poised to serve, and ice clanked in glasses, Parker taking requests.

"The boys" bounded into the room from upstairs, glad to be a part of things. Joey asked Parker for a brandy old-fashioned, sweet, which surprised me, not because of the weirdness of the concoction (something of a standby in Wisconsin), but because I didn't realize that Joey had a taste for alcohol. Thad sidled up behind Joey and told Parker, "Same as my uncle, please."

Parker said, "Hey, Mark?" and Thad knew he wouldn't get away with it.

With lowered voice, I asked Neil, "When they're not boozing, what do kids drink these days?"

Neil shrugged. "Beats me. Pop? Juice in little boxes?"

Clearly, I had a lot to learn about parenting before considering any responsibilities of guardianship. I took Thad aside, telling him with a half-laugh, "Nice try." Hoping we could all keep our senses of humor about this, I said, "Look. Come midnight, you're welcome to have a glass of champagne with us and toast the New Year. Till then, though—"

"Cool," he interrupted, apparently getting more than he'd hoped. "Thanks, Mark." Then he asked Parker for some cranberry juice. I heaved an inner sigh, surprised at the adroitness with which I'd averted a potential crisis.

Soon, Parker had mixed drinks for all present—Scotch for himself, Joey's old-fashioned, Thad's juice, the usual vodka and orange peel for Neil and me. As for Glee (I might have predicted it, though I had never seen her drink), she ordered a breathlessly dry gin martini, vigorously shaken ("at least fifty times," she instructed), straight up in a birdbath, with a pearl onion.

I forgot about Hazel. Just as we were about to exchange our first toast of the evening, Hazel appeared from the kitchen with the caviar service and all its accoutrements—toast, blini, sour cream, chopped egg, and onion. "Hazel, won't you join us with a drink?" I asked, assuming she would decline. To my surprise, though, she accepted a glass of wine, saying, "It might be nice to have something to nip while keeping an eye on things in the kitchen." So the seven of us assembled around the caviar and toasted the future, the first of many such wishful little speeches we would intone that night.

By ten o'clock, Neil, Parker, Thad and I had all taken turns helping Hazel in the kitchen, and it was time to move the party to the dining room. We abandoned our cocktails, all of us on our second, exercising a measure of abstemiousness, save Joey, who finished his third old-fashioned. I poured wine, deciding on an inch or so for Thad, whose company that evening had actually proved pleasant. The table was set, the fire was roaring, the music was now demurely eighteenth century. We all sat down, Neil and I at either end of the table, Hazel nearest the kitchen.

By any standard, the meal was sublime, its centerpiece being a prime tenderloin of beef with a perfect, silky bordelaise. We ate hungrily, as the hour was very late for a Midwestern dinner, also enjoying several bottles of an extraordinary Château Margaux that Neil had sprung from our pantry in the city. Though most of us had lent a hand in orchestrating the feast, the principal cooking chores had fallen to Hazel, whom we praised lavishly. In turn, she offered compliments on our choice of wine, enjoying several glasses of it. So much for nipping.

The mood of the evening was generally merry, but its bittersweet overtones were obvious to all. Despite our best efforts, table conversation kept drifting to the mystery surrounding Suzanne's murder of only six days ago. It might have been a good opportunity for all of us to put our heads together and debate who-done-it, but the identity of the killer was an awkward topic, as three possible suspects—Thad, Hazel, and I—

took part in the conversation. So we focused on Miriam Westerman (an easy target, liked by no one) and Thad's father,
Austin Reece.

"What happened to him?" asked Parker.

No one volunteered an answer, so I told him, "Sheriff Pierce
says he hasn't been seen in over sixteen years, since before
Thad was born." Then I realized that Thad might be troubled
by this discussion—I wasn't sure what, if anything, he knew
of his father. I quietly told him, "Sorry, Thad."

"Thanks, but I'm okay with it, Mark. Mom told me about
never being married, that it was her decision, that my dad loves
me even though I never knew him. He's out there *somewhere*. I
think about that sometimes."

Surprised by the maturity with which he handled the issue,
I wondered if Thad's recent rebellious streak was some sort
of psychological compensation for the repressed anxiety of his
unknown roots. I told him, "The sheriff is trying to find out
what happened to your dad. If they do find him, would you
like to meet him?"

The table was dead quiet as Thad thought before answering,
"I'm not sure."

Glee asked a question that I'd rather not have raised in
front of the boy: "Is Austin Reece a suspect in Suzanne's
murder?"

"No no no," I assured her, trying to downplay the situation
for Thad's benefit. "Doug Pierce feels, and I agree, that Reece
should simply be informed of what's happened. At this point,
there's no reason to suspect him of anything. Without talking
to him, we have no idea whether he had any sort of motive
to—"

"Of *course* he had a motive," Hazel interrupted me, to the
surprise of all present. She sat back in her chair, fingering the
stem of her empty wineglass. Her comment was made with
absolute authority, and I realized at that moment that she was
probably the only person still alive who had been really close
to the situation, except Joey, of course, whose recollections
would not be reliable.

Amid a chorus of throat-clearing from the rest of the table,

I asked Hazel, "What do you mean?" Neil astutely reached to pour more wine for her.

She leaned forward and spoke with a blank, featureless expression. "When Suzanne turned thirty, she was already a successful businesswoman, but she was not yet a mother, and a woman has only so many years. She knew Austin Reece through her work. She was a big executive at Quatro Press, and he was a top salesman at one of the nearby paper mills. When I say that Austin was a salesman, I don't mean that he worked behind a counter somewhere. No, he handled big corporate customers and made a lot of money. So everyone thought that he and Suzanne made a pretty good match— Lord knows I did—but Suzanne had something else in mind all along. She wanted a baby, not a husband. It's funny. Sometimes a woman gets pregnant in order to nudge a reluctant suitor into marriage, but this was sort of the other way around. Austin *planned* on marrying Suzanne. I heard them talk about it, and she led him along, at least until the baby was on the way. Then she told him she would never marry. She would raise her baby alone. Austin was crushed, and I think he felt humiliated in the eyes of everyone who knew him, everyone who thought he was so lucky to be marrying the rich Quatrain daughter. He changed after that, people said. He got depressed, so much so that he was no good at his job anymore. The paper mill had to let him go, and that made things all the worse for him. When he finally left Dumont, it was only a few days before Thad was born. Austin wouldn't tell anyone where he was headed, but he told lots of people, including me, that Suzanne had wrecked his life."

No one breathed. Hazel paused, sighed, and took a hefty gulp of wine, surely not tasting it. She concluded, "There's no telling what a man might do when he feels like that, and there's no telling how long it might take him to do it." A tear slid down her cheek. "Poor Suzie."

"Let's talk about something else," said Joey, banging his empty glass on the table. "That's all I've heard all week— 'Poor Suzie, poor Suzie.' She's dead now! What about the rest of us? What about *me?* For as long as I can remember, it's always been 'Suzie this, Suzie that.' It isn't easy, being the youngest brother."

Astonished by this outburst, Hazel told him, "Joey dear, we're all upset, and I know how hard it is to think of life without your sister. But if we don't talk about it, we'll never figure out who killed her." Another tear. "Ahhh, poor Suzie."

"That's *enough,*" said Joey, stamping a foot under the table. "If we don't stop talking about Suzie, I'll . . . I'll . . ."

Thad jumped to his feet, scooted around the table to his uncle, and started tickling him from behind. Joey immediately burst into laughter as the rest of the table sat watching, incredulous. Thad asked everyone, "Isn't it time for dessert?"

With the tension dispelled, we all agreed that it was time for something frothy. Neil and Parker helped clear the table of the main course, Hazel's protests notwithstanding. In truth, she was a bit shaky on her feet by then, needing any help that was offered. The crème fraîche that Neil had toted from Chicago was put to good use atop cups of fresh fruit, drizzled with Triple Sec—elegant, summery flavors that stood in sharp contrast to the polar night. Savoring this mélange, we ate quietly, offering occasional coos of approval, except Joey, who complained, "This whipping cream isn't sweet enough." Although sorely tempted, we managed not to snigger at his comment, and Neil passed him the sugar.

A few minutes before midnight, Hazel asked, "Shall I serve coffee?"

"Let's have it in the living room," I said. "It's almost time to turn the calendar." So we helped Hazel clear, and the party moved back across the hall.

I twirled a couple of champagne bottles in ice while Glee took charge of chilling the stemware. Joey wanted another old-fashioned, and Parker told Thad how to mix it while he himself refreshed the fire. Neil changed the classical music to a livelier album of swing tunes, dated but fittingly nostalgic, played low. And Hazel distributed cups of coffee, stopping to remember, "My gosh, the cookies." She scampered off to the kitchen.

She returned with a plate heaped with biscotti. Checking my watch, I waved for her to join our circle, glasses raised—

it was very nearly twelve. I told the others, "When Neil and I made the decision to let our lives follow a new direction, we had no idea that these first few days in Dumont would be marred by such tragedy. At the same time, we could never have guessed that we would spend tonight surrounded by so many new friends—friends for life, I'm sure. With friends, the future always holds bright promise. Happy New Year, everyone."

We clanged our glasses in a group skoal, chorused the greeting, and drank. As I swallowed, I knew that in the next few moments, we would begin exchanging the traditional midnight round of one-on-one toasts, hugs, and kisses. And I felt sudden apprehension that Parker might use the occasion as an excuse to get overly affectionate with me. After all, the man had professed his love for me. Would he now be tempted to get physical, assuming that it would go unnoticed in the context of sloppy sentiment. Surely, Neil would notice. How would I explain Parker's behavior to him?

So the coupling began. First, of course, I set down my glass and took Neil in a full embrace, telling him quietly, "Thanks for everything, kiddo."

He laughed. "What's to thank me for? Hooking up the stereo?"

"No"—I kissed him—"for being here for me, and for understanding why I needed to make this move, and for going along with the whole crazy plan, and for never once doubting that I love you in spite of my own insecurities, and for loving me in spite of . . ."

"Okay," he said, "I've got the idea." And we kissed again, seriously.

Involved as I was with Neil, I didn't much notice who else was doing what with whom, but the room was swept into the schmaltz, accompanied by gentle laughter, tings of crystal, and the syncopated measures of something Cole Porter.

Then I noticed Parker standing beside us, as if waiting with a dance card to cut in. Uh-oh. I braced myself and turned to him with an uncertain smile, letting him make the first move.

"Mark," he said, thrusting forth his hand, "happy New

Year. And thanks a million for the opportunity to work with you at the *Register*. I've told you before: this is all I've ever wanted." He gave my hand a hearty shake.

And that was it. I reciprocated with similar sentiments; then he turned to Neil. They exchanged greetings, a handshake, and a hug—Neil got a *hug*, and I found myself feeling slighted, even while recognizing the irony of my reaction. Maybe Parker had been attuned to my reluctance to get chummier that night, and I decided that I should give him credit for his discretion.

Everyone took turns greeting each other, even Thad, who surprised me with his ability to be sociable, almost charming. Perhaps it was the effect of good champagne, which he appeared to enjoy, but did not guzzle. I lifted my own glass and touched it to his. "Happy New Year, Thad. I know these are really rough times for you, and I know I can't begin to console you on the loss of your mother, but the worst is behind you now. Things are bound to improve." I touched his shoulder.

He gave me a wan smile and a tepid nod, as if to say he appreciated my words, however predictable. But he didn't want to talk about the murder. He said, "Thanks for the champagne, Mark. And for borrowing me your car."

"*Lending* me your car," I reproved gently.

"Yeah. Lending." He looked me in the eye. "You've been decent."

Quite a compliment, considering how far we'd come in a week. He seemed to be getting used to the idea of Neil-and-me, so I suggested, "Why don't we go for a run sometime this weekend—with Neil—the three of us?"

He looked at me as if I were nuts. "It's cold!" he said through a laugh. Then he added, "I'm not much of a runner."

"One way to learn," I told him.

"Maybe." He smiled again, this time with a measure of warmth. "We'll see."

Turning to greet Glee Savage, I saw that Parker had beat me to her. This ought to be good, I told myself, wondering if Parker was prepared to fend off the amorous advances that Glee was surely entertaining. Glee told him, "Happy New . . ."

"Don't speak," he said to her, his voice a low, melodramatic purr. Then, to my rank astonishment, he swept her into a theatrical embrace and planted a big sloppy kiss squarely on her lips.

She was no less surprised than I was. Regaining her equilibrium, she spoke over Parker's shoulder to me: "If this guy's gay, I'm confused—not complaining, mind you, just confused."

Before I could comment, Parker told her, intending for me to hear as well, "It's a simple matter of 'transference,' Glee. You have no way of knowing whose mouth, in the skewed depths of my imagination, was really pressed to mine." He pulled a handkerchief from his pocket and wiped a greasy red smear from his lips.

She laughed at this, as did Neil, who had caught it all. I managed a chortle myself, but was left with an uncomfortable inkling regarding the object of Parker's 'transference.' Thad had also witnessed this exchange, and he appeared quietly disturbed by it. I presumed he was previously unaware of Parker's sexual status. Was he now troubled by the notion of spending the weekend under the same roof with *three* gay men?

After the big moment of midnight had passed and we had finished our ritual of toasts and warm wishes, we eventually settled into chairs and sofas near the fire, engaged in quiet conversation, shifting topics at will, finishing the coffee, pouring more champagne. Hazel rose unsteadily, saying, "I'll just clear the coffee service—less to do later."

"Nonsense," I told her, rising to escort her back to the heavily upholstered wing chair she had occupied. "We'll all pitch in later. We'd rather have you here with us." Others echoed these sentiments, and she resumed her seat. Firelight glinted from the lenses of her glasses as her eyes followed my hands, reaching to pour more champagne for her.

The party was winding down. The music ended, and Neil didn't bother to play something else. Sated by the meal and warmed by the fire, we all just shared each other's company, talking. We spoke of the severe weather setting in. We spoke of my plans for the *Register*. We spoke of the long-distance relationship that Neil and I would have to adjust to. And, of course, our discussion kept veering back to the murder. But the mention of Suzanne seemed to agitate Joey, so we tried to avoid that topic.

Safe ground, I assumed, was the more distant past, and since New Year's Eve (now early New Year's morning) makes a fitting occasion for reminiscences, I invited all present to share their memories. I volunteered none of my own. Since arriving in Dumont before Christmas, I'd been constantly absorbed in boyhood recollections of the house and the family that had lived there. So the others took turns airing the past.

Neil told a bit about his early career in architecture, but he insisted, "Life did not begin for me until the night I met Mark," when we were introduced by our lawyer friend, Roxanne Exner. He moved his career from Phoenix to Chicago in order to be with me, and he would gladly endure the inconvenience of our new arrangement if it would ensure my future happiness. This was a story I knew well.

Parker didn't want to say much, and I realized I knew little more about his past than the employment history that was listed on his résumé. He grew up in Wisconsin, came of age during Vietnam, and came out before Stonewall. "Those were ugly times, for society as a whole and for gays in particular," he told us. He didn't really get his life in order till he got serious about his journalism career. He worked a lot of jobs, "searching for something, finally finding it here in Dumont."

Glee's experience was entirely different, though she grew up when Parker did. As a woman, Glee had known no personal threat from the atrocity of Vietnam, and as a heterosexual, she wouldn't know the significance of Stonewall till she read about it years later. As for her career, it was focused from the start. She had worked at only one paper, the *Register*. "That may strike some as a lack of ambition," she told us, "but all these years I have shared a single passion with Barret Logan—we've understood that the *Register* is not just another small-town rag, and we've *lived* to put that paper on a par with any other in the state."

Hazel said she'd never had ambitions for a career, and she offered no apologies. "In my day, there was pride in making a house a home." It was more than enough to keep a woman busy, and the satisfaction of raising a family well was ample reward for the effort. Her only regret was that she and her husband Hank had never had children. "We tried," she told us, her candor induced by the champagne, "but it just never happened." The Quatrain kids had filled that gap, though, and she always thought of them as her family.

Joey told her that she was part of all his best memories. Then he turned to me. "Hazel's always been around, but one of the best times was when you came to visit us, Mark. We were good friends, weren't we? And I showed you the upstairs, and I let you use my typewriter. You were nice then, and you still are. Those were nice times, when I was little. People didn't treat me funny, like they do now. They'd at least listen to me." He got up with his empty champagne glass and ambled toward the cocktail cart.

Thad told him, "I listen to you, Uncle Joey. And you're one of the few people who always take *me* seriously, too. Grandpa Edwin always listened, but he's been dead three years now, and I miss him. Otherwise, I don't *have* any old stories. I'm only sixteen—there's not that much to remember. I never even met my dad, so I sure don't remember him." Thad turned to me. "What did you say his name was? Like, Austin *Reece?*"

I nodded.

"Then I'm not a Quatrain, am I? I mean, not really."

Unprepared for such a question, I stammered, "Well, sure you are, Thad. Half your blood is Quatrain, only it's on your mother's side instead of your father's. We're alike that way— my mother was a Quatrain. But you actually carry the family name. It's on your driver's license, right?"

"Yeah." He laughed, feeling better about it. He pulled a ratty nylon kid's wallet out of his hip pocket and checked, just to make sure.

Hazel assured him, "You're every inch a Quatrain in my book, and it's a good thing, too. The family was never very large. It needed new blood. You're the last of the line, Thad."

He looked up at her from his driver's license, mystified. "What does that mean, 'last of the line'?"

She explained, "Later, someday, if you have children of your own, they'll be Quatrains and carry on the family name. But if you don't have children, you'll be the last—the end of the line—at least in these parts."

He still didn't grasp it. "Why?"

Patiently, Hazel told him, "Your grandpa Edwin had two sisters, but no brothers, so he was once the last of the Quatrains. But then he had three children—your mother, your uncle Joey, and your older uncle Mark, who died long before you were born. Your uncles never had babies, but Suzanne had you, and she gave you the family name. So now you're the last of the Quatrains, Thad, because you were Suzie's only baby."

Tucking away his wallet, Thad nodded, impressed with his new-learned status.

The rest of us grinned or chuckled—the innocence of youth.

But Joey stumbled toward us from the cocktail cart, wagging the empty glass. "Wait a minute," he said. "What about Suzie's *other* baby, the *first* one, when she took the trip?"

Bombshell. "*Joey!*" yelled Hazel, starting to rise from her chair. Then she sat back. Though flustered, she told him calmly, "I think you're confused."

"*No, I'm not,*" he told her, trying to stand straight and defiant, but finding it difficult to stand at all. To the rest of us, he said, "See what I mean? People treat me funny. They don't listen to me."

"Joey dear," said Hazel, leaning toward him, "we're listening to you. But please, don't say anything more."

"Why not? It happened, didn't it? In high school. Suzie was having a baby. But then she went away. And when she came back, the baby was gone, and I wasn't supposed to talk about it. And you're *still* trying to tell me not to talk about it. Why, Hazel?"

By now, Hazel's head was buried in her hands. She wept drunkenly, unable to answer him. The rest of us didn't move—hell, we could barely breathe. A log popped and sparked. Clearing my throat, I said, "Hazel? What's he talking about?"

She looked up at me with teary eyes through smeared glasses. Removing them, she attempted to shine the lenses with the lacy cuff of her sleeve, but abandoned the project as hopeless. Her hands fell to her lap, and she stared blankly toward the center of the room. There she sat—the living, aging, nearly blind repository of Quatrain family secrets, the guardian of a closet door that had just been kicked open by Joey.

I heard a rustle at my side. It was Glee digging in her purse, pulling out her steno pad, ready for some shorthand. I shook my head. With a roomful of tantalized listeners, we would not be apt to forget details of the revelations to come.

I prompted, "Hazel? Tell us what happened."

"When Suzie was a junior in high school," she began mechanically, as if she had long rehearsed a monologue that she knew she would one day recite, "she got pregnant during Christmas vacation. There weren't many options in those days. Bringing the baby to term was unthinkable—abhorrent—and abortion wasn't legal here then. So Suzie's mother Peggy took her to New York that spring. It was legal. Suzie was fine. But everything was different when she came back. She had missed a big, important dance at school. Her attitude changed. She was different toward men. And she never set foot in Saint Cecille's again." Hazel fell silent.

"I knew it," Glee said under her breath, more to herself than to anyone.

Neil told me, "Our theory was correct."

Parker added, "It all fits."

"Mom had an abortion?" Thad mumbled.

I told him gently, "Try not to judge her. I'm sure it wasn't an easy decision. Single motherhood wasn't as common then—"

Fiercely, Hazel interrupted, "It *was* an easy decision. I *told* you: Suzie *couldn't* have that baby. It was unthinkable. Abhorrent."

Uh-oh. I suggested, "Why don't you tell us the rest, Hazel?"

She looked from face to face, then smiled bitterly, as if to say, All right, you asked for it. With her tongue pasty in her mouth, she said, "Suzanne Quatrain had an abortion because she had been raped. It happened here, under this very roof, upstairs in the attic great room where she was killed last week. Thirty years ago, she was raped in that same room—on Christmas morning! And the man who raped her, the devil who impregnated her was her *very own brother*, Mark Quatrain, home on vacation from his senior year of college!"

We reacted to this news with an involuntary chorus of gasps and my-Gods, my own mind spinning at the thoroughness with which she further crushed the once-idealized fantasy of my handsome older cousin. But she wasn't finished. "Is it any wonder," she continued over our confused babble, "that the family threw that filthy bastard out? They never pressed charges against him—of course not, the shame was too great to be made public—but no tears were shed when he got packed off to Vietnam, and damn few tears were shed when he died there! I'm *glad* he got butchered. They ought to pin a medal on whoever sent him straight to hell. My only regret is what it did to his mother. Poor Peggy's heart couldn't take it, and she died shortly after her son did."

Hazel had finished, leaving us in speechless, sickened disbelief.

Joey, though, was unfazed by the telling of his older brother's crimes, unable to grasp their gravity. "Parker," he said, rattling something at the cocktail cart, "the champagne is gone. Can you show me how to make another old-fashioned?"

New Year's morning dawned bright and bitterly cold, but none of the household saw it. The previous night's party broke up around two, when Glee Savage excused herself, assuring me she could safely travel the short distance home—she lived only a few blocks away, and the haze of her earlier martinis had long since cleared. The late meal, followed by Joey and Hazel's revelations, left the rest of us feeling alert and sober by the time we turned out the lights.

Joey and Hazel didn't fare as well. Joey had drunk far more than usual that evening, and ended up spending the night at the house, recovering. Hazel, who almost never drank, had to be tucked in by Glee before she left. We all speculated whether Hazel would even remember telling us her terrible, long-guarded secrets.

So the house was uncommonly quiet the next morning. Neil and I were the first to rise, shortly before ten. The mood was wrong for sex, and the weather was wrong for running, so we got dressed and went to the kitchen to get the coffee started. Predictably, the door to Hazel's quarters was closed, and there were no sounds of stirring within. Parker joined us a few minutes later, also dressed for the day—flannel shirt and his usual chinos.

After a groggy round of good mornings and our first few sips of strong coffee, we began the inevitable postmortem of Hazel's tell-all, keeping our voices low in case she was awake. Parker told us, "The abortion angle came as no surprise— everything we knew already pointed to it. But the rest really blew me away. I don't know *when* I finally got to sleep."

"Same for us," said Neil, pausing to stifle a yawn. "Mark and I lay there talking about it till God knows when."

I nodded wearily. We had already spent too many sleepless hours rehashing Hazel's revelations, and I was not inclined to immerse myself in them again, at least not so early in the day. "I'm going to get the paper," I told them.

Topping off my old *Chicago Journal* mug, a porcelain remnant of my former life, I excused myself and walked to the front hall. Fortunately, the *Dumont Daily Register* had landed right at the threshold, and it took only a second to retrieve it from the arctic air that had settled overnight beyond the door. Hefting the paper, I noted that it was an unusually slim edition, even for a Saturday, traditionally a sapless advertising day. That, combined with slow news and a holiday morning, left little to print.

I carried the paper to my den, spread it open on the partners desk, and sat down to read it, slurping from my mug. Page one was filled with inconsequential wire-service stuff, nothing of local interest—for the first time in a week, there wasn't even mention of Suzanne's murder. With no motivation to turn the page, I slumped back in my chair, sipped more coffee, and gazed at the room vacantly, slipping into thought. The setting reminded me of another New Year's Day, thirty-three years earlier, the morning my boyhood trip to Dumont drew to a close.

I got up early that day to pack, and the house was quiet. Uncle Edwin and Aunt Peggy had been to a big party the night before—the party he had cleaned his tuxedo for—so I was surprised, when I came downstairs and set my suitcase in the hall, to see my uncle sitting at the big two-sided desk in his den. He was dressed really nice, as always, and was reading the morning paper—the *Dumont Daily Register*, it was called. I went to the doorway and said hello.

He looked up from the paper. "Good morning, Mark! Ready to head home?"

"Right after breakfast," I told him.

He swallowed some coffee from a pretty cup that he put back on its saucer. "I'll drive you to the bus, okay?"

"Sure!" Even though it wouldn't be a very long ride, I looked forward to another trip in his big imported sedan. "Thanks."

He glanced back at the newspaper. "Nothing much happening in the world today. Johnson's escalating troop strength in Asia again. Hippies are still on the march. Same old same-old," he said, whatever that meant.

In the kitchen, Hazel made my breakfast and told me that she'd miss me. When Aunt Peggy came downstairs, she looked sick. "I just wanted to tell you good-bye, dear." Her voice was croaky. "Have a safe trip, and give your mother my love." Then she went back to bed. My older cousin Mark never even got up (he must have gone to a party of his own), so I didn't get to see him—I was hoping he'd muss my hair again, and I just liked the way he looked. Suzanne and Joey came down to eat, and Joey seemed really sorry that I was leaving. Then Uncle Edwin appeared in his topcoat, jangling his keys, saying, "Time to get going, Mark. Let's catch a bus."

In the car, I noticed that my uncle was in much better shape than my aunt. The party, or something, must have agreed with him. He talked about enjoying the cold morning. He even whistled now and then as he drove. Then he reached into a pocket behind the car seat and pulled out my folder—the little stories that he'd asked to read the night before. "You wouldn't want to forget this," he told me. "You're a fine writer, Mark. Keep working at it."

There weren't many people waiting for the bus, not on New Year's morning. Uncle Edwin carried my suitcase, setting it next to me on the pavement. Scrunching down so we could talk eye-to-eye, we said all the good-bye stuff, and we hugged. With his arms still around me, he said, "You're a very special young man, Mark. You're not at all like the others." Then he kissed me—right on the mouth.

Some dozen years later, he would repeat himself, almost word for word, when he kissed me at the grave of my mother, Edie Quatrain Manning. That was the last time I saw my uncle Edwin.

But now I sat in his chair, at his desk, in his den, under the roof of the stately Prairie School house he once built with his partner, the man with whom he cofounded the Quatro Press. In an ironic twist of history, if not quite fate, his home was now my home—his desk, my desk. These thoughts led me to the letter he had written to me before he died, stowed safely in the credenza near the desk. Responding to the urge to read it again, I fished a little brass key from a pile of paper clips in an ashtray on the desk, then unlocked the cabinet door. The letter was propped where I left it, next to the box of Suzanne's dossiers delivered by Elliot Coop the previous afternoon.

I immediately lost interest in the letter, which I had read dozens of times, and focused on the files, which I had not yet read, but meant to. Pulling the heavy box from the cabinet, I nudged the door closed with my knee and carried the files to the low table in front of the fireplace.

Settling on the sofa there, I lifted the folders from the box and discovered that they were already arranged into three bundles, which I placed on the seat cushion next to me. The two smaller bundles were labeled SUSPICIOUS and ABOVE SUSPI-CION. The other bundle, largest by far, was labeled INCONCLUsive. Intrigued, I went directly to the "suspicious" files, pulled the first, and opened it.

Parker's theory was correct. It was, in fact, a dossier on a Vietnam veteran, a survivor of the ambush that supposedly killed Mark Quatrain. It included a sketchy biography of the man's upbringing before being drafted, then a detailed account of his activities and whereabouts during the thirty years that had passed since his honorable discharge. The thick file took some twenty minutes to read in its entirety. The report concluded that this subject was "suspicious" because he had family ties to central Wisconsin, but, otherwise, there was nothing in his background to suggest that he was really Mark Quatrain, back from the grave.

Perusal of the next dossier, equally detailed, revealed only that the veteran was "suspicious" because, like Mark Quatrain, he had been an accomplished athlete who also held an honors degree in English. They had graduated from different colleges, however, and there was nothing to suggest that the subject's academic records had been falsified.

The files seemed less interesting now, so I ceased reading them in full. Skimming the next several, still from the "suspicious" bundle, I found nothing to convince me that Mark Quatrain was still alive and had assumed another identity. Immersed in this fruitless research for an hour or so—it was nearly noon—I was interrupted by a commotion in the front hall.

Roxanne Exner and Carl Creighton had just arrived from Chicago, and I was too absorbed in my reading to hear them when they pulled into the driveway. Neil and Parker were now greeting them at the door. So I packed all the dossiers back into their box—including those labeled INCONCLUSIVE and ABOVE SUSPICION, which I had not yet opened—and returned them to the cabinet, locking them away for future study.

Emerging from the den into the hall, I saw at once that I had not underestimated Roxanne's attention to her travel wardrobe. Carl was hefting the last of the luggage in from the porch, and its quantity suggested a stay of a month, not a weekend. A disconcerting thought: Was this a sign not of vanity but of foresight on Roxanne's part? Had she come prepared to stay awhile, assuming I'd need her at hand to defend me against the overzealous maneuvers of a hotdog DA?

"Long time no see," she told me, shrugging out of her fur as I stepped forward to give her a kiss.

Eyeing the Christmas nutria she dragged on the floor, I asked her, "Wasn't it a bit warm for that in the car?"

Carl answered for her, "We had the air conditioner on. And it's *still* ten below."

We all shared a laugh as Neil and Parker stacked luggage at the foot of the stairs. Neil turned to ask everyone, "Hungry? Hazel set up a makeshift buffet in the kitchen. After last night, we're lucky to have lunch at all."

"I'm surprised she's even *up*," I told him. "How is she?"

Parker answered, "Wobbly, but functioning. No signs of life from upstairs yet."

"Good God," Roxanne wondered aloud, "what'd we *miss?*"

" 'Twas a night to remember," Neil assured her. "Let's talk about it in the kitchen." And he led the way back through the hall.

Hazel had set out makings for sandwiches, various sweets, and a potful of noodly soup, made ahead yesterday, simmering on the stove. Her door was closed, and I asked, "Won't we bother her?"

"She said not to worry about it," Neil told me. "She's just fixing herself up." Under his breath, he added, "Frankly, she's got her work cut out for her."

Roxanne repeated, "What'd we *miss?*"

As Neil and Parker began constructing absurdly thick sandwiches for our new arrivals, I related events of the previous night, inching toward Hazel's postprandial revelations.

Roxanne sat at the kitchen counter on a stool, legs crossed, listening, experimenting with the sandwich Neil had given her. Unable to get it into her mouth, she pulled it apart and picked at it with a knife and fork. Splatting a puddle of mustard on her plate, she said, "All *right*, Mark—the meal sounds fabulous, and I'm glad the wine was perfect, but what 'happened'?"

Her impatience was justified. My narrative had given no

hint of the evening's climax. So, while preparing a sandwich of my own, I explained, "After midnight, after the toasts, we all settled into conversation in the living room."

Roxanne mumbled, "Meanwhile, back in the drawing room . . ."

Without comment, I continued. "Both Joey and Hazel had been drinking far more than usual all night, and between the two of them, they managed to spill some extraordinary family secrets."

"How delicious," said Roxanne, licking something from a finger. It wasn't clear whether "delicious" applied to her finger or to the secrets. Carl shushed her, preferring to hear my story.

"Ultimately"—I paused—"Hazel revealed that Suzanne had an out-of-state abortion during high school. We had already suspected as much. This wasn't just a typical unwanted pregnancy, however. Suzanne had been raped. On a Christmas morning. Upstairs in the great room of this house." Roxanne's jaw was already drooping. Was she ready for the corker? "The rapist was Suzanne's own brother, Mark Quatrain."

Roxanne and Carl were of course stunned by this news, losing interest in their lunch. I was hungry, though, and took advantage of the lull to eat a few bites of my sandwich. Roxanne also lost interest, at least for the moment, in wisecracking. "Lord, how awful," she said, slumping on the stool. Whirling her hand, she attempted to piece together the story: "So Suzanne had the abortion, but what happened to her brother? Didn't you say he died in Vietnam?"

"Right," I told her, "but I didn't know the details till this past week. The family never pressed charges against him. They were—what? Conflicted? They just wanted him out of here. A few months later, he graduated from college, got drafted, and, before long, he was off to Asia. There he raped another girl, a local girl, and—this gets worse—he murdered her. Then, while awaiting a military trial, he himself was killed in an ambush."

Parker interjected, while stirring the soup, "Or so the story goes."

Roxanne looked from face to face, confused. I told her,

"Parker has a theory, based on the fact that Mark Quatrain's body was mutilated beyond recognition in the ambush."

Parker crossed from the stove to us, explaining, "Mark Quatrain could have survived the ambush and switched identities with a badly mutilated victim in order to escape prosecution for killing the Vietnamese girl. Years later, when Edwin Quatrain died and the probate lawyers began nitpicking the estate, they may have concluded that Mark Quatrain's death could not be absolutely verified. Even though the estate was settled without incident and Suzanne was its principal beneficiary, she'd gotten wind of the idea that her brother might still be alive. Now, in light of what we learned last night from Hazel, it's perfectly obvious why Suzanne would be motivated to find him—revenge."

Roxanne and Carl, both of them lawyers, were by then fully engrossed in Parker's theory, nodding to each other as he led them point by point through an intriguing legal thicket.

I told them, "Parker's theory took on even greater plausibility yesterday when Elliot Coop delivered to me a pile of private investigators' dossiers that Suzanne had been collecting." I turned to Parker and Neil, confirming, "I studied some of the files this morning, and, sure enough, they trace the whereabouts of veterans who had survived the ambush in which Mark Quatrain supposedly died. Unfortunately, the files I read pointed nowhere."

Parker pressed onward. "Still, consider: The plot comes full circle. Suzanne has had these guys under investigation for a couple of years now. Suppose Mark Quatrain is, in fact, one of them, and suppose he's clever enough to figure out that Suzanne was on his trail. He would then have a strong, obvious motive to kill her."

"Jeez," said Carl, shaking his head at the thought of it, "the brother from the grave." He plucked a pickle from his plate and bit off its end.

Neil asked, "But how would he do it? I mean, Suzanne was killed here in the house, on Christmas Day. We know who was here—at least we *think* we do. Did Mark Quatrain sneak in, kill Suzanne, and sneak out again?"

"Not likely," said Parker, "but he could have paid or otherwise convinced someone—anyone—to do it for him. He may be nowhere near Dumont. Or maybe he's been here all along."

I reminded everyone, "This is all speculation, involving a bunch of 'ifs'. At this point, I'd call the 'brother from the grave' a long-shot suspect at best. I think we need to concentrate on the short list of living, breathing known suspects we've already identified."

At that point we heard footfalls in the hall, and all of us turned to see Joey Quatrain step through the kitchen doorway. He stood there timidly, looking like hell, having slept in his clothes. His suit was wrinkled, tie askew, beard unshaven, hair unkempt. Seeing me, he immediately asked, "Was I bad, Mark?"

"No, Joey, no"—I waved him into the room—"you just had a bit too much to drink. It was New Year's, and no harm was done." I reintroduced him to Roxanne and Carl, whom he remembered from Christmas, but he had little to say to them. I asked him, "Do you feel okay?"

He wasn't sure. He answered quietly, "I'm sort of hungry."

Neil offered, "How about some soup?"

Joey nodded, licking his lips. Neil crossed to the stove with a bowl.

I told Joey, "There's coffee, too. That'll help wake you up."

He hesitated. "Do you have any cocoa?"

Parker laughed. "I'll get it." And he went to the refrigerator for milk.

I asked Joey, "Is Thad up yet?"

He shook his head. "I looked in his room. He's still asleep."

Roxanne eyed me accusingly. "Did you get *him* smashed, too?"

"*No*," I assured her, "he's just sleeping in. You know how kids are at that age."

"*No*," she assured me, "I don't." Then she reconsidered. "Actually, I do recall reading something about their circadian rhythms."

"God, Rox," said Neil, "you make him sound like a locust

or something." He carried the bowl of soup to the counter and pulled up another stool so Joey could join us and eat.

In deference to Joey, we avoided the topic of Suzanne's murder and dropped our discussion of Parker's "brother from the grave" theory. We focused instead on Joey himself, and Roxanne got him to talk about his job at Quatro Press.

"They call us 'human resources' now," said Joey. "We used to be just the personnel department. It sounds more important, I guess, but we don't do anything different."

Carl said, "I assume Quatro is Dumont's largest employer."

"Oh, yes," said Joey, pausing to slurp a noodle, "we're biggest by far."

Parker stepped into the conversation with Joey's cocoa. "I just had a thought," he said. "Joey, I know you find the topic of your sister's murder upsetting, but you know how important it is that we find the killer, don't you?"

"Yes," he answered skeptically. I myself wondered where Parker was heading.

Parker told him, "Before you came downstairs, we were talking about an idea that your older brother, Mark, might still be alive."

Joey dropped his spoon in his soup. "He died a long time ago, Parker. He was killed in Vietnam."

"Yes, we know that," Parker explained patiently, "but there's a slight chance that somebody made a mistake. It's possible that Mark didn't die, and if that's true, he might be able to help us discover who killed Suzanne. But first, we'd have to find Mark. Would you be willing to help us?"

Joey tried his cocoa, thinking over the question. "Sure," he answered, "but I don't know how to help you. Where would we look?"

Good question. I was wondering about that myself. Parker told him, and the rest of us, "Quatro Press is the area's largest employer. If Mark Quatrain were still alive, and moved back to town and needed employment but wanted to get lost in the crowd, chances are he'd apply for work at Quatro. He could quietly keep an eye on things at close range; then, when the time was right, he could act."

"Act on what?" Joey asked. But the rest of us now understood what Parker was driving at, and I had to admit that he had raised an interesting possibility.

Parker said, "The point is, Joey, that since you work in personnel at Quatro, you probably know everyone who works there, at least in passing, right?" Joey nodded, and Parker continued. "So I'm wondering if you could check your files and find out if there are any Vietnam veterans who started working at Quatro anytime within the last three years. We need someone about fifty years old, with an honorable discharge, who may have asked questions about the Quatrain family."

"Allan Addams," Joey said at once, looking suddenly alert. "I don't *need* to check the files, Parker. The person you're talking about is Allan Addams. I hired him about three years ago—it was shortly after Dad died. Allan was hurt in Vietnam, so he walks funny. He works in the credit department, just down the hall from me, so I see him all the time. He's *always* asking me about the family."

The rest of us all looked at each other, astonished. Had Parker hit pay dirt?

He told Joey, "I know this may come as something of a shock to you, but Allan Addams could possibly be your brother, Mark Quatrain."

Joey screwed his face in thought for a moment, then laughed. "No, I'm sure Allan isn't Mark."

Excited by the prospects raised by Parker, I jumped in, noting, "You haven't seen your brother in over thirty years, Joey. People change a *lot* in thirty years. If Mark is still alive, he wouldn't look anything like the way you remember him."

Joey considered this. "Nahhh," he told me, as if he'd caught me in a fib, "they *couldn't* be the same person."

Dingdong. We all looked toward the hall. "I'll get it," I said, then left the kitchen to answer the front door, leaving the others to gab about Allan Addams with Joey.

Even before opening the door, through the narrow sidelight I recognized the figure of Sheriff Douglas Pierce. "Good afternoon, Doug. Happy New Year," I told him as I let him in.

He returned the greeting and removed his gloves to shake my hand. "Mark, I felt awful about declining your invitation for last night. I've got a lot going on right now"—he amplified—"personally, I mean. Maybe we can talk about it sometime."

"How about now?" I offered.

"No." He smiled. "That's not why I'm here. I'm afraid this is business."

With a wave of my hand, I led him into the den. Closing the door, I explained, "There's a houseful of people, mostly in the kitchen."

He hung his coat and told me, "In spite of the holiday, I've been getting a lot of pressure from the DA this morning on two fronts. Harley's still pushing me to make an arrest, and now he's started meddling in Miriam's custody battle for Thad. I can't hold him at bay much longer. We need a new lead, or at least a new wrinkle."

"I can't offer much regarding Thad"—I broke into a broad smile—"but I've got several significant wrinkles regarding Suzanne's murder."

"Oh?" He pulled out his notebook.

I gestured that we should sit opposite each other at the desk. Leaning over the suede blotter, propped up by my elbows, I gave him a detailed account of Hazel's midnight revelations, Parker's "brother from the grave" theory, and Joey's inquisitive veteran credit manager.

"Well now"—Pierce poked a period on his pad—"this ought to keep Harley Kaiser off your tail for a while. It certainly warrants continued investigation. Do you have time to brainstorm a couple of loose ends with me?"

"Sure, Doug." Then I had a thought. It was about one in the afternoon. "Have you eaten yet? We've got a casual lunch going in the kitchen—everyone's out there. Why don't you join us? We can all put our heads together."

While Pierce had turned down my invitation for the previous evening, he showed no reluctance in accepting this one. Maybe he was hungry. So I led him to the kitchen, where everyone looked up from their soup and sandwiches to greet him, save Joey, who had forged onward to his dessert, piling a plate with frosted brownies, a variety of cookies, and a huge gob of leftover crème fraîche. "This stuff isn't bad if you put enough sugar on it," he told us. Then, noticing the new arrival, he added, "Oh, hi, Sheriff Pierce."

"Hi, Joey," Pierce answered brightly. Eyeing the plateload of sweets that Joey was wolfing, he offered a good-natured warning: "Go easy on that, Joey. You could get a serious buzz."

We all laughed, except Joey, who appeared baffled by the comment, shrugged, and took an enormous chomp out of another brownie, smearing frosting on his unshaven cheek. The sight of his mouth devouring the chocolate made my own teeth tingle, but the overload of sugar didn't seem to bother Joey in the least. Presumably, the buzz felt way better than his hangover.

I asked Pierce, "What can I fix you, Doug?"

Noticing an abandoned plate on the counter with a half-eaten sandwich that he presumed to be mine, he told me, "Go ahead and finish your lunch, Mark. I'll put something together myself." And he made himself at home among us.

Retrieving my sandwich, adding a folded slice of cheese to it, I told the others, "Doug is intrigued by our 'brother from the grave' angle, and he'd like to brainstorm a couple of points with all of us."

"Ooo"—Roxanne rubbed her hands together—"I *love* parlor games."

Neil laughed. Carl and I shot her a behave-yourself glance. Parker told Pierce, "We'd be happy to help. What's on your mind?"

Pierce neatly sliced his sandwich with a serrated knife, not on the diagonal, I noted, but squarely in half, top to bottom. He told us, "By now, we should be able to focus this investigation on a key suspect or two, but, instead, our list is growing. The mystery of Suzanne's murder has been dogging us, I think, because the case has too many loose ends. So let's try concentrating on one detail at a time."

Carl nodded. "A sound approach, Sheriff. What don't we know?"

"For starters," Pierce told him, "we're baffled with regard to the weapon. What was it, and where is it?"

I explained to both Carl and Roxanne, "The coroner finally issued his report on Thursday, just two days ago. He determined that the blunt instrument that killed Suzanne was something like a baseball bat, as her wound contained traces of both hardwood and varnish."

"So," said Roxanne, flipping her hands, "let's *find* the baseball bat. Of the known suspects, who would be most likely to have one?" Answering her own question, she asked, "Have you searched Thad's room?"

I waved her off—she was on the wrong trail. "First, Thad's not into sports. I doubt if he owns a bat. Second, and far more important, the coroner said that the weapon was merely something *like* a baseball bat, because he also found that there was a curious pattern of smaller indentations in the fatal wound, which would be inconsistent with the smooth design of a bat."

Even as I explained the coroner's ambiguous findings, I had the sense that I was missing something, that there was something just beyond reach . . .

"Hey!" said Joey, springing up from his dessert. With a wild look in his eyes—had the sugar kicked in?—he suggested, "What about one of those king-things?"

"My God," I said. "Of course."

"King-things?" someone asked. "What on earth?" asked another. Through a half-laugh, Pierce said, "What are you *talking* about, Mark?"

"The artichoke finials," I told everyone. "The finials decorating the banister at the top of the stairs."

Neil looked at me as if I'd lost it. "Sure, Mark. The killer dragged Suzanne over to the stairway, banged her head against an artichoke, then dragged her body back across the room to the fireplace. What's wrong with this picture?"

"*No,*" I told him, all of them, impatiently. "The finials aren't fixed to the railing. They're mounted on dowels about so long"—I measured two feet of air—"that simply slip into the newel posts beneath the banister. They slide right out. When we were kids playing upstairs, Joey liked to parade around with one of them, hoisting it like a scepter, a king-thing. Any of those finials would make a handy, heavy club."

"Let's take a look," said Pierce, pushing his sandwich aside.

Joey didn't need to be asked for a demonstration, though. He was already headed out of the kitchen and up the stairs. The rest of us—Pierce, Parker, Roxanne, Carl, Neil, and I—raced to follow him.

Arriving in the attic great room, we clumped at the top of the stairs, watching Joey as he slipped one of the white-ash finials out of its newel, exactly as I had described it. He raised it high over his head and began his old king routine, strutting around the room majestically.

Turning my attention from Joey's performance to the eight or ten finials remaining on the banister, I noticed that, sure enough, one of them was missing—the one from the far corner, next to the wall. "Look," I told the others, pointing to the vacant spot. We crossed en masse to it, huddling to peer at the empty hole.

"Don't touch any of them," Pierce told us. "The killer may have used a finial from a more convenient spot, then rearranged them so that the absence of the weapon would be less conspicuous. With any luck, he—or she—may have left some fingerprints. But somehow, I doubt it." Somehow, I suspected Pierce was right.

Joey's imaginary procession had by now wended its way to the far side of the room. When he reached the bare stretch of floor in front of the fireplace, where the rug bloodied by Suzanne had been removed, Joey underwent an instantaneous change of mood and demeanor. Until that point, he had played the role of a happy if stately King Joey, hoisting his pretend scepter and waving to the throngs of admiring subjects seen only by him. Now, though, standing on the spot where his sister was killed, Joey was suddenly energized, and he began swooshing his king-thing menacingly, working himself into a frenzy. His actions resembled something of a ninja routine, replete with whoops and grunts as he bashed some hapless opponent with repeated blows of the finial.

Aghast, we watched this eerie performance, inching across

the room to observe him at closer range. Silently, we exchanged a round of astonished glances as he yelped at the victim he bludgeoned on the floor. Fearing that he might soon wreak damage to the room's furnishings, I was tempted to step in and restrain him.

At that moment, though, he snapped out of it. "See?" he told us, panting, sweating, smiling. "You could bop someone real good with a king-thing."

Was Joey's bizarre behavior merely the harmless, playful consequence of a brownie-induced sugar high? Or was he venting a facet of his character previously unknown to us? Did Joey harbor wild and potentially violent impulses that could bubble to the surface without warning? Was he capable of shattering his own sister's skull? What could motivate such brutality from such a benign, simpleminded soul as Joey?

Could it possibly be that the identity of Suzanne's murderer was not nearly so convoluted and mysterious as Parker's "brother from the grave" theory? Could it possibly be that he stood right there in our midst, weapon in hand?

I did not, of course, voice these thoughts. There was no need to. We were all wondering the same thing—our shared suspicions were both obvious and palpable. Sheriff Pierce had witnessed the whole outburst and was capable of drawing his own conclusions. Besides, discussion of this tantalizing new wrinkle would only further spook Joey. If he was the guilty party, we would need to coax proof from him with the velvet gloves of wheedling, not confrontation.

Pierce sat on one of the leather sofas under the chandelier in the center of the room, encouraging everyone else to be seated as well. He took out his notebook, wrote a few words, and told us, "Assuming we've identified a plausible weapon, let's focus on something else. What exactly was Suzanne *doing* up here when she was attacked?"

I told him, "She said she wanted to see if she could 'find something.' She had been sitting in the dining room before dinner, talking with us. I was there when she left, along with Parker, Roxanne, and Carl. Right?"

"Right," said Roxanne. "And it struck me as odd, or at least abrupt, when she excused herself. I had no idea what she had in mind—it didn't seem to follow from our discussion. We were talking about the hate mail Mark got that weekend, and I made a few cracks about Miriam Westerman, not knowing that she and Suzanne had shared a tumultuous past. I didn't get the impression that Suzanne was annoyed with me. She just seemed to be on another wavelength."

"Ohhh," said Parker, enlightened. He told Roxanne, "I was fussing with the fireplace and Mark was helping set the table when you and Carl came into the room. Joey had just been there talking about some toys he'd found, and Hazel wondered if he'd run across the Quatrain children's baby books, which the house's previous owners had set aside somewhere. After that, I, too, noticed that Suzanne seemed preoccupied, or, in your words, Roxanne, 'on another wavelength.' When Suzanne then said that she wanted to look for something, my assumption was that she meant the baby books."

"That makes sense," I told Parker, Pierce, everyone. "There are *lots* of books up here"—I gestured toward the bookcases flanking the huge fireplace—"and that whole end of the room was littered with books when Suzanne was attacked. Maybe she figured that since the Tawkins had left the baby books somewhere, it was logical to start looking up here."

"Why, though?" asked Roxanne. "We've all just learned that Suzanne had been raped in this very room by her own brother on a long-ago Christmas morning. To overcome such demons and return to this room alone, on Christmas, her search must have been motivated by more than schmaltzy sentiment or idle curiosity. But what?" Roxanne crossed her arms.

"Good question," I conceded.

Neil mused, "What if there was something of great value *in* the baby books?"

Carl shrugged. "Suzanne was already wealthy." He closed his eyes in thought.

Parker rose, strolling to the bookcases for a closer look.

Pierce wrote more notes.

Joey fiddled with his king-thing.

Sunday morning, Neil and I awoke shortly after sunrise. Something told us that not a creature was stirring, not yet, save us. Something told us that the cold snap had waned some with the setting of the moon. Something told us that we had both slept well for a change, that we were rested, untroubled by our dreams. In short, something told us that the mood, at last, was right for sex.

The decision was mutual and spontaneous, requiring no discussion. A good-morning hug, a kiss that lingered, tongues exploring each other's teeth—these were the signals that our dance of the dawn had begun. The first few steps were slow and romantic, a full-body caress, a contorted snuggle beneath the down-filled comforter. But soon the pace quickened, with bedding kicked to the floor as our moves became more energetic. Leading and following, demanding and submitting, we traded active and passive roles with the blink of an eye, the probe of a finger, a lick. We moved to the beat as one—linked, to be sure, in the most literal and physical sense, but also in the depths of our brains, where we celebrated a communion of intellect, a shared past, a future fantasy. Together, we whirled to a crescendo that said the dance would end soon, very soon, reaching for that moment of climax. Tensing then, my partner came. In the next beat, so did I. And the music stopped.

"I love you," we said. "We needed that," we agreed. "It's been too long."

It was good—not the stuff of dreams, not the sublime rapture of a first night, but it was decent, solid sex, a much-needed physical release. And we had shared it.

Neil laughed quietly, tracing a finger around my ear, looking into my eyes and through me. "There's been way too much going on in our lives lately."

"That's an understatement." I rolled onto my side to face him, planting an elbow in the pillow, propping my head in my hand. With my free hand, I patted his chin, felt his stubble. "I keep telling myself that once the takeover of the *Register* is behind me, everything else will just fall into place. But that's not the half of it. There's all the uncertainty about the future of our 'arrangement,' to say nothing of Suzanne's murder." I plopped back onto my pillow, staring at the ceiling.

"To say nothing," Neil reminded me, "of Suzanne's son. There's still the whole Thad issue to deal with." He pulled the bedclothes up from the floor, covered us both, then moved in close, his arm around me. "You've had a week now to mull this. Where do you think we're headed with Thad?"

"That depends on Miriam Westerman and the courts," I told him, "but more important, it depends on you. If I take responsibility for Thad, 'we' no longer means 'you and I,' but 'the three of us,' at least for a few years." I turned to face him. "Do you have any interest in being part of a little 'family'?"

"I could handle it," he assured me. "And the truth is, I think we'd make excellent parents. But the bigger question is this: Could Thad ever adjust to the stigma of having 'two daddies'? At his age, that's asking a lot."

"Do you realize," I asked Neil, "that there was a poll a while back showing that most adolescents would rather die— literally—than be known as gay. 'Faggot' is universally recognized among kids as the *worst* possible slur."

"I don't care for the word myself," Neil reminded me, "but for us, it's more than a put-down. It's hate."

"Thad's come a long way in the last week—he no longer reacts to me with the knee-jerk revulsion that he's learned from his peers—but I'm sure it would still be a major leap for him to adjust to the notion of having *us* for parents. Could he do it? I have my doubts."

Neil sat up in bed to ask me, "Have you talked to him about it, point-blank?"

"No, not yet." I thought of something and sat up next to Neil. "Friday night I invited Thad to join us for a run this weekend. He sounded game for it, if not overly enthused. If it warms up today, maybe we should try it, and if the chemistry seems right, we could all have a heart-to-heart talk."

"Sure," said Neil, getting out of bed, donning a heavy

flannel robe. Cinching it, he turned to me, adding, *"After* we get that tree down."

Ugh. I flopped onto my back, whining, "Do we *have* to?"

He stepped to the bed and ripped back the covers, exposing my body to the cold air of the room. "You're the one who laid down the law: 'If we're going to fart around with a damn tree, I want it down the weekend after New Year's.' "

I laughed, hugging myself for warmth. "I doubt if I used exactly those terms."

"Maybe not," he conceded, "but that was the gist of it. Anyway, today's the day. Tomorrow is Suzanne's funeral—we won't be in any mood for it then."

He was right. I'd never been able to stomach Christmas decorations after New Year's, and as dreary as the ritual of detrimming the tree might be, it was the price one must pay to cleanse the house of the holidays. Dry, denuded, and browner than green, our twelve-foot spruce would spend the following night at the curb.

The project began late that morning, with the entire household reluctantly pitching in—even Roxanne packed away two or three of the hundreds of ornaments, between prolonged trips to the kitchen for more coffee. Hazel took charge of making sure everything was sorted into appropriate cartons. Neil and I handled most of the ornaments. Carl and Thad helped Parker with the lights. Finally, in a spray of needles, Parker and Carl hauled the corpse to the street. Then Hazel revved up the Hoover, sending the rest of us upstairs for refuge.

In the hallway, I nabbed Thad. "Hey," I suggested, as if the thought had just come to me, "why don't we go for that run we talked about? Neil can join us."

"Now?" he asked, as if he were ready to go back to bed. It was noon.

"Why not? The day's as warm as it'll get. The dirty work's out of the way. Besides, we can talk."

He knew what that meant. "Okay," he agreed, not thrilled. "Give me a few minutes to change, okay?"

So a few minutes later, Neil, Thad, and I set out through the front door and down the front walk, turning onto the street that led to the park. Neil and I wore our usual cold-weather running clothes—no shorts for me—it was now January, after all. Thad wore a ratty school sweat suit with his beat-up tennies—basketball shoes, actually, so I knew at once that his claim of inexperience was no exaggeration.

We started out at a leisurely jog, adjusting to each other's company as well as to the outdoor air, engaged in some small talk about how far we intended to go. None of the previous week's light snow remained on the ground—it had evaporated in the weekend's bitter cold. And although it was somewhat warmer now, the temperature had barely nudged above zero, so our outing, while sunny, was anything but balmy.

"Let's pick up the pace," I suggested. "It'll keep us warmer." And I broke into a running stride, pulling ahead.

Neil easily caught up with me, running at my side. "Remember that run we took, three Christmases ago on a mountainside in Phoenix?" He turned his head to look at me, grinning.

"Our first run," I reminisced. "We ran without shirts. It got hot."

"I'll say. And when we got back to my place ..." he reminded me.

He didn't need to finish. It was the first time we had sex—the first time, in fact, I had sex with a man. I was hooked. We both were. Within a week, Neil decided to uproot his career and move halfway across the country to be with me. And now, it seemed, I was forcing him to chase me again.

"Hey!" It was Thad's voice. "Wait up!"

Neil and I stopped and turned, running in place. Thad was a half block behind, hindered by bad shoes and atrocious form. Though he was far younger and considerably leaner than either Neil or me, we had the advantage of being much better trained, and he found it impossible to keep up with us. I hadn't meant to lord our performance over him, and I suddenly wondered if we had wounded his pride. On the contrary, though, I found that he was impressed.

"For a couple of . . . old guys," he panted, "you're not bad."

I wondered if the words in his mind were really "couple of fairies," then chided myself for ascribing these prejudices to him—there was nothing in his tone of voice to suggest that his comment was laced with anything darker than good-natured razzing. "Come on," I told him. "No one's trying to win any medals today." And we fell into a less strenuous run together, Neil and I pacing ourselves so as not to outdistance Thad, who trotted between us.

"Try not to move your arms so much," I suggested to Thad. "Keep your forearms parallel to the ground, just above your waist, letting them swing naturally with your gait—no need to pump them like a power-walker." He did so, and his form improved dramatically.

Neil added, "Even though it's cold, don't clench your fists inside your mittens. Focus all your energy on your legs—relax everything else." Thad's stride immediately lengthened.

"The difference between walking and running," I told him between breaths, "is that when you walk, one foot is always on the ground, sometimes both. But when you run, both feet are never on the ground, sometimes neither—there's a moment when you're actually *aloft*. Take those thousands of moments aloft, splice them together, and you've spent quite a bit of time in midair. This may sound a little Zen, but running is a lot like flying."

"Cool," he said, and he meant it. Chances are, he had never thought of running as anything other than school-enforced drudgery—of course it was awful. But when he let himself slip into the primal grace of the act, he saw it in an entirely different context, one of almost hedonistic pleasure. He didn't explain this to me. There was no need to verbalize it. I could recall the exact moment in my life (I was not much older than he was) when these same revelations astounded me and forever changed my attitude toward the simple, innate drive to place one foot in front of the other, fast.

The impact of this discovery was heightened for Thad as our course led us into the park—the timing was perfect. The crunch of our feet on the frozen trail signaled that we had left the minor urban agonies of the town behind us and had entered a tranquil domain of tamed nature, placed there, it seemed, for no purpose other than to please us. Even the sting of cold air in our lungs took on a different quality, a dash of pine that insinuated mint more than sap.

Ahead, around a turn of the lagoon, lay the pavilion where I had taken refuge against the dark a few days earlier with Parker, where he mussed my hair, igniting the same erotic charge that had confused me as a boy when my older cousin, Mark Quatrain, touched me. "Up there," I told Thad and Neil. "Let's rest." Let's talk, I meant, but did not say it.

We soon settled onto the same bench where I'd sat with Parker, in the roofless alcove facing the lagoon. Instinctively, Thad took the middle spot, between Neil and me, as he had done while we were running. We squeezed tight to each other, not only because it was so cold, but also because the bench was only so wide, making looser accommodations impossible. For a long minute, we said nothing, watching the vapor of our collective breath dissipate into the glacial scenery.

"Thad," I said at last, turning to look at him, "we really need to talk about your future." He nodded but said nothing, so I continued. "I know you're not happy that your mother appointed me as your guardian. And I doubt if you're any happier that Miriam Westerman wants the courts to put you in *her* custody. I have to be honest with you—I felt totally unprepared to take on these responsibilities, and let's face it, you and I didn't hit it off very well at first. So I've had mixed feelings about fighting Miriam. But Neil and I have talked it over, and we truly think that you'd be better off with us than with her, and we're willing to go to bat for you. But that would be pointless if, in fact, you want us out of your life. So we need some direction, Thad. Should we save the courts some trouble and just let Miriam have her way?"

Thad's head fell to his hands. "No!" he yelled into his mittens, then began to sob. "God, no—please!"

Neil put his arm around him. "If you don't end up with Miriam, you're stuck with us. So we all need to be blunt about a certain issue and come to an understanding. Please, Thad, look at me. This is important."

Thad looked up. Tears had already made frosty trails on his cheeks.

With the fingers of his glove, Neil brushed the flecks of ice from Thad's face, telling him, "Mark and I are gay, Thad. You're well aware of that, of course. And I think you understand that we're lovers. Maybe you've never known any openly gay people, and your friends may have led you to believe that we're—what?—perverted scum. In the short time you've known us, have you come to understand why we could never tolerate such an attitude—in you or in anyone else? If we're to stand any chance of living together, happily, as a family, you can think whatever you like, but you'll no longer have the freedom to say things that Mark and I find hateful."

Thad broke into tears again and swiped them with his mittens—green wool fibers stuck to his icy lashes. "Neil," he promised, "I'll never say those things again." He turned to me. "I won't think them, either, Mark. I *don't* think them. At least I don't *think* I think them. At least I'll try."

It was my turn to put my arm around him, and I pulled him close, resting his head on my shoulder. "I know this won't be easy for you—at school, with friends."

"They'll just have to get used to it," he told me with the startling insight of common sense.

Neil interjected, "First things first, guys. We've still got Miriam Westerman to tangle with, and from everything I've seen, she can be pretty fierce."

The prospects of life with Miriam dropped Thad into a state of numb panic. I reminded both of them, "We've got Roxanne Exner on our side, and she can be pretty fierce, too. The important thing is: Now we know where we stand, the three of us. Neil and I think we can handle the responsibilities of sudden parenthood, and Thad thinks he can handle the practical dilemma of having two dads. Right?"

Thad and Neil looked at each other, then at me. "Right," they said, decisively, in unison.

I smiled, standing. "Let's head back to the house," I started to tell them, but I rephrased my suggestion: "Let's go home."

They got up, and we all stretched a bit, limbering our chilled joints for the return run. We were about to take off when Thad stopped us. "Hey, guys, just a minute." And he held out his arms, wanting a hug. Cold as it was, Neil and I could have melted as we stepped to either side of him and shared a happy embrace.

So we started on our way, running three abreast, returning to the house that Thad now wanted to call his home. If we prevailed in court and Thad were to end up living there with Neil and me, it would not be the first time that the house on Prairie Street was the setting for an unconventional living arrangement.

I remembered the day three years ago when Elliot Coop and I showed the house to the Tawkins. Elliot told me that the upstairs apartment had been built for my uncle Edwin's original business partner, while he and his young family lived on the lower two floors. "An odd setup," Elliot described the arrangement, "but it seemed to work." At least for a while.

Was the "setup" we were now contemplating—Thad, Neil, and I—any less odd? Would it prove more successful? I assured myself that all three of us seemed determined to build a semblance of a family. Besides, within two or three years, Thad would most likely move away to college and begin building an adult life of his own. Neil and I would be back where we started, just the two of us. For now, though, Thad needed us. And though my commitment to his mother was little more than an empty promise made on the spur of the moment ten years ago, it was a commitment nonetheless. Thad, Neil, and I were doing the right thing, I decided, headed in the right direction.

"Where are *you* headed?" Neil called to me with a laugh.

We had left the park and were now running through our neighborhood, only a few blocks from the house. Immersed in my thoughts, I didn't notice Prairie Street and failed to turn. Neil and Thad stood at the corner, several paces behind me. Chagrined, I returned to the corner, suggesting, "Let's walk the rest of the way."

Our walk was more of a scamper, as the weather was not conducive to strolling. Neil and I discussed dinner plans—we still had a houseful of guests to entertain. Thad walked between us, but did not take part in the conversation, seemingly occupied with thoughts of his own.

Then, suddenly animated, he said, "Mark, I was wondering. Once everything is settled—I mean with Miriam Westerman, the court stuff—maybe I could just move into an apartment with some friends. There's enough money, isn't there?"

"It's not a question of money," Neil answered for me, explaining to Thad that he was too young to live on his own. Thad didn't give up the idea easily, though, forcing Neil to persist in his opposition.

This brought to mind the argument I'd overheard between Thad and Hazel regarding the boy's confrontation of his mother with the same proposal. Now, taken aback that Thad would raise this issue so soon after our heart-to-heart and hug-fest, I had to wonder if he had warmed up to me on the hunch that I'd be a pushover for his plan. Was that it—did he really think of me as a weak-willed sissy pushover? Was he merely using me as part of a scheme to achieve his own independence? Was he *obsessed* with his independence? And how far might he go to achieve it?

As we walked up the sidewalk toward the front porch of the house, Neil told him, "Besides, there's no point in discussing this *now*. Wait until after tomorrow. We'll all have clearer heads."

"Why?" he asked. "What's tomorrow?"

"*Thad*"—Neil stopped in his tracks—"it's your mother's *funeral*."

"Oh. Yeah."

Because New Year's fell on a Saturday, Monday was a holiday, and most of Dumont showed up for the funeral of Suzanne Quatrain, chairman and principal stockholder of Quatro Press, the town's largest employer. Saint Cecille Church was filled to capacity—beyond, in fact, with the crowd spilling out to the street.

Thad, Joey, and Hazel were seated in the front pew. Attorney Elliot Coop joined Neil and me directly behind them with Roxanne and Carl. Parker sat nearby with Glee Savage, publisher Barret Logan, and some other people from the *Register*. Across the nave, on the other side of Suzanne's white-draped casket, the front pews were occupied by Quatro executives, city and county officials, and a pinch-lipped Miriam Westerman, who had caused a scene with an usher to get a decent seat.

The service was lavish if not heartfelt, the music heartfelt if not profuse, the flowers profuse if not beautiful. The whole show was a far cry from the Requiem Masses I'd known as a boy, when I donned cassock and surplice, memorized the Latin, and assisted at such rites. They may have been grim, but those black-trimmed Tridentine funerals at least made it clear that someone had *died*. This memorial struck me as little more than a confused mishmash of feel-good theology, happy bromides, and sappy folk songs. If it weren't for the coffin in the aisle, you'd have thought someone was getting married, not buried.

Father Nicholas Winter, pastor of Saint Cecille's, moved from the altar to the lectern to read the Gospel. At its conclusion, the people sat, awaiting his eulogy.

Having known the priest's name but not having met him, I'd expected him to look something like Santa Claus. The image conjured by the name, however, was quickly dispelled by the man's physical reality. Shrunken, beardless, and dark-haired, vested not in red but in gold, he spoke with an affected accent that seemed more Episcopalian than jolly.

"An allegiant child of the church," he began, "has been brutally taken from our midst. Yet in leaving this life, departing on her journey to the next, she has come home to Holy Mother Church."

Right. I half expected thuds of protest to sound from Suzanne's coffin, but of course she couldn't hear the priest's words—not in this life, nor from "the next." The priest surely knew that Suzanne would have laughed at his tribute. She had broken from the church thirty years ago (long before I myself would bolt), and while I could not say with certainty, I presumed that she had not set foot in Saint Cecille's since. Now, they had to lug her here in a box—"allegiant child," indeed.

Perhaps the priest had taken this tack in order to promote the Big Lie, rewriting the facts of Suzanne's life in hopes that her death might lend credence to his own faith. Did he really believe the nonsense he preached? Or was he merely toying with us? Perhaps his words were chosen to gall Miriam Westerman, to rub her face in the victory he enjoyed, having won the right to preside at this public spectacle. I'd hold it to the man's credit if, in fact, his rhetoric was inspired by petty pride instead of piety.

Whatever his motivation, Miriam reacted predictably. She fidgeted and fumed across the aisle, and at several junctures in the sermon, she appeared ready to stand and dispute the priest's words. I weighed this prospect with mixed emotions. The outburst would lend a nifty twist to the tiresome blathering, but it would only upset those who had genuinely come to grieve. In any event, Miriam summoned the self-restraint to stew privately.

The emotions of others in the church ran the gamut, exemplified by those who sat in front of me—Hazel sobbed openly, Joey sniffled, and Thad listened dully with dry-eyed stoicism. Most of the congregation sat as I did, quietly respectful, but lacking any display of sentiment. It was impossible, of course, to read the minds of the hundreds who filled the pews that morning. The people of Dumont felt the loss of Suzanne in differing contexts. To a few, she was family; to others, a friend; to most, an influential business figure. To some degree, her death was mourned by all—all, I speculated, save one. Chances were, there was a killer in the church, miming grief. But who?

I was tempted to take out my pen and make a few notes, but the priest's words distracted me, and I thought it ill-mannered to flaunt my disbelief.

"Let us pray, then," concluded Father Winter, "that our dearly departed sister"—he filled in the blank—"Suzanne—will look down upon us with favor from her heavenly home, where she enjoys eternal happiness with all the saints, with the Blessed Virgin Mary, with our Lord and Savior, Jesus Christ."

Amid a smatter of amens, the priest returned to the altar and prepared to utter the long formula that would turn bread, he claimed, into God.

The rest of the service was familiar and uneventful, save for the awkward logistics of distributing Communion to the throngs who snaked forward, squeezing past Suzanne's casket. When at last it was over, the organ thundered a recessional, and Father Winter led the casket back to the doors of the church, altar boys churning clouds of incense in its wake. Those seated in the front pews followed him, so I was among those first to leave.

Coughing back tears, caused not by grief but by the pungent smoke that engulfed us, I slowly made my way along the center aisle toward the open doors, eager to breathe the clean, cold air. Everyone turned as we passed, and it felt as if the hundreds of unknown faces were looking at me, but of course it was Suzanne's remains that were the focus of their attention.

The organ continued its somber march, overlaid by horn sounds that mimicked the trumpets of doomsday. While the organist's performance was reasonably skilled, the trumpeter's was not, sounding eerily dissonant above the stately melody, more like a car alarm than music. As we drew nearer the door and under the choir loft, the offensive horn noise grew louder, and I realized that it *was* a car alarm. In the next instant, I recognized that it was *my* car alarm.

Good God. Fishing in my pocket for the key fob, I rushed ahead of the procession and out the door, preparing to silence the damn thing.

Out in the parking lot, across the street from where the hearse and limousines idled at the curb, I saw a couple of squad cars and a group of sheriff's deputies near my car, presumably trying to quell the disturbance. Jogging toward them, I pushed the fob button, and as soon as I was in range, the honking

ceased. Spotting Doug Pierce near the back of my car, I
approached him, mortified, ready to offer profuse apologies.

But then I noticed that the cops wouldn't care that I had
silenced the blaring alarm, for, in fact, they had tripped it. My
trunk gaped open, its lock picked by a police locksmith. Pierce
held something in his arms, bundled in a blanket. Suddenly
apprehensive, I asked, "What's going on, Doug?"

Before answering, he turned to mumble instructions to his
deputies. While I waited, the congregation poured out of the
church and, attracted by the commotion in the parking lot,
herded past the hearse and crowded toward us. Pierce turned
back to me and unfurled the blanket. There in his arms was
the missing artichoke finial, the bloodstained king-thing that
had killed Suzanne Quatrain. He told me, "Just before the
funeral, we got an anonymous tip from a man, traced to a
phone booth. He told us the weapon was in your trunk."

A gasp went up from the nearby onlookers, who quickly
spread word through the crowd that Suzanne's killer had been
caught.

"I'm sorry, Mark," Pierce told me. "The DA wants you
booked on suspicion of murder." Then he began reciting my
rights.

Neil, Parker, Roxanne, Carl, Thad, and Hazel all stood
behind me, astonished, voicing words of support. Roxanne
leaned forward and said into my ear, "I'll do everything I can,
Mark. I'll meet you downtown." Meaning, of course, that I
was about to be hauled away.

I offered my wrists to Pierce, but he shook his head, telling
me, "Just get in the car." He opened the back door of one of
the squads. As I got in, he stood between me and the crowd,
giving instructions to the deputy who would drive us to the
sheriff's department. He was about to close the door for me
and get into the front seat, when Thad poked his head inside
the car.

"Mark," he said, sounding panicky, "what's happening?
They can't do this."

Before I could say anything in response, Miriam Westerman

burst through the crowd and nabbed Thad by the elbow, telling him, "The courts should have an easy time of it *now*, Ariel, deciding whose guidance is best for your future!"

Then Pierce closed my door, took the front seat, and told the driver, "Let's get out of here."

PART THREE

Three Days Ago

I had another dream, which began as a replay of an earlier one.

I'm a boy of nine, visiting the house on Prairie Street for the first time. It's the second day of my visit, and I've met everyone in the household except my oldest cousin, Mark Quatrain, who's returning from college. Then somebody opens the door, and I see him. He's very handsome, with wavy hair, and he's wearing tan pants. Everyone else is hugging him; I want to, but think I shouldn't. Trying to think of something clever, I tell him, "We've got the same name." He smiles and says, "How about that?" Then he musses my hair with his hand.

Later that afternoon, I'm in Joey's room, and I stroll out into the hall and look in on Mark. There he is with his shirt off, unpacking a suitcase and sorting through his records. Seeing me, he says, "I'll find some Mozart." He kneels on the floor, reaching for an album that slipped behind the stereo. His backside is toward me, and I can't take my eyes off him. I feel lost for a moment; then I walk over to him and just, well . . . *touch* him.

Mark gets up fast, laughing, being nice. He says, "Go ahead. Touch me."

I put my arms around his waist and squeeze him against me. He looks at the ceiling with his mouth open, and he puts his hands in my hair, and he pulls, and it sort of hurts but feels good anyway. He says, "I want to touch you, too, Mark."

So I take one of his hands and put it between my legs, and I feel warm and hard there. He looks into my eyes and tells me how green they are, and I laugh, telling him, "Show me your cock. Fuck my mouth."

I'm not little anymore, but his age, eighteen. We're the same height, same build, same name, same khaki pants. There's a twin-thing going on, and it heats up fast. We're on the floor, groping each other. "Mark, oh, Mark," we whisper.

So far, everything is happening the way it did in the earlier dream. But then, things start to get different.

"Hey," says someone, popping into the room. But I can't see him, and I don't care—I'm busy with my cousin, my twin. "Hey!" he repeats. "Back off, Mark. That guy's straight. Worse yet, he's a rapist and a murderer. I don't know what he's up to, but he's dangerous."

Wearing the same khaki pants that Mark and I wear, Parker walks over to where we are sprawled on the floor together, and he stands over me. The way he moves, the way the crisp fabric hugs his butt, everything about him—his body language—reminds me of my cousin Mark, just as it did on the day when I hired Parker. And now I'm doubly aroused, with my fantasy-cousin lying there at my side, with my hot managing editor straddling my shoulders. "Besides," he tells me, reaching a hand down to me, "that guy's just a kid. You need a man, Mark. I'm here for you."

As he pulls me to my feet, I'm no longer nine, no longer eighteen, but an adult. Parker and I are now the same age, same height, same build, same khaki pants. There's sort of a twin-thing going on, and it heats up fast while Mark Quatrain watches us, grinning, lying on the floor. Parker and I share a long, deep kiss as our hands fumble to unbuckle each other's belts. Then I feel Parker's hand lift my balls, and I moan at his touch. With his other hand, he combs his fingers through my hair, mussing it, and my penis stiffens to the point of pain. Watching us, lying there, my cousin Mark unzips his own pants and starts masturbating.

Parker tells me, "Rub your dick in my hair," and he kneels in front of me, thrusting his head at my groin. As instructed, I slide my penis through his curls and instinctively grab his hair with both of my hands, forcing his face to nuzzle deeper into my groin. "Oh, Mark," he groans, "I'm gonna come."

But the voice didn't come from the man kneeling in front of me. It came from the man lying on the floor. It is no longer my cousin Mark, but Parker, in the first throes of orgasm. "This is all I've ever wanted," he tells me, shooting semen that arcs into the air, then lands in puddles that disappear within the wrinkles of his crumpled khakis.

Spontaneously, my testicles clench, and I feel the rush of orgasm pulse through my penis into the hair of the man kneeling before me. My fingers are buried in Mark Quatrain's curls, and as I come, I pull. He yelps, enjoying the pain, ejaculating at my feet. Breathless, I lift my hands from his head and discover strands of his hair wrapped around my fingers.

He looks up at me, smiling with woozy bliss.

I crouch to kiss him, slipping deeply asleep.

Waking in the dark, I glanced at the bedside clock and saw that it was shortly after six. The near silence of early morning was broken only by the sound of the furnace blower and by a low chatter that resembled the grinding of teeth. The weather had turned bitterly cold again, so cold that the brick walls of the house seemed to grate their own mortar in defiance of the gelid outdoor air.

The bed was warm and comforting, heated, no doubt, by the passions of my dream. The dream, though bizarre, was highly pleasurable, and I took it as a signal from my subconscious that despite the horrendous turn of events following Suzanne's funeral the week before, I could now sleep more easily.

The murder charges against me didn't stick. While tests confirmed that the finial found in my car was in fact the murder weapon, it obviously had been planted in my trunk. Even Dumont's hotdogging DA, Harley Kaiser, itching for a conviction, conceded that I was framed. Roxanne convincingly argued that if I had committed the crime, I'd simply have burned the finial in any of the house's fireplaces; the sheriff himself, Doug

Pierce, confirmed that he'd seen several of the fireplaces in full blaze on Christmas Day. What's more, if I *had* been dumb enough to carry the bloodied king-thing around in my car, I wouldn't have been smart enough to clean off all its fingerprints, a task that someone had scrupulously tended to. No, it just didn't add up, so the finial in my trunk could not be used to prove me guilty of Suzanne's murder. But it didn't exonerate me, either, and Kaiser ordered me not to leave town—I was still on a short list of suspects.

Following my arrest, both Neil and Roxanne spent the full week in Dumont, Neil for moral support, Roxanne on legal matters. Her first order of business was to clear me with the DA. Aside from the fact that he couldn't build a strong case against me, Roxanne shrewdly reminded him that I would soon be taking over as publisher of the *Register* and that it would not be in the best interests of his next election to antagonize me. He may not have liked the tone of her reminder, but he was smart enough to know that she was right.

Less easily handled was the matter of Thad's guardianship. As Doug Pierce had warned, Miriam Westerman proceeded with her court action to take responsibility for the boy, and immediately after my arrest, she was granted temporary custody, alleging that my dubious character posed a danger to the child. Roxanne quickly set the wheels in motion to appeal that ruling and have Thad remanded to my permanent custody, but she cautioned me that the process could be time-consuming, the outcome iffy.

With the crisis of my arrest dispatched, and with the custody question temporarily at bay, both Roxanne and Neil returned to Chicago last Sunday, needing to get back to their regular jobs. I felt guilty enough that I had not yet lived up to my end of the "arrangement" with Neil, having spent no time with him in Chicago since my move north during Christmas week. It was now January twelfth, a Wednesday (eighteen days since Suzanne's murder, nine since her funeral), and Neil had already spent three consecutive weekends in Dumont. Since I was now under orders not to leave town, he'd be returning for a fourth.

So all was unusually quiet that early morning as I lay in

bed mulling my dream. Neil and Roxanne were back in Chicago. Thad was with Miriam Westerman. The only others sharing the house with me now were Hazel, in her quarters downstairs near the kitchen, and Parker, asleep down the hall from me in the room that had once been Mark Quatrain's.

Thinking of Parker—not the intruder who had nudged into my dream, but the real person sleeping in my cousin's room— I was grateful he was there in the house. He'd been steadfast in his efforts to help me through the difficult events that had transpired since my arrival in Dumont, and he'd proven himself a tireless worker during his many days of unpaid research in the *Register*'s morgue. Initially, our plan was that he would stay at the house until he was able to get a lease on a suitable place of his own, but the search for alternate housing hadn't been mentioned since his arrival, and I wondered if Parker entertained notions that the living arrangement on Prairie Street might become permanent.

Then I realized (and it was a disquieting thought) that I had not broached the subject of Parker's residence because I myself felt no urgency to have him move out. Reminding myself that I must do nothing to encourage his stated but repressed affections for me, I nonetheless acknowledged that our friendship had grown increasingly close and comfortable over those past three weeks. So I pondered the possibility of suggesting that he plan to stay.

Would such a setup simply be too weird? Unconventional living arrangements seemed to be central to the history of the house, originally designed for both my uncle's young family and his long-ago business partner. Then it passed to Professor and Mrs. Tawkin, an unconventional duo by any definition. Neil and I had recently moved in as its next inhabitants, he and I constituting another unconventional couple, at least by Dumont standards. Add Thad to the mix, as we were now petitioning the courts to do, and our little family would become even less typical. Add Parker, and it would get downright peculiar. How would Neil react to such a suggestion? I could very well guess.

These frets, I told myself, were premature. In five days, next

Monday, I would officially take over as owner and publisher of the *Dumont Daily Register*, with Parker as my managing editor. That, after all, was the purpose of this move—I was giving new direction to my life in journalism, and I was doing so at considerable financial and emotional risk. Put things in perspective, I told myself. For the moment, the issue of where Parker would spend his nights was fairly trivial. If, within the next few weeks, he found his own apartment, the issue would be resolved. If not, I would face some sticky decisions—but it needn't be dealt with now, at this moment, lying in bed, planning my day.

It was time to focus more on business and less on the family matters that had dominated my time since arriving in Dumont. That very afternoon, I reminded myself, Elliot Coop was to meet me at the *Register*'s offices with retiring publisher Barret Logan for the signing of some last bit of paperwork. I needed to phone Glee Savage and ask her to be there. She had already interviewed me for a big feature story that would appear that Sunday, detailing the change of ownership. She might want to describe the "color" of the signing itself—it might make a good lead for her story. And the impromptu ceremony might make a good photo-op as well. I needed to write some notes—it was too early to start phoning people.

I sat up in bed, switched on the lamp, and squinted, waiting for my eyes to adjust to the light. There on the nightstand was my trusty Montblanc and a fresh reporter's notebook—old habits die hard. I wrote a few reminders of things to accomplish that day, and it was refreshing to realize that they all pertained to the newspaper, none to Suzanne's unsolved murder. I felt invigorated. It was barely dawn, I had already accomplished some productive work, and I still felt the energized afterglow of my dream's hot climax.

Maybe (it had been far too long since I'd done it) I should lace up my running shoes, head outdoors to tick off a mile or two before sunrise, *then* come home for coffee. I got up, crossed to the window, held back the curtain, and touched the glass. It was so cold, it burned my fingertips.

So I shrugged into my robe, deciding to pad downstairs

and start the coffee. First coffee, then maybe a fire in the den, then the paper, then the idea of taking a run could be revisited. Maybe.

The idea of taking a run was never revisited that morning. Considering the weather, I neatly nudged the notion from my mind, dismissing it as ridiculous while I settled onto the little sofa in my den. The coffee was brewed, the fire was built, and I was dressed, with the morning paper spread before me on the low table. The sun had risen, bright if ineffective against the cold. Varied house noises (running water, creaking stairs, door thuds) told me that both Hazel and Parker had risen for the day.

Postseason Packers hoopla had made its way forward from the sports section and dominated the front page of the *Register*. My pen was not within reach, but I made a mental note to have a word with someone about that. It was a quiet morning for news—no developments on Suzanne's murder—and the front page also contained a boxed story promoting Glee's comprehensive Sunday feature on the impending change of management at the paper.

As I leaned from the love seat to turn the page, Hazel entered the den with a carafe. "Good morning, Mr. Manning," she told me while stepping forward to refill my old *Journal* mug. "Sorry I wasn't up in time to make coffee for you."

"No problem." I smiled. "Actually, I sort of enjoy performing the morning ritual myself." I sipped from the mug, reconfirming that my coffee was in fact better than hers. "So feel welcome to sleep late whenever you like."

She nodded a wary thank-you, as if she understood the ulterior side of my thoughtfulness. "If you have no objection," she told me, "I thought I'd begin some of the sorting and packing we discussed."

"Excellent," I told her. Having been settled into the house for some three weeks, I'd grown annoyed by the disarray of the extra bedrooms upstairs, which had become virtual dumping grounds during the Tawkins' move out and my own move in. I suggested, "Start with Joey's old room—it's the worst."

She chuckled at my understatement. "Would you care to go through anything before I phone Goodwill for a pickup?" I shook my head. Easy decision. "Just use your own judgment, Hazel. You know this house and its contents better than anyone. Anything of value, hang on to. Anything of interest to Joey or Thad, offer to them. Anything else, throw out."

"Yes, sir. That's clear enough." She retreated from the room, then paused in the doorway to tell me, "I'm hoping I'll run across those items that the Tawkins packed away for us, especially the three children's baby books. With Suzanne gone now"—Hazel paused, letting a momentary pang pass—"I'd really like to look through those albums. Joey should have them. And someday they'll go to Thad."

"Happy hunting," I told her softly. While the lost mementos had no sentimental value to me, they clearly meant a great deal to her, and I hoped she would find them. I added, "You've got a big project ahead of you. If you like, I could pick up the groceries for tonight." Joey and Thad were coming over for a midweek dinner, a family supper we hoped to make a tradition of.

"Thank you, Mr. Manning," she accepted my offer, "that would be most kind of you. I've already made a list. I'll leave it on your desk later."

As she backed out of the room, I heard Parker greet her in the hall. "Morning, Hazel. I started a new pot in the kitchen." Then he entered the den, mug of coffee in hand.

"Hi, Parker," I told him, motioning for him to join me. "You're looking chipper this morning." Fresh from the shower, his hair was still damp. He wore a bulky V-neck sweater over a white T-shirt. Below, of course, were the perpetual khakis. Sitting in the chair across from me, he looked downright cuddly in the glow from the fire, and I enjoyed a fleeting replay of his surprise appearance in my dream. I realized, in fact, that I was aroused by the sight of him—a reaction that was undeniably pleasurable, but entirely inappropriate to the working relationship I would officially establish with him next week.

With a conscious effort to suppress this response to his physical presence, I resorted to a foolish commentary on the weather. "Cold one, huh?"

He nodded, slurping his coffee. "It doesn't really bother me—it's not as if we're out digging ditches." He laughed at the thought of it. Then his visage turned thoughtful. "Truth is, Mark, these have been the most exciting and rewarding weeks of my life. Weather be damned, you and I are about to embark on a career move together that could change the face of small-town journalism. Forgive my broken record, but this is all I've ever wanted."

Yeah, I'd heard that before. For some reason, I told him, "Poor Neil. He'll be driving back up here on Friday evening— four weekends in a row. I owe him so many visits, I'll never live up to my end of the bargain."

"Neil's cool with it," Parker assured me. "Clearly, the man loves you. Besides, you're under orders not to leave town."

"Can you imagine!" I laughed at the irony of the situation. "I move up here, make a major commitment to this town's business climate and its future, only to end up targeted as a murder suspect, a virtual prisoner in my own house."

"Harley Kaiser's a prick."

"Why, Parker," I told him, feigning dismay, "you don't even know the man." In truth, neither did I. In the hours of crisis following my arrest, I never actually met the district attorney, but was handled by one of his assistants. Kaiser himself had to tangle with Roxanne, whose big-city credentials, to say nothing of her adept, argumentative style, forced him to release me on my own recognizance—with the stipulation that I not leave town until the investigation was resolved.

Parker said, "Now that things have calmed down some, have you come to any conclusions? Who killed Suzanne?"

"Good question," I told him, leaning forward, grasping the *Journal* mug with both hands to warm my fingers. "Let's talk it through, Parker."

"Great." He also leaned forward. "Recap. Who's first on your list?"

"Hazel," I told him. "Well, actually she's *last* on my list.

Granted, her inheritance from Suzanne establishes an obvious motive. What's more, she's had ready access to the trunk of my car since the day I arrived, so she would have had ample opportunity to plant the murder weapon there in an attempt to frame me. However, I just don't think she has either the temperament or the physical ability to club a person to death, especially a person she helped raise. She still seems genuinely grief-stricken by Suzanne's death."

Parker nodded. "That's my gut feeling about her exactly. But if Hazel is innocent, why would she concoct that screwy story—*if* she concocted it—about Miriam Westerman bringing a fruitcake to the house at the time of the murder?"

"Two possibilities. First, she can't stand Miriam, so maybe she just wanted to make trouble for her. Second, and more likely, Hazel may have been trying to cast suspicion on Miriam in order to protect Thad, who she fears may be the actual killer. Whatever her motive in blaming Miriam, I think we can still safely conclude that Hazel was not attempting to cover her own guilt."

"Agreed," said Parker. "Who's next on your list?"

I chortled. "I do, in fact, have a list," I told him, rising and crossing to my desk, where I pulled a notebook from a drawer and flipped it open. "Next is Miriam Westerman. She had two strong motives—getting the trust money for her school, and getting custody of Thad, whom she has always considered to be rightfully her own son, 'Ariel.' Adding to my suspicions of Miriam, I caught her snooping around my car a few days before the weapon was planted there. However, Doug Pierce said that it was a man on the phone who tipped the sheriff's department about the finial in my trunk, which casts suspicion away from both Miriam *and* Hazel."

Parker stood, hands in pockets, thinking. "What does Doug think of Hazel's allegations about Miriam's fruitcake visit?"

I shook my head. "He doesn't think that Miriam was in the house when Suzanne was killed. He's questioned her at length about it, and she has an alibi that seems solid. He no longer considers Miriam a suspect, and he suggested that I cross her off my list." As I said this, I uncapped my Montblanc and did so.

With a thoughtful tone, Parker mused, "The sheriff has certainly been accommodating to you throughout this case—in stark contrast to the district attorney. Has it occurred to you, Mark, that Sheriff Pierce might be *gay?*"

Though Parker's question was unexpected, his observation didn't surprise me in the least. I told him, "I've had that thought. He's not married because 'the right girl never came along,' but he's volunteered nothing explicit. Yes, he's *friendly*. My best guess is that this is an issue he's struggling with at some level, but I don't know what level he's at. Maybe he's gay but closeted, or straight but curious, or anywhere in between."

"Keep me posted." Parker smiled. (Was he *interested* in Pierce?) He crossed to me at the desk and glanced at my list. "Who's next?"

"Uh . . . Thad. I don't know what to make of the kid. He was a belligerent, detestable snot on the day we met, which was also the day his mother was killed. Since then, we've warmed up, a lot, and he's actually begged me, tears and all, to keep him out of Miriam's clutches. And now I've got Roxanne embroiled in the legal battle to return him to my custody. So, needless to say, I'm conflicted on this one. I *like* the boy, and I'm taking steps to make a home for him, but I haven't forgotten that there's a possibility, however remote, that he's a murderer."

I gathered my thoughts before continuing. "Consider: He's been obsessed with an adolescent independence kick, and he argued violently with his mother about it, threatening her. He raised the same issues with me only minutes after he, Neil, and I decided we'd attempt to build a semblance of a family together. That was the day before Suzanne was to be buried, and Thad had completely forgotten the funeral. While I recognize that everyone has his own way of dealing with death, I find it worrisome that Thad has yet to show the slightest sign of grief. And finally, there's the issue of my car. I've lent it to him, and he seemed grateful. Yes, he enjoyed driving it, but he also had the opportunity to plant the weapon in my trunk.

The bottom line is: As far as I'm concerned, the jury is still out on Thad."

Parker read further down my list. "It looks like your rogues' gallery has a late entry—the victim's feebleminded brother."

I breathed an uncomfortable sigh. "I'm afraid that Joey Quatrain's chilling performance on New Year's Day has earned him a prominent spot on the list. In front of the sheriff and a roomful of witnesses, he not only 'guessed' the identity of the murder weapon, but also gave a convincing display of its use. When you think about it, he had a couple of feasible motives for wanting his sister dead.

"One possibility is money. He apparently suffers from some serious delusions about the funds that are available to him— he made exorbitant, unbacked offers to buy both the *Register* and this house out from under me, only to learn that he doesn't have a dime of expendable income. The other possibility is resentment. The twelve-year-old brain in his middle-aged body has not dealt well with the fact that the world has passed him by. His sister became the focus of all the attention and adulation that he would have liked to share, but couldn't. His petulant behavior, frequently prompted by the mere mention of Suzanne's name, could be the surface clue to deeply buried anxieties that were vented in murder."

Parker took a seat on one side of the partners desk, asking, "Since Suzanne's funeral last week, how's Joey been acting?"

"Even more erratic and agitated," I answered, sitting in my uncle's chair at the desk, opposite Parker. "I've phoned him several times at Quatro Press, and he's rarely even shown up for his job, though of course he still draws a paycheck. I have to admit that I've grown to feel both suspicion and concern for Joey. So I phoned him at home last night and suggested that he pick up Thad after school today and bring him here to the house for a family supper. Joey perked up. He liked the idea. He phoned Miriam to get permission to spend the evening with Thad—he even had sense enough not to tell her that he was bringing him here."

We both laughed at the ease with which Miriam had been duped by Joey's simplemindedness. Parker said, "This dinner tonight—it's a family thing. Do you want me around, or should I make other plans?"

"By all means, please join us. You're as much a part of this peculiar, extended 'family' as anyone, Parker. Besides, I need you there to help me observe things. It wasn't entirely the warm fuzzies that prompted me to call this meal. Either Thad or Joey may have killed Suzanne, and I want to set them both in a comfortable, unthreatening situation in hopes that someone might drop a useful clue."

Parker grinned—he was impressed. "Good plan," he told me. "Of Thad or Joey, do your suspicions fall more heavily toward either one of them?"

Exasperated, I shook my head. "I'm leaning toward Joey, but there's one major hitch with that theory. In all likelihood, it was the murderer who planted the king-thing in my trunk, but, as far as I know, Joey never had access to my car."

"*Mark*," said Parker, leaning over the blotter toward me, "don't you remember? On the Monday after Christmas, when we were helping the Chicagoans pack up for their return trip, Neil had forgotten a wastebasket or something in the trunk of your car. I went to get it, and Joey went with me to help. But he claimed to like your car so much, he stayed in it, 'playing,' till we called him into the house later."

"God"—my mouth fell—"of course. I'd forgotten that. Thank you, Parker." I uncapped my pen and added a footnote to the page I had begun on Joey.

Parker leaned back in his chair, gloating. "For that matter," he reminded me, "both Neil and I have had constant access to your car, and we were both in the house at the time of the murder. It's important to remain coldly analytical about this, Mark. Leave no stone unturned."

His tone was serious—too serious—and I responded with a laugh. "I appreciate your rigorous approach. Rest assured that I *have* left no stone unturned. I've already considered the fact that either you or Neil could have conceivably planted the finial in my trunk. Outweighing this, however, is the fact that you both met Suzanne for the first time on the day she died.

It's highly unlikely that either of you could develop sufficient motive for murder within the span of an hour."

"Just checking." He nodded, satisfied that my methods had not gone sloppy. Then he leaned forward again, trying to read my notes. "As long as we're exploring long shots, what about Thad's father?"

"Austin Reece is still a possible suspect, but we're working on little more than a hunch—and Hazel's story that he left town complaining that Suzanne had 'wrecked his life.' So far, the sheriff's investigators have not been able to determine Reece's whereabouts."

Parker drummed his fingers on the blotter, thinking. "If I'm not mistaken, that leaves us with only one remaining possibility—the 'brother from the grave.' "

"That's *your* theory," I reminded him. "It's a compelling idea—everything fits. But it's a puzzle with a piece missing, a piece that may not exist. Neither Suzanne's pile of dossiers nor your own retracing of Suzanne's morgue research has revealed a likely new alias for Mark Quatrain. If he's still alive, where is he? *Who* is he?"

Parker tapped my notes. "Joey gave us a lead—that inquisitive Vietnam vet working in the credit department at Quatro Press."

Slumping back in my chair, I said, "Doug Pierce followed up on that last week, the day after Suzanne's funeral. He drove out to Quatro, intending to interview both Joey and the credit manager, whose name is Allan Addams. Joey wasn't there, though—he hasn't shown up at the office since New Year's. And Addams wasn't there, either. It turns out, Addams was finishing up a winter vacation with his family. They were in Mexico, and they left the morning of Christmas Eve. Maybe that's why Joey was so insistent that Addams couldn't be his brother—the man wasn't even in the country on the day Suzanne was killed. What's more, he was still away when the weapon was put in my car. So, unless it turns out that Addams never really took the trip, he's in the clear."

"Hmm." Parker slumped in his own chair, mirroring my

posture. "Suzanne's dossiers—you checked them all, and there was no file on Allan Addams?"

I shook my head. "I've had a chance to study all the pertinent files—those grouped as either 'suspicious' or 'inconclusive'— and there was nothing on Addams. The remaining files, 'above suspicion,' offered no promise at all."

"Do you mind if I take a look at them? A fresh pair of eyes might find something you missed."

"Good idea." I'd meant to have Parker review them anyway, but he'd been spending most of his days at the *Register*. I stood at the desk, forewarning him with a laugh, "There's a hell of a lot of material. It may bog you down for a while."

He stood. "Then I'd better get more coffee. Need some?"

"Thanks." I passed him my empty mug, and he left the den, headed back through the house toward the kitchen.

I took the little brass key from the ashtray of paper clips and opened the credenza near the desk. Hunkering down to pull the heavy box of files from the cabinet, I heard the doorbell. So I abandoned the dossiers and went out to the front hall to answer the door.

It was Sheriff Pierce. "Good morning, Mark," he told me, stepping inside, removing a glove to shake my hand. "Sorry to bother you so early." It was not yet nine o'clock.

"You're always welcome, Doug," I told him, thumping the door closed, "and no appointment is necessary." I helped him out of his coat. "What can I do for you?"

But before Pierce could answer, Parker reappeared in the hall, bearing the two cups of coffee. "Uh-oh," he said comically, "it's the law. 'Morning, Sheriff."

They exchanged some pleasantries, remarking on the bitter weather; then Parker commented, "It looks like you two have some business to discuss."

Pierce told us, "Yes, actually. Mark, do you have a few minutes?"

Parker interjected, "I really ought to get going anyway, Mark. I'll study that material sometime later, when it's more convenient. Meanwhile, there's plenty to keep me busy down at the paper, preparing for next week's transition."

"Fine," I told him. "Just let me know when you'd like to see the files."

He handed me my *Journal* mug, then asked, "Coffee, Sheriff?" Offering Pierce the cup he'd refilled for himself, he joked, "Drink from the back side—it's clean."

Pierce gratefully accepted it, if only to warm his hands. Parker waved a good-bye, retreating down the hall to get his coat, near the back door. I led Pierce into the den and hung his coat; then we took our customary seats on either side of Uncle Edwin's partners desk, with the cabinet door still open behind me. We heard Parker leave.

Pierce asked, "Is there anyone else in the house?"

"Just Hazel. She's probably upstairs, cleaning the unused bedrooms."

Pierce leaned toward me. I noticed the polished shine of the leather shoulder holster under his handsome cashmere blazer. "We're getting ready to make an arrest, Mark. The DA feels this has gone on long enough, and, to an extent, I agree with him. I'm here because I wanted to let you know where this is headed."

"Thanks, Doug," I told him quietly. Leaning close over the blotter, I asked, "So then—who is it?"

"I'm not entirely comfortable with the results of the investigation, but everything seems to point to Joey."

I sighed, sitting back. "I was beginning to reach that conclusion myself, but—like you—I'm not comfortable with it. And I thought Harley Kaiser was reluctant to implicate a Quatrain."

"He is," Pierce assured me, "but let's face it: Joey's not quite 'all there.' I mean, chances are, he'd end up institutionalized someday anyway. It's a sad, tragic situation. On the positive side—if there is one—because of Joey's mental condition and nonviolent past, the law will go easy on him."

Again I sighed. Everything Pierce said made sense, but it was hard to accept. While I felt that Joey was indeed our strongest suspect, I didn't want to believe that he had ruthlessly bludgeoned his sister.

"Doug," I said, holding his stare with mine, "can you wait till tonight to make the arrest? Joey is coming to the house this evening with Thad. It's going to be a family supper that I'd hoped to turn into a weekly tradition. If you wait till then, you'll have the rest of the day to check every possible lead one more time. If you're still convinced of Joey's guilt, just drop by the house during dinner. It'll give you the opportunity to question him discreetly before making the arrest—and it won't be such a public spectacle." I leaned forward, arms propped on the desk. "Please, Doug. What do you think?"

He exhaled noisily. With the slightest nod, he told me, "All right, Mark. That's the plan." Again he exhaled, but this time the noise had the character of a nascent laugh. "It's really ironic. Growing up here in Dumont, knowing the Quatrain kids all their lives, the rest of us thought of them as the luckiest people in the world—hell, just for starters, they were *rich*. Who'd have thought their lives would be ruined by such a heartbreaking string of events?"

I shook my head. "Not I, certainly. Of course, I didn't grow up with the kids—I knew them only from that one Christmas visit. But that was enough to convince me they would all lead charmed lives. Little did I know that it would all begin to fall apart only three years later."

Pierce's features turned suddenly inquisitive, as though he'd thought of something. "It's none of my business, Mark, but is that what it was all about—the letter from your uncle Edwin? You started to tell me the story two weeks ago, and I've been curious about it since. Did he tell you what happened between Suzanne and Mark Quatrain?"

"God no," I answered, allowing myself a weak laugh. I reminded him, "I didn't learn about the rape until Hazel stunned us with her tell-all on New Year's Eve. No, my uncle's letter dealt with something more directly related to *me*."

Pierce's brows instinctively arched, wanting more details. But he surely sensed that we were venturing into very private territory, so he was not about to prod for information that was not offered. It was entirely my decision whether or not to continue. I asked myself what kind of game I'd been playing. Why had I tantalized him with this story? I had opened the door, and, by rights, he deserved a sense of closure. Besides, I knew I wanted to share the letter, and the time had come.

"You'll recall," I told him, "that when my uncle died three years ago, I inherited the house. On the day I came up here to sell the house to the Tawkins, Elliot Coop handed me a letter written by my uncle shortly before he died. I got into my car with it, and was preparing to follow the lawyer to his office to finalize the sale, when curiosity got the better of me. I pulled over to the curb and, in the shadow of the house, opened the letter."

Reaching behind me into the open credenza, I removed the envelope that was kept there next to the box of dossiers, then held it in front of Pierce. "Would you like to read it?" I asked him.

He paused. He didn't answer, didn't nod. He carefully took the envelope from my fingers, handling it as if it were thinnest glass, as if it might shatter at his touch. It was addressed, simply, "Mr. Mark Manning, Jr., Chicago." He slipped out the letter, unfolded its pages, and began to read the words that I'd pondered so often during countless bouts of introspection:

Dearest Mark,

I don't like secrets. They put walls between people. They are lies of omission. But sometimes our best judgment is tempered by our worst frailties, and the laws of conventionality are allowed to rule.

In the name of convention, in the name of "what's expected," a secret has been kept from you. It involves me, and I feel shame—not for my past actions, but for my silence. Perhaps you have already figured this out, but you deserve to hear it, plainly, from me.

It was your father who used to live upstairs on Prairie Street. He and I were more than friends. For years, we were partners—in building the business, in building the house, and yes, most certainly in bed. We loved each other. And I never stopped loving him, not after he moved away, not after he died.

You can be proud to know that your father was openly homosexual—as open as anyone dared to be back in that dark age, that black-and-white era. I worshiped the man, but never had his strength, so I followed convention and married Peggy, naming our first son after him. My sister Edie (your mother-to-be) knew the whole story, but because she loved Mark (your father-to-be) as much as I did, she was happy to be his "armpiece." Though she did not live with us on Prairie Street, she rounded out our daring foursome in public.

Even in a house that was custom designed to fit this extraordinary arrangement, day-to-day life was touchy. But we all determined to make it work, so there were unspoken, inviolable rules regarding the where-and-when of your father and me. Late one night, however, after an urgently needed transgression, all hell broke loose when Peggy caught me sneaking down from the third floor wearing little more than my still-obvious state of arousal. The subsequent uproar utterly shredded our delicate web of contrivance. Under those circumstances, in those times, your father simply had to leave. So he married my sister and moved with her to Illinois, selling out his share of the business to me. But he never sought reimbursement for his share of the house.

So you see, Mark, all along, the house has rightfully belonged more to you than to any one of my own children. More important, you are its spiritual heir. I used to tell you that you were "special" and "not like the others." I assume you have deciphered my meaning, and I hope you have forgiven my presumption.

How did I know? We have a sense about these things, don't we? What's more, you showed me that little story about your infatuation with "Marshall." Though cleverly constructed (for the work of a nine-year-old), it could not withstand the scrutiny of a discerning old closet queen. I hope the passion and honesty of your youthful confusion has long since affirmed itself in a happy and proud self-awareness. Take advantage of these more enlightened times.

Simply be who you truly are, without compromise—even if by some miracle, God forbid, you've turned out straight!

Dearest Mark, I doubt that you will want to live in Dumont. You'd suffocate here. It's a closet—a closet with streets. So, what will you do with the house? If I were you, I'd sell it. Buy a new car. Buy a new house—hell, *buy a houseboy!* And have yourself a ball.

Love,
Uncle Edwin

Sheriff Pierce looked up from the letter. He folded it, returning it neatly to its envelope. I was not sure how I expected him to react, what I expected him to say. When he paused in thought, I felt compelled to comment, "There's been a lot of research lately about a 'gay gene,' and there's convincing evidence that it's passed along through the mother's side of the family. I've long intuited a half-baked theory about gay uncles—so many of us seem to have them—and Edwin's letter places me in those ranks. On top of which, my own father . . ."

Pierce interrupted my genetics lecture with a halting gesture of both hands. "You've done your uncle proud, Mark," he told me. Then he grinned. "I've seen the car. So, where's the houseboy?"

That afternoon, I blustered into the *Register* building, chilled marrow-deep by the short walk from the curb to the door. Greeting Connie behind the receptionist's window, I asked whether Elliot Coop had arrived. Hearing that he was waiting for me, I loped up the stairs to the editorial offices.

The old lawyer had already spread Barret Logan's desk with the last set of documents that would make next week's change of ownership official. I had phoned ahead, asking Glee Savage to be on hand with a photographer, and they were all assembled inside Logan's glass-walled office, ready to witness the moment of transition. Logan was dressed, I noted, in a black three-piece suit—especially austere, even for him—and I couldn't help wondering if his mood was funereal.

Removing my overcoat while crossing the newsroom, I spotted Parker Trent conferring with an editor, and I waved him over, inviting him to join us. "The venerable old *Register* is about to usher in a new era," I told him, "and I want you to be a part of it."

Parker said, "The staff seems psyched for the change now. The rumor mill must have been thrown into high gear when word got out that Logan was selling, but it's been an orderly transition, and everyone seems eager to move onward."

Under my breath, I asked, "Even with two new bosses who are gay?"

"If that bothers people," Parker assured me, "they haven't said boo."

We entered Barret Logan's office to the greetings of all present. Draping my coat over a chair, I wondered where Logan routinely hung his own coat—it was not apparent. Did he have a closet somewhere? Maybe a private bath? Within a few days, this office would be mine, and I had never taken a close look at it.

Elliot Coop told me, "I believe you'll find everything in order, Mr. Manning. The financial instruments have been duly executed, and with merely a few pen strokes, the assets will be transferred." He cleared his throat with a prim cough.

Logan laughed. "Mark, what Elliot means is: out of *your* pocket, into *mine.*" If I had feared that the retiring publisher might react to this ceremony with morose sentimentality, I was wrong. He seemed positively giddy.

"Now then, Barret," Elliot clucked, "don't forget: It's a fair exchange. Both you and Mr. Manning profit from this agreement."

"Yes, Elliot, yes," said Logan with good-natured impatience. "Let's sign."

And with that, he drew a pen from the holder on his desk; I removed the Montblanc from my jacket and uncapped it. Elliot pointed to a series of *X*s marked on the documents, and Logan and I began the ritual of signing them. With Elliot,

Glee, and Parker watching, the photographer recorded the big moment with repeated bursts of his strobe. Other staffers gathered beyond the glass wall, guessing the purpose of the event.

Glee had her steno pad poised. When the signing was complete and we all took a deep breath, she asked, "Well, Mr. Logan, how do you feel?"

"Rich!" he answered without hesitation. He added, "And you can quote me."

After a round of handshakes and mutual congratulations, Logan told me, "If you care to move some things in on Sunday, I'll try to finish clearing out on Saturday." With those words, the change of power was no longer an abstraction, but real, almost tangible. A hush fell over the room.

"Take all the time you need," I told Logan with a smile. As an afterthought, I said, "Are you sure you don't want to stay on for a while on a consulting basis?"

His shook his head—his mind was made up. "No, Mark. You and I both know that I'd just be in the way. You'll be far better off learning to run things without anyone looking over your shoulder. And I have every confidence that you're the right man for the job."

It was a humbling moment. All I could say was, "Thank you, Barret."

Minutes later, Logan was due at an editorial meeting—one of the last of many thousands he had chaired during his career—and Parker left with him, to take notes on the routine that I would soon be assuming. Left alone in Logan's office with Elliot and Glee, I retrieved my coat from the chair where I'd left it.

"Why don't you stick around, boss?" asked Glee. "I thought I might show you the art department's layout for Sunday's front-page feature."

"I'd like to see it," I told her, "but maybe tomorrow. Right now, I have to run out for groceries—Joey and Thad are coming over for dinner tonight. I've got Hazel busy with a cleaning project, so I volunteered to shop." I was tempted to explain to Glee that the evening also held the distinct possibility of Joey's arrest, but I thought it best not to broach this matter in front of Elliot Coop. As the Quatrains' longtime family attorney, he might feel compelled to take preemptive action on Joey's behalf. Whatever was to transpire that night, I wanted it kept low-key, without the involvement of lawyers.

Elliot said to me, "As long as you're leaving, Mr. Manning, I'll walk you to the car. I have a rather amusing story to relate, regarding Joey."

With my curiosity piqued (this "amusing story" was offered by the same man who had handed me my uncle's coming-out letter three years earlier), I slipped my coat on, helped Elliot with his, and we started out the office door together.

But Glee leaned into the hall with more on her mind. "By the way, Mark, I'm looking forward to Monday. It'll be fun."

I stopped, turning back to her, confused. "It'll be *interesting*," I conceded, "but I doubt if my first day on the job will be 'fun.'"

"No"—she laughed—"Monday *night*. Parker invited me out to the dinner celebrating the takeover."

"That does sound like fun," I said, "but I'm afraid I know nothing about it."

"Oops." She blushed. "Gosh, I'm sorry, Mark. I just assumed you'd be part of the party. Maybe it's a surprise— and I spoiled it."

"Maybe it's just the two of you," I suggested.

She gave a low chortle. "I should be so lucky."

She could fantasize all she wanted about the prospects of a cozy dinner with Parker, but her wishful thinking didn't much interest me. Besides, I was already feeling warm, standing there in my heavy winter coat. I told her, "I'll talk to you tomorrow about that layout," then headed through the news-room, toward the stairs, with Elliot.

The old lawyer tittered, "It really was *most* amusing, Mr. Manning."

I smiled, prepared to be amused. "What happened, Elliot? Since Suzanne's funeral, Joey's behavior has been a bit pecu-liar—I mean, peculiar even for Joey. He hasn't been to work in a week."

As we started down the stairs, Elliot agreed, "My yes, indeed. You see, Mr. Manning, he's been off on another of his—how shall I put it?—tangents. As you know, Joey previously entertained unrealistic notions about purchasing both your house and this newspaper." He made a broad gesture, encompassing the building that surrounded us. We now stood in the lobby near the door to the street.

"Well," Elliot continued, "in a similar vein, just yesterday he visited me at my office, wanting to establish an extravagant endowment fund for the benefit of some African orphanage he'd heard about in church last Sunday from Father Winter. He was genuinely distraught by the story of these starving babies in some war-torn banana republic. He said that these poor children needed his money more than he did." Elliot paused, choking back a wave of emotion.

I thought aloud, "He truly is a kindhearted soul. What a shame he's not able to function more realistically."

"Well put," Elliot told me, touching my arm with his gloved fingers. "Moved by his generous spirit, I was at a loss for words, at least temporarily. In the end, of course, I explained to him—once again—that while his own life will always be comfortable, he simply has no discretionary funds. It was sad, but I think he finally grasped the idea that while he was born to wealth, he has no money."

We both shook our heads in silent sympathy for the confusion and frustration that had marred Joey's entire adult life. I swung the door open for Elliot, and we trudged out into the raw afternoon. Already, the sun had slunk behind the barren branches of old trees, inching toward the horizon, anxious for night.

Night fell cold, hard, and fast.

Hazel had spent most of the day cleaning, and by the time I returned home around four-thirty with groceries, the first boxloads of junk were being hauled away by a Goodwill truck, little more than junk itself. Its brittle gears gnashed as the van lurched from the curb and trundled down the street, pausing to belch exhaust at the foot of a hill.

Parker came home from the *Register* shortly after five, offering to help Hazel in the kitchen. It was a simple supper, the main dish being pot roast, which required a lot of cooking but little attention. Joey and Thad arrived sometime after six, keeping me company in the dining room as I set the table. Hazel had agreed to join us, totaling five. I deliberately miscounted, setting a sixth place for Sheriff Pierce, unsure of when he would arrive. When Thad pointed out the extra setting, I shrugged, telling him, "Let's just leave it. The table looks more balanced with an even number."

With the pot roast tucked in the oven, Parker entered the dining room and offered to build a fire. We all agreed that it was a fine suggestion for the cold night, and he set about loading the fireplace with logs and kindling. Propped next to the set of fire tools was one of the king-things, an artichoke finial from the third-floor banister, brought downstairs by Roxanne the previous week, after my arrest. She had studied this duplicate of the makeshift bludgeon while preparing notes for my defense—a precaution that proved unnecessary, once she convinced the district attorney that I'd been framed. Parker now lifted the wooden finial from where she had left it, near the fire, and laid it along the mantel.

Hazel began delivering serving dishes from the kitchen, and I asked everyone, "Shall I open some wine?" Thad's vote, which didn't count, was enthusiastically positive, but both Hazel and Joey declined, having felt no craving for wine since New Year's. Parker and I weren't inclined to commit to a whole bottle that evening, so we opted instead for cocktails, which he offered to fetch from the bar cart in the living room.

At a few minutes past seven, we all sat down to dinner. The meal was excellent, in its homey way, and the conversation pleasant enough, in light of our recent tribulations. All told, it would have been a thoroughly enjoyable evening, had it not been for my knowledge that Dumont County's chief law enforcer would soon be paying an official visit.

I tried to keep this thought at bay as Thad described life

with Miriam Westerman. He hated his new custody situation, of course, but made an effort to lighten the topic with tales of Miriam's at-home foibles. Our snickering at these insights erupted into full-blown laughter when we learned that the charismatic founder of Fem-Snach flushed her toilet but once a day—a practice based on ecological grounds.

Engrossed in this discussion, we sailed through our main course, and Hazel was ready to clear the table for dessert. But Sheriff Pierce had not yet arrived, and I worried that we might finish too early, that he would miss his opportunity to question Joey. "It's only seven-thirty," I told the others. "What's the rush? Let's just enjoy each other's company for a while. Dessert can wait."

Everyone agreed that there was no hurry, but in verbalizing this observation, we seemed to kill the easy spontaneity of our patter. Even the Fem-Snach jokes lost their punch. Finally, silence reigned, save for the idle scraping of Joey's fork on his empty plate. In search of something to say, Hazel raised the one topic we had all been trying to avoid.

"Poor Suzie was always so quick with the banter. She was never at a loss for words. Oh, Thad"—Hazel was getting weepy—"how we miss your loving mother."

"I know, Hazel," he told her quietly. "I know."

Joey scraped his plate a bit louder. He pretended not to listen, but his blanched fingers gripped the fork with mounting impatience.

Hazel persisted, "There's no justice. Suzie's gone, killed, and no one seems to care. Nothing's been done."

Parker told her gently, "That's not true, Hazel. Everyone in town cares deeply about what happened to Suzanne. The investigation is bound to identify the culprit soon. We've all been working on . . ."

Parker's words were interrupted by the slam of Joey's fork on his plate. "That's *enough*," Joey blurted. "I've told you before. I'm getting sick and tired of all the fuss and worry over Suzie. She's *dead*. Stop *talking* about her."

Dingdong—saved by the bell. "Now, who could that be?"

I wondered aloud, checking my watch. Excusing myself from the table, I left the room and rushed to the door.

It was Pierce. "I was worried you weren't coming," I told him as I let him in and took his coat, tossing it on the nearest chair. "Joey was starting to get dicey."

I led Pierce back toward the dining room, and as we walked through the portal, I told everyone, "Look who's here." Turning to Pierce, I suggested, "There's an extra place at the table, Doug. Why don't you join us for dessert?"

"Great. Thanks," he said, sitting. "Just coffee, though."

I also sat. Hazel rose, starting to clear dishes. Noticing that the fire was dying, Parker got up, ready to tend it. Crossing from the table, he said to Pierce, "We were just assuring Hazel that your department has spared no effort in trying to solve Suzanne's murder. Are you getting close, Sheriff?"

"Very close," Pierce answered flatly, looking from Parker, to me, to Joey. Then he told Hazel, "You can set your mind at ease, Mrs. Healy. Suzanne's killer should soon be brought to justice."

"Thank the Lord," she said, hands aflutter. "I haven't slept decent in nearly three weeks." Loading her arms with dishes, she left for the kitchen.

Wide-eyed with curiosity, Thad asked bluntly, "Who *is* it, Sheriff Pierce?"

Pierce shook his head. "Can't say yet." He smiled. "Improper procedure."

Thad nodded, mummed. Then his face brightened again. "Can you at least tell us—was the weapon really the king-thing?"

"Oh, yes, definitely," said Pierce. "The tests were conclusive."

Joey was tapping his plate again with his fork, but Hazel reappeared from the kitchen for more dishes, taking his.

Rising, I asked, "Can you imagine?" Moving to the fireplace, I lifted from the mantel the finial that had been brought downstairs by Roxanne, displaying it to the others in the room. "What could drive a person to such utter brutality?" I hefted the club. The mere feel of it in my hand sent a shiver through me—I couldn't fathom the thought process that could compel a human being to smash the heavy wooden artichoke into another human's skull.

Parker was kneeling next to me at the hearth, stoking the fire. He looked up, telling me, "There are only a handful of classic motives for murder—greed and revenge topping the list. Take your pick."

Greed or revenge, I thought. Did either motive apply to Joey?

His fork and plate now missing, Joey smashed his hand on the table. "I said before, that's *enough*. Suzie's *dead*. I'm sick of hearing about it. If everybody doesn't stop talking about her, I'll . . . I'll . . . *do* something, and this time, I'll die!"

Pierce seemed taken aback by his statement, but the rest of us were merely exasperated by this ploy. Hazel lugged another pile of dishes toward the kitchen, turning to tell Joey, "You behave now." Thad got up and moved behind his uncle, preparing to administer the surefire tickle remedy. Parker stood in front of the fire, brushing grime from his hands while calmly admonishing Joey, "No more threats about turning blue." As for me, something was now troubling me, something in the back of my mind, and, pondering this, I said nothing. Besides, I had seen these scenes of Joey's before, and there was little I could add. So I continued to study the king-thing, taking an experimental swipe at an imagined victim on the floor, grimacing at the gross ruthlessness of the act.

Suddenly Joey recoiled from the table with horror, pointing toward the fireplace. "HEY!" he cried. "It was you all along, Mark! *You* killed Suzie!"

I didn't think my brandishing of the king-thing had been sufficiently dramatic to inspire such a wild reaction, but then, I hadn't seen it through Joey's eyes. Did he really think I had killed his sister? Or was he gaming, making audacious accusations in hopes of deflecting suspicion from himself? Was he that clever?

We all huddled around him trying to calm him down. Thad told him, "Mark wouldn't do that, Uncle Joey. I'm sure. I know I said those horrible things on Christmas, but I was wrong." Pierce assured him, "We have no reason whatever to suspect Mark of this crime." Hazel said, "I've got a nice cake for dessert—you'd like that, wouldn't you, Joey?" Parker offered, "Let me take him up to his old bedroom. He might find that soothing. He could rest for a while." And again, I could think of nothing to add to this overlapping litany of mollification, so I said nothing.

Joey's glance darted from face to face as the others spoke to him, about him, through him. Unable to sort their words, he was numbed by a confusion that verged on panic. Noting this, Pierce said to me, "I think Parker's right—maybe Joey should lie down for a while." He checked his watch. "There's no hurry."

The others seemed momentarily puzzled by this comment, but I understood what Pierce meant—he had made up his mind that Joey was to be arrested that night, and he wanted him to be in a calmer state of mind when he was taken away. I nodded my agreement to Pierce. "Parker," I said, "would you like some help?"

He shook his head. "Joey and I are old friends now, aren't we? Let's go upstairs, maybe look at some of your old toys. And if you feel like it, you can have a little snooze on your old bed. Sometimes that's nice after a big dinner."

Rather than taking comfort from Parker's soothing words, Joey now appeared frightened—as if he understood what the sheriff had in store for him. Trembling, he offered no resistance when Parker grasped his forearm, saying, "Come on, Joey. Let's go up to your room." They left together, Joey glancing back at us over his shoulder. Then they disappeared into the front hall, and we heard them slowly mount the stairs.

Hazel, Thad, Pierce, and I breathed a common sigh of relief, but Hazel and Thad mistakenly believed that the evening's high emotions were now solidly behind them. I thought it only fair to prepare them for what lay ahead, so I suggested that we all sit down around the table.

I told them, "Sheriff Pierce didn't just 'happen' to drop by tonight," then continued to explain that Joey was to be arrested for Suzanne's murder.

Hazel reacted, predictably, with sobs, but acknowledged, "He's been acting so mean and spiteful every time we mention dear Suzie's name, I was starting to fear that he'd done something terrible."

Thad asked Pierce, "Will it help Uncle Joey any that he's . . . not quite right? I mean, don't they go easier on sick people?" Thad rubbed his eyes, and I wondered if he was hiding a tear.

Pierce nodded. "Joey's handicap will certainly be a factor in how his case is handled. The district attorney wants a conviction very badly, but I'm sure he'll be satisfied with a lenient sentence—probably some sort of protective custody." We discussed the sequence of events that would likely follow, leading up to Joey's trial. Now and then we paused to comment on the sadness of the situation.

A few minutes later, Parker returned to the dining room. Responding to our collective gaze, he smiled, telling us, "He should be fine."

I asked, "What happened?"

Parker joined us at the table. "We sat on his bed and talked for a while. I did my best to explain that Mark would never have harmed Suzanne. He seemed convinced. Then I got him to lie down. He was calm, so I left. He'll be fine."

Thad told him, "Sheriff Pierce is going to arrest Joey later."

Parker gave a sorry shrug. "I figured. It was starting to add up."

There was a lull in the conversation. Pierce said, "I hate to be a bother, but I never did get that coffee—and I could use it."

We all agreed that coffee would be good, and Hazel flew into action, embarrassed by the lapse in her service. "I might as well bring out dessert, too," she said while going into the kitchen.

Thad said, "I'll give her a hand," leaving through the portal into the front hall.

Laughing, I called after him, "The kitchen's back here."

He paused to explain, "Bathroom first."

Still seated at the table, Pierce and I discussed the whole situation while Parker got up and stirred the fire again—by now it was little more than embers. Perhaps ten minutes later, Thad brought the coffee service in from the kitchen, followed by Hazel, who carried a big fancy layer cake.

In that moment, I was swept over again by the eerie sense of déjà vu that had hung over me since my move to Dumont. Hazel was now thirty-three years older, but she was the same woman, carrying the same cake into the same dining room where I'd sat with the Quatrain family on Christmas Day during my boyhood visit.

We were all talking about lots of stuff—Christmas (naturally), Suzanne's latest crush (boring), my older cousin Mark's first semester of college (very interesting). Then Hazel popped in from the kitchen with this big frosted cake. You'd have thought it was someone's birthday. She asked, "Everybody having dessert? How about you, Mark?"

"Sure!" my cousin and I answered together, and everyone laughed at the confusion. Trying to add to the fun, I said, "It's a good thing my dad's not here. His name was Mark, too."

Joey thought I was hilarious, laughing all the harder. "That *would* be a mix-up."

But no one else laughed, and the table got quiet.

Hazel now set a similar cake on the same table. "Everybody having dessert?"

"Sure," Parker and I answered together, but without much enthusiasm.

Pierce hesitated. "I'm tempted. But just coffee, please."

Thad didn't even need to answer—of course he wanted cake. So Hazel cut the first slice for him, an oversize wedge with sticky buttercream frosting that stretched from the plate like hot mozzarella.

"Half that," I told her.

When we were all served and ready to begin, Hazel set down her fork, telling us, "This has always been Joey's favorite dessert. He calls it 'birthday cake without candles.' It would be a shame for him to miss it, especially tonight. Maybe he'd like to join the party again." She rose from the table. "I'll go up and talk to him. But please, start without us." And she left the dining room, headed upstairs.

Needing no further prompting, Thad tore into the gooey layers of devil's food. Pausing to breathe, he told Pierce, "You really ought to have some, Sheriff. No one makes cake like Hazel."

Parker agreed, "You can't *buy* a cake like this."

I told them, "I'll never forget the first time she served—"

Hazel's screams interrupted this commentary, and the three of us bolted from the table, rushing upstairs.

"My God! Oh, Joey, dear God!" she wailed from the doorway to his bedroom.

We rushed past her and into the cluttered room—Hazel had been there sorting and boxing things most of the day, but the floor was still piled with junk, the desk stacked with everything from shoes and toy cars to notebooks and an old microscope. And there on the bed, atop the same old plaid bedspread that I could recall so vividly from my boyhood visit, lay Joey, faceup in a pool of light from his desk lamp. He was dead. And he was blue.

I gasped at the sight, freezing where I stood. Thad huddled with Hazel, trying to comfort both her and himself. Parker and Pierce approached the body, circling the bed, scratching their chins, dismayed but curious.

Scrunched in Joey's hands was a folded piece of paper, which Pierce carefully removed. Opening it, he scanned the page, shook his head. Then he slowly read it to us: " 'I'm sorry, everybody. I'm sorry, Suzanne. I'm sorry, God. Money is good, but it makes people do bad things. I was wrong to kill my sister. I've gone to be with her, to tell her I apologize. I hope you can all forgive me. Love—' " Pierce extended the note to me, telling all, "It's signed in his hand, 'Joey.' "

Hazel ran howling from the room as I stepped to the bed and took the note from Pierce. I told anyone, "I saw him pass out once as a kid, and I've heard his threats since, but I didn't think it was actually *possible* to . . ."

"There's your proof," said Pierce, pointing to the note.

I held it under the desk lamp, read it, studied it. Sure enough, the childish message was typed on Joey's old Smith-Corona, its letters half black, half red.

Parker stood over the bed, hands on hips, shaking his head, looking down at Joey. "Christ," he muttered, "we should have seen this coming."

Pierce pulled out his notepad, clicked his ballpoint. "It's an open-and-shut suicide."

And it wrapped up the mystery of Suzanne Quatrain's murder.

PART FOUR

Three Hours Ago

Today is Saturday, the fifteenth of January, three days after Joey's death. His funeral is scheduled to begin at one this afternoon.

Three hours prior to it, around ten in the morning, I sat in the third-floor great room of the house on Prairie Street. The upstairs apartment had been built for my father at a time when he never dreamed that he would one day marry and sire a son, at a time when he was my uncle Edwin's lover. The upstairs apartment had awed me with its stately, masculine beauty when I was a boy of nine, at a time when I never dreamed that I would one day own the house and reclaim those lofty quarters as my private domain. The upstairs apartment had served as an abandoned play space for the three Quatrain children, at a time when Suzanne never dreamed that she would one day be raped there by her own brother—she certainly never dreamed that, years later, the attic great room would also be the site of her own grisly death.

I sat there on the long leather sofa under the roof's central peak, mulling the room's history and the bizarre role it had played in my life. For the first time in weeks, my thoughts were clear and I felt no anxiety, content that a deadly mystery had been solved.

The house was quiet. Both Neil and Roxanne had returned to Dumont for the weekend, but they were each busy with other matters away from the house. Parker planned to put in a couple of hours' work at the *Register* before the funeral. And Hazel was resting up for the afternoon's ordeal, tucked away in her quarters downstairs behind the kitchen.

Earlier in the morning, she had rapped quietly at the doorway to the den, where I sat at the partners desk, once shared by my uncle and my father. Entering from the front hall with something tucked under her arm, she told me, "I've nearly finished clearing out the extra bedrooms, Mr. Manning. Goodwill will send the truck back for a last load on Monday."

I laughed softly. "You've really thrown yourself into that project, Hazel. It wasn't all that urgent, but I do appreciate your efficiency."

"It kept my mind busy," she assured me. "The whole business with Joey was just so . . . *terrible*—I've hated to think about it. I was glad to have something to fill my time." She paused, wiping a single tear from behind her glasses. "Anyway," she told me, composing herself, "the effort paid off. Just this morning, I found the three children's baby books, left behind by the Tawkins." Proudly, she took them from under her arm and presented them to me, placing them squarely on my desk.

The top album was that of the oldest Quatrain child, Mark. Overcoming a moment's apprehension, I flipped it open and found the typical hospital footprints, a lock of hair, his first words, early report cards, school pictures. His childhood photos left little doubt that he would grow into the strikingly handsome eighteen-year-old I met as a boy. Another picture, a high-school track-team photo, showed him in silky shorts and singlet—a frozen moment capturing the same evocative body language that he strutted in life, when he awoke obscure passions within me that I would not comprehend till decades later. Turning back to the front of the book, I felt his lock of infant's hair between my fingers. At long last, I touched him— or rather, I touched his relic, a remnant of the golden child who grew into a monster, a murdering rapist who would slay and be slain. In the den, beneath the desk, my groin burned as I became aroused. Dismayed by my reaction, I closed the book, setting it aside.

The next volume was Suzanne's, the last Joey's, each as lovingly compiled as Mark's, but neither having the same effect on me.

"I hope you don't mind," Hazel talked while I studied the

albums, "but I've already taken the liberty of looking through them. I wanted to have a little visit with the past—happier times, you know—but sad to say, the memories were just too painful. Who'd think? All three Quatrain children, all dead, each a tragic end." She was well into her sniffles again.

I looked up at her. "Thank you for finding them, Hazel. I'll hold on to them for a while. Someday, they should probably go to Thad."

"My thoughts exactly, Mr. Manning. When I began to search in earnest for the books on Wednesday, I had assumed they would go to Joey . . ." More tears.

It was a bitter irony indeed. Not only was Joey now dead, but these were the very books that Suzanne had been looking for in the loft when Joey clubbed her. Why, though, were they so important to her? Were they important to Joey as well? Or was the timing of the murder a mere coincidence? It didn't make sense.

I told Hazel, "You've been through a lot lately—we all have. The funeral's not till one. Why don't you get some rest? You'll feel better."

She mustered a smile. "Thank you. I'd like that." She began to leave the room.

"Oh, Hazel?" I thought of something I'd been meaning to ask.

She turned in the doorway. "Yes, sir?"

"I realize that you've been moving things around upstairs in order to, well . . . dig through everything. But I was up there last night looking for Joey's old typewriter, and I couldn't find it. Do you recall where you put it?"

The color drained from her face. "Good heavens, Mr. Manning, I had no idea. Was it—is it valuable?"

"I doubt it," I answered with a laugh. "No, I was just curious about something. Thought I'd have another look at it." I could tell from the pallor of her face that my curiosity was moot. Saving her the agony of explaining, I said, "It's all right if you threw it out, though—I told you to use your own judgment."

"I'm so *sorry*, Mr. Manning. I just assumed it was worthless. It was trucked away with the first load of junk on Wednesday."

"That's perfectly all right," I assured her. "It wasn't important. Now go get some rest." Flapping my hands, I shooed her from the room, and she retreated down the hall toward the kitchen.

Setting the stack of baby books to one side of my desk, I rearranged the papers I'd been working on before Hazel's arrival. Uncapping my pen, I crossed another item off the checklist I'd prepared for Monday's transition at the *Register*. Two days from now, I'd be sitting at Barret Logan's desk, and . . .

Wednesday? Not possible, I thought. I'd seen the Goodwill truck haul away that first load of junk on Wednesday afternoon. That same night, Joey died, using the typewriter to write his suicide note. Certainly, Hazel was mistaken—the typewriter *had* to have been in the house on Wednesday night.

I rose from the desk and crossed to the door, intending to dash down the hall, fetch Hazel, and question her on this point. Stopping in the doorway, though, I had another thought, walked back to my desk, and fished the little brass key from the ashtray of paper clips. Unlocking the door to the credenza, I slid out the box of dossiers and plopped it on the floor.

I fingered past the first bundle of files, labeled SUSPICIOUS, fingered past the large middle bundle, INCONCLUSIVE, then grabbed the last bundle, ABOVE SUSPICION, the group of Vietnam veterans' dossiers that I had not yet bothered to study. Something told me I had ignored these too long.

There weren't many, less than a dozen, so I fanned them out upon my desk so that I could scan the names of the men profiled in them. At once, I recognized a name. Flipping to the last page of the folder, I read why the investigator had concluded that the subject was "above suspicion." Glancing over the remainder of the files, I recognized another name, then checked inside to see why that subject was also "above suspicion."

I paused as a sense of serenity and closure washed over me. Yes, the mystery of Suzanne's murder had indeed been solved. The case was indeed closed. I needed to make one quick phone call; then I could at last put the tragedies of the last three weeks behind me.

Gathering the files, I returned them to the box, returned the box to the credenza, and locked the cabinet door. Then I placed that one quick call.

Half an hour later, around ten in the morning, I sat in the third-floor great room on the leather sofa under the roof's central peak, mulling the room's history and the bizarre role it had played in my life. My thoughts were clear and I felt no anxiety, content that a deadly mystery had been solved.

The house was quiet. Both Neil and Roxanne had returned to Dumont for the weekend, but they were each busy with other matters away from the house. Parker planned to put in a couple of hours' work at the *Register* before the funeral. And Hazel was resting up for the afternoon's ordeal, tucked away in her quarters downstairs behind the kitchen.

Checking my watch—it was three hours till Joey's funeral— I rose from the sofa and glanced about the loft. Crossing from the center of the room toward the front wall, I stopped at the banister and peered out through the expansive half-circle of glass. The landscape of the town stretched frozen and white to the horizon, motionless as an old oil painting, save for the trekking of a few cars in the distance, the wisping of smoke from chimneys.

There near the banister stood the large worktable that had once served as my father's desk. I had brought some things up from the den with me that morning, and I organized them on the table, making tidy piles—what Neil would call "an artful arrangement." Squatting to check under the desk, I confirmed that the little wicker wastebasket was empty, newly lined with a fresh plastic bag. Satisfied, I stood again, scrutinizing the desktop. I moved a large magazine, an issue of *Wine Spectator*, placing it atop a small stack of books.

Then I heard the sound of a door, followed by footfalls, downstairs in the bedroom hall. "Hazel?" I called down the stairwell. "Is that you?"

"No, Mark," answered Parker's voice, "it's me."

"I thought you went downtown to the office."

He came to the landing and looked up the stairs at me. "Just on my way."

"As long as you're still here, can you stay a few minutes? You'll want to hear this. Come on up."

"You're the boss," he said, climbing the stairs by twos. Arriving in the great room, he asked, "What's happening?"

I crossed to the center of the room, motioning for him to follow. Sitting at the end of the sofa, I gestured for him to take the adjacent armchair. Leaning close—my knee touched his—I looked him in the eye to tell him, "Joey didn't kill Suzanne."

"*What?*" He flumped back in the chair, spreading his legs. "Mark, Sheriff Pierce said it was open-and-shut. The murder is solved; the killer has taken his own life; it's over."

"No, listen," I told him, leaning closer, placing my hand on his knee. "This morning I finally got around to checking the last of Suzanne's dossiers. I hadn't bothered to study them earlier because they were judged 'above suspicion.' I wish to God I'd taken you up on your offer to read them a few days ago."

"Wednesday morning," recalled Parker, "but then Sheriff Pierce arrived."

"Right. This morning Hazel mentioned something that made me suddenly curious, so I got back into the files." I grinned. "Parker, I hit pay dirt. Guess who is not only a Vietnam veteran, but also a survivor of the same ambush that supposedly killed Mark Quatrain."

Parker seemed stunned by my words. He didn't offer a guess.

I told him, "Allan Addams, the credit guy at Quatro. Joey mentioned him."

Parker shook his head, confused. "Addams sounded promising to me, too, but Joey said he couldn't possibly be his brother."

I shrugged. "You know Joey—sometimes his judgment left something to be desired. In any event, Parker, your hunch

paid off. Your 'brother from the grave' theory was dead-on."
Laughing, I added, "In the future, your views will have considerably more weight with me."

Parker leaned forward, smiling. Resting his hand on mine, he told me softly, "My view all along, Mark, has been that you and I belong together. I'm content to play second fiddle, though—this is all I've ever wanted, just to be here for you."

"And I'm here for you." With that, I closed the few inches that still separated our faces. Touching my lips to his, I kissed him.

"Wow." His reaction was more surprised than impassioned. "Where'd that come from?"

I patted his face, then sat back on the sofa. Exhaling a sigh, I explained, "My 'arrangement' with Neil hasn't been working very well—not only the back-and-forth weekends (that failure has been mine alone), but also the commitment, the will to make it stick. Our lives are different now. Since moving up here, I've felt a million miles from him, even when he's here."

Parker asked me, "Just what are you saying?"

I rose from the sofa and walked toward the window. From behind his chair, without looking at him, I told him, "I'm saying that this career move has done serious damage to my relationship with Neil. It's the last thing I wanted to happen, but it happened. I'm also saying that I'm both lucky and grateful that you've entered my life, Parker. On Christmas night, when you told me you loved me, I was shocked. I had never thought of you in any context other than that of my managing editor. But I have to be honest with you: From the moment I met you, that Saturday afternoon at the loft in Chicago, I found you incredibly attractive."

Turning, I saw that he had risen from his chair and stood listening to me, arms crossed in astonishment. I continued. "The past few weeks have been hell for all of us, but you were there for me the whole time, making good on your word to see me through it. What you didn't suspect was that, with the passing weeks, I'd grown increasingly frustrated by the feelings I had for you. There were countless times when I just wanted to reach over and touch you, Parker. I've had dreams about you. And now that the mess and uncertainty of Suzanne's murder is finally behind us, I can breathe, I can think straight. And what I think is this: If you're still interested, I think we could build a future together."

"Mark," he stammered, smiling, crossing a few steps toward me, "this is so . . . well, *unexpected*. Of course I want to plan a future with you, but we have to give careful consideration to the logistics."

"Logistics?" I took a step toward him. "There's nothing complicated about it. You have drives, I have drives. As to the where and the when—what's wrong with right here, right now?"

"Now?"

I stepped to him and held both his shoulders. "Why not? Hazel is resting. Otherwise the house is empty. It's hours till the funeral"—I smirked—"and we only need a few minutes." I took his hand and led him the few steps to the patch of open floor between the central seating area and the desk near the banister. Then I held him close, resting my head next to his, my crotch next to his. I was highly aroused by the feel of him.

Sensing this, he laughed. "I guess you *have* had ideas."

I held his head in my hands and kissed him, feeling the scratch of his trim beard on my face. Then, lowering my hands behind his back, I cupped his ass, feeling its taut muscles through the smooth layer of khaki. Yanking him toward me, I huffed when I heard the clank of our belt buckles. I said into his ear, "Kneel in front of me."

Not sure where I was heading with this, he hesitated, but complied.

Running my fingers through his wavy hair, I pressed his head to my groin. His breath warmed my crotch as I tugged at his curls. Reliving the scene from my dream, I asked, "Do you want me to put my cock in your hair?"

He looked up at me for a moment. "Not particularly."

Winding his hair around my fingers, I pulled harder. There and then, I thought I might come, still zipped.

"*Hey,*" he yelped, not at all the reaction he'd had in my

dream. But just as in my dream, I found that my fingers were now covered with hair I'd pulled loose.

"Sorry," I muttered. "Got carried away." And I moved to the desk for a moment, whisking my hands clean over the wastebasket. Then I returned to him, kneeling with him, facing him. Pressing my mouth to his again, I tongued him deeply, but found his participation disappointingly passive. So I slid my mouth to his ear, telling him, "Feel my cock." His hands groped at my pants, confirming that I was fully erect. Panting into his ear, I waited for him to unzip me, but he just kept rubbing. Lowering my own hands to his waist, I fingered his belt buckle, felt his ass once more, then groped his crotch. He was flaccid.

I pulled back from him, sitting on my heels. With a quizzical look and a tentative smile, I asked, "What's the matter, Parker? I thought this was all you've ever wanted."

He also sat back, mirroring my position. With our knees pressed to each other's, he shook his head, laughing lamely. "Sorry, Mark," he told me, "but it's just not in me—I mean, not right now." Sheepishly, he added, "You see, the house was quiet this morning, and we *have* been under lots of pressure lately, so I . . . just jacked off, not thirty minutes ago." With a self-deprecating smirk, he reminded me, "I'm fifty-one, pal. I'm not as quick as I used to be."

Extending my hand, I rested a fingertip on his lips, shushing his apology. "No, Parker," I told him tenderly, "you're not hard because you're not gay."

"Mark!" he countered, astounded. "I'm *sorry* I wasn't able to get it up, but that doesn't mean . . ."

"No, Parker," I again shushed him, fingers to his lips, "you're not gay—Glee Savage was right. And you're not Parker Trent. You're Mark Quatrain, the brother from the grave."

His mouth drooped open. Lowering my hand, I dragged the tip of my middle finger over the edge of his teeth and pulled a strand of spit from his lip.

Slapping both hands on his legs, he rose to his feet, telling me, "For Christ's sake, Mark, don't be nuts. You're jumping to ridiculous conclusions, *libelous* conclusions—"

I stood, interrupting him. "I'm nine years younger than you, Parker. I was nine years younger than Mark Quatrain."

He shot back, "There were *lots* of us born that year, Mark. The baby boom was revving up, in case you forgot."

"Mark Quatrain was an honors English major, and you're a top-notch editor. Mark was a varsity swimmer and track star, and you're one hell of a runner. Do you still keep up with the swimming, Parker?" Though convinced of his identity, I could not bring myself to address him as Mark—I could not allow the memories of my older cousin to be tainted by what he had become.

He stepped toward the center of the room and perched on the back of one of the big leather chairs, facing me. In a composed, rational tone, he told me, "Those are mere coincidences. You're far too good a journalist to draw such weighty conclusions from such slim circumstances." Mustering a laugh, he added, "As your managing editor, Mark, I have to tell you, I'm disappointed."

"Good"—I nodded—"you should be skeptical. You should demand hard evidence." I strolled toward the front of the room and perched on the banister, facing him. Separated by some twenty feet, I told him, "There's far more to this than coincidence."

"Such as?"

I shrugged. "Just for starters, I felt that I already knew you from the moment you arrived for your interview at the loft in Chicago. Why? Because you reminded me of my cousin Mark—the way you move, your body language." I didn't want to get more specific on this point. Why give him the satisfaction of praising his butt? Why tell him that we were wearing identical pants that morning because he had inspired a lifelong fixation within me thirty-three years earlier? Why tell him about the erotic charge I felt when he mussed my hair the day we ran together, resting at the park pavilion?

"*Body* language"—Parker harrumphed—"that's *evidence?* You undoubtedly made the association because you were preparing to return to Dumont and your boyhood visit was heavily on your mind. But you raise a good point. If I were really Mark Quatrain, wouldn't someone here *recognize* me?"

"Well," I acknowledged, "let's think about that. You'd been gone more than thirty years. Obviously, you're older now, your hair has thinned, you've grown a beard. So the way I figure it, there were only four of us left who stood a chance of recognizing you: myself, Hazel, Suzanne, and Joey.

"As for myself, I've already said that I *did* recognize you, sort of, at least subconsciously. I even had a dream in which you and Mark Quatrain switched places. It just took a while for the true recognition to bubble to the surface.

"Hazel wouldn't be likely to recognize you—she's half blind. She didn't recognize *me* when I arrived in Dumont before Christmas.

"As for Suzanne, when you 'met' her for the first time on Christmas Day, it struck me that you were uncharacteristically reticent about being introduced. You were all bundled up in a muffler, knit cap, and steamy sunglasses, which you took your time removing downstairs in the front hall. When there was no sign of recognition from Suzanne, you breathed easier, but an hour later, she was dead.

"Then there's Joey. He often complained that none of us took him seriously, but we should have. He's the key to all this, isn't he, Parker? He recognized you, and he said so plainly, but I wasn't smart enough to take him at his word."

Parker threw his hands in the air. "Whoa, Mark. You weren't making sense before, but now you're *really* sounding nuts. Joey? What are you talking about?"

I stepped a few feet closer, moving from the banister to sit on the edge of the worktable. I began, "From the moment Joey's body was discovered, his 'suicide' troubled me for several reasons:

"First, I don't think it's possible, even for a determined adult, to make good on a child's threat to die from holding his breath.

"Second, Joey was staunchly—I daresay childishly—Catholic, believing that suicide is a sin. He mentioned it at lunch one day, and you weren't there.

"Third, his generic-sounding suicide note just didn't make sense. The day before he died, he wanted to make a huge donation to charity—he wasn't greedy. But he did harbor a lifelong resentment toward Suzanne, and if he had killed her, *that* would have been his motive, not money, as suggested by the note.

"Fourth—and this gets to the heart of it—I was troubled by something you said, Parker. In fact, you said it twice. I couldn't quite put my finger on what was wrong, but Joey sure did. A couple of weeks ago, I took Joey and Thad to lunch at the First Avenue Grill. Joey made a scene there, and Thad had to snap him out of it. After lunch, I met you at the *Register*, mentioned Joey's snit, and you made a joking reference to 'his threats about turning blue.' Then, this last Wednesday night in the dining room, Joey threatened, 'I'll *do* something, and this time I'll die.' We all tried to calm him down, and you told him, 'No more threats about turning blue.' The point is: Parker Trent never heard Joey talk about turning blue, but Mark Quatrain did, many times, as a child. Realizing this, Joey recoiled from the dining-room table, pointing toward the fireplace, shouting, 'It was you all along, Mark. You killed Suzie.' I was standing at the fireplace with a king-thing, and you were right there next to me on the hearth. Joey wasn't talking to *me*, Parker; he was unmasking *you*. You knew it. You knew you had to act. And you acted fast."

Listening to all this, Parker was no longer taking my accusations so glibly. Pacing behind the sofa, he asked, "And then what did I supposedly do?" His tone now had a distinctly testy edge.

I remained seated on the edge of the desk, idly swinging one foot as I explained, "You took Joey upstairs to his bedroom on the pretext of calming him down. You'd already made up your mind to stage his 'suicide' at some point, bringing the investigation to an end and taking the focus off the 'brother from the grave' theory that you yourself had promoted—very clever, by the way, very bold of you. So you had prepared a generic suicide note on Joey's old typewriter, making the wrong guess as to his most logical motive. You knew where the machine was, and you had access to it anytime since Christmas. What you *didn't* know was that Hazel threw the typewriter out with a load of junk on Wednesday afternoon, hours before Joey could have used it to write his note. So you took him upstairs that night, and you could've gotten him to sign the note on some pretext, and then you could've suffocated him, and then you could've placed the note in his hands."

" 'Could've, could've'." He stepped to within six feet of me. "That's still a hell of a lot of speculation, Mark. Besides"— he smiled with a sense of relief as something dawned on him— "what about Allan Addams? Only minutes ago, you told me Suzanne had a dossier on him."

Nodding, I reminded him, "Yes, Allan Addams was a survivor of the ambush that supposedly killed Mark Quatrain, but Suzanne's investigator deemed Addams to be 'above suspicion' as an alias for Mark Quatrain."

"It all fits, though," Parker insisted. "He came to Quatro shortly after Edwin's death. He asked Joey about the family all the time . . ."

"Allan Addams is black," I told him. "The investigator, like Joey, easily concluded that Addams never had a former life as Mark Quatrain."

Parker reacted with a blank expression, but a ripple of his bearded cheek betrayed the clenching of his jaw.

I lifted a file from the tabletop where I sat. "I discovered another dossier of interest this morning. Here." I stood, handing it to him. "A summary of the life of Parker Trent since his honorable discharge from Vietnam following a gruesome massacre that he survived. Mr. Trent has established a successful career as a newspaper editor, though it seems he's done a lot of job-hopping, at least until about three years ago—about the time of Edwin Quatrain's death—when he began his most recent stint as editor of the *Milwaukee Triangle*. The report concludes that Mr. Trent is logically 'above suspicion' of the rape and murder of a Vietnamese girl because he is gay."

Parker tossed the file on the desk—there was nothing of news to him in it. "Look," he told me calmly, "it's time to level about this." He tapped the folder. "Yes, I was there. Yes, it was awful. Yes, I committed a lie of omission in not telling you this background, because yes, I came to fear that it might incriminate me as an impostor who had a motive to kill. But I'm not Mark Quatrain. I couldn't be." He tapped the report again. "I'm gay."

I crossed my arms, shook my head. "You've been *posing* as gay, and you've been doing it for three years, since the time when you first got wind that Suzanne suspected you were alive. Glee sensed that you were straight from the day she met you— she had vibes that you were flirting with her. Then I saw that kiss you gave her on New Year's Eve—'transference' indeed. And now I hear that you've made a *date* with Glee for Monday night—what the hell's that about? With my own suspicions aroused, I knew there was one way to determine conclusively which way you swing. Parker, I know what makes men tick, and, believe me, there's no way you could have survived that grope session without a hard-on if you were gay. Hence, the surprise 'seduction.' I had to know."

"You don't know *shit,*" he said, spitting the words. It was the first time he freely vented anger toward me. "If you know so damn much, get to the bottom line and tell me why I'd kill Suzanne—on Christmas Day, an hour after meeting her, in a crowded house." He folded his arms.

Hooking my hands in my pockets, I strolled a few paces in thought, recapping, "Suzanne had discovered the possibility that her brother Mark was still alive, and if he was, she was hell-bent on finding him and bringing him to justice for the murder of the Vietnamese girl—motivated largely, no doubt, by revenge for her own incestuous rape. So it's clear enough why Mark would want Suzanne dead. But what hasn't been clear to me, until today, is why the murder occurred when and where it did."

Pacing back to Parker at the desk, I explained, "When you 'met' Suzanne on that Christmas afternoon, she chatted with you about her research project, mentioning an interest in DNA, and you offered your help. Later, she came up here to the great room to see if she could 'find something,' and we surmised that she was looking for baby books. But her search wasn't

motivated by sentiment, was it, Parker? She was after something specific, and you would risk anything to prevent her from
finding it. So you joined her up here, perhaps pretending to
help her in the search, waiting for the opportunity to smash
the life out of her skull with one of these"—I rested my hand
atop one of the banister's artichoke finials—"a king-thing, a
handy makeshift bludgeon whose existence would be known
only to someone who grew up in this house. A fire was in full
blaze only feet from where she fell, and you could easily have
burned the weapon, but, instead, you kept it, planting it in the
trunk of my car. Your purpose was not to cast serious suspicion
on me—it was an obvious, inept frame-up. No, the point was
to help build the case against Joey (the king-things were *his*
toys), so that everything would fall into place when he confessed
to the crime through his suicide note."

Parker eyed me with a steely gaze throughout this, clenching
one fist, gripping the table's edge with his other hand. "You
seem to have missed the point," he reminded me. "What was
she after? What was so important that I couldn't let her find
it?"

I stepped to within inches of him at the table. I slid aside
the copy of *Wine Spectator*, revealing the stack of three baby
books. "She was looking for this," I told him, opening the
cover of the top album. "A lock of baby's hair, Mark Quatrain's.
She knew that the DNA in a single strand could be used to
provide positive identification of someone now posing to be
someone else—someone who was already under investigation
as one of the subjects of her dossiers. Can there be any doubt
that the strands of your hair that I collected this morning will
match this baby's lock?" With my foot, I slid the wastebasket
from under the desk. Its plastic bag held a generous sample
of his hair. "Parker Trent," I said, "I accuse you of hiding
your true identity as Mark Quatrain. Far worse, I accuse you
of the murders of three people—the girl in Vietnam, your
sister Suzanne, and your brother Joey."

There was a moment's silence. Then, with our faces still
only inches apart, he said flatly, "You smart-ass cock-sucking
queer."

"Watch your language, Parker."

"All these years," he said, turning away from me, his tone suddenly pensive, "I've lain low, moving from job to job, just so no one could really get to know me, fearing that one day Suzanne might figure out that I was still around. And sure enough, right after Dad died, she began her investigation."

Turning, he explained to me, "I'd been so attuned to the possibility, I was smart enough to smell the investigation when it got near. So, yes, I landed the gay job in Milwaukee as a means of putting myself above suspicion. But I could tell that Suzanne was on my trail, and it was no longer sufficient to lie low—I had to take more aggressive action. Coincidentally, while I was weighing my options, it became public knowledge that you were moving to Dumont to take over as publisher here, and I saw the spark of opportunity. My plan, which succeeded, was to get myself hired by you. That would allow me to keep tabs on the whole situation from very close range, and I could take decisive action if Suzanne got too close to the truth."

He stepped toward me at the desk. "Then what happened? On Christmas Day, within minutes of meeting me, she started yapping about DNA, and within the hour she was tearing up this place in search of baby books. So I followed her up here, offered to help, asked her why the albums were so important. She said she was nostalgic—she *lied* to me—dragging a chair to the bookcase so she could search the upper shelves. Kneeling by her chair, I asked her to describe the books as I searched the lower cabinet. While describing them, her tone of voice turned wary—as if she suspected me of looking up her skirt. Which of course I was."

Leering, Parker sat proudly on the edge of the desk. He asked me, "You just don't get it, do you? You have no idea what kind of power a beautiful woman can have over a man— a *straight* man, a *real* man. And believe me, Suzanne had that power. Victim, indeed! She got exactly what she wanted on that Christmas morning as a girl. I did, too," he gloated, instinctively rubbing his crotch, which now displayed a hefty lump. "It was the most rapturous fuck of my life. And it would never be that good again."

Then his eyes flashed toward me with another recollection. "That whore in 'Nam cried rape, just as poor little 'abused' Suzie had. That whore in 'Nam paid the price for her lies; now it was Suzie's turn. And she never knew what hit her— she never figured out that the 'gay' editor from Milwaukee shared her intense interest in those baby books."

He tapped the stack of three albums on the desk. "*These* baby books." He fixed me in his stare. "I couldn't let her have these, Mark. Obviously, I can't let *you* have them either."

Then, with one deft move, he sidestepped to the banister and yanked a king-thing from its newel post, wielding it in the air, gripping the dowel with white fingers. I moved to wrest it from him, but a kick to my shin sent me sprawling. He straddled me, pinning my shoulder with one of his feet, practicing a golf swing with the finial, taking aim at my head. Sneering, he asked, "Any last words, fag?"

"Doug?" I said. "I hope to God you're there."

Doug Pierce said, "Freeze, Parker."

Parker didn't even turn to see Sheriff Pierce emerge from the shadows of a bookcase at the far side of the room. Instead, he spat on my face. "You *son* of a bitch." And the artichoke finial began arcing toward my ear.

The single shot caught Parker in the hip, sufficient to throw off his balance and ruin his swing. Still, I barely managed to roll out of harm's way when he dropped the king-thing, which crashed next to me on the floor. Then Parker himself dropped, falling on top of me, bleeding. Snarling some unintelligible epithet, he tried to grab me by the neck. But Pierce had rushed forward, and before I was able to scramble to my feet, Parker's hands were cuffed behind his back, with Pierce's knee planted between his shoulders.

Pierce looked up at me as I stood, telling me, "Glad you found time to make that one quick phone call."

"And *you* thought it wouldn't work." I looked myself over, checking for blood. My khakis were in bad shape, but Parker's were worse—they had a hole in them.

Pierce stood, hoisting Parker to his feet. Parker whined and complained, bleeding (the rug was probably a goner, as well as the pants), while Pierce told me, "Jeez, Mark, that groping business got a little steamy. I don't mind telling you, I was starting to sweat."

I laughed. "Anything for a story, Doug. *Anything* for a story."

EPILOGUE

This Afternoon

My new life seems bogged by funerals, peppered by the last rites of passage into some vast unknown. The mourners who surround me are watching the spectacle of grief played out at the altar. With a numb sense of detachment, they mime the prescribed motions and mouth psalms about sheep, lost in their memories, as I am lost in mine.

The priest drones through the script of his fill-in-the-blanks sermon, eulogizing "our brother Joseph, an allegiant child of the church." Though Father Nicholas Winter was prepared to fight in court for the right to bury Suzanne Quatrain from Saint Cecille's, he had taken a distinctly different view of her brother Joey's funeral. The wealthy and powerful Suzanne, remember, had fluffed off the church at sixteen, sneaking out of state for an abortion, while Joey had remained steadfast in his faith till his death this week at forty-three. The problem, of course, was that Joey had confessed to murdering Suzanne. And a more serious wrinkle, at least in the eyes of the good Father Nick, was that Joey had taken his own life, blackening his soul with a mortal sin that sent him straight to hell, case closed. Compounding the priest's dilemma was the historical fact that the Quatrain family had practically built this parish—in fact, they did finance the most recent addition to Saint Cecille School, and he prayed nightly that young Thad Quatrain would one day be inclined to carry on the family tradition. So accommodations had to be made. Meeting with Thad and me on Thursday, the day after Joey's death, Father Winter condescended to take on the unsavory duties of officiating at Joey's funeral, but insisted that the service was to be quick and simple—"No choir, no public spectacle, just get him buried, and get it over."

I really didn't care, but I knew that Joey would have, and I was appalled at the priest's arrogant behavior in the presence of Thad. It was a stupid move politically—the kid would surely remember this incident in future years when the priest or his successor came begging for loot—but an even more offensive aspect of the priest's pompous air of infallibility was that it *hurt* Thad. The boy truly loved his uncle Joey, looking past his simplemindedness and focusing on his kindness and affection, thinking of him as a friend and a peer. The last thing Thad needed to hear was that his uncle had committed two truly unforgivable sins, but that's exactly what the priest told us that day.

Now, of course, Father Winter views Joey's passing in a different light entirely. Word has spread quickly since Parker's arrest this morning, and everyone understands that Joey did not bludgeon his now-sainted sister, that, in fact, they were both victims of their evil older brother, who was thought, till today, to have been heaven-sent some thirty years ago. Ah, the fickle ebb of eternal rewards—easy come, easy go.

If the priest is at all confused by this turn of events, he doesn't show it. To the contrary, he seems positively giddy that the man whom he eulogizes was murdered—a tragic though passive demise thoroughly acceptable to God, while suicide is not. "This gentle soul was a gift to our community," Father Winter preaches, "inspiring us with the childlike quality of his faith. Clearly, he was put on this earth to walk among us as an example to all mankind. Let us rejoice in our knowledge that . . ." To hear him gush and babble, you'd think it was Christmas.

I recognize, though, that some of the man's words carry the ring of truth. Joey *was* a good person, and I do mourn his passing. During these few weeks since my move to Dumont, I came to know Joey quite well, and I wish I could know him better still. I'll miss him.

When I first came to this town, during my visit as a boy, it was Joey who glommed on to me and claimed me as his friend.

In fact, I saw too much of Joey during that visit, prompting me to seek refuge upstairs on Prairie Street, where I honed my early skills as a writer.

I hardly saw Suzanne at all during that trip, and, as adults, we spent only an hour or so in each other's company on Christmas Day. Now I'm executor of her vast estate, preparing for a custody battle so that I might serve as father to her son.

As for my oldest cousin, Mark, I didn't see much of him during that long-ago visit, but his impact on my life was immeasurable. For starters, we shared the same name, and our namesake was the same man, my father. But my shared history with Mark Quatrain truly began the moment I met him, when he mussed my hair and aroused within me boyish confusions that would later flower into adult passions. He has lived in my memory, adorned my dreams. And three hours ago, he brought our shared history to a close when he tried to kill me.

Father Winter preaches on, cribbing many of the same sentiments he used to bury Suzanne twelve days ago. Those words, however, are the only similarity between her funeral and Joey's. According to the priest's plan, there is no choir today, no public spectacle—this is a far cry from the royal send-off accorded Suzanne, a stripped-down service for her younger, half-wit brother who supposedly died in shame and sin. When the priest learned the truth, only an hour remained before the unpublicized service was to begin, and it was too late to change plans. So, although Joey's casket rests in the center aisle on the same spot where his sister's body had lain, the pews this afternoon are nearly empty, and the priest's words echo to fill the void.

Again I have taken the second pew, flanked today by Neil and Roxanne. The last few years have seen many changes for the three of us, but the greatest of these is surely the life that Neil and I have begun together, and I can never forget that we have Roxanne to thank for introducing us. Without comment, I stretch my arm around her shoulder, pulling her close, sharing the warmth of her fur coat.

Neil sits quietly on my other side, listening without reacting to the sermon. Obligingly, without complaining, he has returned to Dumont for the fourth—or is it fifth?—consecutive weekend. I'm way overdue to visit him at the loft in Chicago, and I told him as we drove to church today that I would begin living up to the "arrangement" without fail next week. "But, Mark," he said, "that's your first week on the job at the *Register*, and you just lost your managing editor. How can you possibly get away? Don't come to Chicago—I'll be back." And that's typical of how he's put his own life on hold while I've tried to get settled here. He's the man I love. Without comment, I stretch an arm around his shoulder, pulling him close. He, Roxanne, and I snuggle patiently in the cold air of the cavernous church, waiting for the sermon to end.

Ahead of us, Hazel, Thad, and Miriam Westerman are seated in the front pew. Thad is in the middle, in front of me, and he sniffles at the priest's words. The loss of both his mother and his uncle has finally caught up with him, and I hope he has learned that he needn't repress sentiment in the name of manliness. He's learned a lot since I met him three weeks ago, and so have I. It's uncertain whether Neil and I can claim the right to build a family with Thad—that's an issue for the courts to decide—but I have learned, to my utter amazement, that the idea is appealing to all three of us, and the thought of taking responsibility for the boy has shaken my own view of how the next few years may differ from the last.

Miriam Westerman couldn't care less about Joey's passing, but she's happy to flaunt her temporary custody of Thad by perching next to "Ariel" in the front pew, as family. Though she'll have a tough time battling Roxanne in court over this issue, she hasn't let that uncertainty stand in the way of plans for her Fem-Snach school, mistakenly endowed by Suzanne's forgotten trust fund. Miriam has already transferred the endowment into a building account, and the groundbreaking is scheduled for next week, in spite of the impossibly cold weather.

That same cold weather has finally nudged Hazel toward a decision that's been too long delayed. Before we left the house this afternoon, she told me that she would be moving somewhere warm. She's sixty-seven, with failing eyesight, financially secure due to the generosity of Suzanne's will.

Except for Thad, the Quatrain family is gone—there's nothing to keep her in Dumont any longer, and there's certainly no reason to endure these winters. She's out of here.

Across the aisle, on the other side of Joey's coffin, the first few pews are peopled as before with a group of Quatro executives. Behind them are a few city and county officials, including the sheriff, Douglas Pierce. I haven't been able to decide whether Pierce is gay. He's been more than accommodating, and he's spoken several times of our future friendship, but his reticence to reveal details of his private life has made it impossible for me to get close to the man. I'm content to know him at arm's length, of course—he's dedicated to his profession and will be an important contact for me at the newspaper—but I sense that there's more to the man, and I wonder if he'll ever feel ready to tell me about it.

A few other people are scattered about the church— acquaintances of Joey, no doubt, or perhaps curious locals, lured by the still-fresh news that both Suzanne and Joey were murdered by their "brother from the grave." What a headline! Chances are, tomorrow's big front-page Sunday feature detailing my takeover of the *Register* will be seriously eclipsed by this morning's unmasking of Parker Trent. And with good reason. This story has it all—deceit, greed, secrets, and lust. Not to mention murder.

Tempted to make a few notes, undoing my snuggle of Roxanne and Neil, I reach beneath my topcoat and remove from my pocket the wonderful old pen I carry everywhere, even here. Rolling the Montblanc in my fingers like a fine cigar, I remove the cap and examine the gold band beneath the nib. Engraved there in tiny letters is the name MARK MANNING, barely legible through the years of wear. Pulling a notepad from my coat, I flip it open and poise my pen, searching for the first words of a story that wants to be told. But my mind is focused on the pen itself, and, once again, one last memory-flash invades my return to Dumont.

I recall one afternoon shortly after my college graduation, a year or so after my mother died. I had recently interviewed with the *Chicago Journal*, hoping to land my first reporter's job, but not daring to hope that the *Journal* would actually take me on. To my astonishment, they did, and I would begin my career there in several weeks.

That afternoon, a small package arrived for me in the mail, and I saw from the return address that it had been sent from Dumont by my uncle Edwin. I had met the man only twice— during my boyhood visit, then much later at my mother's funeral—and I would never see him again. The oblong package was about the shape of a wristwatch, which seemed a good guess for a graduation present, so I opened it greedily, hoping to replace the battered watch that had seen me through high school as well as college.

But instead of a watch, the package contained a fountain pen, an old one. The note with it read:

Dear Mark,

Your mother used to say that we Quatrains must have ink in our blood—there have been so many printers in our family. Now I've learned that you have just been hired by the *Chicago Journal*. You won't be printing, but you'll be writing, and I'm gratified to know that there's ink in your blood, too.

A writer needs a pen, and a great writer needs a great pen. I have treasured this one for years, and I want you to have it. If you look closely at the engraving near the nib, you will see that it belonged to your father.

If you ever have the inclination to visit Dumont again, I'd like to introduce you to my good friend Barret Logan, founder and publisher of our local paper—a pretty good one, by all reports. Who knows? If things don't work out for you at the *Journal*, I might be able to pull some strings and find you something at the *Dumont Daily Register*. (Just kidding, of course.)

Best of luck, Mark, and congratulations!

Love,
Uncle Edwin

Glancing up now from the blank page of my steno pad, I notice that Father Winter is at last wrapping up his sermon, but my thoughts are still with Uncle Edwin. His suggestion that I consider working at the *Register*, which I found laughable twenty years ago, has proved prophetic. And while I didn't rely on him to pull strings on my behalf, it was his money (passed on to me through Suzanne) that allowed me to buy the paper. Looking about, I wonder if Barret Logan is here in the congregation today.

Though there is no choir, an organist begins plodding through some homely hymn that no one sings. Again I grope for the opening phrase of a story I want to write, but the words seem to resist the tangibility of ink. Then it dawns on me. I'm too close to this. This is family. This is *me*. Though page-one material, this will never carry my byline. This is a tale I can spin only in my mind. So, closing my notebook, I cap my father's pen.

When the Mass has finished and all of us rise, Father Winter escorts Joey's casket down the center aisle toward the back of the church, accompanied by another hymn on the organ, badly played. Those of us in the front pews are the first to follow, giving me a clear view of the others waiting to leave. I notice that Barret Logan is indeed among the small crowd, accompanied by Glee Savage, who wears a big-brimmed black hat with mourning veil—she looks like a beekeeper. Standing nearby is Elliot Coop, the Quatrains' longtime family lawyer.

"My God," Roxanne says into my ear, tugging at my sleeve, "look over there." She jerks her head toward one of the back pews. "Isn't that Lucille Haring?"

"Hey, Mark," whispers Neil, tugging my other sleeve, "it's Lucy."

I peer toward the woman, squinting. She's lean and mannish, with a bright shock of short red hair, wearing a drab-colored double-breasted topcoat, its styling vaguely military. Sure enough, it's Lucy. "What's *she* doing here?"

Lucille Haring is the woman I worked with on my last big story at the *Journal*. She applied for the managing editor's job here in Dumont, and although she was extremely qualified, I was reluctant to consider her because Gordon Smith, my mentor at the *Journal*, found her indispensable there in the publisher's office. Then Parker Trent came along, and . . . well, here we are back at square one.

Catching her eye, I acknowledge her with a nod as the procession wends its stately course toward the doors of the church.

In accordance with Father Winter's initial no-fuss strictures regarding this service, there will be no graveside liturgy for Joey—he'll be buried without ceremony at a later date when there's a break in the cold weather. So Joey's casket is carried outdoors to the waiting hearse, but the mourners remain inside, beginning to mingle in the vestibule.

Father Winter, his duties dispatched, turns and claps a hand on Thad's shoulder, telling him, "I wish we could have done more for your dear uncle, but we had so little notice—I'm sure you understand the circumstances."

Thad won't answer the man, but flashes him a look of disgust. With a wry, proud grin, I tell myself, That's my boy . . .

Roxanne hugs herself through her fur, saying to me, loudly enough for the priest to hear, "For a Quatrain, that wasn't much of a show—I'm surprised the good padre even bothered to turn on the lights."

Jabbing her a silent behave-yourself, I turn to Thad, intending to offer some encouraging words for the future, but Miriam Westerman has already pulled him toward the door, fussing at him. Approaching them both, I tell them, "We're having some people over to the house. I hope you'll join us."

Thad's features immediately brighten, but Miriam snuffs the notion, telling him, "You've already spent quite enough time on Prairie Street, Ariel. I'm taking you home." As she yanks the big gnarled handle and opens the door, a gust of dry, frigid air furls her cape.

I poke my head out the door to call after them, "I'll be in touch, Thad. And I'll see *you* in court, Miriam." And they are gone.

Back inside the vestibule, Elliot Coop guides me a few feet beyond earshot of the others. Through an excited whisper, he tells me, "In spite of the tragic events we've gathered to mourn today, I have a morsel of news you may find a tad . . . 'heartening,' Mr. Manning."

That's intriguing. "Yes?" The recessional hymn has ended, but the organist continues to improvise funeral-parlor background music, replete with a cheesy electronic tremolo.

The lawyer bubbles, "I've just learned that Thad's custody case will *not* be going to trial. On the basis of Miss Exner's written memoranda, the judge threw out Miriam's petition as groundless—and he's *furious* with Harley Kaiser for having meddled in the first place."

Having not expected the issue to be resolved so neatly, I break into a smile, asking him, "How soon does the decision take effect?"

"At once," Elliot tells me. "If you like, I'll inform Sheriff Pierce—Thad should be back under your roof by nightfall."

Before I can respond, Elliot continues, "I hardly need to add, Mr. Manning, that with the custody issue resolved, those dangling questions regarding Suzanne's will are now moot. Which means: you're a very wealthy man."

With an effort to control my excitement, I tell him offhandedly, "Well now"—fake laugh—"that *is* 'heartening,' isn't it? Thanks for all your efforts, Elliot."

"I am but a humble servant," he assures me, feigning the obsequious manner that serves as his style of humor.

I sidestep in Neil's direction, eager to fill him in. But I find him already occupied with Roxanne, introducing Lucille Haring to Barret Logan and Glee Savage.

"Ah, yes," says Logan, "I vividly recall the role you played in Mark's big astronomy story last summer. Wonderful work, wonderful exposé."

I butt in, "Lucy! My God, what brings *you* up here?" I offer her a little hug, but her response is predictably stiff—she'd prefer to shake hands.

"It's rather a long story," she tells me, all business, "but Gordon Smith is moving from the *Journal* down to the JournalCorp paper in Orlando. He was *acting* publisher, as you know, and the board has passed him over in favor of younger blood. The upshot is this, Mark: I'm seeking a position else-where, and my first preference is here, with you. So I tore up here this weekend, hoping we could talk face-to-face about it. Arriving in town, I didn't know where to find you, so I phoned the newsroom at the *Register* and learned . . . well, everything." Then, with uncharacteristically cynical humor, she adds, "I hear things didn't quite work out with Parker Trent."

"*My dear,*" gasps Glee, stepping into our conversation, "he fooled us all. He asked me out to dinner with him this coming Monday, and I *accepted.* God *knows* what his intentions may have been. He was devilishly attractive, of course, but I can't believe I fell for the guy!"

Lucy deadpans, "I doubt that *I* would have."

Neil and I struggle to stifle a laugh (we're in church, after all), knowing that Lucille Haring's interests focus more on the likes of Glee than Parker. From previous experience, Roxanne knows this, too, and her reaction to Lucy's comment is consid-erably more reserved than Neil's and mine.

I tell Lucy, "As for job prospects, your timing couldn't be better. We're having a little reception over at the house. Why don't you join us? We can talk."

"Thanks. Perfect. I'd love to."

I suggest, "Roxanne, maybe you could ride over with Lucy and show her the way. There's something I need to discuss with Neil."

Roxanne deadpans, "Thanks. Perfect. I'd love to." And she escorts Lucille Haring toward the door.

As they are leaving, Lucy tells Roxanne, "I see you've grown your hair longer. I liked it better short."

I ask Glee Savage and Barret Logan, "Care to join us?"

"For a brief while, surely," says Logan. "I haven't quite finished cleaning out my office downtown, and I want to wrap it up today."

Glee reminds me, "You said that when all the facts were in, I'd get the assignment to write Suzanne's story. I'm anxious to get cracking on it, Mark."

"It's all yours," I tell her. "But you'll never make today's deadline, so you might as well join us for a drink."

"Might as well," she admits, and, after she offers Logan her arm, they stroll together from the church.

By now the organ has stopped warbling, and an altar boy has snuffed the candles in the sanctuary. Father Winter has retreated to the sacristy, where he noisily flips circuit breakers; the lights hanging from the Gothic-arched ceiling blink out in sequence, marching from the altar to the door. The old boiler drones pathetically from the basement. "Guess it's time to leave," I tell Neil.

Sheriff Pierce breaks away from a clump of people near the door. He takes us aside, telling me, "I didn't want to talk to you about it while Thad was still here with Miriam, but the department got a final report on Austin Reece, Thad's father."

I nod, recalling, "You mentioned before that you were having trouble tracking him down."

"With good reason," says Pierce. "Reece died years ago. Car accident. Too bad—I got the impression Thad might want to meet him. When the time is right, could you let the kid know?"

"Sure, Doug. Thanks for the word."

Judging from his tone, it's clear that he doesn't know that the custody issue has been resolved. I'll let him hear this from Elliot Coop—I've yet to tell Neil about it.

Joining a few stragglers who button their coats and don their gloves, Pierce, Neil, and I brave our way out the door and into the bright but arctic afternoon. Traipsing down the broad front steps of the church, I ask Pierce, "Coming over to the house?"

"Can't," he explains. "On duty." Then he shakes our hands in parting, walking off toward the parking lot.

Neil and I cross the street, headed toward my car. As our feet crunch the pavement's rutted ice, I mention, "By the way—I've got some great news."

❑